D1526901

A SELDITH CHRISTMAS

William R. Vaughn

William Vaughn

Redmond, Washington USA

http://BetaV.com

First Print Edition Published
September 29, 2023

Copyright © 2023 William R. Vaughn

All Rights Reserved

Also available in Kindle™

ISBN: 9798862890655

Imprint: BetaV

V121.1 A Seldith Christmas (Final Draft).docx
10/7/2023 11:18:00 AM

10 9 8 7 6 5 4 3 2 1 0

❧The Author❧

William Vaughn is an award-winning author, dad, and granddad who has written over twenty books and many dozens of magazine articles over the last forty years. He's also an avid nature photographer and traveler capturing natural beauty all over the world. While once a technical writer, he currently publishes novels in the young-adult and new-adult genres. He has chosen the Pacific Northwest as his home and source of inspiration.

❧ The Series❧

The Seldith Chronicles series begins with *The Owl Wrangler,* a story introducing Seldith elves no taller than a mushroom. Each member of the clan has a unique talent, their own magic, their own integral place in society. The first story of the series follows Hisbil, a teen uncertain of his destiny, but determined to discover what has befallen his father. *Guardians of the Sacred Seven* and *Quest for The Truth* continue his epic saga.

❧ This Book ❧

While *A Seldith Christmas* includes a few characters from *The Seldith Chronicles* series, it can be read on its own. It is primarily set in a small town on the coast of Maine in 1939. It's a time of world tumult, where life seemed simple for some, but could be deadly dangerous for those fleeing oppression or those seeking to expose the truth. We follow Trudi, a young woman raised and apprenticed by Opa, her grandfather. He's an aging clocksmith—the last of a long line of Austrian clock masters. While Opa's creations are beautiful and entertainingly animated, the old man has closely guarded the secret behind their seemingly magic jewels, gears, and tiny inner workings.

❧ Acknowledgements ❧

None of my books could have been brought to readers without considerable help from a small army of talented, generous, and patient friends, editors, proofreaders, beta readers, and artists. Each contributor has their own unique talent—not unlike the members of a Seldith clan. I will endeavor to mention each of these individuals and catalog their contributions; my apologies if I missed your name.

Beta readers are those individuals who volunteer their time to provide viewpoints on every aspect of the manuscript. They provide guidance on the prose and provide their opinions on character development, and believability and anything that comes to mind. Thank you again for your diligent work. These individuals include Sue Shellooe, Jennifer Swift, Michelle Poolet, Dr. Stephen Gresham (Auburn University), Julianne Mitchell, Melissa Alexander, Margot Ayer, Amy Baker, Darrel (DB) Baker, Rebecca Putnam, and Dr. Donald Stewart – whose name I borrowed for the kindly Dr. Stewart in the story.

Developmental Editors Richard Gibney and Charlene Mertz took a near-finished manuscript and helped me restructure and polish it before publication. They focused on historical accuracy, exchange rates, timelines, and a litany of details this author and the reader might get confused. Thanks a million.

Foreign language Editors the individuals who edited the non-English text considering the story includes snippets of several foreign languages. Thanks to Géraldine Vigoureux, Margo Ayer, and others who helped craft dialogs in other languages.

I would also like to call out another influential beta reader: Charlotte Neward. While I was all but ready to commit the manuscript to final edit, Ms. Neward returned a comprehensive, and frankly critical review. Fortunately, I recognized that every criticism she made had merit. The next year was spent recreating the book you're about to enjoy.

❧ Cover Art❧

In the past, I took pride in incorporating my own photographs in my cover art, but this time, I strove to do something different. To that end, I spent several months trying to rekindle my fledgling watercolor painting skills. But COVID dampened that ambition. While considering an AI-generated cover, I soon realized that this would deprive a human artist of their chance to contribute to the cover, so I put out a call to my friends and soon found Bobbie Halpenny who took on the task. She spent considerable time trying to paint what I envisioned for the cover, but unfortunately it was not to be. I would like to thank her for her dedication and efforts.

Timelines and other factors forced me to return to my own photographs and Photoshop skills. So, yes again, the cover is my own creation.

❧Use of Artificial Intelligence❧

This manuscript was written entirely by the author on Microsoft Word without the help of an artificial intelligence (AI) text generator. And no, the cover was not created by an AI program, but by the human author using his own photographs augmented with Photoshop.

❧Dedication❧

This book is dedicated to four intelligent, imaginative women: my daughters Victoria Ballard, and Christina Vaughn (AKA to their dad as George and Fred), and granddaughters Mary Ballard, and Katherine (Katie) Ballard. May they find inspiration and enjoyment in these pages.

One—The Chargé D'affaires

*R*ichard St. James, a gray-templed man about forty, scanned the December 9th, 1938, edition of The Times. *They don't get it*, he fumed, flipping through the pages. His fingers tightened around the newsprint.

As deputy to the chargé d'affaires of the American Embassy in London, he was tasked with gathering intelligence that could impact his country's foreign policy or put citizens at risk. While the paper was peppered with war news, there was little solid information about what the United States would do about Herr Hitler's thinly veiled threats. Rumors, wild speculation, and distortions flavored almost every story, but he needed to know more. While his tattered copy of the New York Times brought him six-day-old news, it didn't help understand today's political climate back in the States as his government and citizens reacted to rapidly evolving events abroad. Muttering to himself, he refolded the paper and filed it with the others he had kept.

But today, Richard was distracted by a more pressing ordeal he and his family were about to face. The final straw that made it imperative that he act at once had occurred only an hour ago. Richard had planned to meet Henri, a Frenchman, a longtime friend and reliable informant. But the meeting did not turn out as planned. It seems Henri was desperate to find, in his words, "Someone who could help change the course of history and save countless lives." His urgent plea echoed in Richard's mind. For reasons he didn't fully grasp, Henri was convinced that he, 'Rishard', was the right man, the only man, he could trust for an exceptionally dangerous job.

He recalled their clandestine meeting in a nearby park. "You really have *all* of this?" Richard whispered as he studied the document Henri had given him concealed in the folds of a tabloid. It appeared to be a catalog of documents and photographs detailing behind-the-scenes treaties and subversive activities that implicated men and women at the highest levels of government on both sides of the English Channel and the Atlantic.

Henri nodded, his eyes studying the few people strolling nearby. "Oui. And more," he said, patting a bulge in his coat.

"Where did…?"

"Do not ask too many questions, mon ami. Too many people have sacrificed their lives to secure them."

"But, Henri, I'm not nearly important enough, not politically connected, not…" Richard protested, admitting to himself that he was probably not the man Henri needed.

"The cause needs someone we can *trust*, that *I* can trust. So many important people are involved. You were my best man and my son's godfather."

"But you really know so little about me. About my past. How can you trust me with something this important?"

Henri looked him in the eyes. "We all have a past that we're hiding from. Rishard: You *must* help us."

"But wouldn't someone… someone like my boss, be better…?"

"No, mon ami. I don't trust him for reasons I need not explain."

Richard had to agree. The chargé d'affaires was of questionable character and a political appointee, but he said nothing. What Henri was asking him to do would put him and his family in grave danger, but the mission would be equally important to their native countries and to the world.

"Au revoir, mon ami. I must go. They may be watching," Henri said, putting one arm around his shoulders and sliding a packet under Richard's coat. "Get this into the right hands, and be careful," he whispered. "Bonne chance."

As they parted company, Richard secured the packet deep inside his coat. Thirty steps away, he looked back. *Oh my God.* He watched in horror as a pair of men dragged Henri into a car. When one of the assailants looked his way, Richard froze for an instant before nonchalantly blending into a crowd of tourists being led by a woman holding a small blue flag. Staying with them until they were out of the park, he walked at a good pace for a block and ducked into a menswear shop's doorway where he hid behind a rack of tan raincoats. Peering through the coats, he saw them. *There. Two men pushing through the pedestrians and moving his way.* He was being stalked by jackals. *German agents? Scotland Yard? MI5?*

Richard casually donned one of the raincoats as a disguise and moved off, not daring to look back. *Not too quickly. Be casual. I'm just out for a stroll.* He pulled down the brim of his fedora and focused on escape while his heart threatened to leap out of his chest.

There it is. On the other side of Grosvenor Square stood his refuge: the American Embassy. Looking back one last time, he didn't see the men but never doubted they would keep looking for him. If Henri was still alive, Richard accepted that his friend would have little choice but to betray him—at least eventually. Richard knew that he had to leave the UK and hand-carry these documents back to the States. *And protect Catherine and the kids.*

Inside the massive embassy doors, he leaned against the marble wall to catch his breath.

"Mr. St James, sir, are you all right, sir?" the Marine guard asked.

Richard just looked at him and nodded and held up his hands. "I'm… fine. Someone may be… chasing me."

"I'll alert the commander," he said, reaching for a phone and motioning to the men at the gates to lock them down.

Richard wasted no time making his way to his office, fending off conversations as he went. As he passed his secretary, he leaned over and whispered "Rachel, will you please call my wife?" He closed and locked his office door. He gazed up at the old clock on the wall which pulled his thoughts to a distant, unforgotten place in his past. His concentration was broken when his phone rang. "Catherine?" he began. "Hi. I'm fine. Dear, I thought we should visit your cousin in Blackburn. Yes. The car will be there by four this afternoon. Please get the kids ready. Sorry for the short notice." Catherine had not said another word, but he could hear her catch her breath.

Richard hung up and carefully upended the contents of the envelope Henri had given him. A sheaf of documents dropped to his desk along with a small metal canister, which he opened at once. It contained a thin strip of photographic negatives. Handling them by the edges, he held them up to his desk lamp; he could see images of documents, and photographs of what seemed to be military emplacements, and annotated photographs of people and maps. *Oh my God.*

He returned everything to the envelope, sealed it, and hid it in a secret compartment in his valise. *What's next? Oh. The currency.* Going to his safe, he worked the combination. The safe didn't open--*merde*--. Taking a deep breath, he turned the dial again but far more carefully before hearing the final click. Once the safe was open, he extracted a banded stack of banknotes and a small bag of coins. *Damn. It's all British.* Looking again at the clock, he realized he would not have time to get to the bank to exchange it himself. He needed to trust this task to someone reliable. Returning to his desk, he penned a note on embassy stationery detailing the instructions and giving his home address.

Someone tapped on the door. Richard cleared his desk quickly.

"Sir?" his aide asked. "Are you all right?"

"What is it, Cedrick?" Richard said through the door.

"I have your American newspaper and an important dispatch."

Richard opened the door and returned to sit behind his desk. The aide followed and stood before him.

Cedrick, a young man whose whiskers had just begun to appear, looked down at him, his boyish face contorted with a forced smile that tried to hide his concern. He held a neatly folded newspaper and a typed report.

"Is that my New York Times?" Richard asked, taking the paper. "It's late."

"Yes, sir. I'm sorry sir. And there is this dispatch from our agents in Berlin—it just came in."

While Cedrick had only been with the embassy eighteen months, he had already risen to a moderate level of trust. In these troubled times, people who could protect a confidence and keep a cool head were hard to find but easy to lose.

"We've also had more reports of incidents in Munich," Cedrick began, "… and several more in Berlin, and the Sudetenland. Are you sure you should continue with your plans to ?"

"Yes. It's set. They're expecting me in Balmoral tomorrow. I'll be departing momentarily, but I have something vitally important for you to do. Are you ready for additional responsibilities?

"Of course, sir," he said, standing at attention.

"I have written out the instructions here," Richard said, handing Cedrick the envelope and the currency. "This currency needs to be exchanged for US money and delivered to my residence by three this afternoon. The address is in the envelope."

Cedrick nodded and took the bank notes and the envelope.

"This is *vitally* important. Repeat your instructions."

"I'm to take this currency to the bank. They will exchange it for American bills. I will take it to your house by three."

"Without fail."

"Without fail, sir. You can trust me."

"I know I can." *I hope I can.* "The American currency is to be delivered into my wife's hand *personally*."

"Yes, sir. Personally. Can I take your bag down?" Cedrick said, picking up the large valise next to the door.

"No, I'll take it."

"It's no trouble, sir. Really."

He's too eager. "No. I want to add another few things before I go," Richard said, waving Cedrick away. "Get started for the bank. You don't have a lot of time." A sinking feeling came over him as he raced through the instances when he had trusted his aide—and perhaps should not have. *It's nothing. I'm being paranoid. But for want of a nail the battle was lost…*

When Cedrick closed the door behind him, Richard wasted no time loading selected irreplaceable personal effects into the bag. He knew he was not coming back. Looking up at the ornate clock over the door, he gave a heavy sigh. All at once, a flood of memories brought him back to a simpler time, a happier time, a time that had slipped away from him. *I can't take it with me.* He left a note to Cedrick to return the London Fog coat to the store with his apologies and to have his office clock carefully packed and sent to his residence. He stood by his desk, staring as the clock's secondhand ticked away the time he had left. *My pistol.* He retrieved his service revolver from his desk and, opening the breach, verified it was loaded with five rounds. He lowered the hammer on the empty chamber and slid it into his coat pocket along with a box of cartridges.

He looked back into his office one last time. *That's it.* Carrying his valise, Richard walked calmly through his outer office where Cedrick and other members of his staff wished him well and a safe journey. By happenstance, they thought he was heading for a meeting at Balmoral Castle in Scotland. This gave him a perfect chance to slip away before anyone knew he was gone.

Out on the busy street, Richard pulled down the brim of his fedora, opened his umbrella, and blended in with the hundreds of other dark-suited men carrying identical black umbrellas through the rain. For once, the cold December weather had been a blessing. Hailing a cab, he gave the driver an address across London, and added an extra instruction. "Someone may be following me. Can you do something about it?"

"I can gvnor," the cabbie said, touching his brim. A moment later, the cab's maneuvers pushed him against the door as the driver made a hard right, accelerating through gaps in the traffic.

Richard looked behind them and didn't see another car in pursuit. "Perhaps you lost them."

"But not if they know where you're going."

"I expect you're right."

"Stewart. Me name's Stewart. I'll make sure, but it might be best if you hoof it the last block or so to be sure."

"A good plan," Richard said, settling back into the seat but still checking behind them every few moments.

"This is it, gvnor. Your address is in the next block."

"Here. And keep the change," Richard said, handing the cabbie a five-pound note.

"Thank you, guvnor," he said with a big smile and tipping his hat.

"You never saw me. Right?"

"Right," Stewart said with a wink.

As the cab had disappeared into traffic, Richard hailed another and, using a thick French accent, had the cabbie take him to King's Cross station where he disappeared into the crowd.

Richard's office staff had expected to hear from him later that day. They wouldn't. No one would.

Two—The Escape

*B*ehind her locked bedroom door in a pristine Georgian townhome located in an upscale part of London, Mrs. Catherine St. James packed her journal and a few clean clothes into a strangely heavy traveling bag. As she stood considering what else to include, she checked her watch just as someone knocked on the door. *Three forty-five.*

"Madam? There is a person here with a package." It was Mrs. Rutledge, her housekeeper.

It's here.

"He insists on delivering the package 'Into Mrs. St. James' hands.'"

Catherine's stomach tightened. "I'll be down directly."

"Yes'm," her housekeeper said.

Catherine listened until Mrs. Rutledge had descended the staircase before unlocking the door and entering the hall. As she locked the door behind her, two teenagers accosted her.

"Mother, may I take my new blue satin?" Fredricka, her seventeen going on twenty-year-old daughter asked, holding the dress up under her chin.

"Freddie, I expect Cousin Gerald would like it, but not this trip."

"If she gets to take that fancy dress, I can take my—" her fifteen-year-old son George began.

She held up her palm. "We talked about this. This is a quick trip, and we all agreed on what you can take—everything must fit into one small bag. Let's stick to the plan." Her voice was firm. Looking over the rail at the foyer, she saw a neatly dressed man holding a package wrapped in brown paper and tied with cord—it might just as well have been a package of laundered shirts. "Finish your packing. The car will be here in less than a half-hour," she said to her teens.

"Yes'm," they said in unison, turning to go back to their rooms.

Steeling her courage, the lady of the house descended the stairs as if making her grand entrance at a formal ball. "You have a package for me?"

Her butler, Mr. Smithers, stood a discreet distance away but seemed poised to intercede if necessary. "She's addressing *you*, man," he said.

"Are you Mrs. St. James?" the man asked.

"I am," she said.

"Please sign here." He handed her the delivery receipt and a pencil.

Catherine carefully inspected the package, ensuring the seals were undamaged. "Thank you, young man," she said, signing the form. "Mr. Smithers, please take care of him."

Returning to her bedroom, she didn't hear his reply or anything else except her own thoughts as she locked the door behind her. Inside the package, she found a packet the size of a brick, and several sacks of coins. Opening the packet, her expression changed. *Pounds. It was supposed to be dollars.* She shook her head and inspected the small bag. *British coins. Someone's head will roll. Probably that idiot Cedrick.* She hid the currency and coins in a side-compartment in her bag. *It will have to do.*

Sitting at her desk, she wrote notes and sealed them in envelopes—each addressed to a different member of her household staff. As the last envelope was sealed, she retrieved the Colt 1903 pistol from her bag, ensured it was loaded and a round was not chambered. She slipped it into the outer pocket of her overcoat and stood for a moment. *I've forgotten something. My tools.* Extracting a black leather pouch the size of a thin wallet from her lingerie drawer, she slid it into her coat pocket alongside the pistol. *It's begun.* She took a deep breath and walked out into the hall. She left the key in the lock.

సౌసౌస

A few minutes after four, everyone, including Catherine's four-year-old daughter Annie, had assembled at the front door. "Do you have everything?" Catherine asked the children as Mr. Smithers brought down the last of their luggage.

"I have Katie," Annie said, holding up her irreplaceable doll.

"That's *good*," Freddie said. "We would all be lost without her."

Annie raised her hands and Freddie obliged by lifting her into her arms. A heartbeat later, the child's head plopped on Freddie's shoulder.

Catherine smiled. The mild sedative was already making this journey easier—and safer. "The car is here, let's get loaded." She handed Mr. Smithers an envelope. "Mr. Smithers, as we discussed earlier, you can reach us at Blackburn, my cousin Peter's country estate, for a few days. While you may contact us there in case of dire emergencies, I fully expect you to handle any issues on your own."

"Of course, Ma'am," he replied, sliding the envelope into his inside coat pocket.

"Everyone else, Mr. Smithers is in charge."

Mrs. Rutledge and the others nodded.

Alfred, their driver, loaded the luggage into the boot of the Bentley and held the door open for the family as they descended the front steps.

"Mr. Smithers, I'll depend on you to manage things until we return," Catherine instructed. "And see that Mrs. Rutledge and the rest of the staff get some rest once the instructions are followed."

"Of course, Ma'am," he said. "You needn't be concerned."

I wish, Catherine thought as she settled into the car with her most precious cargo—her children.

❧❧❧

Twenty minutes later, as they reached the outskirts of London, she realized that they were making good time. Annie rested her head on her sister's lap, Freddie read one of her books, and curious George asked questions about what he observed out the window.

"How much farther?" he asked, gazing at the sunset.

"About that," Catherine began. "We aren't going to Uncle Peter's."

Freddie looked up at once. "We aren't?"

"No. You're both old enough to know the truth, especially since it will affect your lives as well. Your father and I are leaving the country—tonight. And there's more—"

"What? What about my game? I'm supposed to start at mid-field on Saturday," George interrupted.

"I'm terribly sorry, but there…" Catherine had struggled with how much to tell her teenagers, but in time, they would have to know most of the details, anyway. "Listen. Your father and I feel that we can't be safe in the UK, so we need to return to the States. The problem is, we can't travel by conventional means, so we can't just get on a train or board a passenger liner and sail back to the States."

"Why not?" Freddie asked.

"We don't want anyone to know where we are. It's just a precaution."

"You think we might be kidnapped or something?" George asked, his voice trembling.

Catherine thought for a moment. "There is a possibility that someone might try," she answered, watching her children's eyes. Freddie clutched her little sister a bit tighter.

George just stared at his mother.

"It's not at all likely that anyone will be able to find us. Your father and I have taken elaborate measures to make that especially difficult. We'll be fine. Think of it as a grand adventure."

"Why did you tell the servants we would be back?" George asked.

"Oh, I left them notes explaining as much as they need to know," she said. "The less they know, the better."

"So, an adventure," Freddie said, putting on a brave face. "How exciting!"

"Will we go back? What about my cricket bat and cleats?" George asked.

"Perhaps, someday. We'll see how things go."

"But...why didn't you tell us before?" Freddie asked, closing her Jane Austen. "I would have said good-by to my friends."

"Your father just decided this morning. Something really important must have happened. And no, your friends cannot learn that we've left the country—no one can."

"It's not fair," George pouted.

"I agree," Freddie echoed.

"And I also agree. But sometimes, life isn't fair."

"It's the curse of the diplobrat," Freddie moaned. "Having to start over every time your father has to leave town."

"Sadly, true," Catherine said. "It's the price we pay for the opportunity to live comfortably and learn abroad. We find ways to make friends quickly and still try to keep them once we're separated. It can be a hard life, but a rich experience."

"Can't we just—" Freddie began.

"It's settled. We've been planning this for some time and there's no turning back. Right now, what I need from you two is steadfast cooperation and courage. I'll need you to watch out for each other and Annie and remember that we love you."

The teens just stared at her in disbelief.

"Do you understand?"

"Yes, mother," they both said softly. Freddie retreated to her book and George to his window.

Catherine knew she would have to make it up to them. In the glow of the dome light, she flipped back in her journal. Here she had recorded nearly every step of their journeys, challenges, and adventures through the years, ending in their current assignment in England. The preceding pages spanned the idyllic years when she and her husband Richard lived in Boston, the city where she was born and raised in privileged society. It was at an embassy soirée where she and Richard first met. He was a dashing junior diplomat with a reputation for sowing his wild oats. Once they were engaged, she managed to rein in his wandering spirit—or she had hoped so. He had not shared much about his years before they met, but she sensed a longing for something or someone in his past. She chose not to pursue the issue feeling he would tell her in time.

Several months ago, she recalled the evening he came home from the embassy with troubling war news.

"Could we be trapped here in the UK if war breaks out?" she asked, holding his hands.

"Yes. I'm afraid so. Hitler is likely to drop bombs on London. We would have to move you and the children north or perhaps back to the States."

"But could we get back? Won't the seas be extremely dangerous? Remember the Lusitania? They might do the same if war broke out again."

"They might…" he said. His gaze drifted away.

"What can we do? Should we leave now while it's still safe?"

"I can't leave, darling. Not yet. You know that. There is far too much to do and leaving my post would ruin my career."

"We need a plan," she said.

Catherine and Richard spent that entire night and the next week formulating an elaborate plan to flee the country at a moment's notice if the need ever arose. With months to prepare, they hoped their plan would mean their family would be able to escape to safety—assuming it could be executed flawlessly. The codeword *Blackburn* was their signal to get family away from London and make their way back to the States. Special bags were packed, arrangements made, and lists of essentials checked off in preparation for that day they both hoped would never come. That was in September.

Starting a new entry, Catherine recorded how the chauffeured car was abusing her otherwise good nature as she and her children had bounced around inside like dice in a cup.

"Alfred, can you drive more carefully?" she asked.

"A bridge washed out, ma'am, so we've been detoured to an alternate route," he said. "We need to keep moving to arrive on time."

"I understand, but please drive like we're eggs, not dice."

"Yes'm."

"Kids, do you remember Uncle Peter?" Catherine asked, wanting to get their minds off the ordeal she had imposed on them.

Freddie looked up. "I do. Isn't he the one with the scary machines in the old castle tower?"

Catherine smiled. "Yes. He's quite proud of his castle."

"I recall him teasing me about my choice of reading material."

"That Jane Austen you're reading would not raise his ire, but you might remember during our last visit; he caught you reading that John Cleland novel about Miss Hill."

Freddie blushed and closed her book. "I suppose he's right. Fanny Hill was somewhat racy."

"And inappropriate for a girl of your... tender age."

"Seventeen is not a *tender* age. Juliet was only thirteen when she took Romeo as a lover."

Catherine frowned. "In any case, you should be more circumspect when around people from outside our immediate family. And hiding from the world in your books keeps you from enjoying and experiencing the real world around you."

"I thought you didn't *want* me to experience real life? Didn't you just chastise me for reading about underage intimacy?"

Catherine painted another stern look on her face, but she knew that she was losing the argument.

"Yes, mother," the girl said.

Catherine closed her eyes and realized that she might never again see her London friends and (albeit distant) relatives on this side of the Atlantic. And *they* did not have the luxury of fleeing the country in the face of another world war. They would have to stay and take whatever Herr Hitler threw at them.

"Why didn't father come with us?" George asked.

"He needed to travel on his own." She didn't tell them that he planned to lead their adversaries away from his family. "You know he's an important diplomat, so he has considerable responsibilities."

"An assistant isn't *that* important."

"I beg your pardon; your father becomes the American ambassador if the ambassador and Mr. Armbruster, his boss, cannot serve. That's *critically* important."

"Oh," George said. "Does he not *also* have responsibilities to his family?"

"Why has the car stopped? Are we there?" Freddie asked.

Catherine lowered the window and noticed that the car had indeed stopped behind a black bread truck. She opened the partition so she could converse with Alfred. "Alfred, is there a problem?"

"I'm afraid we're having a spot of bother with the motor," Alfred said, through the partition.

"I see. Can you see if the driver just ahead can assist us?" Catherine asked. She glanced at her watch. *Right on time.*

"Of course, Madam," he said, getting out and walking over to the black van touting the name of a local bakery. He returned a moment later. "He is more than happy to accommodate."

"Thank you. All right, my darlings, we need to get out. Take your things with you. Alfred, if you will be so kind as to assist with the luggage?"

"What's going on?" Freddie asked.

"We're switching vehicles," Catherine said as she gathered her things.

Freddie hesitated. "Must we?"

"We must, it seems," George began.

"Less sniping, more loading," Catherine said. "And don't leave your sleeping sister behind."

Catherine got out and gazed out into the night. They had stopped on a bluff high above a port city, its lights twinkling in the distance. In the filtered moonlight, a boundless body of water stretched out before them, but she did not recognize where they were.

Catherine approached the truck driver. "Good evening. How is the weather in Paris?" *I hope he gives the correct countersign.*

"It's warmer in the winter," he said. "Good evening, Madam. My name is François."

Perfect. She knew better than to give him or anyone her name. "Do you know where we're going?" she asked.

"No, madame, I am only instructed to take you to the next rendezvous," he said quietly.

"Je comprends," she said. And she did understand. The fewer people who knew their identities and ultimate destination, the better. She moved to the rear of the truck where Alfred had finished loading their few pieces of luggage and the teens were arguing and negotiating the seating arrangements. Annie was asleep in Freddie's arms. "Let's get going."

"Madam, I was instructed to give you this," Alfred said. He handed her a sealed envelope addressed in her husband's hand. "Ma chérie, pour lire quand tu es seule." She translated: *My love, to read later, once you're alone.* She read the words again before slipping the sealed envelope into her inside coat pocket next to her pistol.

"Will there be anything else, madam?" Alfred asked.

She pressed an envelope into his hand. "These are your instructions and enough money to keep you comfortable until you can secure another position. We have included a glowing letter of recommendation. We only ask that you wait a week before reappearing, at which time, return the Bentley to the residence.

"Very well, madam. Safe journey."

"Thank you, Alfred."

Turning to her children, Catherine took a deep breath. "Let's get aboard." With a helping hand from the driver, she and the kids got into the bakery truck. Inside, they found a large crate with bench seats and ropes dangling from the top.

"Please take a seat on the benches," the driver began. "Strap yourselves down and hold on tight. Comprenez-vous?"

"Je comprends," she said.

Now all she had to do was convince her kids that this frightening part of their journey sealed inside a crate would be all for the best.

"Freddie, George, I need you to be brave," she began before telling them what was expected of them. "I'll take Annie. Get yourselves situated."

Not knowing if it was the terrifying prospect of being sealed up in a crate the size of a hall closet, or their maturity, both teens complied and fastened themselves to the crude bench with little protest. Annie, still sound asleep in her mother's warm embrace, was oblivious. Only then did Catherine realize that they might have to spend hours or longer locked inside. *Surely not. Dear God, I hope not.* She took Freddie's hand. George took her other hand. She was immensely proud of her diplobrats.

We're all at this truck driver's mercy—a man I've never met. The knot in her stomach tightened a bit more.

"George and Fredricka, I want you to be the diplomats your father taught you to be. I expect we're still some distance from our next destination, so make yourself as comfortable as possible."

A moment later, the truck pulled back out onto the road— or at least that's what it felt and sounded like. Sometime later, the rumble of cobblestones under the tires told her they had entered the city.

"We're near a fish market," Freddie said, holding her nose.

"Quietly. Talk quietly," Catherine whispered, checking Annie. She was still asleep, nursing her thumb.

"That's the sea, you ninny. We could be in Southampton by now," George whispered. "Or Felixstowe."

The new sounds around them confirmed they were in the seaport Catherine had seen from the bluff—and a busy one at that. *But which one?* Their elaborate plans had not specified which port would be used, the ship, or any other detail that could derail their journey in case their plans were compromised.

When the truck stopped, she heard a few voices nearby spoken in hushed tones; she could only make out a few words. In the darkness, she was unable to read her watch, but thought that it had taken far too long for someone to come for them. Someone whispered, "We are moving you all. Please hold on and remain completely silent."

In the shadows, a man dressed as a seaman slipped into a dark, unoccupied office. He picked up the phone, dialed a number, and in a few moments began to whisper. "Cedric? They're going out on the Sutherland. They sail on the tide. I understand," he said, hanging up the phone.

Catherine held her breath and pinched her eyes closed. Moments later, the crate rocked and pitched.

"Woah," George said.

"George," Catherine whispered, "we must keep exceptionally quiet. Please—for everyone's safety."

"Mother?" Freddie whispered, her voice trembling.

She squeezed her hand. "I'm scared too, honey."

A trickle of dust fell through the cracks as just before the crate lurched off the ground, swinging and spinning. *We're being hoisted by a crane.* All around them, she heard men's voices shouting commands. Wishing these unseen men would be more careful with their fragile cargo, she realized that to the longshoremen, all they were manhandling was a crate of nothing more delicate than frozen fish. Hopefully, no one would discover they were inside.

With another lurch and a thud, the crate came to rest. Freddie leaned over and put her head on Catherine's shoulder as someone disconnected chains. *We must have been loaded somewhere.*

Catherine lost track of time as they waited for what seemed like hours, listening to the clattering sounds of other cargo being stacked all around them. From time-to-time, a flash of light crossed the darkness, letting George, whose eye was glued to a knothole, get a snapshot of what was going on outside. She was glad he was not giving a minute-by-minute account, as it might betray their presence; at the same time, she wished he was.

When it had been quiet for what seemed like an eternity, she broke her silence. "What can you see?" she whispered.

"We're in the hold of a cargo ship," he said.

"That much I could tell. Do you see any men around?"

"Not anymore. Hush. Someone's coming."

The sound of tortured wood pierced the silence as nails were pulled from the sidewall of their crate, but no words were spoken. Seconds later, a different flood of smells and fresher air blew by her face as the crate wall was taken away.

Have we been discovered?

"Madam, s'il vous plait, if you would come this way. Only a bit farther, but you must be absolutely quiet." A man holding a crowbar spoke from out of the shadows.

"Untie yourselves," Catherine whispered into the darkness, not realizing that Freddie and George had already done so. It seemed they were more than ready to get out of their stuffy pine closet.

With Annie now in Catherine's arms and the teens following close behind, the man guided them up and down a series of metal stairways, through watertight doors, and finally into a corridor with what appeared to be passenger cabins. When they reached cabin four, they were ushered inside.

"Et voilà, Madame," the man said.

"Merci," Catherine said. The door closed before she could ask the name of the ship or where they were bound.

"Well, this is far better than that splintery box," Catherine said, after gently laying Annie on one of the bunks and covering her with a blanket. She rubbed the stiffness out of her backside as they perused their accommodation.

"It's not the Queen Mary," George said.

"We're safe and alive," Catherine said. "You should be thankful."

Understandably, Freddie seemed dazed. Inspecting their new surroundings, they found themselves in what appeared to be a lower-class, inside stateroom, without a porthole. Catherine was thankful the men who were facilitating their escape had been… no, not quite as kind as the stewards on the White Star Line Oceanic which had initially brought them to Liverpool, but at least they had not been harmed, abused, or molested—so far—just bounced around a bit. Their bruises would heal.

"Mother, what's going on?" George asked as Freddie turned to hear her answer.

"You know as much as I," she deftly lied. "I already told you that these men are taking us to some other port—hopefully in America, Canada, or the Caribbean."

"Well, I'm not going to stay here. It reeks, and it's filthy," Freddie said, nearly in tears and tugging at the cabin door handle. The door was locked. "There *must* be better cabins."

"Fredricka, *yes*, you are. Both of you are—as I said, your jobs are to look after each other and your sister, and stay calm—like diplomats in an uncomfortable, delicate situation."

Catherine's hands were trembling as she took a sip of water. A single tear ran down her cheek, which she quickly brushed away. She sat in the only chair and closed her eyes. While she had been trained in basic covert operations, never had her own children, her babies, been put at risk. *Never.*

"Mother, it will be all right," George said. "I won't let anyone hurt you or anyone." He knelt and embraced his mother, trying to comfort her.

Freddie joined in the group hug. "I'm sorry. I was being an entitled brat."

Across the cabin, Annie had awakened from her 'nap.' "Me too," she said, hopping down and wrapping her arms around her mother's legs, with Katie sandwiched in the embrace.

"Think of this as a grand *adventure*," Catherine told the children. "Now, who gets to sleep on the top bunk?"

"That's mine," said George as he kicked off his shoes and hoisted himself onto one of the upper berths.

"And this is mine," said Freddie patting the other upper.

"But *I* wanted to sleep in the sky," Annie said mournfully.

"Okay, let's see if you like it way, way up here," Freddie said, lifting her up. An instant later, Annie began to protest.

"Oh, okay I'll give you the bunk that's closer to mom," Freddie said, gently setting her little sister back on the deck. Annie plopped on the lower berth and began to bounce.

"And Annie and I will sleep together if I get scared," Catherine said lovingly to her toddler.

Someone knocked, the cabin door swung open and their suitcases were brought in by a small tan-skinned Asian man dressed as a cabin steward. His name badge read "Bing."

"You tell me you want something. I bring. Just ring bell." He pointed to a button mounted next to the door. "I bring breakfast at eight."

"Xiè xiè Bing—thanks," Catherine said in English-accented Mandarin. "Please, what time is it?"

"Early. Five forty in morning. They call me 'Mr. Bing'," he said with a smile. "You rest now. We sail on tide." With that, he closed and locked the door.

"Was that Chinese?" Freddie asked.

"Mandarin," Catherine said. "I only speak a few phrases, but a few kind words can open doors and soften hearts anywhere you go."

"Assuming he speaks Mandarin," Freddie said.

"No, you're right, not all people from Asia do. Let's get settled."

While Freddie retreated to the head to change for the night, George helped Annie get ready for bed and find a special place for Katie. Annie needed no encouragement to pull back the covers and burrow in, falling asleep before her head hit the pillow. It was almost as if someone had given her a sleeping potion early in the ordeal and it had not quite worn off.

Catherine took this opportunity to retrieve her journal and continue logging their story. As she gazed about the cabin to compile her recollections, she saw an ashtray with the name of their ship. *The Sutherland.*

December 10th. Day one on board the Sutherland. 4:50 AM. French (?) courier delivered a letter from Richard enroute. Boarded the ship hours ago. Every effort was made to hide our identity. On schedule. Expect to sail on the morning tide. Still haven't told the kids the entire plan. Accommodations spartan, but clean. Mostly. Kids are doing well. Annie's sedative has not worn off.

"Mom, are we in danger?" Freddie asked as she came out of the head tying the ribbons of her nightgown.

"We'll be fine. Get some sleep," Catherine gently reassured her. "It's still very early." She wound and set her father's watch to five forty-two. The precious keepsake made the cramped berth seem as appealing as a warm beach in the Bahamas while her thoughts drifted off to idyllic times before and after being married.

"You were as courageous as ambassadors; all of you," Catherine said, getting up to tuck in Freddie's covers and kiss her on the cheek.

"Like father?" Annie asked.

"Yes, like father."

"Go to sleep. We need to get as much rest as possible. We might have a long trip ahead of us," she said. She already knew they did. She snapped off the last cabin light. Suddenly, darkness enveloped her. With her eyes wide open, her mind began to conjure terrifying shapes and swirling phantoms all around her. Every sound, no matter how subtle, added to her angst. She had been warned about interior cabins, but never realized that she too would be affected by the absolute darkness.

"Mommy?" Annie cried. Reaching out, she realized that she was standing next to her bed, her daughter's face wet with tears. She clutched her to her breast and tried to soothe her.

"Mother, can we leave a light on?" George asked.

"Of course, it gets pretty dark in here," she replied, and got up to turn on the light in the head. The light was like a miracle tonic that seemed to soothe everyone. *It's going to be a long trip.*

Catherine knew she couldn't sleep. There was still a chance Richard would be able to make it to the ship before it sailed, but when the engines started, that hope evaporated. A few moments later, she felt the ship rock with the swell. *We're on our own.* She glanced at the time. *05:50.*

When the children's breathing told her they were finally asleep, she fetched the letter from her coat pocket and slipped into the head. Sitting on the facility, she broke the seal on the note. It was encrypted using their private cypher, which she knew by heart. She translated as she read.

> My darling, I fear they've found me. I cannot travel with you as planned so I will stay behind a bit longer . I trust these men. They will take you somewhere safe. When you're settled, let me know in the usual manner.
>
> We both knew this day would come. Use your training and wits to keep yourself and the children out of reach of those who would harm us.
>
> Your loving husband. Richard.

She began to sob quietly and kissed the paper, smearing the ink. Closing her eyes, she washed the ink off the page, shredded it, and flushed the bits into the sea.

"Mother, are you all right?" Freddie whispered through the door.

She took a deep breath. "Fine, darling. I'll just be another minute."

Three—The Protégé

*I*n a quaint clock shop in Klippenburg, Maine, two score clocks struck noon two seconds before the clock tower over City Hall echoed their chimes. Trudi, the clockmaker's granddaughter, didn't look up while every chime, ding, animation, and whirring gear made the shop seem like the finale of a kindergarten music concert. Having been born and raised here, she had grown accustomed to the shop's rhythmic heartbeat and the discordant concert held every quarter hour for each of her nineteen years.

As the echo of the last chime faded away and the final cuckoo had retreated, a bell over the shop door tinkled. Trudi rose to greet her grandfather. *Late, but safe.* "Any problems, Opa?" she asked, taking his bulky package.

Without a word, the old man tottered over to a clock that had finished chiming two seconds slower than the rest. Stroking its wooden side as if caressing a child, he whispered. "Try to keep up, Georgianna. I'll give you a warm bath, I promise."

"What took so long? I was beginning to worry," the girl asked as she hung his coat and hat. She noticed his face was slightly redder and his eyes drooped a bit more than when he left. While already concerned about his health, she had witnessed a steeper decline of late—his gait shorter, his breathless spells more frequent, his appetite waning, and his moods darker. Something was draining his energy and dampening his spirit.

"Holzkopf eines Metallverkäufers."

"English, Opa," she said, but understood his German phrase berating the shop owner where they bought their raw materials.

"That wooden-headed fool did not have our order ready. He made me wait."

"Mr. Dunson was supposed to *deliver* it yesterday. I'm sorry, he said he—"

"Macht nichts. I have most of it. Dunson will deliver the rest once he is paid."

Trudi shook her head. "Let's get you settled in front of the stove and a warm cup of tea. You must be frozen." *Why wasn't he paid?* she thought.

"I saw Mrs. Vandergelder," he said breathlessly as he moved toward the counter. "Her husband's not doing well so, I told Martha—"

"Sally Jo," Trudi corrected softly. "Don't tell me she badgered you to fix her clock next."

He nodded. "I promised I would fix it by this evening."

"Oh, Opa. There are so *many* left to repair ahead of hers. Please don't make promises we can't keep."

"But Frau Vandergelder is a good customer," he began. "While it costs quite a bit to win a new customer, it costs far more to get a disappointed customer to return. I'll make the time." It was one of his favorite expressions.

"She hasn't paid us for that ornate metronome, or her custom glockenspiel." She recalled her grandmother's words: *with more good customers like her, we would have to close the shop forever.*

"She will…" he said, heading toward the stool behind the counter to read the morning mail. "She will."

Experience had taught Trudi that Mrs. Vandergelder wouldn't pay, not without bribery or more concessions. She had already tried insisting and begging to no avail. Lately, the job of collecting what the shop was owed had fallen almost entirely on her young shoulders. She had already decided to try a new tactic with recalcitrant patrons like Mrs. Vandergelder. Those who paid promptly would be given precedence over those who procrastinated. The only problem was getting Opa to go along with the scheme—that would be even harder than collecting overdue bills.

At Trudi's feet, her tabby Clarence wove through her legs, begging for either attention or food, or perhaps just out of boredom. She picked him up and gently scolded his nose for being a pest. He just purred and nibbled her finger. "Shoo. Go catch a rat," she chided. The tom looked back as if spurned by a lifelong friend and strutted off, his tale twisted into a question mark. She knew he would be back before long.

Gazing out the front door, she frosted the glass with another heavy sigh. Outside, the world passed her by one or two people at a time. Klippenburg was a small village, so she knew many of the townsfolk and the stories of their lives, but as overwhelmed as she was with the shop, she yearned for time for herself—especially since her grandmother had passed away.

With a twist of his winding key, Captain, one of her favorite wind-up toy soldiers, came to life in her fingers. Setting him on the display cabinet, she watched him wave his tiny hand at the people passing by and come to attention and give a crisp salute. Captain was one of a cadre of intricate mechanical creatures she had conceived to keep herself company and entertain the customers' children. Outside, Mrs. Clancy, with her three-year-old in tow, paused as the little girl with red ringlet curls returned Captain's salute. Trudi looked up and smiled, Mrs. Clancy did the same and kept walking. When children came in the shop, she would let them play with Captain and the other wind-up toys, but his predecessor had mysteriously disappeared, so she was more careful now to ensure that they did not get scooped into a child's pocket.

Across the winding cobblestone street, Trudi saw a handsome young man linger at the corner. *Phillip*. As he looked toward the shop, his face widened into a warm smile. For just an instant, she returned the smile, but before she could wave back, a girl Trudi's age in a mink-collared coat appeared. *Ada.* She was a classmate from a well-connected family. The couple embraced, kissed, and strolled off, her arm in his—her fashionable skirt flipped up by the breeze.

Trudi returned to the counter where Clarence had climbed up begging for attention again, and where her grandfather was still thumbing through the small pile of letters and flyers. He gently stroked the cat, which purred in appreciation.

"Liebchen, isn't the awards dinner tonight?" Opa asked.

"Oh, you may be right." She pretended to be unconcerned, despite having scoured the mail for weeks, searching for an invitation that had never arrived.

The old man paused a moment and gazed at her with eyes that had seen so much, witnessing both tough times and good, and had watched Trudi's mother die in childbirth and his own wife fade away and leave him.

"Is there something you need?" she asked, touching his wrist to subtly feel his pulse. His skin felt cold, and his heartbeat slow. "A warm cup of tea? Something special for lunch?"

"We need to talk."

"I would like that," she replied.

"It's important—" he began. "But I'm too tired just now."

"Can it wait until after your nap?" she asked, leading him through the beaded curtain toward his overstuffed chair in the workshop. Draped over the chair's arms was the afghan Oma had crocheted for him thirty Christmases ago. As usual, Clarence waited patiently for his warm lap.

"Just a few winks," he said, tossing the mail into the trash basket as he passed.

Trudi stifled her sigh. She would have to forgo her plans for lunch if Opa could not watch the shop as usual. He didn't like to close at midday as some shops did. After she got him settled, she returned to the counter and picked up the phone, tapping the hook.

"Ernestine?" she said to the operator, "Can you ring Chrissy? Thanks." Trudi waited a moment for her friend to answer. "Hey, it's me," she whispered into the receiver. "Sorry, Opa is too tired. Perhaps another time. Yeah, I know, we need more help. Would *you* work for two bits an hour?" Trudi smiled at her vulgar retort. "Neither would I. Let's try again, later in the week." Trudi nodded her head at the response as a frown darkened her face. "I understand. Just come by the shop sometime, I would love to visit." She nodded again, said "bye," and hung up. She paused for another moment before returning to the workshop where she picked up Clarence and covered her grandfather's legs with the afghan. The cat immediately settled into his favorite resting spot.

The old man, his hand trembling on her arm, gazed into her eyes. *It must be important,* she thought. A shudder ran down her spine and a flood of ominous premonitions washed over her. *He's been to the doctor. He has cancer, it's his heart or...* "What is it?" she asked, but she was far from certain she wanted to know. If it were what she feared, life as she knew it would be over after his next breath.

"I need to tell you about the... the little people."

"The little people Opa?" *Not again.*

Her grandfather had at times hinted about his helpers or "Seldith," as he called them, and those fanciful stories had been more frequent of late. While sometimes she could feel subtle vibrations and other unexplained sounds from below the floorboards in the shop, he would never fully explain their source.

"Opa, really? You've told me stories about the Seldith since I was a little girl."

"Not everything."

"Why not? If they're real and not just some bedtime story, you need to tell me all about them."

"Because up till now I've had to keep them secret."

Trudi realized that Opa must be spinning another one of his tall tales. On countless occasions, he would weave elaborate fairytales as easily as Rumpelstiltskin wove gold from straw.

"A secret? Why? Are they dangerous?" she said, to humor him.

"Dangerous? They would never bring harm to us in any way. But you and I, Clarence, and the rats are their greatest threat. You must promise, *swear* to never tell anyone about them." He tightened his grip on her arm and glared into her eyes. "Not anyone."

"Well, that will be easy because I have no earthly idea what you're talking about. Perhaps you should just show me."

Opa looked down at Clarence purring in his lap. "I will. Soon. After I rest," he said with a yawn, which the cat echoed.

"All right, you two take your nap. You can show me after lunch."

Trudi's mind raced at the possibilities, given what negligible information her grandfather had revealed about these little people. *Perhaps he's gone mad?* She certainly wouldn't tell anyone. *What or who could I tell? Perhaps just Chrissy or Sally. Hardly. Sally never keeps any secrets. She would tell Bogart, who would tell his brothers, who would pass on the story with many embellishments all over town before the first light of dawn. No, I mustn't tell anyone. I need to think of something else. The mail...*

Kneeling by the trash bin, she retrieved the mail Opa had tossed away. Thumbing through it, her heart ached as she found more unpaid bills and unanswered correspondence. She added all but the ads to the stack she kept for Opa when he wasn't so tired. She realized that she would have to take over the books entirely if the old man could not keep their debts paid.

And no, there still was no sign of the invitation. *Something from the city, and the metal monger.* She opened the letter. The word "Overdue" had been stamped in red across the invoice. *No wonder they hadn't filled the order.*

While Opa napped, Trudi's day continued in earnest. She listened for the doorbell while she tried to work on the books and later, when the customer traffic waned, she repaired clocks in the adjoining workroom. It was midday when the bell in the shop tinkled. Returning to the sales floor, she found a middle-aged man browsing among their more ornate clocks; he was dressed as if he could well afford anything in the store. She greeted him with her friendliest smile. "Good day, sir. Can I wind up your interest in a fine clock?"

"Perhaps. Cute. I get it. 'Wind up,'" he replied, chuckling.

Trudi led him over to the better, more elaborate clocks most sought after by tourists and collectors where he picked up a small mechanical frog—one of Trudi's toys. "Can one still access the bay from up here?"

"They say the passages are long-since abandoned as they aren't safe," she said. She knew about the seldom-used door which she dared not open thanks to Opa's admonitions, but she suspected it led down to the bay.

"That's a shame," he said, "How much for this delightful frog? Is a dollar fair?"

Trudi hadn't really intended to sell the unique one-of-a-kind toys, but a dollar was indeed generous and sales had been slow. "Sure. Perhaps I can also interest you in Dora? She's one of our nicest clocks. She chimes in three octaves."

"A dollar it is," he said, admiring the delicate artistry of the frog before handing it to her. "Can you wrap it for me? My wife will love it."

"Perhaps you could kiss it and become her prince?" she said with a smile as she wrapped the mechanical toy. "Be a good frog. I'll miss you," she furtively whispered to it. "Anything else?"

"Not today. We'll be in town for another couple of days, I'll bring back the missus. She's the clock connoisseur."

"I look forward to meeting her. Have a good day," she said as he left.

For some reason, the tourist's curiosity piqued her own. *I simply must get Opa to show me behind that door.*

Not long after the clocks struck one, Trudi heard Opa working in the shop. When she joined him at the workbench, he made no mention of wanting to tell her any more about his little friends, and he seemed content, so she didn't press the issue. Around five, the last of the customers had left, so she closed the shop. Opa was still at work when Trudi rejoined him.

"Ready for some dinner?" she asked, kissing him on the cheek.

"I managed to get Mrs. Vandergelder's clock working. She had wound it too tight and broke the mainspring. Again."

"I know she'll be happy. Perhaps happy enough to pay us this time."

"I wouldn't go that far," he said, with the tips of his mustache curling up.

Trudi began reassembling one of the clocks her grandfather had repaired. Opa didn't tell her what needed to be done or how to do it, but just to get him talking, and to make him feel needed, she asked him a question: "Is this the right bearing jewel?"

"You know very well that Dianne insists on rubies," he said.

"Oh, yes, I forgot," she lied. "Rubies." Trudi knew the name of each of the clocks, which had been named like Opa's children when they were first built. The two worked in silence for a while before Trudi spoke again. "Are you ready for some supper?"

"About," he said. His voice was barely audible, and she could tell he was beyond ready to end his day.

"Then let's stop here for supper. We have much of it done. I can finish up after we eat."

"Got any of that stew left?" he asked.

"Enough for both of us. I'll bake a few biscuits too."

"Sounds good. I'll quit when it's ready."

The clocks chimed seven when Trudi called her grandfather into supper. She helped him to the kitchen table, draped a napkin under his chin, and sat in her place across from him, as always. While they ate, Opa told her how his trip to the supply shop had gone and complained that the price of sheet brass had gone up again.

They retired to sit in front of the small stove in the workshop as Trudi worked on the clocks and Opa read one of his books in German. As the clocks struck ten, she helped him get to bed. She was relieved that the nightly battle to get him settled was no more than a brief skirmish.

Once Opa's bedside light was turned off, Trudi quietly reopened his door a crack so she could hear him if he fell or called out in the night—as he sometimes did. She returned to the workbench and surveyed what was left undone. While she tried to keep up, as of late, there were many unfinished jobs and so few hours before patrons returned to demand their precious clocks, metronomes, and music boxes. Now that she was all but running the shop on her own, she rarely promised a quick turnaround. This meant people did not bring their clocks by as often for cleaning or minor adjustments, which didn't help business. It also meant the clocks that came into the shop needed more extensive repairs and deeper cleaning when they finally stopped working.

Given the amount of work yet unfinished, Trudi knew just what she had to do. Using a silver key hung on a chain around her neck, she quietly unlocked a cabinet in a dark corner of the workshop. Inside, a polished brass and steel figure as tall as a six-year-old sat patiently with his hands folded in his lap as if waiting on a park bench for his mother to return. His brass face had been modeled after a young boy who regularly stood at his mother's hip when she visited the store. The mechanical boy's eyes remained closed until Trudi pulled a lever on his shoulder and brought him to life. At that, the mechanism clicked, whirred, and for a moment, he looked up at her with trusting eyes. Using a crank inserted into his back, Trudi wound his mainspring, and after twenty turns, no more, no less, he sat upright, his back as straight as a choirboy. A moment later, his gears whirred again, and a narrow strip of paper inched out of his brass lips.

WORK NOW?

"Yes, Privi. Now we work."

The mechanical boy stood up, walked to the bench, and began to work. In years past, Privi would spit out innumerable questions and Trudi would show him what to do or make an adjustment in his mechanism, but lately, he had been working on his own without much guidance. Ironically, she wished Privi was a bit more talkative and less robotic. He helped pass the time and kept her mind off her own life's curvy road. It was also nice to have someone who would listen to her troubles and not criticize her decisions.

"What do you think about the mayor?" Trudi asked, not really expecting an answer.

Privi paused, albeit briefly, and looked at her before reattaching the clock's mainspring with his mechanical fingers and spinning tiny screws with a screwdriver built into his other hand. He printed another note:

`NO IDEA`

That was his default answer when he didn't know how to respond—or, (as she had begun to suspect), didn't want to. Privi really didn't seem to enjoy discussing politics.

"I think he's a bit scary. He acts like he's a self-coronated king. And his wife—she's certainly not like any of the other prudish mayor's wives we've ever had before. She dresses and wears makeup more like a streetwalker."

Privi nodded in agreement but never quit reassembling the clock Trudi had just repaired.

"Don't you think we should replace the chime spring too? I thought I saw a tiny crack."

Privi nodded and printed a short message.

`NO HAVE`

"We don't have a spare?"

`NO HAVE`

"Put the clock aside. I'll look for a new spring in the morning."

`I MAKE`

"You'll make it? Can you do that?" Up to this point, Privi had never done any steel spring fabrication, but he had watched her do it many times.

Privi looked up at her.

`I MAKE`

"Okay. Give it a try," she said, raising an eyebrow in disbelief.

Privi took a tightly wound coil of steel from a long row of drawers in the wall behind them and in a few moments, had fashioned and deftly rewound a new chime spring. He looked up at her again as if asking for approval or praise for his work.

OK?

"That looks fine. *Perfect.* Go ahead and install it," she said with a smile. Privi had come a long way and had progressed in his skill far faster than ever expected. It was as if he had acquired an intelligence well beyond what gears and wind-up motors could provide—almost like magic.

As Trudi watched Privi, she noticed one of her mechanical toy soldiers had walked over to them, as if he was curious and wanted to inspect their work. The soldier nodded in approval. "I'm glad it meets your standards," she said with a smile. The tiny mechanical man walked back over to his box on the edge of the workbench and sat, where he wilted as if going to sleep. When Trudi turned her back, Privi reached over and wound up the toy soldier and stood him up next to his box. Privi looked up as if asking for approval. Trudi nodded and smiled.

For the next few hours, Trudi and Privi repaired, reassembled, and tested the remaining clocks long past the point of being weary. Trudi's head sagged, and sometime later, she awoke with her head on the workbench. Privi was still sitting beside her, quietly boxing up the last of the clocks—their night's work stacked neatly at the end of the workbench, tagged, priced, and ready to deliver back to the customers when they called the next day.

"What time is it?" she asked, brushing brass shavings off her cheek.

0132

"Is that the last one?"

Privi nodded and placed the last box on the stack.

"Let's get some rest."

Privi nodded, but just stood next to the bench as if waiting for further instructions.

"Go on to bed, Privi. Thanks."

BED

Trudi watched Privi put himself back in his cabinet, pull the door closed, and lock it from the inside. Heading for her own bed, she looked in on Opa. He was still sleeping quietly with Clarence on guard at the foot of his bed—the cat's right eye opened briefly as she pulled up Opa's blanket. She did not remember climbing the stairs, changing into her nightdress, or getting into bed.

∞∞∞

About two in the morning, Clarence walked his nightly rounds, scanning the baseboards for telltale signs of rodents, and visited the dripping faucet in the kitchen for a drink. It wasn't long thereafter that he had the neck of a fat rat in his jaws. As was his custom, he left the inedible remains under the kitchen table and returned to Opa's bed to clean himself. His eyes nearly closed a few minutes later.

Four—The Last Day

As a warm ray of sunshine kissed her cheek, Trudi awoke to a new dawn—or she tried to. Hours before, as her body struggled in vain to get a few more minutes of rest, her mind had already begun clearing the pathways through the forest of her challenges.

"Get up," she told herself aloud. Reluctantly, she arose, washed, dressed, and made her way downstairs, all with her eyes barely open. Spotting a small furry lump under the kitchen table and cursing under her breath, she bent over to pick up the half-eaten rat carcass with her fingertips. Trudi appreciated that she didn't have to deal with live vermin on her own. Holding it by the tail as far as her arm would extend, she tossed it out the window toward the river five stories below.

Sleepwalking through the shop, she retrieved the newspaper spiked through the mail slot. The news included another mixture of scandals and intrigue which passed her by like a mute parade. Few of the stories ever affected her life, but this morning, a bold headline caught her eye.

AMERICAN DIPLOMAT'S FAMILY DISAPPEARS

Somehow, this story touched her heart.

> *London: Mrs. Catherine St. James and her three children Fredricka, age seventeen, George, age thirteen, and Annette, age four, have not been seen since they were collected at their London residence two days ago. Their driver is also missing. Mrs. St. James, the popular wife of the American chargé d'affaires, The Honorable Richard St. James, is a respected member of society. He has been unavailable for comment. While unsubstantiated rumors imply she and her children have been kidnapped, Scotland Yard has neither confirmed*

nor denied these reports. Anyone with information on their whereabouts should contact the American Embassy, Scotland Yard, or the American State Department. A substantial reward has been posted for information leading to their safe return.

Those poor souls. They must be terrified.

She scanned the headlines and noted the continued tensions in Europe as well as stories of unrelenting attacks against the Jewish communities in Germany. *I wonder how much they're offering as a reward?*

Refolding the paper, she laid it out for Opa to read at breakfast as part of his morning regimen. As usual, she lit the Franklin woodstove with the ads she had discarded and made their breakfast. Working like a machine, she ensured her routine didn't vary. Teakettle and frying pan on the stove, apple cored and sliced, toast in the toaster, butter, eggs, teapot, tea, and warmed plates at the ready. It would take exactly twelve minutes and eleven seconds to prepare and assemble it all. Just like clockwork. *I wonder if Privi could be taught to make breakfast?* Her mind wandered away to work out the intricate problems of such a task.

When she heard Opa stirring, she looked up from his sizzling bacon and yawned again. Pouring herself another cup of strong tea, she took a sip, a deep breath, and renewed her efforts to make sure his favorite breakfast was ready, knowing he liked to keep to his own rigid schedule. So did she.

And then, out of the din of ticking from the shop in the next room, she heard something—or more precisely, it's what she didn't hear that caught her attention. One of the clocks in the shop had stopped. After having spent nearly two decades listening to the constant, asynchronous ticking and chiming and cuckooing, it was as if the tick-tock symphony had ingrained itself into her very being. When any clock in the shop slowed down, or simply counted out the seconds unevenly, and especially if one stopped, she could almost always tell which one had failed, even from the next room.

Many had remarked on Trudi's exceptionally sensitive hearing—to her it was both a blessing and a curse. Sometimes it was better not to hear what people were saying when they thought they were alone. Trudi imagined it was like a mother being able to recognize the cry of one of her children from across the house, or a symphony conductor knowing which piccolo player had a late night. Her grandfather said her gift came from being born to a fourth-generation clockmaker's daughter, in a clock shop, at the stroke of midnight, when the clocks celebrated her birth with a twelve-chime salute with Westminster flourishes.

She returned to the shop and yes, Juliette, one of the older clocks, had stopped. She carried it back into the kitchen like a mother cradles a feverish baby, and laid it on the table. "Juliette, I'll see to you after breakfast," she said, patting the clock.

"Guten Tag, liebchen," Opa said, his cane clicking on the hardwood floor. He sounded as if his throat was encrusted with barnacles.

"Sleep well?" she asked, laying his plate of eggs, bacon, and apple slices on the table.

"Gut genug," he said, as he often did. She understood—"good enough."

"Englisch, Großvater," she reminded him with a smile. While Trudi understood her grandfather's German, she challenged him to use English—as had her grandmother whom he had brought over from the old country. Oma often chided, "…now we were living in the America, it is important to speak English." Opa was a hard case ("Lasst sie Deutsch lernen!¹"), still proud of the old country and his traditional ways. "The fatherland and Austria taught me all I know about clocks and

¹ Lassen sie Deutsch lernen: Let them learn German.

mechanical devices," he would say. "I dishonor that heritage by not speaking the language of the fatherland."

But both Trudi and her grandmother knew there was enough prejudice against foreigners as it was, without them speaking a different language. With the newspaper filled with more unsettling news from Germany, she knew it would be better to have their heritage remain in the shadows. But Trudi also knew that everyone in town was well aware of her family's ties with Germany and Austria—a fact that Opa did not let them forget. Vocally condemning the Nazis who had spread across his homeland like a plague of ignorance and hate, he knew there were plenty of Germans who disavowed Hitler's tyranny, when they dared. She said a silent prayer that fascism would not spread to these shores.

Opa opened the paper and studied one article after another. He pointed to the article of the missing family. "We need to remain watchful for these people. Perhaps they're Jews trying to flee that, that, Arschloch," he said, rattling the dishes with his fist.

"I would not be surprised. There are many hundreds of thousands trying to escape to freedom," Trudi said while refilling his teacup.

"That dream haunted me again," Opa said, peppering his eggs.

"Oh, I'm sorry. Was it the one where the elves and Faeries come in at night to fix your clocks?"

He nodded as he stirred in a dribble of honey with the handle of his fork. "It seemed very real this time. I thought I heard them working in the shop—tap tap tapping with their tiny hammers." She saw the corner of his bushy mustache turning up.

"Oh? I'll see that they work more quietly in the future," she said, placing a rack of warm buttered toast on the table before taking her place at the table.

"About dawn," Opa began, "… a clan elder came and stood on my bedside table. He told me a change was coming."

"The weather *is* turning colder. Winter will be here soon. Perhaps we'll have a white Christmas this year."

Opa's imaginative dreams were not that unusual, so Trudi was unconcerned. He often recalled his dreams of the forest elves, the Seldith, not much taller than his palm, coming to him in the night, offering help in exchange for protection and food. But as with other fanciful stories parents and grandparents tell their little ones, Trudi pretended to believe them to maintain the aura of mystery and the illusion of magic in their otherwise monochromatic lives. She herself dreamt of fairies tiptoeing between the shadows in her room. One night, they promised to whisk her away to their magical kingdom and make her their Queen and benefactress but she never shared the dream with Opa for fear of stoking his delusions.

"No, not the weather. Some other kind of change," he insisted. "Is there more bacon?"

"A change? What did they mean?" she asked, with feigned sincerity. "And no, no more bacon today."

"I'm not sure. They just said I should prepare for a change." He took a sip from his cup and stared into his inky tea. "Wait. We're out of bacon?"

"We have more bacon, but Dr. Stewart said to ration you to two slices a day."

"Harrumph," he said, eyeing her slice.

Trudi quickly snatched up her last piece and gobbled it down before he could distract her and take it. She didn't dare tell him that was the last slice in the house and it would have been the last of the grocery money for this week if it weren't for the what she got for her toy frog. She also knew that at forty cents a pound, bacon was a luxury they could barely afford.

"Perhaps the Seldith elder was right—I *should* retire and let the elves do *all* the work from now on. Since we've sheltered them all this time."

"Really?" This *was* great news—if he weren't kidding again. It would be a relief to let him live out his years at a slower pace. She could keep fixing the clocks and he could take his time in the park and sleep in, go play chess more often at the pub, and...

"Wait. Do all the work?" she asked. "Would they make your breakfast, do your laundry, clean the toilet, wash up, run the shop, and help you get in and out of the bathtub?"

"Don't be silly. They're terrible cooks."

"I wouldn't talk so loud; you might offend them. Perhaps they're great cooks," she whispered.

"Oh, I expect you're right." He feigned a worried look as he savored the last morsel of his bacon. "But their soup tastes of blueberries and sand," he whispered. "And you know how much I dislike blueberries."

"So, they came again last night?" She wondered why he knew how their soup tasted.

"They must have. I see that the clocks are all repaired and neatly stacked in the workshop. I thought I left a few unfinished."

"You left a few, but I'll admit, the elves and I finished up after you went to bed," she fibbed. *Did he really not know about Privi, or is he just pretending?*

"If I'm to retire, I need to talk to you about a few things... important things."

Someone knocked on the shop door. The old man frowned. "Let them wait," he growled. "They should know we don't open until nine."

She picked up the breakfast plates. "Yes, I'll be right back." Hearing another more insistent tap on the shop door, she turned to leave. "I'll bet that's Mrs. Robbins. She said she might be early."

Trudi laid the plates in the sink and hurried into the shop—still ten minutes before opening time. Shaking her head and unlocking the door, she discovered it was indeed Mrs. Robbins, and her work day had begun.

"I'm sorry to make you open early," Mrs. Robbins began, "but I'm here to pick up the clock—it's my husband's birthday and I wanted to surprise him at breakfast." She didn't wait to be invited inside.

"Of course, Mrs. Robbins. It's ready. I'll get it for you."

"I brought you that new novel I spoke of—it's ever so good. It's one of those pirate romances you like."

"Oooh," Trudi squealed, as she bagged the clock.

"Are *you* doing the repairs now?"

"Oh, hardly," she lied. "My grandfather does most of the work. I just do the final cleanup." She didn't want Mrs. Robbins to spread the word that Opa was barely able to keep up. After all, they were coming to the shop for *his* skill and *his* reputation as a master clockmaker, not hers. Trudi handed Mrs. Robbins the invoice—smiling when she paid in cash along with a nice tip. Mrs. Robbins was one of the good ones. Now she could pay some of the bills stacking up below the counter—and she could even buy more groceries and bacon.

By the time Trudi got back into the workshop, her grandfather was already tinkering with Joleen, a newer clock which included an elaborate music box that played different chimes each day of the week.

"Opa, the shop is quiet. Did you want to tell me something?" she asked.

Her grandfather didn't answer at first, still focused on a tiny part under the magnifier.

"Opa?"

"Ja, liebchen, it's time," he said, turning off the work light. Taking Trudi's hand, he led her across the room as if she might hesitate to follow him like the time he first took her to the dentist.

"Did you ever wonder about the drawers?" he asked.

"Where you store the replacement parts? Not really. I just assumed we bought them like the other raw materials, or you made them yourself."

"That's… not… They're made by…" Her grandfather began.

"Opa? Are you all right?" she asked. But she could see his face was pale, and a moment later, she had to keep him from falling.

He didn't answer, but took another step toward his room. "I think…"

Without warning, he grabbed his left shoulder and staggered—nearly losing his balance and pulling her over with him. Even in the dim light, his face told her he was in considerable pain. All at once, his knees failed, and she could do nothing to keep him standing.

"Opa? Opa!" He did not answer. His hands felt as cold as raw meat, and his pulse beat like a metronome with a broken regulator. "Sit. Just rest," she said, helping him sit upright. Her mind sifted through countless ways she could help, but they all seemed impractical, or meant she would have to leave to get help and she might never see him again. Holding his hand, she finally felt his pulse slow and settle to a slower, irregular rhythm. *Thank God.*

"I need to tell you the rest of the secret," he whispered, barely able to speak.

"Not on your mainspring. You're going to rest here quietly while I count to three hundred."

Opa nodded and closed his eyes, and she kept counting.

"Twenty-two...twenty-one..." she continued.

"Trudi, your father..." he began. "He's—"

"No. Don't try to speak. We can talk once I get you in bed and call Dr. Stewart."

Trudi didn't take her eyes off her grandfather until she felt it was time to take a chance on getting him into his bed. When she glanced up, she saw something move. "What was that?" she asked.

Opa didn't answer.

"Opa, I thought I saw a...a little man with a hat, about four inches tall. He was watching us, but then he ran into the shadows."

"I told you... about them," he said in a whisper.

"Your imagination is getting the better of both of us. Let's get you into... bed," she said, getting to her feet.

Something buzzed by Trudi's ear. *Bats?* She swatted it away, and she thought she heard a tiny voice cursing her. *Talking bats?*

Getting Opa to lie down took a Herculean effort; she had to help him across the room and into his bed, but they finally made it—almost as if someone were helping her. Once he was breathing steadily, and she thought he was out of immediate danger, Trudi rushed off. "I'm getting Doc Stewart. I'll be right back," she said over her shoulder.

All but out of her mind with fear and grief, Trudi darted into the street and screamed for help. While the pigeons roosting on the eaves fled in terror, there was almost no one on the street. Trudi kept calling for help until the beat cop, Officer McNally, appeared out of nowhere.

"My...grandfather. He's...he's not ... well."

"Does the shop have a phone?" he asked.

"On the counter," she said. *Why didn't I think of that?*

"Let's ring…"

"Doctor Stewart. He's not far."

"Fine, come inside before you catch your death of cold," the officer said softly, leading her back inside. He picked up the receiver and tapped the hook. "Ernestine, this is Officer McNally. Yes…yes, please send Dr. Stewart to the Sanduhr Clock Shop on Riverview. Yes, it's an emergency. Thanks," he said, and hung up.

"Is the doctor coming?" Trudi asked, her voice breaking.

"Yes, she'll get him. I'm sure he won't be long. Let's see what we can do until he gets here."

Trudi nodded and hesitated before pushing through the beads hanging down across the doorway. As she reached for the doorknob of her grandfather's bedroom, she heard someone talking—or thought she did—from inside. She paused and tried to listen.

"You don't have to go back in," McNally said. "Just sit here and I'll check on him."

"No, he'll be frightened. I need to be there… if…"

"Perhaps that's best," he said. "You *should* stay with him."

Brushing away a tear, Trudi followed the officer into the bedroom and immediately looked around. Opa's eyes were closed, and he had a thin smile on his face. Officer McNally's fingertips palpated the old man's neck. He pulled out a small pocket mirror and placed it on Opa's upper lip. Looking back at Trudi, the officer put on a brave smile. "He's breathing, but slowly. Hopefully, the doctor can tell us more."

At that moment, the reality of her grandfather's plight hit Trudi like she was stepping in front of a speeding car. She collapsed, and her world went black.

⁂

"Is she all right?" a voice asked. It was barely audible over the ticking clocks.

"I expect she's fainted," another tiny voice said.

"So, there's nothing we can do for the old man? Should we get——?"

"It's too dangerous. We've known for some time that his heart is far too weak for her skills. I wish it were otherwise."

"I expected as much. I've talked to him about his health for years and told him if he didn't take care of himself, he would only have himself to blame."

"We had better tell the others. A change is indeed coming…"

ele ele ele

Trudi felt a cool cloth on her forehead and opened her eyes. She was sitting on a chair while two men hovered over her grandfather—Doctor Stewart, using his stethoscope to listen to Opa's heart, and Officer McNally.

"He's alive, but I fear he's had a heart attack. He's too weak to be moved to a hospital. Let's step out to let him rest."

"He *is* going to be okay, right? If he rests?" Trudi asked as the doctor led her into the workshop and closed Opa's door.

"I don't think so," he said softly. "I expect his heart is failing. It will take a miracle to undo decades of poor diet, too much work, and not enough rest. If he makes it through the night, we can move him to the hospital. All we can do is wait. I'm so sorry."

"Is there someone who can come take care of you?" the officer asked, looking worried. "I can have my mother drop by."

Trudi shook her head. "I'll be all right," she said, but at this moment, she was not certain of anything. She glanced over to Privi's closet and saw him watching her through a crack.

Doctor Steward left her with a few tiny white pills to give her grandfather if he experienced any further chest pain, making her write down the instructions. "There is little else we can do but watch and wait," he said, squeezing her hand. "And pray."

Trudi kept the shop closed and spent the afternoon reading to Opa from one of his favorite books—H.G. Wells' *The Time Machine*. She would not let him speak of his secrets or the mysteries they held, fearing it would further agitate him.

"Later, Opa, later. We'll talk when you're better." He was too weak to protest.

That evening, she made them both a light supper, which she brought to his bedside. She was encouraged that he did seem to be feeling better and some color had returned to his cheeks. *Rest. That's the ticket.*

About eight, she adjusted his pillows and kissed him on the forehead. "Tomorrow, when you've had a good night's sleep, perhaps you can just *tell* me about your secrets."

"Ja. In the morning," he said. "Gute Nacht," he said, smiling.

"Gute Nacht, Opa, sweet dreams, Ich liebe dich. "

"Und ich liebe dich auch. "

Trudi fed Clarence and gave him a hug, wishing he would keep her company for the night, but he insisted on his usual place at Opa's feet. He wasn't the only one keeping watch.

Five—The Silence

*T*rudi's dreams were a confused tangle of leprechauns, rats, and street urchins huddling around a small fire. But, as frightened as she was, there were no comforting arms to embrace away her nightmares, and there hadn't been since her grandmother had passed years ago. Opa, as much as she loved him, could never fill her shoes as comforter and confidante.

Having thought she heard voices, Trudi opened her eyes and stared into her darkened room. As her eyes focused, she thought she could see two tiny people on the windowsill, framed in the moonlight. It was as if they were tiny figurines, escapees from a clock. Thinking that was strange, she snapped on the bedside lamp. When she looked back, they were gone. *Dreaming. I'm dreaming… I'm…asleep.*

In the quiet hours before dawn, Trudi found herself barefoot in the shop where every clock had stopped. The silence was deafening. In a panic, she raced from clock to clock, trying to restart their pendulums, but they would not swing for more than a few ticks. Suddenly, she heard loud metallic ticking, but it was irregular—unlike a clock ticking… more like a…

Trudi forced her eyes open and awoke to a woodpecker jabbing at the metal flashing outside her bedroom window. She scolded the bird, but it showed no fear of her protests. She was thankful to be brought back to reality, even though her feet felt like she had been skating barefoot on a frozen pond.

"I'm up, I'm up," she shouted at the bird. Thinking she had overslept, she scurried to prepare Opa's breakfast and was ready to lay it on a tray just as he lowered himself into his chair at the kitchen table as if nothing had happened. Incredulous that he hadn't stayed in bed, she wound up her lecture mainspring, but took a deep breath instead, deciding to revel in the fact that he was feeling strong enough to walk to the kitchen. *He's going to be fine.*

"Guten Tag liebchen," he said with a weak smile. He looked more tired than usual, his hair seemed grayer, and the skin on his hands and face looked as dry, mottled, and wrinkled as a sandy riverbed after a winter drought.

"Sleep well?" she asked, laying his breakfast on the table. She hoped he wouldn't notice the absence of bacon.

"Did *you*?" he asked, meticulously spreading a thin pat of butter on his toast.

"A few strange dreams…" she began. Something was troubling him, but she dared not ask. Her mind was elsewhere as well—mostly with concerns for his health and her future.

"What's left to get done before we open?" he asked.

"Not much. Just sit there and enjoy your tea while it's hot. Is there something *you* want done?" She dared not tell him that she didn't plan to open the shop until he was better.

"Just… just the secret. We need to finish our talk about the parts, and about your father."

"My father? You never mentioned him before. What about him? Didn't he abandon my mother before I was born?" But then she paused. She did not want to trigger another heart attack. "Your secrets can wait until you've regained your strength."

"But perhaps I can just—"

"Finish your breakfast and don't get out of that chair until I get your paper." She kissed his cheek and stepped into the shop. Not finding the paper inside the door, she pulled her robe closed and slipped outside to collect it. Leaning over, she smiled and nodded to Mrs. Porter peeking out her kitchen window. Caught snooping again, she snapped shut her curtain.

Scanning the headlines as she pushed through the doorway beads, "The world is still ending," she said aloud. "...the usual drama, His Honor the Mayor is in financial trouble, and another member of the legislature has been indicted. They still haven't found the missing diplomat's wife and her family. Nothing new." She laid the paper on the table.

Opa's eyes were fixed on Amser, one of his oldest clocks. Then Trudi heard it, the same as in her dream. *Silence?*

She turned back toward the shop. "Opa? The clocks have stopped!" She gently nudged his shoulder. "Opa?" She felt his cheek, but he didn't respond, his skin was cool to the touch. "Opa!" Her knees wilted as she knelt to listen to his chest. *Nothing.* She pressed her fingers on his neck as the officer had done. *Nothing. No pulse.* She embraced him—her tears flowing onto his flannel shirt. "No. No. No," she wept.

Feeling something on her shoulder, she turned to see Privi standing by her side.

OPA BROKE?

Through her swelling tears, Privi's face looked as human as ever—and somehow, immensely sad. "Yes. I'm afraid so."

I FIX?

"I wish you could. I wish *I* could."

❧❧❧

Sometime later, Trudi spoke on the phone to Dr. Stewart and then to the police. Officer McNally came promptly, as much to care for her as her grandfather. He organized men to move Opa to his bed, where the doctor closed Opa's eyes and reverently laid his time-worn hands over his chest.

The next few days leading up to the funeral were especially challenging. She had expected this day to come eventually but prayed that it would be years away—and not until she was ready. She remembered Opa telling her the fates rarely wait until one is ready to accept what happens next. He was right. She wasn't nearly ready. When the newspaper informed her that his obituary would cost money she didn't have, she decided to forgo that luxury, but she couldn't bear to post a sign on the shop door. It seemed too final.

Kneeling in prayer on a hard wooden bench while the priest gave the funeral Mass, Trudi felt little solace or comfort from the cleric's all-too-familiar words. Her mind wandered as she calculated how many times she had heard these same prayers that bookended every Mass. *Nearly a thousand times over the years.* When she heard heels lightly clacking on the stone floor, she turned to see the small chapel was populated by a few familiar faces. The old woman who spoke to Opa most mornings on his walk had taken a seat near the back—Trudi didn't remember her name. Chrissy, her friend from school, whispered a few words and sat behind her, and even Mrs. Peabody and Mrs. Vandergelder had put in an appearance.

Officer McNally and Dr. Stewart sat nearby, but the officer soon moved to sit next to her. She wished that he would put his arm around her, but he did not.

The funeral Mass was all but identical to Oma's. In both services, Trudi heard very few of the words as she tried to reach through to wherever Opa's soul had gone. She only wanted to say a final good-bye. *I pray Oma is there to comfort you.*

She felt a hand on her arm. "It's time," Officer McNally said softly. He helped her to her feet to process behind the hired pallbearers who took her grandfather's simple coffin to the churchyard, where an open grave waited.

One by one, she and Opa's friends stepped forward to express their soft condolences. She barely remembered anything they said, their sentiments washing out of her mind as if they were drawn in sand at her feet and swept away by waves of grief.

Mrs. Peabody hung back at the gravesite, and once the priest and the others had said the same words they said at her grandmother's funeral, she approached.

"Did he… is my clock fixed?" the old woman whispered. "My husband—"

Trudi looked into her eyes. "I'll see to it." Her fists tightened into stone mallets, while she lingered at her mother's and grandparents' final resting place. She didn't remember how long she stood in the soft rain, trying to make sense of it all, until Officer McNally appeared at her side, shielding her from the rain with an umbrella.

"Come home, Miss Trudi. You'll catch your death out here. It's time to carry on your grandfather's work."

She wasn't ready to do either, but she reluctantly accepted a ride back to the shop and was about to take refuge under her bedcovers when she heard it. The clocks in the shop had restarted. It was as if they had all paused for a long moment of silence…

కుకుకు

"Is she all right? I'm very worried about her," a female voice whispered.

"The Master's death has struck a heavy blow, but she's a warrior," another voice replied.

"Let's let her sleep. I'm glad we got the clocks restarted."

"I was afraid that might happen. Each one of them seemed to be quite attached to him."

Six—The Crossing

*A*bout eight in the morning, Mr. Bing awakened Catherine and her children with a tray of unfamiliar, but edible, food, and a pot of warm coffee for which Catherine was most grateful. "You eat. You try not make sound," he said.

"Where is the ship taking us?" George asked, but he made no attempt to get past the little man.

Mr. Bing said nothing as he retreated into the passageway and locked the door.

"George, please don't speak to Mr. Bing. It… it will make things more complicated," Catherine said.

"But where *are* we going?" he asked.

"We'll find out when we arrive," she said, inspecting the tray. She also realized why their door was locked. It was to protect her and her family from the crew—a thought that was both comforting and frightening at the same time.

George looked like he was about to ask another unanswerable question but thought better of it.

"Well, we won't starve." Catherine said, dividing their rations. "There are only two cups, so we'll have to share until we get more." She expected the teenagers would complain and squabble over their portions, but she was relieved that they were behaving civilly—better than some adults in a similar situation. *Fright has strange ways of affecting people.* Her training and experience in the field had taught her that.

"Mother, can I have a cupcake?" Annie asked.

"*May* I have a cupcake," Catherine corrected.

"You can have one too. I want chocolate."

"Sweetie, there are no cupcakes."

"Then ask Mr. Bing," the child commanded, stamping one foot.

Catherine gave her a medium serious glare. "Perhaps we should, but this is what we have now. Aren't you hungry?"

"For a cupcake."

"A chocolate one. Yes, I know. We'll see. Eat your porridge before George eats it."

"He better not!" she cried, and spooned in a mouthful.

Catherine managed to keep the children occupied with word puzzles and George made a checkers game on the steel deck with bits of paper, chopped carrot coins, and soap to draw the lines. Before noon, the carrot slices proved too tempting for hungry tummies.

But the hardest part of inside cabin life was fighting off the claustrophobia—her's and the kids'. It took only a few minutes to realize just how dark and scary the cabin became when the last light was extinguished. Their minds conjured terrifying imaginary beasts and goblins which seemed to appear out of the absolute darkness. To allay their fears, Catherine left the light on in the head as a night light and this seemed to help everyone except Annie who needed to sleep with her mom.

Thankfully, meals (with more barely edible raw carrot rounds) were brought with a modicum of regularity. Except for the rubbery celery, the food was palatable, but fell well short of the first-class fare to which they had become accustomed.

On the second day, Mr. Bing brought them a chess set, a tired deck of playing cards, a short stack of books, two more drinking cups, and—kept warm under a napkin—a few freshly baked iced cupcakes. As usual, he laid them on the table without a word, stepped out, and locked the cabin door behind him. And as usual, Catherine thanked him in Chinese through the door. Before she had turned around, Annie had devoured one of the cupcakes—and yes, it was chocolate. *How did he know? He must be listening. Of course, they are.* She looked up to see an air vent leading off to who-knew-where.

"Mother, may I have half of one of the cupcakes?" Freddie asked.

"You know what sweets can do, but perhaps a half won't push you over the edge," Catherine said.

Freddie grinned and carefully parted the cupcake in two, offering her brother the plate. "I cut, you choose," she said.

George quickly reached out but at the last instant, took the slightly smaller portion and decided not to eat it, giving it to his mother. "I'm not hungry," he said.

Catherine thanked him and noticed that he did look a bit green. She felt his head, but he didn't seem to be overly warm. Clammy, yes. *Seasick?*

They were all thankful for their own facility (which Freddie informed them was a "head") and sink, so they could access relatively fresh water for their personal needs. It seemed their captors had thought of everything—even passable towels. After two days, Mr. Bing came in with clean linens. Without a word being spoken by anyone, he made up the room. As usual, Catherine thanked him in Mandarin.

But this time, Mr. Bing smiled. "I no Chinese. Chan ben khoun Thai," he declared.

"You're Thai? From Siam?"

Mr. Bing nodded. "Captain and crew think I Chinaman."

At that point, a stream of Thai flowed from parts of Catherine's mind that had laid dormant since her days as a schoolgirl in Bangkok. Mr. Bing revealed his name was an impossibly long series of sounds that made it clear why he preferred "Mr. Bing."

He finally said he needed to attend to his duties in other parts of the ship before he was missed. He put his hands together in a wai and said, "Sawat de krap" with a low bow, indicating his respect for her social standing.

Catherine replied. "Kop koon maak. Sawat de ka," she said with a slight bow, as was appropriate for a woman of her elevated status.

Mr. Bing smiled and nodded as he stepped out, locking the door behind him.

"Mother, what was *that?*" Freddie asked.

"You didn't know I spoke Thai?" she said with a grin.

"No. Not at all."

"Well, neither did I, but something clicked when he said he was Thai."

"What did he say? Did he reveal where we're headed?"

"He told me his name and that he's from the north—a small village near Chiang Mai. He wanted to see the world, so several years ago he got hired on when the ship was in port near Krung Thep, which is Bangkok."

"And…?"

"Oh, I didn't ask him where we were going. He wouldn't know," she lied. She had asked and Mr. Bing said, "Mai lou," which meant he didn't know.

"It's a strange language—like singing," Freddie said.

"Most westerners don't have an ear for it and if you don't learn as a child, you might never learn to hear the vocal tones," Catherine continued.

This exchange opened a floodgate of language duels between Catherine and the teens in German, French, Spanish, and Russian, leaving Annie confused at first, until they found that she too could learn simple phrases. They decided to teach her how to ask for help, "Where is the toilet?" and "Where is the American Embassy?", phrases which they agreed every diplobrat should know in several languages.

"Now teach me to ask for a chocolate cupcake!" she demanded.

As the afternoon progressed, Catherine refreshed her children on her early childhood as an embassy worker's child. "I was also a diplobrat," she admitted. She told her children that she had lived on the outskirts of Bangkok and had to learn conversational Thai from the day their family met their staff, who spoke only a few words of English. It wasn't long before she became the family's translator and a real hit at the lavish parties hosted by her parents, which were teeming with diplomats, politicians, and generals. Her servants were meticulously careful that she only use more formal Thai, and never the street slang or the pronunciations she overheard from the staff. It seemed she was to speak the "proper" Thai used by important, high-ranking people, and not use their working-class words or phrases.

"Like in the UK," Freddie said. "I overhear an entirely different dialect of English on the streets and from our own staff on occasion."

"Exactly," Catherine said. "The way a person speaks brands them by class faster than their dress or mannerisms."

"Pygmalion," George said. "They just released Pygmalion, a film about a flower girl passed off as a mysterious duchess."

"Perhaps we'll get to see it. It should be fun," Catherine said.

"Weren't you afraid to go into the dark underbelly of Bangkok?" Freddie asked.

"At first, I never went alone, but I soon overcame my fear. I tagged along when the embassy driver took my mother into the city on errands. I remember the traffic was overwhelming and chaotic, clogged with pedal bikes and motorized tuk-tuks, pedestrians, and massive trucks gayly decorated with lights and festooned with horns," she began.

"Tuk-tuks?" Freddie asked.

"Tiny three-wheeled cabs that run on smoky motorcycle engines. Shall I continue?"

Her kids nodded in agreement. "But once I arrived at the shops, the owners invariably treated me and my parents like visiting royalty. I remember one such visit...

"Sa wat dee ka. So nice to see you again, Miss Catherine," the owner's daughter said, offering me a deep wai. "Please, come sit down and have something cool to drink. Cha yen?"

"Chai. Kop coon maak," I would reply. "Yes, please." The sweetened Thai iced tea was a delicious treat, and I knew the jeweler boiled the water before it was prepared, as the ice might be contaminated.

"Knowing the language opened many doors for me, helped me make and keep more friends and allies in important places. It also made it easier to be aware of my surroundings and avoid situations where I might be put in jeopardy. Whenever I was out walking, I would listen intently to the people around me who assumed I didn't speak their language."

"Why didn't they think you spoke Thai?" George asked.

"Well, most westerners didn't take the time to learn the local language, and when they tried, they shredded the words. It was like listening to a first-grade band concert abusing a Bach concerto. And I didn't have straight black hair like most Thais. They just assumed I was an ignorant 'farang', a foreigner."

It was then that Catherine realized that she had become a career diplomat almost from birth. What she didn't share with her children was that this international experience made her attractive to intelligence agencies at a prodigiously early age. After the embassy parties, little innocent Catherine would be asked to replay the conversations she had overheard. It took years for the guests at these parties to catch on and not share their confidences and secrets within her earshot—but by then, her family had moved on to another post, where she quickly absorbed new languages and dialects. She didn't share stories about how she worked in the field for a number of intelligence agencies and received considerable training and experience well before she met Richard.

After the kids settled into their beds for the night, Catherine caught up with her journal.

> December 11th: Day two. Discovered our "Chinese" Mr. Bing is Thai, but even so, he has not been told where we're headed, or he isn't saying. The kids didn't know I spoke Thai, so we played a game that exercised their own language skills. I'm so proud of them. Someday, they'll make great diplomats, or perhaps spies. Seas seem calm and we're finally getting some rest.

Just after Bing had brought them breakfast on the third day, cups and dishes began sliding around and bouncing off the table's metal rails before crashing to the floor. At first, the kids thought it was fun, until Freddie complained of a queasy stomach—just before emptying her breakfast into the head. The smell triggered most of the rest of the family to follow suit, one-by-one—all but Annie, who seemed unfazed by the rolling decks. Before long, the rest were clinging to their bedrails. Thankfully, Mr. Bing had foreseen this eventuality and supplied a mop and bucket as well as several large bowls to deal with the side-effects of living onboard a ship tossed about on the sea like a cork in a storm drain.

After another day of this, Catherine was happy that she and her offspring had finally discovered their sea legs and their mal de mer had abated. It was only then that they discovered Annie had found a new pet, which she had been feeding and hiding in her pocket: a small brown rat.

Over the next two days, Catherine overheard Freddie and George spend considerable time hatching and incubating elaborate plans to overcome Mr. Bing, steal his keys, and escape. At the same time, Catherine did her best to keep them otherwise occupied and not frighten Annie. Nevertheless, the seemingly endless days and nights tended to ratchet up their boredom and anxiety.

December 14th: Day Four (I think). We've all been seasick, all but Annie. Our only respite is to hold on to our berths, hoping we can get through this. Freddie said she had a whole new appreciation for the poor souls on the Mayflower. I think we can forget our anniversary cruise. I'm really missing Richard, and my idyllic life in London.

જજજ

About midnight on the fifth night, Freddie's screams woke everyone. Catherine rushed to her bedside, trying to soothe both her and Annie, who also sat up crying. "It's just a dream, darling."

"Mommy, are they going to sell us into white—?" she whispered.

"I won't hear any talk like that. We're safe and everyone has been exceedingly kind."

"But I'm frightened. I want to go home," she wept.

"As do I, but we must be brave," Catherine confessed. "Please, just try to sleep. We're all so tired."

Catherine retreated to the head and opened her journal.

December 16th. Day Six. We've had about all we can take locked away in this dark, cramped, smelly, rat-infested jail-cell of a cabin.

Seven—The Subfloor Clan

*I*n the dim space beneath the floorboards and between the joists of the clockmaker's workshop, Alred, an elf no taller than a large mushroom, waited in silence with a handful of other Seldith[2]. They knew they had to remain especially quiet while the umans[3] were in the workshop directly above. Rumor had it that something important had changed. The closely knit clan of about five-score elves knew they needed to be ready for whatever came next.

Like his father and grandfathers before him, Alred had been born with the Wizard herditas[4]. He knew it may be time to work his powerful magic once again but wondered if the incantation would be his final spell. As a senior Elder, it was also his duty to mentor the Seldith through this, and every, crisis. It helped that his copious experience with umans made him especially valuable to every level of the Seldith clan.

Over the last several days, the clan could not help but hear Trudi's mourning cries, but they had already known their uman benefactor's health had been failing. It had been a topic of discussion for years. Listening behind the walls and watching over the umans from the shadows, their spies had kept the clan leadership well informed. Lately, the news had been especially grim.

For the last couple of days, the thump of uman boots had kept the clan awake at all hours, as they worried about the dreaded event that would ultimately dictate their fate. As much as he would have liked to have helped cure the old uman, the

---

[2] Seldith—An ancient clan of magical forest elves.
[3] Uman— The elven term for a human.
[4] Herditas—An inherited task or magic ability passed from one's parents.

clan leadership had reluctantly agreed there was nothing they could do.

A handful of sems[5] squatted nearby, some also standing around Alred as more gathered, seeking news. "Is it true? Has the uman passed?" one younger sem said.

Alred nodded, and a wave of trepidation and uncertainty washed over them all. He could see it in their faces and their tears. Out of respect or fear, they uttered not a word. "Just do your work and remain quietly vigilant in your homes. We'll soon know what comes next. Speculation is pointless. All we can do is be patient and wait."

When the uman's living space above them finally fell silent, the sems huddled together more closely, buzzing with questions. Alred raised his hand and silenced them. He wrapped his arm around Kenezer, a middle-aged nesem[6] standing by his side. He brushed away her tears.

"Should I have tried to heal him?" she asked, gazing into Alred's tired eyes. "Didn't you tell us a story about the healer saving a uman back in Stone Valley?" Others nodded at the suggestion.

"While it's true that Herachel did heal a uman, no one can be brought back from the dead—even the most skilled healer cannot perform *that* miracle. We also know that the old uman was well past any healer's skills." Alred recalled the indelible memory as if it were yesterday. A misguided, over-ambitious healing had taken the life of someone quite close to his heart.

"I could have *tried*," Kenezer said, squeezing his arm.

Alred could feel the power of her gentle touch pulling away his pain. Kenezer's herditas of empathic healing, passed down from her mother, gave her the power to absorb pain and injury with a touch—taking on her patients' afflictions as her

---

[5] Sem: An adult male elf—as 'man' when referring to humans.
[6] Nesem: An adult female elf—as 'woman' when referring to humans.

own. If the injury or illness was not too severe, the healer could recover in time, but sometimes they would sacrifice themselves and not survive.

But Kenezer was not unique when it came to magic. Almost every member of the clan had a power of some kind, some subtle, some ordinary, and a precious few, like Alred, quite profound and ever-growing. While Alred had unique and exceptionally powerful gifts, he was loath to display or use them for reasons he kept to himself.

Alred shook his head at the troubled healer's eyes staring up at him yearning for reassurance. "I'm afraid not," he began. "Mr. Sanduhr told me we should let him pass. He knew it was his time," Alred said softly. The old man had been a loyal friend and Alred trusted precious few umans—for countless reasons that hard experience had taught him.

"What of our jobs?" one brave sem asked.

"What about our food?" asked an anxious nesem.

"We agreed long ago to help him and his family whenever and however we could. His passing does not change that agreement."

"My father says the clockmaker was killed by the rats," a teenage yesem[7] said bravely.

"Nonsense. He was just an old uman at the end of his days," Alred said, his eyebrows pushed down, furrowing his brow. "They usually don't live longer than their eighties."

"Really? My grandfather is over three hundred winters old. Aren't you older than that?" the yesem asked.

"Sometimes I feel far older than my years."

"My father says the rats have been poisoning the old uman for years and biting his toes at night," said a yesem standing nearby.

---

[7] Yesem: A young male Seldith elf.

"James, have your father come see me. I don't want *any* of you spreading these made-up stories. It's immoral and against The Book[8]." With a look, the yesem wilted and scurried away. By the time he reached his home, his father had mysteriously lost the power of speech.

"If the old uman isn't going to give us food, how are we to eat?" a voice from the growing crowd asked.

"We can make do. Seldith always have—long before living on handouts from umans, and we still have our river-side gardens and fish traps."

"Will the uman girl want to help us?"

"Miss Trudi? Perhaps," he said; Alred was far from certain she would be willing to take on her grandfather's responsibilities as provider, but Alred knew it would be his job to find out. Some time ago, the Grand Council had tasked him to be their liaison with the uman clockmaker, given his extensive experience with the giants. As a result, he had been charged with managing the agreement which specified the clock parts the uman requested. In exchange, the uman would provide food, protection from the outside world, and, from time-to-time, access to his fermented ale and wine. This symbiotic relationship had been going on for generations—long before Alred had arrived and, for that matter, before the old uman came to the shop as an apprentice.

And Alred already knew about Miss Trudi, as he called her. Once he was made liaison to the umans, he pledged to look after him and the old uman's granddaughter, and that he had done. Her 'mechanical' assistant was built from parts she had designed but Alred had enhanced with a bit of his own magic.

---

[8] The Book of Truth details everything the Seldith hold as true—every law and every explanation of the world around them. Think of it as a holy book and encyclopedia in multiple, massive volumes.

He had never told her, or anyone, for that matter—not even the old uman.

Now that the old uman, the master clockmaker had passed away, he knew the Council would call on him to resolve this crisis. But almost everyone had expected the uman to live long enough for his granddaughter to bear a son to take over the shop. According to their Book of Truth, no Seldith had ever negotiated with a *female* uman—much less a teenager. Alred was not encouraged by this prospect.

At that, several elves asked a flurry of questions.

"And what about the machinery?"

"Who will want the clock parts we've been making and repairing for him?"

"And all that scrap metal?"

"And the coal? Who will bring us fuel to stoke the forges and keep our homes warm?"

Alred held up his hand again to mute the restless crowd as it grew more anxious. "We simply don't know. I'll be meeting with the Council to formulate a plan. In any case, we should stop using coal anyway. The noxious fumes are making many of us sick."

Another round-faced yesem spoke up. "Are we going to starve? My papa said we will…"

The yesem's mother reached out to pull him closer but Alred shook his head to dissuade her. "No, we won't starve," he said softly. "We'll do what we always do. We'll forage and fish, and adapt, and if we *really* must, we'll move out of River House," he said, using the calmest voice he could muster—as if relocating the clan would be as easy as organizing a summer picnic. Alred smiled and reached over to tussle the yesem's hair. "When I was your age, our clan moved quite often—

south for the winter, north for the summer and many times to escape umans or belluas[9].

Given that grumbling dissent and fear were spreading like a brushfire, Alred understood that he and the Council would have to devise a workable plan, at least something to get them through the next few days—and quickly. He had seen this before. Uncertainty and change foment fear and dissent.

Sondrah, an attractive middle-aged nesem with a delightful twinkle in her eye, stepped forward. "May I speak?" she asked, raising her hand.

"Please. Any of you. Feel free to comment or ask questions. The Council and I want to hear what you think. Just keep your voices down. We can't be sure the umans won't come back."

"I don't think anyone wants to move," Sondrah began. "We have been here for generations, long before you joined our clan. Almost none of us have lived like nomads. Some have rarely gone outdoors." Her tone wasn't sharp, but not particularly supportive. "The uman girl might still feed and protect us—it's in her best interest. We simply need to ask her for help. Perhaps she'll be amenable to the old arrangement."

"Are you volunteering?" Nonbon, one of the older Council members, interrupted.

Sondrah just glared at him and stepped back.

"I thought not."

Alred expected Sondrah, like most sems, was understandably afraid of the umans. Who wouldn't be? As far as the Seldith were concerned, umans were loud, clumsy, oafish giants with large, smelly bodies, and noisy boots. While Alred had spoken to umans before, negotiating, arguing, and even going into combat against them, he had seen them toppled,

---

[9] Bellua: Any aggressive creature. Raccoons, opossums, bobcats, rats, dogs, or cats.

wounded, and killed, but he still showed umans a considerable degree of respect and prudently kept his distance. He had also learned they were much like the Seldith in most things but size. Some umans were good, and some evil, some smart, and some challenged with the complexities of dressing in clean clothes.

Dumold, an orange-bearded sem in gold-braided robes with flashing ornate rings on every finger, entered from the Council chambers. He was flanked by several uniformed, sword-wielding sems—members of the Council Protectors. Mounting the dais, Dumold pushed aside several other members of the Council and raised his hands as if to stop applause, but there was none—just a low contemptuous grumbling. He raised a scroll and began to read—haltingly as if it was a skill he had barely mastered.

"My fellow River… Housians," he said, looking down again at his notes. "Thank you for… assembling." He scanned the scroll again, looking for his place. "… to deal with this is a very serious matter. No matter… what I decide to do myself, I promise you it will be the best decision. I always make the best decisions. So when I decide what to do, whatever it is I do, I assure you River House will be kept safe. Since I was elected to head the Council by the widest of margins without the help of any other party…"

At this point, the volume of dissenting voices grew louder which prompted Dumold's Protectors to loosen their swords and scan the crowd for trouble.

He rambled on, apparently too focused on the scroll, and either didn't hear or ignored the rumblings from the onlookers. "…we have had to make a number of important changes to tighten security and protect us from the umans above. For this reason, I am ordering that the trap door be sealed to form an impenetrable wall between us and the umans…until I have decided…what to…do." Rolling up the scroll, he looked toward the dwindling crowd, but he did not make eye-contact with anyone.

"Are you mad or just stupid?" someone called out from the back. "What do you plan to *do?*"

"Do we need to move? How can we get our supplies, fuel, and food if you seal off the umans?"

Nonbon leaned in and whispered something to Dumold who nodded and raised his tiny hands. "The Council will retire for... one week while we... we study this problem which I did not create." He and his cadre turned at once and withdrew to the chamber with the other Council members. Alred stayed behind.

"What? Wait. We need to hear from the council. What is it *they* want to do?" the crowd shouted to the council member's backs as they retreated into their inner sanctum.

Alred just shook his head. Once their elected leaders and their sycophants had disappeared, the clan slowly dispersed, returning to their own lives and jobs with their children in tow, but the grumbling didn't stop.

"Something needs to be done," Sondrah said.

"I agree. I doubt if we have much time," Alred said.

"How so? We've been fine so far."

"If we're found accidentally by someone from outside the old uman's family or if his granddaughter starts to ask the wrong questions, we have no idea how she might react."

"Has she ever seen us?" Sondrah asked.

"Perhaps. The old uman insisted that we remain hidden whenever we met but it's high time we were introduced," Alred said.

"Yes. Long overdue. It would have been far easier if all three of you had met when he was still alive," Sondrah said.

"I agree—far less dangerous as well."

Eight—The Will

$\mathscr{T}$rudi's next day arrived like the morning train carrying her through life—a conveyance she had no choice but to board and ride where life's tracks took her. Struggling through the morning routines of bathing and dressing, she tried to keep her thoughts focused on the next minute—fearing to contemplate what might appear out of the darkness at the end of this interminably long tunnel.

Staring at the leaves being bullied by the wind in the street below her window, she realized that not only had she not opened the shop, she hadn't even made it out of her bedroom. She ran a brush through her hair, then, still standing at her washbasin looking at a sad young woman in the reflection, she asked herself *why?*

Clarence appeared at her feet, and as she sat back down on the bed, he made his way to her lap. "He's not coming back, hon." The cat's large gold eyes stared up at her in disbelief. "I'm so sorry." Embracing him, she closed her eyes and began to cry again. "Neither of us got to say goodbye. I know I wanted to tell him I loved him, and I know he was trying to tell me something…"

When she opened her eyes, she heard someone tapping on the shop door beneath her window and calling her name. Clarence hopped down and raced out as if expecting Opa to be returning from his morning walk. "Coming," she said, loud enough to be heard. Wiping away her tears, she patted out the wrinkles on her dress and went downstairs to mute the annoyance.

Outside the shop, a well-dressed stranger peered through the door, his breath fogging the glass.

"What is it? The shop is closed," she said from across the room.

"Miss Sanduhr? I have important business to transact."

"Can't it wait?" she begged, not really wanting to talk to anyone.

"Please. May I come in and speak to you privately? It's really important."

Relenting, Trudi nodded and let him in, locking the door behind him.

The intruder, holding his case and his bowler hat in one hand and a business card in the other, seemed troubled—as if he were the bearer of sad news. "I'm so sorry to trouble you Miss. I'm Mr. Raymond Brook, Attorney at Law," he said. "I'm your late grandfather's attorney." He offered his business card.

"Nice to…" Trudi began, accepting the card. *No, I'm not happy to meet you.* It was his voice that reminded her she had seen him meet with Opa. "We should go to the other room so we can speak without being disturbed," she said, leading him toward the kitchen.

"Again, I apologize for disturbing you," he said. "I know this must be an especially difficult time for you."

I was wondering when you vultures would start circling.

She offered him the guest chair at the kitchen table. "I'm sorry, I don't have anything to offer other than tea, and that's cold." Feeling a chill herself, she lit the stove as Clarence took up a guard post across the room.

"A cup of warm tea would be most appreciated. I've been waiting quite some time and, it's unseasonably cold out there."

"I'm sorry, Mr. Brook, I did not intend to open the shop today," *or perhaps ever.* Trudi tried to focus on making tea—she needed it as much as this blue-lipped attorney. "Why is it my grandfather never mentioned you?"

"He was—"

"Besides your business card, how do I know you are who you say you are?" she interrupted.

"I have his witnessed signature on your grandfather's last will and testament. Can you recognize his moniker?"

"Yes, Mr. Brook, I help with his books and have him sign all of the checks," she said with measured tones. "Can you show me the document?" She didn't mention that she had been forging his signature out of necessity for many years.

"I didn't mean to offend you Miss, it's just that—"

"Yes, I know. Too many people don't know how to read. No offense taken," she lied with a thin smile.

Mr. Brook opened his case and extracted a document yellowed with age. He smoothed it flat for her and pushed it across the table.

"Yes, that's how he signed documents—down to the drawing of a clock." Trudi carefully studied the paper. It took a moment, but like winter rain on a thin cotton coat, the frigid reality of her grandfather's words soaked through to her soul. *How could he?* Opa had left his entire estate to his deceased wife, Trudi's grandmother, his deceased daughter, Trudi's mother, and…

"Wait. He left everything to my father Dick Heiliger? The scoundrel who left my mother after I was born? That's unbelievable," Trudi said.

"Yes. I'm afraid that's what it says—at least as far as the inheritance."

"That's just not fair, it's not right, it's immoral," she said, holding back tears and shoving the will back into Mr. Brook's lap. "I was told that after my mother passed in childbirth, my father disappeared, never to be heard from again. That was nearly twenty years ago. I have no idea where he is or if he's even alive."

"I hate to tell you, but that's not completely true. Your father did not marry your mother and only knew her in passing. I can only assume that putting Mr. Heiliger in the will was an enticement to encourage him to return and accept responsibility for your and your mother's welfare."

Trudi just stared at the man sitting across from her, his eyes unable to meet her face.

"I'm sorry, but his will was executed about the time his daughter Maria was found to be carrying Mr. Heiliger's child, and I expect he was included in the will as a dowry or enticement of sorts. While an atypical practice—this old-country tradition is still performed from time to time. I encouraged your grandfather to amend the document several times, and again in the last few years, but he never did."

"So, my so-called *father* was to be bribed to marry my mother?"

"One could interpret it that way."

"But he never did. Not exactly a saint."

"Exactly. He simply failed to return, and your grandparents lost touch with him."

"Did he know my mother Maria was carrying his child?"

"That's not at all clear. I expect not, which might explain his behavior."

Trudi's mind was reeling with these revelations. Opa had never told her the truth. *Why? Was that what he was about to tell me before he passed?*

"Miss, your grandfather, Mr. Sanduhr, appointed my firm as the executor and instructed us to hold his estate in trust for you until your twenty-first birthday, or until your father, Mr. Heiliger, comes forward to claim his inheritance."

"That's less than two years. I'm twenty in March."

"Yes. Once you turn twenty-one you will no longer be a minor and the estate will revert to you and your heirs."

"I look forward to that day," she said, getting up to fetch the now-steaming kettle.

"Is there some reason you don't use your father's surname?"

"Why would I? As far as I'm concerned, my grandparents raised me. I've always used their name. And as you said, Heiliger never married my mother. By some chance, do you know where my so-called father is?"

"As I said, we lost touch long ago so, no, we do not. My firm is, however, required to make a concerted effort to make him aware of the inheritance. I did enquire about his whereabouts the last time I met with Mr. Sanduhr. That was over two years ago. We now suspect Mr. Heiliger might have been using an alias when he dated your mother. If he was an important person, that's not uncommon."

"Or a scoundrel and a rogue. What's been done to find him?" Trudi asked.

"We have posted advertisements in every major newspaper in the country—seven papers so far."

"I see, and has he answered?"

"Not so far, but it's been too soon. In cases like this, it's not unusual for individuals and confidence tricksters to fraudulently claim an inheritance, so even if someone responds, it will be our duty to verify their identity and veracity."

"How will you be able to tell the criminals from my real father?"

"We were hoping that you had photographs, an example of his handwriting, or any identifying marks that could help."

"Identifying marks?" Trudi asked, as she poured from the kettle to fill the teapot.

"Tattoos or birthmarks. Perhaps he had a deformity like webbed feet, a missing finger, or a scar?"

"Or a forked tongue and hooves?"

Mr. Brook smiled. "That might make identification easier."

"I wouldn't know about any of that. My grandparents never spoke of him—it was a sensitive subject. Milk or sugar?" she asked, pouring the tea.

"Just black. Please. Are there papers he might have signed or photographs of him and your mother?"

"I… I don't know. I have not thought about much of anything since my grandfather's passing." She handed him the cup, which he used to warm his hands, still red from the cold.

"Thanks. Of course. I'm willing to leave a copy of the will with you. He does say some kind things about you in some of the accompanying documents. He made it clear that we were to do what we could to protect your interests, and that is our intent."

"But my 'father' still inherits the shop, the clocks, and this old tyrolean pile of stone."

"Yes, I'm afraid he does, and rights to the clock designs. But we can appeal to the probate court, and perhaps, since he abandoned you so long ago, you might very well win a favorable judgement, or even have him declared dead."

"I see a 'but' in your expression."

"But… you are still a minor and a female. Both will limit what the court will grant. Without a guardian, without–"

"A man, a husband, the court will not give me what's rightfully mine, what I've worked nearly twenty years to earn, to rightfully inherit. That's utter balderdash, if you'll pardon my language."

"I can't agree more, but that's the way of the world until the laws can be changed," Mr. Brook said.

"Changed by men in Congress."

"Sadly, I'm afraid so. Please let me know if you find any documents or photographs that might help locate and identify your father."

Trudi nodded "I will. Is there any other legal advice you can give me?"

And there was. While Mr. Brook recovered from the cold, they discussed the rudiments of keeping the shop in the black. Showing her competency would go a long way in court. Hours later, Trudi called him a cab.

"Have a good day, Miss. I wish I had brought happier news," he said.

She locked the shop door behind him.

Men really know how to kick a girl when she's down. A single tear, then two, then a torrent, flowed down her face as she collapsed to her knees in the center of the shop. There she wept, immersed in the comforting ticks and tocks which had punctuated and comforted her days and nights for as long as she could remember. These staccato sounds were the very heartbeat of the shop—of her life. She was no longer sure how she was to keep them all ticking or why she should even try.

Nine—The Shop Reopens

*A*bit after noon, on Mr. Brook's advice, Trudi had rewound her courage and managed to get her face washed, herself and Clarence fed, and the store ticking again, three hours late. Thankfully, only Mr. Thompson had been kept waiting outside.

"It's after *noon*," he began, pulling off his gloves and rubbing his hands together.

Trudi looked up at the wall of clocks. "Why yes, you're right," she replied with a cheery voice. *This is all I need.* "I hope you didn't have to wait long."

"Not long. I need you to look at my cuckoo," he said, laying his animated clock on the counter.

Trudi smiled and bit her tongue. *Too easy.* "Elvira? Have you been misbehaving?" she said, speaking to the clock like a naughty puppy.

"Her cuckoo sounds hoarse. Could she have the flu? There's a lot of that going around."

Trudi looked up. His smile told her he was kidding. "I expect she's coughing from the tobacco and coal smoke."

"Guilty, I'm afraid, but simply *everyone* in my house smokes. Even the dog."

And so, her day began. Almost all of her clients were unaware that her grandfather had just passed. *Without an obituary, why would they know?* She dreaded having to share the news when patrons asked to speak to the clock master.

Around three, a few customers came to shop, browsing for Christmas presents. She was showing a young woman one of her better music boxes when Mrs. Brown, the police chief's wife, came in with Esmerelda under her arm. As she laid the clock on the counter it immediately began to cuckoo madly, as if celebrating its return to its nest. Trudi quickly returned to the counter to help.

"Good morning, Miss Trudi. I'm glad you decided to reopen," Mrs. Brown said, seemingly embarrassed by her demented clock. "Esmerelda, hush," she admonished. The clock kept chiming and the little cuckoo kept popping out unabated.

"I'm sorry if you were inconvenienced, Mrs. Brown. So, what's ticking with Esmerelda? She seems a bit excited this afternoon," Trudi asked, hanging the clock on a stand that let the clock's counterweights hang over the edge of the counter. It fell silent the instant Trudi touched it.

"You have a magic touch, Miss Trudi," Mrs. Brown said. "As strange as it might appear, Esmerelda seems to be… blue. For the last few days, her song has been a tone lower, and she didn't chime or sing at all this morning. And now, it's like she's been into the chief's brandy."

"I see," Trudi said with a thin smile. "I expect a gentle spa oil treatment will help. If you can leave her with me for a few days, I'm sure I can brighten her spirits." *And mine.* Esmerelda cuckooed as if she agreed. Trudi and Mrs. Brown laughed.

"Since Esmerelda agrees, that sounds like the best plan," Mrs. Brown said, looking askance at the clock. "I expect both of you could use some pampering. How are you doing, Miss Trudi? You look tired, my dear."

"I'm okay." *I'm holding on by my fingernails.* "I can also scrub off this tobacco smoke residue—no extra charge," she said, using a cotton swab to wipe off a bit of the oily smoke residue that had accumulated on Esmerelda's face.

"Chief Brown so loves his pipes and cigars, and I dearly love him, so I guess it makes sense that I bring her in more regularly."

"Yes, I think it would be wise," Trudi said, "and easier than getting someone to give up smoking." She placed

Esmerelda into a small wooden box with a slip to remind her of what repairs she needed and who owned her—even though she knew every clock in town.

"How is your grandfather? He seemed to be moving slowly the last time I was here—late last summer? Can he spare a moment to chat?"

Trudi took a breath and sighed. "I'm afraid my grandfather passed away a few days ago. His heart just—"

"What? Trudi, I'm so sorry for your loss. I know how close you were."

"Thank you," she said, gripping the counter to fight back tears.

"Do you plan to keep the shop open?"

"I should be able to, as long as we have loyal customers like you."

"So, who will be doing the repairs? Have you engaged a new clocksmith?"

And there it was—the question Trudi feared the most. She closed her eyes, thought for a moment, and replied. "My grandfather took me on as his apprentice about fifteen years ago—when I was tall enough to reach the workbench. I fervently hope to maintain his standards of quality and carry on his work."

"But you're a girl, a mere child, and now an *orphan*," she said, as if uttering an expletive.

"Mrs. Brown, I'm nearly twenty and since when does my gender or having living parents have any bearing on my ability to do skilled work and provide good customer service?"

The older woman paused a moment and smiled. "Not a thing. I apologize."

"I agree. Not a thing. But if my work does not meet your standards or I treat you disrespectfully, you have every right to take your business elsewhere," Trudi said, her voice beginning to break.

"I see. Well, I sincerely wish you the best of luck," Mrs. Brown said. She stood for a moment, staring at Esmerelda.

Is she thinking about taking Esmerelda elsewhere? "Keep in mind that I have cleaned and lovingly cared for Esmerelda a half-dozen times in the last decade, just like every clock in this shop and hundreds more all over town."

Mrs. Brown paused for another moment. Trudi looked up and noticed two eavesdroppers focused on Mrs. Brown. *As influential as she is, if she walks out with Esmerelda, I may as well close the doors forever.*

"No, of course my dear, I had no idea you were so heavily involved. I'll leave Esmerelda in your loving hands. But first, I would like to look at the music box I saw the last time I was here. It will keep me thinking of Esmerelda while she's going through her spa treatment."

Trudi's knees got a bit wobbly for a moment, but the look of concern on the faces of the others in the shop kept her upright. She took a measured breath and brushed away a passionate tear. "Thank you so much for your continued support and confidence, Mrs. Brown. Yes, I think I know just the music box you admired. It was one I made with a new four-octave design. It's especially nice."

"You made it?"

"I've designed and fabricated about a third of the clocks in the shop—leveraging some of my grandfather's training, designs and guidance, of course. And I've maintained them all."

"I'm impressed, my dear. Most impressed," Mrs. Brown said. The other two women nodded in agreement. "One other thing, Trudi," she began in a whisper.

"What is it?" Trudi asked.

"I didn't see an obituary in the paper. Wouldn't that help everyone know about your grandfather's passing and explain how you plan to keep the shop open?"

"Perhaps," Trudi heard herself say.

"But you couldn't afford it."

Trudi nodded.

"I would be happy to do that for you, my dear," Mrs. Brown said, touching Trudi's arm. "Let me take care of it."

"You don't have—"

"But it would be a fitting recompense for all the joy your grandfather's clocks and music boxes have brought into our lives. Think nothing of it."

"Thank you so much. I'm incredibly grateful," Trudi said, fighting back tears.

After that, Trudi's day was more like a pleasant dream, not the nightmare that had haunted her for weeks. She realized that from this day on, she would have to work hard to maintain her customers' trust, strive to never disappoint them and to repay their kindness.

Nearing the end of that long day, she had informed customer after customer that she planned to keep the shop open. Her fervent desire to continue her grandfather's work solidified her convictions to carry on the family tradition, even if she had to do it alone. Unfortunately, by the end of the day, she had made too many promises. The answer to exactly *how* she could keep the shop ticking, do the repairs, and still have a semblance of a life would remain one of her life's mysteries.

Trudi's feet felt like they had been trampled by goats. As the sun went down and the streetlights came on, she was more than ready to turn the "Open" sign to "Closed" and lock the front door; the joy of working in the shop again and helping her clients had been muted by her grief and Mr. Brook's visit.

Thankfully, the only customer now lingering in the shop was Mr. Philip Wembley III, a handsome travel writer from the UK. On an earlier visit, Mr. Wembley had bought enough to tire out his assistant, so Trudi didn't want to rush him. But Philip was a talker and loved to pass the time as he gathered what he called 'color' for his travel articles.

"I so enjoy this old place," Philip said, laying a wad of crumpled bills on the counter as if they were discarded tissues. "It reminds me of the quaint villages in the Austrian Alps. Judging by the architecture, it must have been built in the late 1700s."

"Yes, the town and this building are quite old," Trudi forced a smile as she flattened the bills. "Especially the ancient plumbing and electricals. The steam heat and boiler must date back to Napoleon."

"Yes, those old steam boilers are a mechanical nightmare," he said.

"My family settled here from the old country around 1890, long before indoor plumbing. Thank the stars my grandfather put in a bathroom upstairs, but I have to say five Hail Marys to get hot water up there."

"Funny. The building looks like it was carved into the side of the mountain. Was it?" Philip asked.

"That's what they say. At the time, the cliff was a ragged outcropping of rock that no one really wanted, despite having a commanding view of the harbor and a central location in the town. In the early days, some entrepreneur carved a covered spiral stairway into the cliff, and built docks, a warehouse, and here on top, a small inn to service the ships and sailors coming from all points of the globe."

"Location, location, location, they say."

"It is a good spot. Of course, my family were not the first owners. We found evidence that blaggards, bootleggers, and bordellos had occupied the building."

"Fascinating. Are there rooms below?"

Trudi shook her head. "Just a long stairway that leads to what remains of the dock. I don't know much about them."

"Intriguing. This could prove to be a profitable venture with a bit of capital investment."

"There's even talk of pirate hideouts, and during the Revolutionary War, they say the townspeople opposed to the insurrection held clandestine meetings here to smuggle loyalists up to Canada." Philip seemed enthralled with her stories. "To this day, we still hear strange noises at night." It had been a long time since she had been alone in the shop with an attractive man—even if he was old enough to be her father—*well, almost.*

"Haunted too? How marvelous. Speaking of human smuggling, have you seen them?" he asked, pointing to the newspaper on the counter. "I hear they're offering a big reward."

"Who?"

"The St. James family. Scotland Yard is very worried about them. I expect they were kidnapped by German agents or worse. Rumor has it that Mr. St. James has gone into hiding or has met with foul play."

"I saw it. The story's been in the paper for days. And no, I haven't seen the family. I wish I had; I could use the dough," Trudi said, "I doubt they'll just show up on my doorstep. Will that be all, Mr. Wembley, or can I interest you in a nice music box? We have a delightful selection against that wall," she said.

Philip shook his head. "Ah, no. I've reached the end of my souvenir budget, and my wife's patience. She'll be worried."

"Of course, I can send these items to your hotel if that would be convenient." *Married. It's for the best.* She was nowhere near ready to let a man into her life.

"Yes, yes, that would be appreciated," he said, handing her a card with the hotel's address. "My wife and I plan to eat at the restaurant just up the road—it overlooks the bay. Is it any good?"

"It is," Trudi fibbed. She had never eaten there, but hadn't heard anyone complain, except for Mrs. Vandergelder. After she saw Mr. Wembley to the door and watched him walk out of her life, Trudi noticed a familiar cabbie parked down the street. *Oh, good. Chad.* She waved him over.

"Miss Trudi? How has your day gone?" he said through the passenger window. "How's your granddad? Feeling better?"

Trudi steadied herself on the door and released a deep sigh. "I'm okay, I guess." *He doesn't know.* "But my grandfather passed away a couple of days ago."

"My Lord. I had no idea," he said, getting out of the cab and standing next to her. "I've been out of town visiting relatives upstate. I'm so sorry for your loss." He touched her hand.

"He was a big fan of yours, Chad. You were always so helpful."

"Is there anything I can do for you?" he asked. "Anything."

"Sure… sure. I have a delivery to the Stonewater. Can you take them over now?"

"Yes, of course. Are they inside?" he said over his shoulder, heading for the shop.

Once Chad gently laid the packages on the front seat, he gazed into Trudi's eyes. She could tell he wanted to say more, do more, and be more to her, but she wasn't ready; even with a young man this nice. "Thanks so much," she said, reaching up to hug him. He returned the embrace and, a long moment later, he was off. Before the warmth of his embrace faded, she realized she had not paid him. *I must repay his kindness.*

Ten—The Sea Door

*W*hen the clocks stuck seven, Trudi looked up from the music box she was repairing and realized her day had slipped away like memories of happier times. As she clicked off the last light in the shop, a sound like a creaking hinge ran a cold shiver up her spine. Now that she was living alone, every squeak, every banging sash, every branch tapping on the glass, evoked visions of villains, ghosts, and elves trying to spy on her—or worse. *Someone's in the shop.*

Walking cautiously toward the counter, Trudi's imagination spun like tires on an icy hill, conjuring all sorts of beasts and intruders with bad intent. Peeking over the counter in the dim light, she expected to find Clarence coiled and waiting to pounce on her—one of his favorite ploys to get attention. She saw nothing. Mrs. Robbins had warned her to keep a baseball bat, a loaded pistol, or a dagger nearby. Now she wished she did.

There. Something scurried away into the darker shadows. She only got a brief glimpse of it out of the corner of her eye. *A big rat?* "Clarence! Where are you?"

A moment later, the tom ambled out of Opa's bedroom where he must have been waiting for the old man to return. It seems he refused to believe the clockmaker would not be back.

"There's a big rat in the workshop. It's your job to keep them out of the house," she said.

Clarence just stared at her for a moment before sliding up to her, purring—as if to say he was sorry.

"Well, do your job. I was scared to death," she said, her voice trembling. She picked him up and turned on the kitchen light. "Do you see any critters in *here?*"

He just purred.

"Well… okay. I'll get your dinner."

At that, Clarence wanted down and waited patiently at his bowl for all of seven seconds before returning to urge Trudi to hurry.

"What was that?" Trudi spun around, but Clarence seemed disinterested. *Something's in the workshop.* She snapped on the workroom light and felt a cold draft on her bare leg. *Sweet Mary, the door is open.* And indeed, it was.

The sea door, as Opa called it, was almost never used, but now it was open wide enough for something the size of what she saw pass through. She had no reason nor desire to cross the massive door's threshold given the unappealing aroma of bat guano, rotting fish, and the rank seashore wafting into the workshop. The key still hung on its hook above the door. *Maybe Opa opened it, or the wind? Perhaps that's what he was trying to tell me.* She took the key down and tried it in the lock. It turned easily. *Interesting. It's been used regularly—otherwise the lock would be stiff.*

Dropping the key into her pocket, she fetched a candle and matches and pulled on the door; it protested with a low moan and barely moved. If her grandfather had opened it, she could see why he wasn't able to open it any wider. With her back against the wall, she used her legs to push it just wide enough for her slender body to get past the doorway and into the dark space beyond.

She took a breath. "Clarence, are you coming?" she asked, looking for her mouser, but he was nowhere to be seen. *Coward.* "It's just us three then. Me, myself, and I," she said aloud, as if to deter someone lurking nearby. Once her trembling fingers managed to light the match, she could barely light the candle. Stretching her arm out ahead of her, Trudi took another tentative step inside. *Wait. Are those wires?* She followed a pair of thin wires from the ceiling to a switch located right where it should be—at her left shoulder. A snap later, the passageway ahead of her was illuminated, revealing a steep spiral of stone steps disappearing into the darkness. Worn smooth over the centuries, they looked as slippery as wet grass after a flock of Canada geese have lingered.

Her senses on edge, Trudi took another tentative step forward as her fingertips brushed the damp cold of the stone wall and felt what must have been lettering chiseled into the stone—its meaning long since lost to history. Five steps later, the scent of bat guano and musty air encouraged her to cover her mouth and nose with her sleeve.

As her eyes adjusted to the dark, she felt her way down the first three steps when something ran across her foot. After only a brief shriek, she looked down to see a mischief of brown rats, their red eyes glaring up at her as if she were intruding on their private domicile. "Just passing through. I mean you no harm," she said, wishing Clarence wasn't such a coward. The largest of the rats stood on his hind legs and squeaked in reply as if to answer. At that, the rats parted to either side of the stairway. *Strange. I really need to keep that door closed.*

Ahead, with the cold sinking into her bones and the damp, odoriferous breeze still in her face, she tentatively descended another step and another and another, toward an uncertain end. Twenty steps down, she came to a wider section and a rectangular opening in the outer wall. She paused to look out on the angry waters of the bay and felt the fresh, albeit cold air slapping her face. Turning to continue her descent, she saw a great wooden door, crisscrossed with iron. *A locked storeroom? More mysteries, but not tonight.*

In the distance, she heard a low rumble. Looking back, she realized the rats were following her but keeping a safe distance. *Waiting for me to fall?* Ahead, she heard the rumble again followed by a rush of water, like waves crashing on a beach, and then silence. All she could see were more and more steps spiraling down into the darkness.

The lights blinked once, twice, and finally went out altogether, immersing her in absolute darkness. *Not good.* Retrieving her candle, she managed to get it lit again on the third match. Holding it up, she could see only a few paces ahead. *Forward or back? Well, I've gone this far.*

Ten steps further down, she tried to use her candle to ignite an old torch impaled in an iron ring, but it would not take the flame. The candle would have to do. *I need to be better prepared next time—assuming I survive.*

Her legs protesting, she was relieved to find the stairs finally leveled to a landing, and she saw it—a door, with rivulets of water pushing in at its foot. The irregular, but now louder rumbling roar was followed by a crash. Her feet were suddenly covered with frigid water. *It's just the sea. That door holds back the sea at high tide. Of course, don't be a ninny.* Only then did she see a metal plate next to the door offered a bit of advice, but unfortunately, only the word "WARNING" in enormous letters was still readable. *Perhaps it's warning folks about a sea monster. I wonder what it looks like outside. The air must be fresher. Better not. Why not?*

Her curiosity finally got the best of her. Waiting for the water to recede, she tried to pull open the heavy door. *Locked?* But it resisted as if it knew better. With another pull, she got it unlatched and barely open—just in time for another wave to crash against the door, knocking her against the far wall. The last thing she felt was the icy water soaking through her clothes, just before everything went swirly and black.

ぺぺぺ

Trudi was awakened by something jabbing her in the leg. Half awake, a dream about frozen lakes and sea monsters still lingering in her mind, she opened her eyes to find the sea door key bruising her leg. *The workroom? How... how did I get here?*

Then she recalled her tumble at the bottom of the stone stairway. With considerable effort, she got herself on her feet and immediately felt the effects of lying on the unforgiving workshop floor. Slowly sitting up, she rubbed the painful lump on the back of her head and a few of her other bruises. While relieved that she was not bleeding, nonetheless, every joint, every muscle, every part of her body hurt, except for her hands, which were numb and blue from the cold. Sitting there soaked to the skin didn't help.

As the shop clocks struck eleven, she stumbled her way to the kitchen and relit the stove. Peeling off her wet dress, and wrapping herself in a blanket, she waited for the crackling blaze to bring feeling back to her hands and feet. *Mental note. Don't lay on the shop floor in wet clothes.*

As her mind and body slowly warmed and her teeth stopped chattering, Trudi tried to make sense out of what had happened. *But how did I get back up here?* Still cold, wet, and smelly, she decided she had to rid herself of the rank aroma of dead fish and stagnant saltwater. *At once.* Before heading upstairs, she made sure the sea door was closed, locked, and the key hung back on its peg. *I'll have to go down again and check the lower door—but not now.*

At the foot of the stairs leading up to her warm bath and dry clothes, Trudi heard rustling behind her. She spun around but saw nothing. *Again?* A moment later, Clarence begged for attention. "You scamp. You keep scaring me! Where were you when I needed you to scare off those horrible rats?" He complained when she picked him up, but she held him tight in her arms until he purred.

"Yeah, I'm kinda smelly," she said, carrying the big tomcat upstairs. She put him down as she closed the bathroom door, leaving him to stand guard. "No boys allowed."

Once the bathwater had turned cold, she got out and dried herself, still pondering her tumble and ascent up the stone steps. She still had no recollection of how she got back to the workshop but guessed that she must have crawled up on her own—somehow. She mulled over this mystery during her light supper and her novel until it was time for bed and sleep, hoping to forgo her recurring nightmares. Then she remembered: *The repairs.* She didn't make it between her sheets until after one in the morning.

Eleven—Another Beginning

*T*he next morning came too early. Wishing she could just stay in bed, Trudi had to force herself to push her feet out onto the cold floorboards.

Finally ready to dress, she realized the long black dress she had worn for the funeral and every day since was still wet and reeking of rotten fish. *It's a sign.* She chose another and hesitated before pulling on the black armband the funeral home had given her. She decided to wear it for a while longer.

Regrouping her mettle, she headed downstairs. Halfway down, she stopped and sat on the stairs. Each step down felt like it was taking her away from her old life with Opa and toward an uncertain future. Two score ticks later, she resumed her day, dusted the merchandise, swept the shop floor, organized the finished repairs, and opened the shop—*the shop I don't own.*

Even though Mrs. Brown had bought the music box, business had still been slower that week than it should have been as they approached the holidays. In the breaks between shoppers, chatters, and the curious, Trudi went over the books trying to decide if it even made sense to keep the shop open. Fiscal reality dampened her enthusiasm as the increasing challenges she faced came into focus and multiplied right before her eyes. At the rate things were going, despite one less mouth to feed and less bacon to fry, given the price of supplies, utilities and taxes, she could only keep the shop open for another month or so. Since the tourist season had been hobbled by the news of war, she didn't expect as much business—other than the normal dribble of repair orders and Christmas shopping. But so far, even those had not appeared. She feared, once people learned of Opa's fate, old clients would be hesitant to come by to chat and shop—Opa had been very personable and popular. *The Christmas season will be my salvation or downfall.* She decided to postpone the decision until after the new year.

The more she worried about the problem, Trudi surmised her shop's clientele may not be hers at all, but Opa's—they might return out of loyalty but after that, who knew? She told herself they had come to listen to his fascinating stories, and sometimes, to buy his clocks and music boxes and walk out with his unique designs and distinctive artistry. How were they to know it had been *her* sharp eyes, nimble fingers, and inherited skills that had kept the shop's shelves and walls filled and the shop ticking for all these years?

The bell over the door announced Mrs. Robbins.

"Trudi are you all right?" she asked, crossing the floor and laying the shop's afternoon edition of the newspaper on the counter.

"I'm fine," Trudi lied, forcing a smile.

"Really? I saw the notice in the paper seeking information on Mr. Heiliger in the personals. Haven't you heard from him all these years?"

"Not a thing." Trudi saw the headline.

DIPLOMAT'S WIFE AND FAMILY STILL MISSING. REWARD FOR INFORMATION.

She all but ignored it and skipped over to the personals, looking for the ad Mr. Brook had placed. "Perhaps this will get his attention. I wish we could afford to offer a reward."

"After nearly twenty years? There's a chance. Yes, a reward would help, but also risk bring the charlatans out of their hiding places."

"I expect you're right," Trudi said.

"Word on the street is that he took passage to New Zealand or Australia and never looked back."

"The diplomat?"

"No silly, Dick."

"Dick?"

"Your father. I think he said his name was Dick Heiliger."

"Opa… my grandfather, never said anything about where he went."

"That must be hard," Mrs. Robbins said, patting Trudi's hand.

"It was a long time ago, Mrs. Robbins. I never knew him or any of my relatives besides Opa and Oma. Did you know him?"

"Oh, I briefly met Dick when he was dating your mom. At the time, he seemed to be a gentleman, ambitious, and exceptionally smart. Your mom was totally smitten." Mrs. Robbins paused. "I'll have to admit, I would have snatched him up if your mom hadn't stood in the way."

"Then why did he run after I was born?" Trudi asked, nearly in a whisper.

Mrs. Robbins laid her hand on Trudi's. "That's not how I remember it. He had left town months before your mom started to show."

"Why? Do you remember?"

Mrs. Robbins closed her eyes. "Your mom said it was something important. Something Dick could not talk about, but that he would be back. When days became weeks with no word, Maria and I were very worried, but didn't know how to reach him. When Maria found out she was pregnant, she broke down completely and begged her father to find him—to get him to come back."

"Did he?"

"He searched frantically, but Dick had left no forwarding address at his hotel and your grandfather never found him."

"Wait. Dick didn't know my mom was carrying his baby?"

"I can't see how he could."

"I had never heard *any* of this. Opa and Oma never spoke of him to me. It was as if he was dead or living on the moon, never to return."

"Or in Australia," Mrs. Robbins quipped.

"About the same," Trudi said.

"Don't you have other people? A distant aunt, uncle, or cousin or two on either side?"

"Not that I know of. So many of our kin were lost around the end of the war when the Spanish Flu passed through here. Others have just passed away. Even Oma was quite sick. I think she lost a brother and a sister before they had any children."

"I remember all too well. I lost many dear friends and most of my family in the Midwest. None of them would wear masks even when the doctors said it would help slow the spread. They said God would protect them—with their dying breath."

"That's a shame," Trudi said, not really wanting to chat about people dying.

"So, your world is just in limbo until…"

"Until he's found, or I turn twenty-one."

"When's your birthday?"

"Two years away."

"Do you plan to keep the shop open?"

"If I can. What else can I do? Hop a steamer to Australia or take a rocket ship to the moon?"

"Sweetie, Ginger. Call me Ginger. After all, we're both independent women, and your mother and I were lifelong friends."

Trudi felt tears welling up again at this expression of friendship. Ginger's warmth was just what she needed, what she had longed to hear. A moment later, she enjoyed Ginger's comforting embrace.

"Wait. *You're* the one who fixes the clocks?" Ginger asked.

"I am. It's not that hard. The mechanisms are fairly simple once you break them down into pieces."

"I find that hard to believe; clocks look so complicated inside. And the tiny, tiny parts, do you make those too, or do you have magical fairies come in at night or one of those lens things?"

"A jeweler's loupe? Sure. We also have a microscope and special tools in the shop for especially intricate clockworks."

"It sounds so… so… so un-ladylike. Something that a man would have to do."

"Don't man-parts sometimes get in the way of intelligence, artistry, and the will to learn?"

Ginger's jaw dropped and a broad smile crossed her face. "You're right, my dear."

"I have been able to do everything a man can do since I was able to walk; from splitting the firewood, to keeping the books, and working alongside Opa. The only thing I haven't mastered is spitting tobacco juice."

"And…"

"And inheriting my own shop."

"And that," Ginger said, shaking her head as she turned over the newspaper.

"They still haven't found her?" Trudi asked, nodding at the front-page headline.

"Not a sign. She has to show up somewhere unless she's also on her way to Sydney."

"Sydney?"

"Australia. It's a big seaport—it's where most folks go when they head Down Under or want to disappear."

Trudi wondered if Mr. Brook had placed an ad in the Sydney newspapers. She would ask him to do so as soon as Ginger left.

"You know you're going to need help," Ginger said.

"Help?" Trudi asked.

"You can't keep working in the back when there isn't anyone up front to mind the shop. If that's your plan, you'll have to cut back on your store hours to give you time to make the repairs. Or…"

"Or what?"

"Or hire someone trustworthy to watch over the shop and sell while you work—or train an apprentice, like Opa trained you."

"You volunteering? I can pay you two bits an hour," Trudi said with a grin.

"I'll think about it. It might be fun, and I'd be doing a favor to an old friend and her daughter. But not as much fun as working in a chocolate shop. You can't nibble on clock parts."

Trudi's mind turned to Privi. He could almost work on his own—or she thought he could. *Perhaps.* "I do have a bit of help in the back, but how could I pay someone to help? We're just barely breaking even."

"Room and board? Any apprentice would be grateful for the chance."

"It is something to think about," Trudi said. "But taking a stranger into my home and shop would be…"

"Frightening. He would have to be chosen carefully."

"Him? Why not hire and train a smart girl? Women are far more skilled at fine needlework and can focus far better than men and boys with testosterone poisoning."

"You have a point there," Ginger said.

The afternoon went more smoothly after Ginger's visit, which lasted over an hour. As she walked her to the door, Trudi felt better, and her confidence renewed—right up to the point of realizing she didn't know where Opa sourced those tiny parts he used in the clocks; she hadn't been the only one to recognize their uniqueness. While she and Privi were fully capable of making the larger parts such as the gears and wood-work, it still took a lot of intricate work on a metal lathe to make a single gear set. But Opa's clocks and animated music boxes were different—quite different. And many of the parts were unbelievably tiny and Opa had never shown her how he had made them. He just reached into a small drawer in the parts cabinet and took out the needed replacement, dropping the old piece into another drawer. It was as if he had them shipped in from overseas or, as he sometimes joked, from the land of the elves.

As she was about to close, Trudi stood in the shop's door-way, gazing out at sable clouds crying raindrops pelting ripples in the puddles. A couple walked by arm-in-arm under a shared umbrella. This too, was missing from her life. The shop was her only lover, and a jealous one at that.

Ever since Opa passed, Trudi had to make supper for her-self, but tonight, she was not that hungry and making food for one was… depressing. Instead, she locked up and pushed past the bead wall into the workshop. There, she inspected and in-ventoried the parts and supplies in each drawer and rewrote the faded labels. Thankfully, there seemed to be several of each—enough for about three or four weeks of typical repairs. But then what? When those were gone, what would she do? Perhaps another clock shop could offer some advice, but that would not look especially good. She picked up one of the more complex parts used to coordinate clock figure animations. As it was the size of a lima bean, she had to examine it under the microscope. *Hammer marks? How can that be?* Shaking her head, she put the part back and slid the drawer closed.

And then, on top of everything else, she realized Attorney Brook had given her homework. She had been tasked to find photographs of her father or documents, letters, or news clippings that would describe her father in more detail to aid in the search. There was no way she could have any memory of the man who may come to claim everything she owned. *None at all.* Armed with Ginger's idea, she used the number on Brook's now-dry business card to call him.

"May I speak to Mr. Brook?" she asked the older woman who answered.

"Whom should I say is calling, Miss?" the voice asked.

"Ms. Sanduhr."

"Miss, I'm so sorry for your loss. I met your grandfather several times, and he was such a nice man. I'll get Ray, Mr. Brook, for you."

Trudi related the details Mrs. Robbins passed on to her and her idea about Sydney. Mr. Brook assured her he *had* written to papers in Sydney, Melbourne, and Adelaide, and suggested including Christchurch in New Zealand, but their conversation didn't last long after he asked if she had found time to search her father's papers.

"I'm still looking," she said, feeling guilty that she had disappointed him—and lied.

Intimately familiar with Opa's workshop, Trudi knew there were no personal papers that she hadn't read before—none mentioned her father—not even a signature, as if he had been systematically expunged from their lives. There were a few old papers in the bookkeeping desk upstairs taken over from her grandmother, but again, she found nothing useful except a few faded pictures of her first days at school and a few photos of her mother, bound in a small scrapbook.

The tears returned as she studied the picture of her mother and saw her own resemblance, but she must have inherited her father's height, as her mother was a bit shorter. *If Opa had wanted to hide anything, where he would keep it? But why wouldn't he disavow him, purge him from his life? Tomorrow's agenda: Look for Opa's hiding places.*

As she slid the desk drawer closed, she felt it catch on something. Pulling the drawer out, she looked behind it to reveal what it was hiding. *A secret compartment.* Tucked inside, she found a packet tied with a wide blue ribbon. Snapping on the desk lamp, she carefully untied the ribbon binding what appeared to be a stack of letters and a few faded photographs, their edges frayed as if they had been handled a million times. A tiny smear of red *lipstick?* marked the picture of a young man in a suit—his arm around a pretty girl. They both looked like they would never part. *Dick and my mom?* Trudi gazed deep into the picture, studying his every feature, his eyes, the familiar shape of his face, his smile and how he and Maria looked at one another. *Yes. They were in love.* She clutched the photo to her heart and set it aside to study the letters.

Some were addressed to Miss Maria Sanduhr, others had been sent to Mr. Dick Heiliger at several addresses; all of these were stamped: "No such person at this address."

Trudi found the letters sorted by date, so she began reading them one at a time, revealing a long-standing relationship beginning with a casual meeting at one of Ginger's parties, and over many months evolving to plans for a romantic evening when Dick returned to Klippenburg. The final letter brought tears to Trudi's eyes. Dick had poetically spoken of their intimacy and his desire to return as soon as his mission was complete, even hinting at a proposal. And then… nothing.

Frantically, she searched the interior of the desk, but Trudi was unable to find any other letters, pictures, or anything but dust. Carefully, lovingly, rebinding the letters and pictures with the ribbon, she held them to her heart. *Why didn't Opa or Oma tell me? Dick was going to marry her. He was going to come back and take her for his bride.*

She lost track of time, but eventually realized that these letters might be just what Mr. Brook needed to locate her father. She promised herself to take them to him tomorrow. But now, she had to finish Esmerelda's and Georgiana's bath. "Come on girls, let's get you cleaned up," she said, as if the clocks were old friends at a spa.

Twelve— The Seldith's Plan

"*W*hat happened?" Alred asked as he stood on the second step of the broad staircase leading to the Council Chamber.

Vincent, a middle-aged sem replied quietly, looking around to ensure they weren't overheard. "One of the rats complained about the uman girl invading their space but had fallen and was unconscious at the bottom of the stone steps."

"Do you think they had a hand in this?" Alred asked, pulling Vincent aside.

"The rats? Well, someone chewed through the wires that power the lights, so I expect they were involved."

"I see. Is she still down there?"

"No. No. We organized a team and got both levitation sems and a team of others to float her back to the old uman's workshop."

"So you left her on the floor of the workshop?" Alred's voice sounded increasingly angry.

"It was *exhausting*. They hadn't lifted anything that massive before and she was soaking wet—that made it even harder. One of the firestarters got the workshop stove lit to keep her warm."

"Let me get this straight. You left this poor girl unconscious, cold and wet on the workshop floor. You might have killed her. Why didn't you come and get me?"

"We talked about it, but we knew you don't…"

"Don't what?" Alred said under his breath.

"You don't have many spells left. The Book says each time you cast a spell it… it subtracts from the spells you can… cast, in your…lifetime." the sem said, his voice fading to a whisper.

Alred just glared at him. "Let me worry about my longevity. You should have called me. Has Kenezer examined her?"

"The healer? No, we decided to come and ask… you."

"Get her. Ask her nicely to see what she can do."

Mickey, a yesem[10] ran up, out of breath. "She's gone. The uman girl is gone!"

"Gone?" both Alred and the Vincent said at once.

"The pair on watch said she lit the kitchen stove. She had some tea and went upstairs."

"So she's all right?" Alred asked.

"It appears so. Should I get Kenezer?"

"Let her sleep. She needs it after that flu case last night. Just keep an eye on the uman girl, and don't get caught."

"What about the rats? The sea door was open, and they might have gotten inside," Vincent said.

"We'll need to have a talk with her bellua. Post a few more sentries to make sure the rats don't go unnoticed. Let me know immediately if they try to go upstairs."

"Yes, yes. Of course," Vincent said.

"This isn't over," Alred said as Sondrah walked up and took his arm.

"Let's take a walk," she asked sweetly. "It looks like you need one."

Alred obliged and followed along, her arm in his, knowing he was helpless in her grasp as they strolled back toward the small east-facing window set into the outer wall. He wondered if she had taken his arm as a sign of affection or to steady his

---

[10] Yesem: A young seldith male before reaching adulthood. Equivalent to 'boy,' or 'kid'.

gait. He wished for the former but suspected the latter. He so enjoyed every quiet moment they spent together—it made him feel young. It crossed his mind that perhaps it was her herditas to do just that—make others feel young again. Was it that she reminded him of Rachele, his first love? Perhaps it was because she was one of the only ones in the clan who was not intimidated by his position of authority or bewitched by his considerable power as a wizard.

"I don't want you going up there," she began, using that tone the friends and (especially) females in his life used when they were trying to protect him.

"Up where? To talk to the uman girl?"

"Yes. Send one of the others."

"Whom do you suggest? It's too important and very few of them have ever talked to a uman."

"Others say we should send one of the younger Council members or a Protector, but they're so…"

"I understand."

"This is not a job for…"

"A tired, old wizard?" Alred said with a frown.

"A younger one, perhaps. They're more agile. And we can't afford to lose you."

"We?" he said softly.

"I. You know how I feel."

He smiled and thought about kissing her on the cheek.

She closed her eyes for a moment and continued. "We need mature leadership—someone who has seen the outside world—above the floorboards and beyond these stone walls."

"I'm quick enough."

"Of course you are, but why did someone have to help you fill your wood box last night?"

Alred looked through the sleet pelting the dirty glass. Below, he watched a small party of umans pulling nets out of the river. "My back was acting up."

"Alred, you're one of the oldest and wisest sems in the clan. We would have lost you last spring if Kenezer had not pulled you back from that infection."

"Then who? You?" he asked. "I won't have it."

"Your grandson."

"He… no. Never. He's too young, brash, impulsive, takes too many chances, and he's only fourteen." Alred's grandson Martine had only come back into his life a few years ago; suddenly showing up at his door with a story about a harrowing escape from the distant Faerie Kingdom. He spun a wild tale of what was left of the survivors of the Stone Valley clan.

"Like Hisbil?" she smiled.

Alred's only son Hisbil had indeed been foolhardy, but courageous and almost seventeen when he confronted and awakened the bellua which changed their lives forever. "Hisbil was older and nearly killed a dozen times—he was lucky to…"

"Save the Stone Valley[11] clan? You yourself told us it was he who led them to safety. He's a legendary hero—so are you."

She was right. Perhaps it was time for someone with Hisbil's courage to step forward, but at his age, was his grandson ready for a task this important? "I'll think about it."

"I'll send—"

"No. Let me talk to him. I'm still not sure he's the best choice."

Sondrah offered her hand to help Alred stand. With some difficulty, he rose to his feet unaided—she handed him his

---

[11] The story of the Stone Valley clan is told in *The Owl Wrangler*, book one of *The Seldith Chronicles*.

walking stick and squeezed his hand. "You know I love you, and I don't know what I'd do without you," she whispered.

"You'd manage." He wasn't sure he would last long without her. Putting his arm around her, he pulled her closer and shared a tender kiss. They lingered at the window, standing as one, until someone came by.

"They're looking for you," the sem said in passing, apparently not wishing to linger.

"I need to deal with this. It can't wait."

"Will you consider…?" she began.

"I will. Consider it." After another quick kiss, Alred sent her on her way and made his way past the small houses tucked between the floor joists. He looked over their living space with pride. With the help of others in the clan, each family had erected their own home—their metal stovepipes ultimately connecting to the building's stone chimney, smoke folding in with the fires built on the uman level. Some homes were just a shed or a lean-to, others elaborate mansions with glass windows, central heat and copious electric lights fashioned from tiny Seldith-crafted bulbs. Most of the larger homes had traditional round doors with an axle hole in the center. For ages, their doors had also served as cartwheels when the clan was forced to relocate, but here they had not been used for that purpose in a very long time—if ever. Alred doubted if they could again—or even if this clan could stand the rigors of living out in the elements. Too many had rarely ventured outside or felt rain in their face, touched a blade of grass, or seen a live squirrel or a butterfly outside a picture book. And yes, Alred thought that was sad and campaigned to get people to explore what lay beyond their own sheltered world, while the more conservative Council resisted.

As he walked, Alred was greeted by as many smiles as worried looks while the Seldith went about their lives. It seemed that some never concerned themselves with what they called "politics" or "false news," the day-to-day issues that shaped the way they lived. Some washed dirty faces, others tended to their chores, while others still practiced their favorite pastime—idle gossip where shards of the facts were spun and twisted into yarns alongside falsehoods and woven into believable stories.

Alred's hearing was not what it was in his youth, but he didn't have any trouble eavesdropping. "Should we be packing?" someone asked a neighbor as he passed.

"There will be time for that," he said without stopping.

"Are you going to have the uman part the sky?" a nesem holding a broom asked him.

"I hope it won't be necessary," Alred replied, "but the uman girl is young and curious. Perhaps she'll want to see where we live. It might help her understand us better and sympathize with our lifestyle."

"It's a messy belluas' nest down here," the nesem said, pushing her broom a bit harder.

"Do what you can. First impressions are the most lasting."

Mr. Hershel's toddler twins nearly knocked him over as Alred turned into another long corridor of homes. He steadied himself on his stick as their father followed in close pursuit. He decided against casting a buffer spell to keep them a safe distance away—something he was known to do fifty years ago.

"I'm sorry, Your Honor. They're just excited," he apologized.

"Perhaps you could keep them better corralled until this is resolved."

"I'll try," Mr. Hershel said over his shoulder, snagging the closest twin. The other was already out of sight, but its shrill squeals could be heard in the distance.

When Alred reached the red door just down from the water spigot, he paused and touched the valve to let a few drops of water fall into the common cup. Putting it to his lips, its brackish taste cleared his mind. He knew what needed to be done, despite the objections and obstacles.

Alred and his grandson did not see the world in the same way, and he did not look forward to talking with him. Although muffled, he heard the shrill, whining sound of metal-on-metal coming from inside. *He must be running the lathe.* He waited until the sound had stopped before knocking.

A moment later, the door opened a crack and a pair of eyes glared out at him from the dark. "Yes?" Alred didn't say a word; he just looked at the yesem wearing a dirty shirt, pushing unkempt hair off his face. His hard, callused hands held an experienced steel hammer, his arms rippling with blacksmith's muscles. "Is there something wrong?" the youth asked impatiently. "I have work to do while the workshop is quiet."

Uninvited, Alred pushed open the door and picked his way across the room, spotting a suitable chair. He wondered how anyone could live in a tight, cluttered space like this—the walls covered with mats meant to dampen the sound, while the lack of windows and the heat from the forge made the room unbearably hot. With some effort, Alred set aside a large sheet of brass and sat down. "Martine, we need to talk."

"I'm busy. We're almost out of intermediate gears and I'm two days behind." He had already turned back to the lathe, but he hadn't switched it on.

"I know how busy you are, and how vital your work is, but what I have to ask is also important."

"Why is it that *your* emergencies are always more important than my deadlines?"

Martine sounded very much like Alred's long-lost son Hisbil. Alred studied the yesem from head to foot—he had grown to be quite a handsome specimen—nearly matured to a sem over the two years since he had shown up at his door, cold, soaked to the skin, and nearly starving. Surprisingly, he had no dark rings, tattoos on his arms—at least none that he could see. Perhaps he didn't have the Wizard herditas. Perhaps he wasn't really Hisbil's son—and perhaps his only grandchild. What he really suspected is the young sem's lack of training as a wizard. He would not be the first yesem to turn away from his herditas as his father Hisbil had.

"Well, what is it?" Martine asked impatiently. He switched on the lathe, showering the room with filings and noise.

Alred waited until after the shrill noise had stopped. "We need to convince the uman—the clock master's granddaughter—to let us live here."

"Then go meet her. Isn't that *your* job? You're now the Chief Elder, the Viceroy as you keep reminding me." Martine didn't look up from his work.

"Some say it should be done by someone younger."

"And some say you're not fit for the job—you should just retire. Look in the mirror."

Alred said nothing. Of course, Martine was right—the truth hurts most of all. His detractors in the Council were right. He *should* give up his duties, set aside his robes, and retire. He just wasn't quite ready to be a ward of the clan—his food brought to him, and his needs met by well-meaning folk. He wasn't going to give up that easily. "Do you have any tea?" he asked.

"Tea?" The yesem frowned. "Yes, of course. I have hot water on the stove." Martine turned and stepped over one obstacle after another, making his way to the steaming kettle.

"How is your… friend?" Alred asked, trying to be diplomatic. It was another sensitive subject.

"Glenda? She's better. The herbs Kenezer gave her have helped. While we're on the subject, have you reconsidered the expedition to rescue her family?"

"I've thought about it—a great deal."

"But you still won't let me go."

"You barely made it back here."

"I made it. I've regained my strength and I want to go back and help get them out of that *place*."

"Glenda doesn't want you to go."

"She's just afraid I won't come back."

"So am I. And if you did somehow find your way back to the Faerie portal, what makes you think you could get in and get her family to return here with you?"

"I just can. I know I can."

Alred slowly shook his head. "We don't need to go over this again. We've talked about it ever since you found me here at River House."

"For years," he grumbled, handing Alred a mug of steaming tea. Martine's eyes were pinched with anger.

"Thanks." Alred took a sip but never took his eyes off the yesem who called himself his grandson.

"I'm going anyway—as soon as I collect enough supplies and find a few more to go with me."

"I know. You've said."

"What is it that you need me to do? Build another machine? Fix something?"

"Not this time. I want you to talk to the uman girl. Besides me, you're one of the only ones who have talked to umans."

"And lived?"

"And lived."

"Hisbil told me all about them. Umans are evil—even the ones who claim to be our friends. I met too many of them on the way here. I want no part of this."

"You're right. They can be unpredictable, greedy, and evil. The old uman who cared for us for decades was not. He and his wife kept our secrets and sheltered us for generations."

"Then *you* go. He was *your* friend."

"I want *you* to."

"You're commanding me to go?"

Alred nodded. A tear formed at the edge of his eye. "If that's what it takes."

"As the Viceroy of the Council, or as my grandfather?"

"Both."

"And if I don't? Will you exile me?"

"I hope it would never come to that," Alred said, looking down. He knew exile was the harshest of all penalties. Those ejected from the safety of the walls of the settlement were often never seen nor heard of again—by anyone.

"Martine?" The voice came from a dark-haired yenesem[12] standing in the doorway. About Martine's age, she was slender and dressed in clothes more likely to be seen on a yesem her age. Her hair was braided and woven into an intricate spiral around the back of her head. Her bright eyes said a lot about her. Alred saw intelligence, curiosity, courage, and wit. She had been a welcome addition to the clan and Alred had grown quite fond of her. He treated her like the granddaughter he never had.

"Glenda?" Martine said, taking a clumsy step toward the door. He tripped over a stack of metal scraps making an awful clatter. He immediately got to his feet, and everyone listened for a moment to ensure the noise hadn't alerted the uman presence above them.

"I heard Alred was looking for someone to talk to the uman girl," Glenda said softly.

"You heard right," Alred replied. "I asked Martine to go talk to her, but he has—" Alred said, offering Glenda his chair.

---

[12] Yenesem: A young Seldith female.

"I'll go. I've talked to umans before," she said, taking Al-red by surprise. "I'm *sure* I can convince her if she's halfway amenable."

"*No*. No. No. You are *not* going up there," Martine insisted, shaking his head and charging toward her as if she were about to leave.

"Seriously? Since when do *you* get to tell me what to do?" She pushed him away.

"I'll go," Martine said. "It's settled. She's staying here."

"Good. And I'm going too. You would only foul it up," she said, stepping away from him. "Remember that day on the trail when you nearly got us both killed?"

"Which time?" he asked.

"Exactly," she smiled.

Alred just stood back, silently watching the youngsters work out their issues. So far, his unplanned scheme was working very nicely. Or was it? He saw Sondrah's hand in this. Two *would* be better than one. He realized that the two of the most important people in his life were heading into the path of a giant. He would have to do something about ensuring their safety—but what?

๑๑๑

It took some encouragement, cajoling, dire warnings, and a few threats to get the clan to cooperate, but River House was put back in a reasonable semblance of order—it had not looked this polished in… well, ever. Yes, many of the older elves had scurried away into hiding with their children tucked away, too frightened to deal with a face-to-shoe encounter with a uman—something they had spent their lives avoiding.

Howard, a middle-aged sem, appeared out of the group of elves milling around the narrow stairway leading into the uman rooms above them. "Alred, are you sure this is wise?" he asked, grabbing Alred's arm. "You're going to get these two and a lot of other good sems killed."

"I've talked to the Council…" Alred said, staring at the sem's hand. He withdrew it and waved it in the air as if it had caught fire.

"And they all agree?" Howard said, rubbing his palm and backing away.

"Do they agree on anything?"

"We should just lie low and hope she does not notice us."

"Really? Sure, we could hold on for a few weeks if we ration our remaining food, but every time we go out into the world to forage, we run the risk of some hostile uman or bellua discovering us and the entire River House settlement."

"You can always erase their memory—like that couple who stumbled upon our fishing party last month."

"Sure, that uman forgot he had seen us but he also didn't recall he had asked that nice young lady to marry him. That took quite a bit of fixing to put right."

"I… I didn't think about it that way, but I thought Dumold said the Council was going to—"

"It's been decided," Alred said, turning away. He knew he was taking a big chance. It wouldn't be the first time. "Are you ready?" Alred looked around at Martine and Glenda standing at the base of the ladder.

"I guess so. What's it we're supposed to ask her to do?" Martine asked. "Fix us three meals a day and serve them on a tray?"

"Don't be disrespectful," Glenda said. "I know what to ask her to do. Why don't you just stay here, Martine?"

Martine glared at her. She just smiled.

Alred handed Glenda a scroll, sealed with wax and tied with a blue ribbon. "This document details the previous agreement. It was signed off by the Council and Mr. Sanduhr."

"Well, we're off. Wish us luck," Glenda said, stepping onto the ladder and tucking the scroll into her waistband.

"Luck," Alred said. "Just explain the barter arrangement we had with her grandfather and his fathers before him. As before, we promise to keep providing the parts she needs for her machines." As they pushed on a lever, a latch above them clicked.

"And Martine?" Alred said.

Martine turned.

"Take care of her. She means a lot to me—and so do you. Don't take any unnecessary chances." He reached out and held their shoulders for a moment and closed his eyes. Martine looked back for a moment.

"Wait," Alred said, holding out a scabbard and sword. "Martine, you forgot this."

"Hisbil's sword? I don't expect any magic dragons up there."

"You never know. It came in handy for your father. Take it."

Martine looked up to Glenda, already on the ladder. She nodded and he strapped on the sheathed blade.

Thirteen—The Benefactress

*W*hen Martine had nearly reached the top of the stairway, he heard another whirr when a small door above them opened—almost as if it had sensed their presence. Cool air cascaded down the stairway smelling of strange food odors, machine oil, and… something else. *Umans.* He had never grown used to it. Like the unmistakable aromas of wildfire and belluas in the forest, he knew nearby umans meant mortal danger. He could feel the hair on the back of his neck stand on end. Glenda clutched his hand—it was no steadier than his and just as clammy. Climbing the stairway, he examined the dimly lit room as if were a wild forest overflowing with dangers.

The room *seemed* empty, but Martine wasn't taking any chances. His few years of experience in the forests had refined his sense of smell (which had saved him on several occasions) but another sense which he could not fully understand was tightening his stomach as he climbed. It wasn't fear. Alred had explained it as 'awareness' or 'cognizance.' He remembered being told fear is how one feels when facing the unknown. Cognizance is what one feels when facing something you at least partially understand. He knew what he was about to face. It was still terrifying.

Martine was relieved that the uman didn't seem to be in their *immediate* vicinity. *Good.* He took a deep breath. He wanted to talk to the clockmaker's granddaughter on his own terms, but not unduly startle her or stumble into another uman and especially not a bellua. Yes, there were confirmed reports of a large toothy bellua—four times the size of the largest rat he had ever seen. And yes, its odor salted the air, and its pheromones marked every door jamb and chair leg. This was its private territory, and he knew they were intruding.

As they crept forward, with Glenda close behind, he hoped she would cooperate. After having spent over a month together in the forest and searching through the uman town trying to find Alred's new home, they had developed a relationship which could be best described as strained but strangely symbiotic. She always seemed to have a contrary opinion about everything, but it irked him that she was right too often to ignore. While they were together, they could hardly be called a team, but Martine knew he would not be standing here without her—more precisely, they would not be standing here without each other.

When they approached the far wall, he wanted to say, "Let me do the talking," but dared not. Alred clearly trusted her— and she had the scroll tucked into *her* belt.

But Martine's uninvited intrusion into the uman's living space was different—it could be seen as a violation of the agreement. He and Glenda were unexpected. Not wanting to be caught out in the open by the uman or the still unseen bellua, he quickly crossed over to the wall. Following in his shadow, Glenda nearly made it there ahead of him, running on soft feet that made not a sound over the noisy clocks in the next room.

"We must find her, before she finds us," Martine whispered. "I don't want her stumbling onto us by accident."

Glenda nodded. "Given the time of day, she's probably making breakfast. Let's try that way." She motioned beyond the beaded curtain.

"How do you know the kitchen is in that direction?" Martine asked.

"Because I studied the map. Didn't you?" Glenda asked.

Martine realized she was right. Again. He shook his head. "No. Are you sure?"

"The aroma of food is coming from that direction," Glenda said.

Martine could hear clattering. *Pots and dishes.* "Someone's in there," he whispered, catching his breath. "I can smell her." *And something else…*

When Glenda nodded, he skirted around a row of beads, trying to keep them from moving. He cautiously stepped into the next room and listened again. *Footsteps.* He pushed his back against the wall and waited. Glenda tucked herself in under his arm, shivering.

"Want to go back?" he whispered, his lips nearly touching her ear, his breath caressing her cheek.

She shook her head—vigorously. "No. I'm just cold," she whispered, turning her face to his.

He gazed deep into her eyes. *Focus.* Pausing for a moment, Martine turned to look back toward the kitchen. "Let's go." Moving nearly as one toward the kitchen, they hugged the baseboards and turned the corner. *There she is.* To the Seldith, Trudi was as well-known as one of their own children, and many had witnessed her growing up within these walls.

While Martine had seen umans a dozen times before, even negotiating and arguing with them, it was no less terrifying seeing one twenty, now fifteen, now ten, elven paces away. While he had planned to somehow get up on the kitchen counter, he didn't see a way to climb the slick table leg. Down here on the floor, they could be easily trampled and the uman girl would barely notice.

As Trudi laid down her dishtowel and turned toward them, she released a deafening scream and jumped back.

Roach dung. She's seen us!

Momentarily turning her back on them, Trudi swung back around, waving a large kitchen knife like a medieval swordsman preparing for a duel.

"Run!" Martine whispered.

Glenda grabbed his arm. "Freeze," she hissed.

Not given a choice, Martine let himself get pulled deeper into the dark corner between the dish cupboard and the wood box.

Trudi was out of sight, but from the sound of it, she was still thrashing around the room in pursuit. "Get out of there!" she screamed. He heard her knife clang against the stone wall and then the wood box.

They dared not move—cornered, there was nowhere to run. *Brilliant strategy, Martine,* he chided himself. Glenda seemed every bit as frightened as he was. *What have I gotten her into— again?*

Inexplicably, Trudi had turned her back on them, more interested in slashing and chopping at something above them on the counter. Still hidden, they did not see what she was chasing, what had violated her personal space, and what she was trying to mince with the knife, but they were relieved *they* did not seem to be the object of her frantic attack. Whatever it was, she was bent on violently ending its life. Martine figured if it was horrible enough to frighten a uman, it would be far more than *they* could handle. He was glad he had accepted Hisbil's sword—a lot of good it would do against something which was terrifying a uman over twenty times their height— even one using a blade as long as the uman's forearm. Some inner sense told him to draw the sword; once exposed to the air, it felt strangely warm in his hand and in the dark, it gave off a soft orange glow. Holding the blade in front of them, he planted his feet and braced himself, pushing Glenda behind him.

"What do you plan to do with that? Cut her shoelaces?" Glenda whispered.

"Just in case," he said, now feeling foolish at having brandished it.

Realizing Trudi was distracted, he took a chance and looked around the corner. "Now!" Martine tried to pull away, but Glenda still would not budge, holding his arm in an unbreakable grip. Her eyes did not show fear as he might have expected, but a grim determination he had seen before—a look he had grown to respect.

A heartbeat later, a large black rat with fiery red eyes jumped down from the counter carrying a chunk of bread in its teeth. It landed two strides away in front of them.

"You!" the rodent hissed through the bread and his sharp yellow teeth.

"You!" Martine said, tightening his grip on the sword. He recognized the rat at once—Brewater, a notorious troublemaker and bully. "You're violating the treaty by coming up here."

"And what are a pair of snowflakes going to do about it? Report back to your bumbling Council?" he replied with a sneer.

"Oh, that's exactly what we'll do, and if the uman doesn't slice you in two, the Protectors will," Glenda said.

"You pesky fleas, you won't be telling anyone once I eat your liver and drag your carcass back to feed my kids." As the enormous rat charged, a blinding aura formed around Hisbil's sword like a shimmering umbrella. Martine instinctively thrust and drove the blade into the beast's neck and up through its head. It collapsed and thrashed for a moment—its warm lifeblood flowing over them.

"My God!" the uman girl screamed. "Leprechauns! Sweet Mary! Opa was telling the truth," she said, taking a step back.

"Are you okay?" Glenda asked Martine, pulling herself out from under the beast's body while trying unsuccessfully to stay clear of the pool of blood seeping through the floorboards.

"Mmmff?" Martine cried from under the bulk of the limp carcass.

Glenda looked up and saw Trudi. She seemed ready to flee or jump up on a chair. "It's all right, missy. I think it's dead. It can't hurt you." It didn't occur to Glenda that the girl was now just as frightened of them.

"You can t...talk?" she said, with a trembling voice.

"Yes, mistress. We can speak, but we aren't leprechauns." Glenda said as loud as she could without yelling.

"To rats? You could understand it?"

"Some of them, yes—the awakened ones. The rest, not so much," Glenda explained.

"Is it...dead?" Trudi asked.

"I think so. Are *you* hurt?"

"No, not at all—just startled. I've never seen...little people before," Trudi said, her voice a bit less agitated.

"I was a bit scared myself," Glenda said with the color returning to her face. "And this is not the first time we've almost met. You nearly got a good look at Martine and me the other night."

"So, there *was* someone on my windowsill?"

Glenda smiled and nodded. "The Seldith have watched over you as you grew up from a tiny baby. Who do you suppose keeps the belluas out of your crib and the pantry?"

Martin, still buried under the corpse, called out. "If you ladies are done chatting, could you get this bloody bellua off me?"

"Oh, sorry," Glenda said as she pulled on the rat corpse while Martine pushed, but the lifeless hulk would not budge.

A moment later, Trudi reached down and picked up the rat by its tail. "And who are you?" she said in a not-so-steady voice, holding the rat at arms-length. Martine's sword was still impaled in its head.

"You're holding Captain Brewater, head of rat security, and we're just a couple of Seldith—friends of your late grandfather." Martine said.

"He's Martine, and I'm Glenda—at your service, Miss Trudi."

"Are you the elves Opa talked about? I thought they were just bedtime stories," Trudi said as she deftly removed the tiny sword from the rat's skull. Almost in a single motion, she opened the window and tossed the carcass out toward the river. "That's the third one this week."

"I wish she hadn't done that," Martine whispered to Glenda, knowing the rats would be doubly offended by having to collect the body before high tide.

"After Opa died," she continued, "...they seem to have grown bolder."

"Really?" Martine asked, catching his breath but not taking his eyes off Hisbil's sword. He knew he would have a lot of explaining to do if it was lost. And there would be more explaining when Brewater's body appeared on the beach.

Martine watched Trudi lay his sword out of sight on the counter.

"You said you were *Seldith*? I can't say that I've heard of you."

"We live a very quiet existence; didn't your grandfather explain what we do for him?" Glenda asked.

"No. Sadly, I think he tried, but no one believed any of the stories he told us—while granny humored him, I always thought he was addlepated or trying to be funny. He talked about Faeries too."

"He was telling the truth about us—or I hope he was," Martine began.

"Mistress Trudi, we would like to discuss something important with you; if it's convenient," Glenda interrupted.

Trudi smiled. "Would it be better if we spoke face-to-face?" she asked.

"Of course, what do you suggest?" Martine asked.

Trudi turned to the sink and placed a teacup on the floor. "Hop in."

Glenda looked at Martine for a moment but didn't move.

Thinking Trudi seemed tame enough, Martine decided to take a chance and crawled into the cup. "Are you coming?" he asked Glenda. He extended his hand.

Glenda had her all too familiar 'I'm not so sure' look on her face, but she nodded, and with his help, climbed in. "What stewpot did you get us into now?" she whispered.

Martine shook his head. *She's right.* He had probably been too impulsive again—just like his father. Once in the cup, he realized they were at the uman's mercy. They held on while Trudi carried the cup aloft. After the first second, Martine didn't see much through his pinched-shut eyelids, and only opened them when he felt the cup settle on the kitchen counter. Peering over the cup, the view from inside the teacup on the counter was terrifying, to say the least. He had never liked heights—a fear he had not discovered until he was forced to the edge of a stony cliff during their harrowing escape from the land of the Faeries. He looked over at Glenda. Face-to-face, he saw her eyes were still squeezed shut as she embraced him as if for the last time, her breath coming in quick puffs.

"There. Isn't that better?" the uman girl said.

No. No, it's not. Put us down, his mind screamed. He forced a smile and felt a warm hand squeezing his. He squeezed back and relaxed—a bit. When Glenda's eyes opened, their lips were all but touching.

"It *is* high," Glenda said, pulling away. *Really high.* "But sure. Better. Can you hear us all right?"

"Much better," Trudi said nearly whispering. "But what brings you to my kitchen? Surely not just to rid me of rats, and for that, I'm grateful."

"No, we've come to ask a favor," Martine said, now wanting to get this over and be safely back home beneath the floorboards.

"A favor? Well, why not? You've already done me a service. That took great courage."

"You're quite welcome. The belluas have been a problem for us as well. We were glad to dispatch it for you." What he didn't say is that killing the bellua might very well have other, more dire consequences, as the killing doubtless broke the terms of the truce the Seldith had with the colony of river rats. *Today must be the day to break and make treaties.*

"Well, I can't thank you enough," Trudi said. "What is it I can do for you?"

"We want to… well, we want to renew the arrangement we had with your grandfather," Glenda said, pulling out the scroll.

"Arrangement?" Trudi said, opening the tiny parchment scroll with her fingertips. She pulled out her jeweler's loupe to read the tiny print.

"Basically, it says that we, the Seldith, make clock and machine parts. Your grandfather…" Martine began.

"It's all in the agreement," Glenda said, crawling out of the cup and helping Martine do the same. They both moved further from the edge. He could see Hisbil's sword about ten paces away on the counter.

"Are you two a couple?" Trudi said, still trying to read the scroll.

Glenda blushed and shook her head. "No…" she said, softly, wiping the blood off her face.

"We're just… friends," Martine said, his voice trailing off.

"Martine, do they call you 'Marty'?" Trudi asked.

Glenda laughed. "Not unless you want to raise his hackles."

"Then, *Martine* it will be."

"Well, what did you want in exchange for your clock parts? I had always assumed my grandfather had made them himself or somehow bought them in the city."

"The clock master, and his fathers before him, obtained them from us. Hundreds of years ago, we were shown designs—we've been manufacturing and refining them ever since. The clock masters gave us changes and improvements from time-to-time, but not for many years now."

"Really? So where do you get the raw materials?"

"Materials?" Martine asked.

"The metal and the jewels—the metals and precious stones used as bearings."

"We take melted down broken or worn-out parts and re-cast them. Precious little is wasted, but Wilhelm provided whatever we needed."

"Amazing. How do you—?"

"We have our own sound-insulated forges and metalworking shops beneath the floorboards, mostly in the lower levels. Martine is one of our best machinists. He's exceptionally talented," Glenda said with pride. "He seems to have a magical gift for the work."

Martine made a gesture to keep Glenda from giving away too many secrets—especially concerning magic. Thankfully, she nodded and seemed to understand.

"Where are your workshops?"

"Very nearby," Glenda said with a smile.

Martine gave her another sideways look. He wasn't sure they should divulge everything—not yet.

"Can you show me?"

"We would be happy—" Glenda began.

Martin's eyes grew narrow, but Glenda didn't wilt from the glare.

"We need to come to an agreement first," Martine interrupted, watching Trudi's eyes. She was still smiling, seemingly oblivious to his concerns.

"I understand. How did Opa, my grandfather, compensate you for your work?"

"Protection," Glenda said, "…like it says in the document."

"And food," Martine added.

"And scraps of cloth, thread, and notions," Glenda added.

"Yes, of course," Trudi said. "That sounds fair."

"I thought I recognized the material in your apron. I once had a dress made of that cloth," Trudi said with a smile.

"But mostly protection," Martine said. "From the outside world. And bacon."

"I suppose you'll want your tiny dagger back," Trudi said, holding out Martine's sword.

"Yes. Please, Grandfather Alred would be most upset if I lost it."

"Again," Glenda whispered.

જ્જજ્

Beneath the kitchen stove, pressed against the back wall, a small brown rat sat shivering. Her mother stood by her side.

"They *killed* him," it wept. "He was just looking for food."

"It's what daddies do. It's the risk they take."

"But why?"

"Because we have to eat."

"The giant has so much—it won't miss that bit of crust."

"I'm sorry, child. We need to go. I'm about to pop."

"Your babies are coming?"

The pregnant rat nodded and shuffled off, pulling her swollen torso through the small hole chewed through the baseboard. Following close behind, her daughter looked back one last time, perhaps to get a glimpse of her father's killer, the father of her forty-five brothers and sisters who would have to fend for themselves from now on. They had already started making plans to take over the house—from within. Those horrible Seldith would be the first to go. And then the human.

Fourteen—The Negotiation

*T*rudi followed the two Seldith elves as they scampered across the floor, back through the beaded curtain, and into the workshop. It seemed the elves had been there all along—all these years and she had never seen them. Thinking back, she realized that wasn't true. She had seen *signs* of them, tiny footprints in the dust that she thought were made by rats, the pinky-sized hat she found as a child, and other hints, such as mysterious sounds of mouse-feet darting out of sight. Opa had told her the hat belonged to one of his elven friends, but at the time, she had just humored him. "Perhaps you'll return it one day," she remembered him saying, giving it back to her and returning to his work. The hat had disappeared a few days later from her bedside table without explanation. She suspected it was the tooth fairy.

Even then, Trudi was not one of those children who *really* believed in Santa Claus, the Easter Bunny, the tooth fairy, or that her father would return someday. And there they were, little elves, as real as life—unless she was dreaming. She stopped mid-stride and pinched herself hard. *Ow. I'm awake. Perhaps other dreams can come true.*

Martine knelt on the floor and tapped on the boards with the butt of Hisbil's sword. A moment later, the stairway door opened, and he peered into the darkness before exchanging words with someone below.

"Show her the trapdoor," Alred said from below.

"They want you to open the trapdoor," Martine said.

"What trapdoor?" Trudi asked.

"It's hidden under the rug."

Although skeptical, having never seen a trap door any-where in the workshop, she did as Martine asked. Kneeling on the floor, Trudi rolled up the dusty old Persian rug. Under-neath, Trudi could just make out the outline of an opening—if she hadn't been looking for it, she might not have seen it at all. Judging by the dust lodged in the cracks, it had not been disturbed in ages. "What's down there?" she asked.

"You'll see," Martine replied with a sly grin. "Open it care-fully."

"But please," Glenda said. "Try not to frighten anyone. So many of my friends are deathly afraid of Umans."

"Umans? Oh, you mean *me*? I wouldn't dream of hurting anyone." With some effort, Trudi finally freed the large ring and, giving it a tug, the floorboard panel twice the size of her oven door came loose, and she pulled it open.

Astounding.

Trudi could not believe her eyes. Beneath the workshop where she had worked and played her entire life, row after row of tiny houses had been built between the joists, no two the same. It reminded her of Opa's model railroad town, long since dismantled and stored upstairs. Strangely, there were no elves or any sign of movement. Even Glenda and Martine had slipped away.

Worried she might have frightened them, she lay on her side to wait while she studied the houses more carefully. Fear-ing the homes might be fragile or she might further alarm the inhabitants, she did not try to touch anything. She marveled at the intricate maze of what must be stovepipes, water pipes, and wires strung between the houses—apparently used to carry away smoke, bring in water, and electrify each home. Growing impatient, she whispered. "Hello? Please come out. I mean you no harm."

At first, nothing happened. And then, the smallest walking creature she had ever seen appeared behind the crack of a round doorway. Dressed in a darling jumper and neatly fitted blouse, the child's hair was tied in a ribbon. The little creature looked up at her—completely fearless.

"Who are you?" Trudi asked softly.

"My name is Betty. I'm two. What's your name?" she asked bravely.

"What a pretty name. My name is Trudi." As she spoke, a frantic mom dashed out, scooped up her daughter, and disappeared inside, slamming the large round door.

"Wait. Don't be afraid," Trudi cried.

"Uman! How dare you violate our domain!" an angry voice shouted from the shadows.

Looking carefully, Trudi spotted an older Seldith dressed in a long red robe standing out of the light beyond her reach.

"And you are?" Trudi asked, rising to her knees. Unable to see clearly, she fetched a flashlight from the workbench. When she returned to the opening, she directed the light into the darkness, illuminating a handful of Seldith standing on the edge of the shadows, showing (almost) no fear of her. Several others were as brave as chickadees on a porch railing, and stumbled over each other in panic when Trudi redirected the light toward them.

"Dumold, stop this at once!" another voice cried out as another somewhat shorter Seldith strode out of the darkness. Martine and Glenda pushed their way through the now-growing throng of robed and uniformed elves carrying spears and swords—a few even had crossbows aimed up at her.

"Who authorized the opening of the hatch?" the red-robed elf demanded.

"I did," Alred said boldly.

"And who gave *you* that authority?"

"We did," several of the other robed elves said almost in unison, pushing their way to the front of the gathering. "We decided to act to resolve this issue."

"This is outrageous," Nonbon said, his face turning red.

"It's in the Book of Truth, Nonbon—which you are bound by oath to uphold. Article seven clearly dictates that the Council can show a no-confidence vote and overturn a decision of the President by a two-thirds majority."

"And we have the votes," Alred said.

Dumold stood his ground looking dumbfounded. As the group of spectators grew, the unrest and number of sems pushing, shoving, and threatening one another increased. When a knife appeared, Trudi gasped and without thinking, shouted. "Stop it. All of you." At that, she scattered the crowd with an enormous puff of breath. Alred, Martine, and Glenda were not spared, along with the rest of the Seldith Council, the spear-bearing Protectors, and their minions.

"Oh, I'm sorry," Trudi said at once. "I hope no one was hurt…" As she watched, Alred was helped to his feet by Glenda, and Martine was dragged out of a barrel where he had taken cover. "But can't we speak civilly? I have no intention to defile you or your homes, but I will only enter into this agreement if you can behave peaceably."

"I think you have everyone's attention," Alred said, with some authority.

"And you are?" Trudi asked.

"I am Alred—Viscount, a member of the Council, and wizard."

"It seems your own children are more mature than your Council," Trudi chided.

"I apologize again for the Elders' behavior," Alred said.

"I expect they're just frightened," Trudi said softly. "I know I would be."

"So it seems. I understand being afraid of threats, but ignorance is a far greater danger."

"You say you're a wizard?" Trudi asked, appreciating the wisdom of this quiet elf's words.

"It's my herditas—my inherited calling. My father and his father before him as far back as the Book of Truth records show, we were born with a gift of…magic, sorcery and, some say, wisdom."

"I see. My name is—"

"Mistress Trudi. Yes, I know, we all know," Alred said, smiling and taking a step toward her. "I've known you and your grandfather for many years. He and I have talked many times."

Trudi laughed. "Then you know I come to discuss the arrangement."

"That we do. The Council and I will be happy to go over the details with you. And then we shall feast."

"A feast? I feel unprepared. I have come visiting and brought nothing as a gift. In human culture, a houseguest brings wine, a home-cooked meal, flowers, or sweets to share."

Alred smiled, and the crowd breathed a collective sigh of relief and began a happy murmur, excited that their worries were unjustified—and the unfolding news could not be much happier.

For the next hour, Trudi studied the agreement with her jeweler's loupe. They went over the minute details along with the procedure for delivering the parts Trudi needed to repair the clocks. In exchange, she was to supply food and other sundry supplies the Seldith needed to keep them warm, safe, and their larders well stocked. It seems she had inherited quite a few new tenants.

The clan's many scribes took copious notes so as to transcribe the new agreement into the Book of Truth. This led to another history and culture lesson as they described this combination of sacred text, law book, and massive journal of the Seldith clan. Trudi found it equally contradictory and interesting.

"And we will need better steel," one of the Council said solemnly.

"For the mainsprings?" Trudi asked.

"For swords and arrowheads."

Trudi took a breath and pondered her response for a moment. "Because? Who do you intend to impale on these swords and pierce with these arrow points?"

"And spearheads."

"And spearheads? Who do you plan to battle? Other elves? Leprechauns?" Trudi asked.

"It should never come to that," Martine said, solemnly.

"They're concerned about the belluas," Alred said.

"Belluas. I saw Martine killed a large rat in my kitchen this morning. Is that what you call them?"

A hush came over the crowd. *What have I said?* Trudi asked herself.

"Yes, rats as you call them. They're an increasing problem. Your grandfather kept them in check using his own magic," Stephen, one of the Protectors said.

"I knew that he once set traps, but he had grown too frail to do that for some time. If I continue that practice, I expect they can be kept in check."

"Or we can," Stephen said. "We're very well equipped. We simply need better weapons."

Given the volatile (and juvenile) nature of the Council, Trudi was unsure about making any promises about weapons-grade steel that she expected could be used against her. "I'll think about it," Trudi said.

"Are we ready for the feast?" Alred asked. Trudi could see the residents of the Seldith village hovering at the edges of their meeting, eagerly awaiting the successful end of negotiations.

"Almost," Trudi said. "I still have a question."

Alred looked up at her with a troubled look on his face. "Perhaps I can answer it."

"Do you know, how did I get back to the top of the spiral staircase? I barely remember being knocked down by the door, but I don't know how I ended up in the workshop."

Alred smiled. "Magic. We carried you up with considerable difficulty, aided by a bit of levitation."

"I see. I find it hard to believe, but I've learned a lot about your clan that I would have never believed before today."

"Consider that everyone in the clan can perform *some* kind of magic. Some subtle, like the ability to make delicious cookies, others more powerful and difficult to believe."

"I guess I have a lot to learn," Trudi admitted.

"Are there other questions or concerns?" Alred asked.

"Well, it seems I trespassed on the rat's territory when I went down the stairs. They didn't seem a bit happy I was down there."

"We have a treaty with them as well. They have promised to remain on their side of the sea door, and we stay on ours."

"Interesting. So why is it I have rats in my larder? They didn't seem to be much of a problem when Opa was healthier."

"Then that's a serious infraction. We'll have to deal with them."

"I would appreciate any assistance in that regard. Really."

"So, any further concerns or questions?"

"None. Let's party," Trudi said with a smile.

While the negotiations had proceeded, the clan had set many large round tables lined with sparse plates of food, a few loaves of bread, and elaborate centerpieces decorated with tiny candles. Exotic smells floated in the air, bringing back fond and long-forgotten childhood memories. Thinking back, Trudi realized that she might have met these tiny creatures when she was a child.

"It all smells delicious. Let me get some wine, bread, and cheese and perhaps some stew meat left over from yesterday's supper. It's the least I can do." She really didn't want to take food from the mouths of their children.

When she returned, laden with a bottle of Chianti, a long loaf of bread, a plate of lamb stew, boiled potatoes, butter, and a round of yellow cheese, Trudi laid out the food on the workshop floor. She positioned a few lanterns that illuminated much of the village and opened the wine. With their help, the food was distributed to the tables in the clan square. She carefully filled several tiny wooden barrels like the pleading mouths of so many baby birds. In a similar fashion, she grated the cheese—the strips tumbling to the round tables where the Seldith children forgot their manners and picked off enormous pieces to devour. She could tell this was a fabulous treat for them—she had no way of knowing that alcohol and abundance brought out both the best and the worst in the elves. Thankfully, the feast and celebrations ended peacefully, well into the wee hours of the morning.

Trudi thought she would sleep better knowing she was not nearly as alone as she once feared. She would no longer worry about the whispers she heard in the night or the patter of tiny feet scampering around after dark.

Finishing her second glass of wine, she bid the Seldith a good night, carefully closed and covered the trap door, and dragged herself upstairs where she crawled into bed and closed her eyes.

৵৵৵

Once the clan had settled into their own beds, Alred, Sondrah, Martine, and Glenda sat around a quiet table in the back of the all-but-deserted tavern.

"*You* could have done that," Martine said. "You could have gone up to confront the uman. Easily."

Glenda touched his arm and shook her head, mouthing "Don't."

"I expect so," Alred said, looking up from his glass of wine.

"Why didn't you? Have you lost your courage?"

"Leave him alone," Sondrah said. "He's the most courageous sem *you'll* ever know."

"Then why didn't *he* go negotiate with the uman girl? It's *his* job. Instead, he hid down here, shivering in fear."

"He's done his part. Look at his arms. Just look," Sondra said, pulling up Alred's sleeve, revealing dark chevrons from wrist to shoulder—some thin, some wide, some elaborate, some dark red like arterial blood. "And these," she said, pulling down his tunic to reveal his striped tattoos had nearly reached his heart.

Martine just stared in disbelief at his grandfather.

"Hisbil had those too, but not as many," Glenda said. "I saw them. He confided in me they appeared each time he used his magic."

"So? We all know Alred's a wizard and so is his son; even more reason for *him* to go up and confront the uman." Martine said, reaching for the jug of wine.

"And so, it seems, is my grandson," Alred said, covering his tattoos.

"What?" Martine said.

"Face it. You're a Wizard, Martine," Glenda began. "Look at your arm. That dark ring on your wrist above your sword hand; it wasn't there this morning. Each time you use your magic, a new ring appears. When there is room for no more, your days as a wizard end."

Fifteen—The Summons

*T*rudi spent a fitful night. By morning, she felt like she had just finished the last mile of a marathon. Her usual nightmares had been replaced by an entirely new storyline. These disjointed and confusing dreams took her back in time, recalling every story Opa and Oma had shared about the little people that seemed as real as the Tooth Fairy—until now. *They're real—very real.*

Surrendering around two in the morning, she got out of bed to study the agreement she had signed in her own blood. Nursing a tiny pinprick in her finger, she realized she had taken on the care and feeding of an entire population of living, breathing, sentient beings who before yesterday, she never knew existed. Their existence was still hard to accept.

She had assumed a sobering responsibility—and a secret she *must* keep. If the wrong people found out, it would mean her charges, the Seldith elves, might well be in mortal danger. But it was more than hiding the existence of the Seldith and feeding them. Much more. If she was unable to keep the shop ticking, she could not continue to fulfill her part of the agreement. If she could not pay the taxes, the bills, the utilities, and do the upkeep, they would all face exile and she would be driven into poverty.

But what choice do I have? I can't very well turn them down. My ancestors have sheltered the Seldith for generations and without their help, I can't keep building our clocks.

Hearing the clocks strike six, she began her day with an entirely new motivation but was held back by a mind-numbing hangover—her first. Mercifully, the shop was quiet most of the morning, so she got caught up on the laundry, a few repairs, and her bookkeeping. *Bills, final notices, warnings, and more dunning notices.* She shook her head in frustration. Making a quick tally, she looked at the sum. With a deep sigh, she closed the ledger and looked for some aspirin.

About three, Trudi was helping Mrs. Robbins shop when Chad came into the store. She was delighted to see another friendly face who wasn't on the list of people to whom she owed money. He was carrying a small envelope sealed with red beeswax. *Wait. I do owe him money.*

"Hi, Chad. Don't I owe you for that delivery?"

"Don't worry about it, Miss Trudi," he said quietly, removing his cap and revealing his shock of curly black hair, which he pushed back into submission with his fingers.

"Thanks. I'll make it up to you. What brings you back?"

"I have a note for your grandfather. It's from the *mayor.*"

"I'll take it," Trudi said, beckoning him to come to the counter. She had already palmed a half-dollar coin. As he handed her the note, she distracted him and slipped the coin into his jacket pocket.

"The mayor said it's supposed to be handed directly to Mister Sanduhr."

"Chad, you know full well my grandfather passed away."

"I *tried* to tell him, but he can be as hard to convince as a… a…"

"Politician," Trudi injected.

"Yeah, when it comes to facts contrary to his beliefs, he never accepts… I guess it's all right if you read it." He handed her the note with the mayor's insignia stamped into the seal.

Trudi mused at the seal, shaking her head. Their infamous mayor was known for these pretentious gestures that had long-since gone out of practice.

"I'm to wait for an answer, Miss Trudi."

The message, written in a hurried but readable scrawl, summoned Master Clockmaker Wilhelm Sanduhr "forthwith" to City Hall to deal with a "matter of critical import." *What has Opa done?* Trudi pondered, re-reading the note. *Back taxes? Some kind of shady deal?* She kept reading. It said Mr. Sanduhr should bring his tools.

"I'm to go with you. Now?"

Chad nodded. "Yes'm."

"But I have customers," she said.

Mrs. Robbins looked up from her browsing and eaves-dropping. "Go. Go. It's the mayor," she insisted. "I was just passing the time."

"Thanks."

"And Trudi," Mrs. Robbins continued, "make sure you aren't alone behind closed doors with that… *man*. He collects the reputations of young girls like children collect pretty sea-shells at the beach."

"I'll be careful," Trudi said with a smile. While she waited for Mrs. Robbins to leave, she wrote a note for the door, and once Ginny had given her a few more words of wisdom, she left, and Trudi locked up. "I'll be ready in a bit," she said to Chad.

Trudi pushed through the beads into the workshop and made a quick search of her card index for anything sold to City Hall and especially to the mayor. She found two—both were sufficiently valuable or large enough to require an onsite visit. She packed Opa's wheeled traveling case prepacked with eve-rything she might conceivably need, including tools, lubri-cants, and a few spare parts for these clocks. She also found a stack of overdue invoices for work done for the city. Adding them up, she realized the city owed them a considerable amount of money. *I wonder why Opa never collected on these invoices. Was it a payoff or protection money?* She tucked the papers into her case.

"Are you ready, Miss? His Honor said to return at once. He's not a patient man," Chad said from behind the beaded curtain.

"I'm ready," she said, closing her case.

"I can take that," he said, reaching over to pick up the case. He nearly dropped it. "H…heavy. Are you bringing lead counterweights too?

"No, just tools and parts—delicate parts," she said, donning her coat.

"Yes'm," he said. With considerable difficulty, Chad lugged the case out to the cab and managed to get it into the trunk. He rushed around and held open the door for Trudi. A moment later, they were on their way toward the center of town at breakneck speed.

"Chad, take it easy."

"Yes'm," he said after skillfully dodging a truck crowding his lane. Trudi breathed a sigh of relief. She had rarely ridden in cars, so it was a relatively new experience for her—and somewhat thrilling. Her mind filled with what might be amiss with the mayor's clocks, so she didn't pay attention to the route Chad was taking or that he was speeding up a dark, narrow alley, raising a cloud of debris.

"I greatly admire your…clocks," Chad said, stealing a brief look at her in the rearview mirror.

"Oh? Do you own one?" she asked.

"Oh yes. My father bought one for my mom many years ago. It plays a lovely tune on the quarter hour. Or it did."

"Is it broken?"

"Here we are, Miss." Chad said as they pulled up to City Hall with a screech of the tires. "I'll get your case." He hopped out and muscled the case out of the trunk. By the time he had lugged it up the thirteenth step, Trudi thought he had earned his tip. "What's this weigh, Miss? Seventy pounds?"

"Oh, only about fifty pounds I expect," Trudi replied. "I usually do this." She tapped a button that released wheels on each corner.

"Oh, now you tell me," Chad said, out of breath.

"The wheels aren't much good on stairs. I'm working on a redesign to solve that problem. What do I owe you?"

"Oh, the mayor is paying me—I hope."

"Well, he didn't figure on dealing with that tool case." She handed him a coin and noticed the boy's shoes. The uppers had been polished, but the soles were paper-thin. "Your mother's clock? Bring it by the shop. There's a good chance I can fix it."

"We couldn't possibly. We're barely making ends meet on what I make with my cab and my dad's policeman's pay. I have a sister and a baby brother with—"

"Perhaps in exchange; you can do me a favor someday," she said with a smile.

"Thank you, Miss," he said, tugging at the bill of his cap as he held open the enormous door and followed her in.

Inside, Trudi found the marble-floored foyer all but deserted. Each step on the polished floors echoed through the corridor. A sign near the entrance told her why.

HOURS: 10:00 TO NOON TUESDAY AND THURSDAY

2:00 TO 4:00 PM MONDAY AND WEDNESDAY

This is Thursday—the place is closed. She just shook her head and turned to leave.

"Can't you read?" a voice bellowed out of the dark.

Trudi looked up and spoke toward the voice. "I was summoned by the mayor."

"I was expecting *Mr.* Sanduhr some time ago," the voice said. "Not a girl."

"My grandfather passed away. I'm Trudi, his granddaughter. I have taken on his clients."

A cadence of noisy footsteps later, a middle-aged man dressed in a three-piece suit approached her from the shadows. "I see. I'm Mayor Babcock. Try to be more punctual, miss."

"Nice to meet you, Mr. Mayor." She lied. Trudi noticed the mayor's professionally shined shoes and their high heels. *A few inches taller, but no higher in stature.*

"How proficient are your repair skills?" he asked over his shoulder as he walked away.

"I get very few complaints," Trudi said, being uncomfortable with self-praise. She followed, but Chad took charge of the cart.

"Of course, I would prefer someone who received no complaints."

"If you would prefer an older man with brittle, arthritic fingers, I'm sure you can find one. I expect Mr. Hastings in Boston is still working," she lied, knowing the 85-year-old clockmaker had retired years ago.

"No, you'll do. Come right this way."

"What's this all about, Mr. Mayor? I had to close my shop." The mayor just strode off into the dimly lit corridor without a reply. Trudi and Chad followed.

"Oh, I'm sorry, didn't the boy say it's an emergency?" he said.

"In this case, shouldn't you contact the police, the fire department, or a doctor?"

"Your grandfather would have been far more qualified to deal with this emergency than any doctor. I hope *you* are. The patient is in there, my dear," the mayor said, touching the small of her back and ushering her into an ornate office twice the size of her shop leaving Chad and her tool caddy in the hall.

Behind her, she heard the door close with a thud. She turned to see His Honor locking it and pocketing the key. "So we won't be disturbed while you work," he said with a smirk.

"Unlock it. Now. And leave the door ajar." Her tone and glare were unmistakable. She had heard many rumors of the mayor's predilection for impropriety, long before Mrs. Robbin's warning. She didn't want her reputation to be added to the list of those left behind in this office. "And I'll need my tools."

"If you insist." The Major stepped back and did as she asked. He motioned for Chad to bring in the tool caddy, shooing him away like a stray goose.

"I'll be right outside," Chad said.

Trudi was amazed at the gilded opulence: Persian carpets, an enormous mahogany desk, a long red velvet divan, cut-glass windows with a panoramic view of the city square, and yes, one of her grandfather's finest clocks stood like a sentry centered on the north wall so it could be seen from the entire room. *Carmalita, long time no see.* "*This* is your emergency?"

"Yes. I'm afraid it's ticked its last tock," he said with mock seriousness. "It was running slow, and the chimes seemed muted and irregular, but now it's stopped entirely." The mayor poured himself a drink from a crystal decanter. "Would you care for a fortifier?" he asked, holding out a brandy snifter.

"I'm afraid not. Mr. Mayor, this 'emergency' does not sound that serious, and certainly not enough to have me turn away paying customers."

"The city will reimburse you generously for your losses *and* your time, I assure you."

"In that case, I'll need a deposit up front and also for the city to clear up its arrears before I get started," Trudi said, looking him in the eye and handing him one of the overdue invoices. One bit of advice her grandfather had passed down was to be wary of the city and get what's owed *before* they rack up more charges. It seems he had not followed his own advice.

"Oh?" The mayor's right eyebrow raised to a sharp point as he looked menacingly over his glasses.

"Your Honor, my grandfather and I have done work for the city many times before." She laid each of the unpaid invoices on his desk one at a time. "Many... many... many times."

"I'm afraid you'll have to take that up with the city accountant once he returns from celebrating Christmas in the Bahamas."

"With all due respect, your *Honor*, your bean counters take far too long to pay, if they pay at all. All too often, they begrudgingly pay fifty cents on the dollar and make us go to court for the rest. As it is, and I should know as I do the books, the city owes us $29.50[13]. I have a business to run, and my *own* creditors to pay."

"I see. Can you work on the clock here and now, or will it have to be taken into the shop?"

"I won't know until I inspect her."

"Her?"

"That's Carmalita—one of my grandfather's finest clocks. She's a masterpiece of engineering and innovation."

"Not much of a masterpiece if it can't keep time." The mayor took a sip of brandy. "Are you sure you don't care to join me?"

"I would *care* to go back to my paying customers," she said, turning to go.

"Then please begin. I will get your money." He opened a large checkbook on his desk and inked a pen.

---

[13] Consider that in 1938, $29.50 is equal to about $640 in 2023.

"No offense, but in cash, Your Honor. In *cash*."

"Do you know who you're speaking to?" he said, his tone hardening, the pen still hovering over the checkbook.

"I'm speaking to a man who has taken advantage of my grandfather's generosity too many times, and who has lost the respect one would ordinarily afford an elected official."

"In cash," he said under his breath, putting down the pen and walking across the room. He swung back the portrait of a stern-faced woman, exposing an older wall safe. Trudi realized it must have been an older model, as she could hear the tumblers click and the bolt-release drop into place from six feet away. "Fifty now, and fifty when you're done?" he said, tugging open the iron door.

"$29.50 now to cover your outstanding bill, $10 for a deposit on the repairs, and the balance when Carmalita is fixed. Call it $40 to get us back on an even keel," Trudi said, still holding out the city's unpaid invoices. "I have no idea how much time it will take or if I'll have to fabricate replacement parts. Carmalita is an exquisitely crafted clock. There's not another one like her in the world, so many of her parts were hand-made."

"Carmalita?" he asked, handing her a stack of crisp bills.

Trudi counted while she replied. "All our finer clocks are given names so we might better remember how and when they were made and in whose hands they were placed. Grandfather treated them like his children—perhaps better." ... *10, 20, 40.*

"Now I need you to sign a receipt. Let's make it out for $50 to cover any future issues."

"So you can claim $50 from the city? I'm not that kind of a businesswoman, your Honor."

"Oh, I thought I was doing you a favor."

"Thanks, but no thanks," she said, writing Paid in Full on each of the invoices, keeping the carbon copy for herself.

"I'll get to work at once. I should be able to tell what's wrong in a few minutes." Trudi turned to the clock and opened the case. Examining Carmalita's history card, she found that she was built when Opa was about twenty-five. It was one of his more sophisticated clocks and had been in service for over sixty years, and in previous administrations, had received regular maintenance. Lately, she had been neglected, and it showed.

Carefully removing the access cover, Trudi raised her lamp. *And that's the trouble.* "It's no wonder you're having problems. From the looks of it, this clock hasn't been cleaned since you've been in office."

"It's been cleaned—it's dusted every week, almost," he said, refilling his snifter.

"Yes, cleaned on the outside, your Honor, but it must be cleaned on the *inside*. Every clock like this needs regular cleaning, lubrication, and maintenance. Given the amount of coal dust, dander, pollen, wood, coal, and tobacco smoke in the air, any mechanical device can get corrupted."

"What do you suggest? Can you clean it here?"

"Not a chance," she said, "I expect the mechanism needs disassembly and a long soak in cleaning solution and any worn-out parts replaced. I would have to take it back to the shop for that. Let's see how bad it is."

Using another one of her inventions, Trudi wound up an automated bellows and used the flexible hose to drive dust out of the clockworks. While she worked, she thought she heard a tiny cough over the hum of the blower. She turned it off and listened.

After the dust cloud had settled, she listened again but heard nothing. But she could see something had made a home amongst the mechanism—literally. *Straw, bedding, and a tiny candle?* Using a pair of needle-nosed pliers, she extracted it all and turned her attention to what appeared to be a bit of fabric wedged between the gears. If she didn't know better, she would have sworn it was a tiny vest with buttons, collar, and lapels, but with an unusual gap in the back. It was the right size for a person about four inches tall. And then she heard it again. A tiny sneeze. *Seldith.*

Stifling a scream, she repositioned the lamp until she saw a tiny creature crouching behind the clock's mainspring. The girl put one finger up to her lips and begged with pleading eyes, covering her chest with her forearm. She reached out and mouthed that she wanted her vest returned. Trudi smiled and nodded, handing it to her, but as she pulled it on, Trudi noticed the girl's back had what appeared to be… *wings.*

"I'm afraid it's thoroughly… corroded, corrupted, really a mess," Trudi said to the mayor. "I'm going to have to make some major repairs back at the shop," she said.

"Really? What's wrong?"

"The internal framis gear is stripped and the idle horologium secunda is hopelessly jammed," she lied.

"That… sounds bad. What's it going to cost?"

"This clock was a custom design, hand-made decades ago and in today's market, it's worth a fortune. I expect I can bring it back to life for a fraction of that—say about, $50." *Better to shoot for the moon.*

"Is it really worth that much to repair?"

"Given its provenance, Carmalita would easily be worth many thousands to a collector—but not in the shape it's in. It's a shame you didn't take better care of her—she would be worth a small fortune." *At least that much is true.*

Trudi could almost see the mayor's eyes turn into golden coins as he wrung his hands. "I'll need half now, and half when I'm done."

"On top of the forty?"

"I'm afraid so."

"Fifty bucks seems—"

"Fair. You won't find another clockmaker anywhere who knows this clock better. If you take it to another shop, they'll just bring it to me because only we make the special parts. My grandfather crafted it long before my mother was born, but I've regularly seen clocks like her in the shop and worked on them many times."

"Done. Can you start on it tonight?"

"Is this Thursday?" she asked, looking up as if she were figuring. "For an extra ten… twenty percent. But why the rush?"

"The… the Council meets in this chamber and depends on the clock for parliamentary functions."

"To time the speakers. Yes, I know—it's one of her features."

"So, you understand why it's so important."

"I can begin work as soon almost as I get back to the shop." She regretted pushing her other customers to the back of the queue, but this fee would put her in the black for the first time in months. *I might be able to afford a temporary assistant and pay a lot of bills.*

"How long will it take?"

"As long as it takes, but with a deep cleaning, best case at least two days."

As she spoke, the elf crawled out to the edge of the clock and scrambled up Trudi's arm and into her breast pocket, gesturing "Thanks" with her outstretched hands.

Meanwhile, the mayor had stepped over to the safe again. Trudi already knew the combination, not by watching him spin the dial, but by being able to hear the gears and tumblers inside the old lock. Her acute hearing let her "see" through the safe door, and she knew the numbers as each lever inside fell into place. *5 9 18 65. Wait. I know that… date…*

The safe clicked, and he swung open the door. Inside, Trudi spotted stacks of cash and the spine of a black leather ledger. A moment later, the door swung closed, and the mayor handed her another stack of bills. After he made out a receipt, she checked to see if it was the right amount. It was. She was tempted to put some of the cash in her pocket but stashed it all in her tool bag.

"Chad is waiting to take you." At that, the mayor left Trudi to disassemble and pack up the clock.

Before she started, she held her hand next to her pocket. "Hello?"

A little face appeared.

"Who are you?"

"They call me Weeset, Miss Trudi. You're the clock-maker's granddaughter, aren't you?"

"That I am. How did you know?"

"Oh, my, you're quite famous. Your grandfather doted on you no end."

"I see. As it turns out, I've just met your clan. We've come to a renewed understanding."

"That's comforting," Weeset said softly. "We were worried that we might have to move out after your grandfather died."

"What's wrong?" Trudi asked. She could tell the girl was upset about something. "Are you afraid of me? I would never hurt you."

Weeset looked up with eyes full of tears. "I'm not afraid of you. You have a kind soul—I can tell."

"Then what's wrong?"

"We can't talk here. The mayor has large ears."

"Perhaps you're right. I'll take you back with me."

Weeset just stared into Trudi's eyes.

"Seriously, are you okay? You can confide in me," Trudi asked again.

"We were all so sad when the old uman passed."

"He was all I had," Trudi said.

"Hardly. You still have us. You'll always have us."

When the door latch snapped, Weeset tucked away her wings and scrambled back into Trudi's pocket.

Trudi worked quickly to disconnect the massive counter-weights and unlatch the mechanism from the ornate clock housing. It slid out into her waiting arms. "Come to mama," she whispered.

"How are you doing?" the mayor asked. "I asked Chad to take you straight home."

Chad appeared in the doorway, holding his hat.

"I'll need help carrying the clockworks and my tools," Trudi said to the mayor. "The counterweights can remain here."

"Chad?" the mayor gestured but didn't offer to help.

"Of course, Your Honor," Chad said. "Has this gotten heavier since I hauled it up the stairs? Wait. Didn't you push a button or something?"

"You need to start working out more. Here, let me help," she said, extending the wheels again.

Chad smiled. "Thanks."

"That's marvelous. I've never seen anything like it," the mayor said.

While proud of her grandfather's inventions, Trudi didn't want to encourage the mayor with more idle conversation. "Let's go," she said to Chad.

Chad turned for the door, pulling the toolbox behind him like a heavy child's wagon. Trudi followed close behind with the clockworks in her arms, wanting to keep the precious contents of her bag in sight. The money was not her only concern—the custom tools and clockwork components were irreplaceable and beyond value in the hands of her competitors.

The mayor followed Trudi out to the cab, but she sensed his eyes seemed more focused on her than the precious clock. "Do you have dinner plans, Miss Sanduhr?"

"Have you asked your wife? I expect she has something prepared and might not be expecting a dinner guest," Trudi said with a wry grin.

Trudi watched Chad reload the tool case in the trunk and regretted not keeping the cash on her person. "Let's get home before it gets any later. The shop has been closed too long as it is."

Chad turned the key. "Let's go Harvey." The cab's engine cranked and sputtered as if to say, "You talkin' to me?" It took several tries to get the engine started and on the road.

"Harvey?" Trudi asked.

"My horse was called Harvey. When I stepped up to this old gas buggy, it inherited much of Harvey's personality. Temperamental, doesn't like the cold, and unwilling to climb tall hills. I still love him."

"I see," Trudi said with a giggle.

"I think he likes you," Chad said after a long silence.

"Harvey?"

Chad laughed. "No, the mayor."

"I think he's old enough to be my father."

"Older."

After that, the conversation relaxed and Trudi revealed the reason for the mayor's "emergency" call to City Hall.

"He seems to think everyone in town is at his beck and call."

"He is the *mayor*," she said, using the word as a pejorative.

"He's a lowlife. I'll be lucky to have a position tomorrow."

"Well, I've come into some…" she began, but hesitated to say what was in the bag. "If you don't mind me asking, what does the mayor pay you?"

"You mean *when* does the mayor pay me? Not much, and not regularly. I just do odd errands for him."

"I understand. Jobs are hard to find, and good, steady jobs are as scarce as a sunny sky on your day off."

"Unless you have connections. That's why I put up with him. I'm hoping some well-to-do businessman will tread some of their mud on my floor instead of leaving it all in the mayor's office."

"What's that supposed to mean?"

"Oh, I hear things from time-to-time. His *Honor* has me wait in his outer office like he did today, but sometimes the door is left open, or when the heat register is set just right, I hear a few tasty morsels."

"I see…"

"And when I take people from place to place, I often over-hear news of an untoward nature."

"Like what?"

"I shouldn't say."

"But you're going to," Trudi said with a coy, flirty lilt in her voice.

"Well…" he began.

As Chad and Harvey picked their way through the evening throng of traffic and dodging pedestrians trying to survive crossing the street, Chad described a few backroom payoffs, illicit affairs, vote-buying schemes, and more. "I expect His Honor is involved in any number of iceberg scandals."

"Iceberg scandals?"

"Where the whole truth is hidden well beneath the shimmering white surface—only a small part is visible. That's all I ever hear—just bits and pieces—the tips of the icebergs."

"Well, I've heard enough," Trudi said, holding up her hand. Her estimation of this mild-mannered and polite young man had changed. He was a lot smarter and wilier than her first impression. It seemed Chad was another intellectual iceberg. While only a few years older, he might prove to be a valuable resource for her and the shop. The fact that he was cute didn't hurt.

"Do tourists ever ask about where to find unique things to buy as souvenirs?"

"Oh, all the time, Miss."

"If you were to get them into my shop, I could make it worth your while," she said.

"Oh, I already do," he said.

"Why thank you. You're sweet. Be sure to bring your clock to the shop."

Chad smiled back at her in the rear-view mirror.

As they waited at a traffic light, Trudi began thinking about what Chad had said. While she was already cynical about their "elected" city and state government officials, if true, these rumors would confirm what Trudi and her grandfather had suspected for years. Chad had mentioned the names of a few people she knew as patrons, or through her grandfather's inventors' society. Of course, the stories might *not* be true, or only half-truths. As her grandmother had taught her, "nothing is really one hundred percent true, but some people, and especially politicians, seem to accept statements as fact if they're only ten percent true. It's like calling something 'apple juice' when the only apple in the bottle is on the label."

As the cab pulled up to Trudi's shop, she recognized a few customers milling around talking to one another, but a man in a tailored suit stood apart from them. At first, she thought he was studying a clock in the window until she realized he was watching her in the window's reflection as she got out of the cab. Once his subterfuge had been discovered, he recast his gaze. As she moved toward the shop door, an older woman in a long black dress pushed forward. *Mrs. Vandergelder.* "Where have you been?" she demanded. "You promised my music box would be fixed this afternoon. I must have been waiting here in the cold for twenty minutes."

"Mayor Babcock summoned me to City Hall to fix his clock." Trudi politely pressed through Mrs. Vandergelder and the other more patient customers to open the shop, letting the three women go in ahead of her while the gentleman hung back. She turned on the lights and noticed that Chad had the clockworks in his arms. *The bag. Oh my God, he's left it on the curb.* She turned and sprang for the door, only to run into the gentleman.

"Miss? I don't think it's wise to leave your things where strangers might—" He was holding her tool bag as easily as a hatbox. His gaze was fixed on her face, as if he expected her to recognize him. She didn't, but motioned for him to put the tool case on the counter. "Thank you, kind sir. Oh, what a relief. That bag has…" she turned her back and checked inside. Both the tools and the money were still safe inside. She put the cash in the drop safe under the counter and turned back to wait on her customers.

"Now, who was first? This gallant gentleman must be," she said, looking up with a smile.

"Well, I *never*. I've been here for just ages," Mrs. Vandergelder huffed.

"Madam, I'll be more than happy to permit you to precede me," the gentleman said. "I can see you have a pressing need for your…"

"Music box," the old woman said indignantly.

The man executed a low bow and a flourish, as if he were addressing royalty.

"That's quite noble of you, sir. Might I deal with you after I help Mrs. Vandergelder?" Trudi said, with her own attempt at a curtsy.

The gentleman smiled and stepped aside.

"Now, Mrs. Vandergelder, I have your music box. It's as good as new."

"Well, I hope so. It certainly didn't hold up very well," she complained.

"From the appearance of the damage to the case, I might suggest you not let anyone use it to crack walnuts. That will be fifty cents to refinish the case and another dollar to repair the mechanism."

"How did you...know?" the old woman asked sheepishly as she dug into her coin purse.

"Oh, I have my sources," Trudi said with a smile. "I'm just glad I was able to bring it back to life and remove the bits of husk wedged in the gears." Trudi knew that some might suspect she could listen in on her customer's homes, but the truth of the matter was less mysterious. Mrs. Vandergelder's maid had mentioned the incident when she checked on the music box earlier in the week.

Once the repair fee had been paid in full (for once), Trudi looked up, but discovered the mysterious gentleman, her helpful knight, had left the shop. *I wonder who he was?*

"Will there be anything else, Miss?" Chad said. He was standing by the door, holding his hat.

Trudi had completely forgotten about him. "Sorry, no. But check back here tomorrow—especially if the mayor finds your services are redundant." She pressed a couple of coins into his palm. His hands felt delightfully warm as their fingers touched.

"That's for helping. Bring your clock by. I'm certain I can fix it."

"Thank *you*, Miss Trudi. I will," he said. "I certainly will." A broad smile covered his face as he discovered the half-dollar.

"Chad, do you know that gentleman who helped with the case?"

"No. He's new in town. I can't say that I've seen him before."

She watched as Chad left the shop and giggled as he boasted to Harvey about his windfall. This time, Harvey started right up.

Wait! Weeset.

Sixteen—The Stowaway

*T*rudi carefully patted her breast pocket, but the Faerie didn't pop up as she had in the mayor's office. *Oh my God. I've killed her.* She gently slid her hand into her pocket and was somewhat relieved to find it was empty. *She must have fallen out—or worse.* She spent the next few minutes searching high and low (but mostly low) in the shop—quietly calling her name, to no avail. When the shop bell tinkled, she was on her hands and knees searching through the dust bunnies under the music box cabinet.

"Miss?"

She looked up into the eyes of the gentleman who had helped her with her tool bag. Her knight had returned. *Oh, dear Lord.*

"Is this an inopportune time? I can come back later." He extended his hand to help her get back to her feet.

"No, no, I was just looking for someone… something," she said, scrambling to her feet with his assistance.

"He must be very small to fit under the case," he said with a warm smile.

"A winding key. I dropped an ornate… winding key. I'll find it later."

"Of course."

"Is there something I can help *you* with, Mister…?" she asked. Catching a glimpse of herself in the mirror, she blushed when she realized how bedraggled she appeared. Her face and dress were smudged with dust, her hair a tangled mess. She frantically brushed back her hair and smoothed the wrinkles out of her dress as she stood.

"Mr… Sanders. I was interested in a nice clock for my… daughter. She never stops talking about your marvelous time-pieces," he said, strolling over toward the more elaborate, more expensive models.

"I'm flattered, Mr. Sanders," Trudi said. "Is there a particular style? A mantle clock, a cuckoo, or a free-standing grand-father?" she asked. *I'm babbling… settle down.*

"This one especially appeals to me," he said, studying one of Trudi's favorites."

Her heart sank. "That's Anastasia, one of Wilhelm's earlier masterpieces." The lovely clock they had named Anastasia was a treasured piece, but as Opa had told her, they were not running a museum. "She's one of our most beloved. Her chimes are like none other."

"Was Anastasia commissioned by the Tzar, or perhaps his daughter?"

"No, but she was inspired by the Grand Duchess' beauty." Trudi would hate to sell it, as it was supposedly one of her and her mother's favorites. It was one of the few pieces that re-minded her of her mother, a woman she had never met. Trudi's head was spinning, her pulse racing. "What brings you into to the shop?" she asked.

"I have an associate with a lovely vacation home nearby. I come up from Boston sometimes to think and unwind—so to speak. I love this little town, but this is my first visit to your shop."

"I suppose you know my grandfather passed a few—?"

"Yes, I know. Sadly, I only saw the notice in the paper but could not attend his services. I would like to offer my sincere, albeit belated, condolences. I hear he was quite an artist and craftsman, and that you inherited this talent. I know he would be so proud of you."

"Thank you. That's most kind," she said sensing his sentiment was heartfelt.

"What will you take to part with Anastasia? I'll give it a loving home."

Before Trudi's trip to the mayor's office, she would have taken far less for this masterpiece—money was that tight. But now that her immediate cash-flow problems were behind her, she decided she could risk asking considerably more. "She's an especially fine piece, and a treasured family heirloom. I really hate to part with her." *Especially to a stranger.*

"I agree, so, quite a bit."

"I can show you a number of other special pieces which are far more reasonable."

"Humor me. I have my heart set on Anastasia."

Trudi swallowed hard. "Ninety nine ninety five."

Her knight continued to study Anastasia as if he were playing poker. "I assume she runs."

"Of course, but she'll need regular maintenance. I'll include the first year."

"The first five years. It will give me a reason to return to your shop."

"Two, and I'll clean it before you take her."

"Can I have it by tomorrow morning? It's her birthday."

"Her?"

"My daughter. She's turning five."

"She's a bit young for something this nice." *Incredibly young.*

"All right; it's for me—let's pretend tomorrow is *my* birthday."

"Nice try," she said with a smile. "I'll need a deposit and the balance on delivery."

"Of course. I'll write you a check." He pulled out a tooled leather checkbook.

Trudi's stomach turned over. Having been swindled before by seemingly "honest" clientele, even handsome, gallant men, she searched his eyes for a glimmer of truth. Unlike the face and sounds of a clock, she found people were harder to read, harder to tell if they weren't ticking exactly right, but so far, he hadn't missed a beat.

"So, no checks," he said, apparently noting her expression. "I don't blame you. Let's say I give you…" He thumbed through his wallet. "I have… five, ten, yes, there's a twenty. Thirty-five. It's all I have on me. Will that be enough to hold it until it be morrow?"

She nodded and smiled at the olde English. "That will be satisfactory. Good night, good night! Parting is such sweet sorrow, that I shall say good night till it be morrow."

Sanders smiled and nodded.

It was too good to be true. Even if he never returned, she was more than a hundred dollars ahead.

"All right, when should I come by? Say noon?"

"Noon is… fine. I should have it done by then." Suddenly, it occurred to her. *The mayor's clock.*

"Adieu," he said as he departed.

The shop door had just closed when Trudi heard a familiar, albeit tiny, voice.

"Miss Trudi?"

Trudi looked up to see Weeset was now seated on the porch of a large animated clock designed to look like a mountain chalet. She could have been sitting there a week before someone realized she wasn't one of the clock's costumed wooden figures.

"*There* you are. I was worried you might have been…"

"I'm used to being around umans, although I've had some close calls."

"Can I get you something to eat or drink?"

"I'm fine. Clarence and I are old friends and he showed me where I could find some bread and cheese."

"Good. How did you get him to—"

"Not eat me? Let's just say I have a way with all God's creatures. He also knows I can change him into a squirrel—or he thinks I can."

"I see. Being as tall as a minute hand, I can see how that would be a useful skill. Wait. You can talk to him?"

"No, he's not been awakened. I can arrange that if you want me to."

"Awakened?"

"The Seldith have the ability to awaken creatures so they can understand speech and even be understood by umans."

"Really?"

"Yeah. But in Clarence's case, I would not recommend it. He's quite demanding."

"I expect you're right."

Weeset flew up and made a dainty landing on Trudi's shoulder. "I was just wondering how you plan to work on both clocks at once."

"Privi will help," Trudi said, reverently taking Anastasia down. "Assuming I get to work on them."

"Wait a tick. Tell me again, why were you stuck inside Carmalita?"

"The mayor's clock? It was my turn."

"You take turns?"

"Well, the Faeries do. The Seldith aren't allowed to go into town—at least not among the people. It's too hard for them to stay hidden."

Trudi gently placed Anastasia on the workbench next to Carmalita and began to work while they chatted. "Faeries. Really. So you aren't one of the Seldith?"

"Oh, we Faeries visit down there too when it suits us," she said, pointing to the trapdoor.

"I'm confused. Why not live down below? It seemed quite nice."

"There is one window. It smells of coal dust and Seldith armpits. So, no, not so 'nice'," she said.

"Don't you get along? You have so much in common."

"Besides being small and magical? No, not really. We try to stay out of each other's way. Over time, the Faeries and the elves have… well, we get on one another's nerves."

"That's kind of sad," Trudi said, gently tugging out Anastasia's works.

"That we don't trust each other?"

"Yes. That would be a real problem. Opa taught me trust is like gold in your pocket. Once it's spent, you'll find it impossibly hard to recover."

"He was a wise man. I will miss him greatly. He had quite a bit of work yet to do."

"And so do I," Trudi said, opening Privi's closet and winding his mainspring. Once she pulled the activate lever, he came to life and went to work. "Privi, would you get these two cleaned up?"

I CLEAN

"Hi Privi," Weeset said, hovering above the mechanical helper.

HI

"Oh, you've met my mechanical friend?"

"I have. We're chums."

I CLEAN

Trudi was dumbfounded. *How did I miss seeing these tiny creatures right under my nose? Magic?*

Privi picked up Anastasia's clockworks and gently lowered the mechanism into the chemical bath and adjusted the kerosene heater. He turned back to the workbench and retrieved Carmalita.

"Did you… create this… him? I've seen him work from time-to-time, but the elves didn't tell me much about his innards."

"I did. He's amazing, and a lot of help."

Weeset just shook her head. "I didn't know you made him. I thought he was magic—made by the elves."

"Magic? To me? Sure. Mechanical magic. I just have a talent for it. I get an idea in my head and things just seem to come together."

BROKE GEAR

"Yes, I know. The A4 gear is stripped. See if we have a spare. It looks like type six. If not, I'll mill one on the lathe."

"It's a type seven," Weeset said.

Trudi turned to see Weeset was sitting on a drawer knob across the workshop. *How did she know which gear?*

"It's in here," Weeset said.

"Yes, I know. How did *you* know?"

"Oh, sometimes I help my boyfriend mill these parts. Maybe you've met him? Martine?"

"Wait. You know Martine? I thought he was sweet on Glenda?"

"Don't make me laugh. They hate each other."

Trudi didn't say anything as she didn't want to get in the middle of this love triangle, but based on how she saw Martine and Glenda behave, she expected Weeset was more delusional than psychic. She opened the drawer and fingered through the brass A4 gears carefully sorted by type. "Four, five, six, there. Seven."

"So, you know about clocks?"

"Seriously? I've been living with the elves for… well, a long time. They're a boring lot. All they ever talk about is clockworks and wars with the rats."

"Really?" Trudi said, not looking up from her clockworks.

"And you'll probably want to replace a few of the bushings as well."

Trudi remembered Privi printing out something about the bushings, so she was not that amazed that the fairy knew they needed repair. In any case, it was a delight to talk to someone who knew her craft.

"Privi had better get those gearboxes out of the bath. You don't want them getting wrinkly."

Trudi heard the shop bell ring. "Customer. Privi keep working," she said, heading toward shop.

I WORK

Trudi found Chad standing at the counter with a clock in his arms.

"Chad, is that your family clock?"

"It is Miss. I must insist on paying to have it repaired. If possible, can it be ready by Christmas morning? Is that too much to ask?"

"Not at all—that gives me plenty of time. I'll get right on it and call when it's ready."

"Do I pay you now?" he said, fingering his wallet.

"We'll discuss that when it's fixed…" She couldn't help but notice Chad could not keep from staring at her face. "Have a great day," Trudi said.

ৡৡৡ

"I see you're quite a chatterbox," Weeset said, sitting on the workbench watching the mechanical boy work on the newly cleaned clockworks. "Learned any new words? Know any jokes?"

I WORK

"I've always wondered how you're bolted together inside," Weeset said, taking off her jacket and laying it on the workbench. In a flurry of wings, she was fluttering like a moth over Privi. "Let's see… access port… there."

In fewer ticks than it takes to count the jewels in a cheap pocket watch, Weeset had opened the tiny door and made her way inside. "Amazing. Absolutely amazing," her words echoed inside Privi's brass skin. She dodged a lever that appeared out of nowhere, but she didn't see the swinging shaft that controlled the mechanical boy's powerful arms. A crushing blow pinned her against his main gear. Two ticks later, Privi's mechanism had mercifully ground to a stop. A small thread of blood flowed down his brass chest.

Seventeen—The Rescue

"*H*ow are we doing in here?" Trudi asked as she returned to the workshop a few minutes later.

BROKE

"Yes, I know, the clock is broken," Trudi said, examining the clockworks Privi had cleaned and partially disassembled. She was puzzled why he was standing motionless over his clockworks. Disassembly was one of his specialties.

I BROKE

Puzzled at his response, Trudi examined Privi and saw the crimson fluid running down his chest. She touched it and realized at once it was blood. "Holy Mary Mother of God," she cried. An instant later she spotted Weeset's tiny jacket. "Weeset? Where are you?" She knelt next to Privi and immediately noticed that one of his access panels was open. *She's inside. Oh, no. Oh, no...*

"Is Weeset here?" a small voice behind her asked.

Trudi turned to see Martine standing by Privi's foot. Perhaps it was Trudi's highly sensitive hearing that let her hear these tiny voices—it was like magic that she could.

"She was here when I went to wait on a customer. I... I think she's... she's trapped inside Privi," Trudi said.

"I'll get in there and look. Help me up," Martine said.

"*No*. You *can't*. It's too dangerous," Glenda said, grabbing Martine's arm."

"She's right," Trudi said, "I'll get her out, if that's where she is."

"Please hurry," Martine pled.

"Privi, full stop. No move. No talk," Trudi commanded.

Everyone held their breath, hoping Privi would not answer. He didn't—standing perfectly still.

Trudi began spinning a screwdriver to remove Privi's chest access panel, held in place with eight screws.

"Can you release the mainspring? If she's still alive, Weeset could be …" Glenda asked.

"No. That might make things worse," Trudi said, her fingers working feverishly. As the last screw fell, she gently lifted away the panel.

Trudi peered into the complex mechanism and … *yes. There she is.* "I see her. She's wedged in there tight."

"Is she…?"

"I can't tell. She's not moving. I'll have to remove his entire chest plate to get to her." Trudi knew that would take a dangerously long time to remove over thirty screws to get the plate off. She dared not share that cold fact with Weeset's companions.

"Let me try," Martine said.

"Martine, please, no," Glenda cried.

But it was too late. Climbing like he was being treed by a raccoon, Martine scaled the mechanical boy and ducked inside the opening Trudi had exposed.

"I need a lever—something twice the length of my leg and twice as strong," Martine said, his head sticking out.

"Here," a voice said.

Trudi looked down to see Alred holding an l-shaped Allen wrench. "Thanks." She handed Martine the tool and he disappeared again inside the gears, springs, and levers. Five ticks later she could hear the metal-on-metal sounds of him working.

"What's going on? Why are Martine and Glenda up here?" Alred asked.

"Why are *you* here?" Trudi asked. Alred looked especially worried—and then she remembered: *Martine is his grandson.*

"We heard you talking to Weeset," Alred said. "A few of us came to help as soon as we knew she was in trouble."

"I think she has lost a lot of blood," Trudi said.

"Let's hope it's not too much," Alred said.

"Where's the patient?" another little voice asked.

Trudi spotted an older Seldith woman running across the workshop carrying a cloth bag hung over her shoulder.

"Miss Trudi, this is Kenezer, our healer," Alred said.

"Martine is trying to get her out of the mechanism," Trudi said softly.

"That little pixie has always been curious."

"Oh?" Trudi asked.

"She's been trapped before. Twice. And stuck down an inkwell. And carried off by a sparrow. We warned her curiosity and wings would get her in trouble. We urged her to keep them tucked away."

"After this, perhaps she'll listen," Trudi said.

"I doubt it. It's not in a pixie's nature," Kenezer said.

Trudi wondered if she should be removing Privi's front plate while Martine worked and she was about to begin when Martine appeared at the opening carrying Weeset's seemingly lifeless body, his shirt red with her blood, his tears streaming down his face. "I got her out. She's alive, but in pretty bad shape."

Trudi gently placed them on the floor next to Kenezer and leaned back to give the Seldith their privacy. She ached to do something, but all she could do was watch—and deactivate her robot. "Privi, release rest," she instructed.

Privi came to life but didn't move. He printed a single word.

BROKE

"I'll fix you. For now, unwind and wait," Trudi whispered in Privi's ear.

BROKE FRIEND

"No, not at all. It was not your fault."

None of the Seldith said a word as Kenezer embraced the limp body of the fallen faerie before letting out a pained cry of her own. Alred laid his hand on Kenezer's shoulder. A warm glow flowed from his arm to encompass the healer and her patient.

"Is she…gone?" Trudi whispered.

Alred said nothing, but turned up his face wearing a thin, hopeful smile.

Trudi didn't know what to think, what to hope for, what to dread, as she had no idea what was taking place. Opa had told her a few fanciful stories of these magical creatures, but, like so many of his tales, she didn't know which to believe and which to discount as whimsical bedtime fairytales. Weeset's wings fluttered—just a bit. *Is she all right?*

But to Trudi's dismay, Kenezer's arms fell limp. While Martine and Glenda helped Weeset sit up, Alred, kneeling beside her, cradled Kenezer in his arms. She had turned quite pale. As Weeset's eyes fluttered open, Kenezer's eyes closed, and her breathing slowed. Sondrah appeared and handed Alred a steaming mug of broth. He held it to the healer's lips. *Yes, she's breathing.* A tick later, Kenezer took a sip and began to stir. *She's coming around. Thank the stars.*

"What just happened? Are they all right?" Trudi asked incredulously.

"We caught her just in time. Kenezer was able to save Weeset, but she still has some healing of her own to do," Alred said softly.

"Save her? I still don't understand."

"Kenezer is our empathic healer. She treats her patients by literally absorbing their illness or injuries—even painful, massive injuries, as you just saw."

"But wouldn't that kill her?"

"Healers *can* die while healing, but the experienced ones, the ones with the most power, can achieve everything short of miracles. Others, sadly, can't, and sometimes die trying."

"That's simply amazing. Too bad she can't heal humans," Trudi said without thinking.

Alred just looked at her. "But she *can* if she's called in time. I've seen it done. However, when the patient is too far gone, it's nearly impossible to heal them—not if the healer expects to survive herself. Sometimes neither survive."

"Humans, like my grandfather."

"Like your grandfather, your grandmother, and even your mother. Your Opa was critically ill and quite old… for a uman."

"My mother too? Was she that far gone?"

"After you were born, her midwife could not stop the bleeding. To make things worse, they say she had a rare type of blood that made things more complicated. By the time we got to her, she had lost far too much blood. No amount of magic could have saved her. I'm terribly sorry. We all felt heartsick. She was a lovely soul."

A tear fell from Trudi's cheek. She was happy for Weeset, and the healer, but sad for her mother, grandparents—and Privi.

Weeset gently landed on Trudi's shoulder and whispered in her ear. "Miss Trudi, thanks. I won't forget how you saved me."

"I'm glad we were able to get you out. Are you feeling all right? You scared us to death."

"I'm a bit weak. Can I have my vest?" She asked, covering her chest with her forearm.

"Of course," Trudi said, fetching the tiny vest.

"It was Martine who risked his life. Thank him too."

"Oh, I have grand plans for Martine," she said with a grin.

Trudi immediately turned to Privi and began assessing his damage. Once she carefully removed his large front plate and exposed the bulk of his mechanism, she could easily see where Weeset had been trapped. One of the levers was bent, but there was no real damage—except for the blood. That would have to be carefully removed.

As the Seldith helped Kenezer get back home, Trudi went to work gently cleaning and reassembling her only mechanical offspring and indispensable helper. She spent the rest of the day working on him before she was ready to bring him back to life.

After tightening the last screw, she gently wound Privi's mainspring, and pulled his activate lever. *Nothing.* Privi just stood there. "Privi?" Trudi asked. "Are you okay? It's all right to wake up. Weeset is unhurt; she's safe."

A long tick later, Privi blossomed back to life.

"Feeling better now?" Trudi asked.

BROKE FRIEND FIX?

"Yes, yes, Weeset and the healer are going to be fine. It wasn't your fault," Trudi said, hoping he would understand.

"Is your mechanical helper going to be okay?" Martine asked, "I had to bend a few levers inside to get her out."

"He's tough and relatively unscathed," Trudi said as the clocks in the shop rang nine. "Stars. Is it that late? I need to get these clocks fixed or there will be problems galore tomorrow. Will you all excuse me?"

"Of course, of course," Martine and Glenda said.

"Can I help?" Weeset asked, apparently feeling perkier after her ordeal and a full mug of the healing brew.

"I think you should probably rest. You were badly hurt," Trudi said.

"Don't you think you've done enough as it is?" Glenda snapped.

"It wasn't entirely her fault," Martine said.

"Oh, it was *entirely* my fault," Weeset said. "And Glenda's right. I shouldn't let my curiosity get the better of me."

"Again," Martine and Glenda said at once.

"Again," Weeset agreed.

"Well, I can use all the assistance I can get," Trudi began, knowing Weeset and Martine both knew a lot about the innards of these clocks. "They're both due back to their owners by noon tomorrow, and I have other patrons waiting as well. I never turn down competent help. Are you sure you know what to do?"

"I had better get started reinstalling that main gear," Martine said.

"And I'll finish the cleanup on Anastasia," Weeset said.

"If you're sure," Trudi said.

"And I've learned a thing or two about cleaning clocks and resetting bearings and jewels," Glenda said, slicing off a bit of cloth.

Trudi looked down and realized the floor around the workbench was covered with sems assisting others to scale the workbench. It seemed there was another hidden staircase against the wall she had never noticed.

By the time the clocks in the shop struck ten, the workbench was covered with elven work parties fixing clocks, music boxes, and a postal scale that had come in for repairs a few days ago. It seemed that everyone wanted to help. Before long, food was brought up, and some paused for a late-night snack while others kept working. Trudi was relieved that Privi was able to do his magic again and seemed quite content working alongside the elves as if he always had.

As they worked, Trudi and the elves exchanged stories of her grandfather, and their own lives as Seldith. The tall tales and over-long stories told her a lot more about the elves who had helped Opa and his ancestors before him. She was amazed that a few were alive when the shop was first opened hundreds of years ago. The Seldith stories were the most imaginative of all, having been told and retold over the generations—of course, with a few embellishments added to each retelling. One of her favorites was the epic tale of a young Owl Wrangler and how he was able to rescue the entire clan from a pair of stray cats—Mink and Ink.

By midnight, Trudi was exhausted, but the workbench was cleared off, cleaned up, and, with Trudi's and Privi's help, the day's repairs neatly stacked and labeled. Once the lights were doused, Trudi smiled and fell asleep before her head touched the pillow. She had all the excitement she needed for one day. It wasn't long before dreams of a mysterious knight coming to her rescue helped her get the rest she so sorely needed.

Eighteen—The Debarkation

*S*econd Officer Plutarch, standing watch on the Sutherland's bridge, signaled "Slow" on the ship's telegraph. The engine room answered a full ten seconds later. As the rhythmic thud of the engines subsided, the ship slowed, barely making way over the current. "Steer one four zero," he ordered.

The helmsman rolled the wheel to turn the bow into the current, further slowing the ship. "One four zero, sir."

"Drop the starboard anchor," Plutarch ordered over the intercom. He watched as a couple of sailors ambled toward the bow.

Even without his binoculars, Plutarch could spot the light blinking from the top of a cliff about a mile to the west. He stepped outside to the rail and uncovered the Aldis lamp. While his Morse was rusty, he dared not have his signalman send the acknowledgment; according to plan, the man was drunk below decks. He blinked what he thought was the recognition signal. He was much relieved when he saw the correct reply.

It's done.

"Isn't this your watch, Mr. Plutarch?" said a voice from behind him.

"It is, Captain."

"Why aren't you on the bridge?"

"I … I had spotted what I thought was a skiff heading out toward us from the harbor," Plutarch lied. He hoped the Captain did not notice the Aldis light had been uncovered.

"Where away?" the captain asked, raising his binoculars to scan the milky fog surrounding them.

"Sou… southeast. There," he motioned with his arm, away from the cliff where he had seen the light.

"I don't see anything." The captain kept looking. "How could you spot anything in this soup?"

"Nor do I, now, Captain. It must have slipped behind one of the other ships at anchor."

"Drop the starboard anchor," the captain ordered.

"Aye, Captain."

"I'm returning to my cabin. Keep a close watch. We don't need any surprise visitors. Not tonight."

❧❧❧

Catherine lifted her pen. *Have the engines stopped?* Opening her father's pocket watch, she wound the stem. *Nearly four A.M.* Her children were finally asleep—they had endured a restless night. She opened her journal and penned a brief note.

December 16th: Day six 3:58 A.M. We must be close. Sea calm. Engines slowed. Sounds of nearby ships. Foghorn? Freddie feeling better, still worried. George, still being George. Annie oblivious, it is just another holiday. Still no clue as to our destination. If only we had a port-hole. Did we do the right thing?

A moment later, she heard a loud bang and a clattering of chains, followed by a splash.

"What was that?" George asked, sitting up in bed and banging his head on the overhead.

"Go back to sleep. I need to think," Catherine whispered.

He didn't. Neither did Freddie. They both got up and dressed. Catherine acquiesced and laid aside her journal to put on her traveling clothes as the kids tried to roust Annie. She would have none of it. "Let her sleep."

Once the ship had settled into an eerie silence, Catherine suspected their odyssey was about to take a new path. Before laying down her pen, she made a final entry.

We have arrived. But where?

As Catherine sat on her berth feeling the ship gently rock on the swell, she realized this was the time they had been waiting for. Their plan was to get the kids to shore quickly and quietly, where she hoped to find refuge. *But how?* She picked up the last half-eaten cupcake and noticed something written on the paper wrapper.

Starboard side gangway 4 A.M. Bonne chance.

The handwriting was clear, and the grammar correct. It was not from Mr. Bing. *Good luck.*

Fortifying her mental state with the last of the cold coffee, Catherine whispered what they had all been wanting to hear: "We're going ashore."

Freddie and George were almost dressed and eager to go. Annie, not so much.

"Get up, honey," she whispered into Annie's ear.

"How are we to escape?" George asked, tying his shoelaces. "The door is locked."

"Is it?" Catherine asked with a wink.

Freddie tried the handle. It was unlocked.

"How?" she asked.

Catherine, with a coy look on her face, said nothing, reasoning Mr. Bing or some unknown collaborator must have left it open.

The teens continued packing and bundling up for the cold, needing no further encouragement or prodding. Freddie helped Catherine dress Annie and pull on her coat. Standing ready in the middle of the cabin as if sleepwalking, the child remained remarkably compliant—for once; a small blessing.

George picked her up like a lawn statue and moved her out of the way.

Catherine packed her journal and a bundle of papers into her shoulder bag. She checked her pistol, made sure a round was not chambered, and slid it back into her coat pocket.

Freddie tucked her book inside her coat. "Mother, did you pick the lock?" she asked in a whisper. "I'm impressed."

"George, don't bother packing; we can't take the suitcases—they're too bulky."

Freddie looked crushed.

"Empty Annie's bag of everything. It's the smallest. Leave her a change of underwear, stockings, and a clean dress. And don't forget Katie. Each of you pick one essential item that will fit in your pockets, then pack your toilette, a set of clean underthings, and one change of clothes in the bag. If it doesn't fit, leave it behind."

"But mother…" Freddie began.

"Just *do* it. We must move fast, and we can't carry that lot with us."

Begrudgingly, Freddie and George each found their keepsakes—a pretty scarf Freddie had received from her aunt, and the ornamental letter opener George had bought in London. Freddie tucked Katie, Annie's favorite dolly, deep into her sister's coat pocket. "Keep Katie safe. Okay?"

Annie nodded and seemed to be coming back to life.

"So, we're going to swim for it?" George asked.

Freddie just made a face at him.

"The water is probably about forty degrees this time of year," Catherine admonished.

"I've raced in icy water before," George whispered.

"In a pool. With a lifeguard. Don't be an idiot," his sister said.

Catherine knew it was true that George had placed in outdoor swim meets, but her youngest, Annie, had never been in water any deeper or colder than a warm bath. While Freddie could sail and swim, Catherine hoped it would not come to that. But before they could jump overboard, they needed to get on deck—and before the rest of the ship's company was awake enough to stop them or discover they were missing.

"She didn't need the key," Freddie whispered to George.

"Really? How did you plan to escape without rousting the whole ship?" George sniped.

"I could pick the lock on any door—with this," Freddie said, holding up a hairpin. "I read about it in one of Sir Arthur Conan Doyle's stories."

"What makes you think you can use *that* to pick a lock? You're not Sherlock Holmes," George whispered, with his little-brother voice.

"I used it to break into your room a dozen times," she said with a sneer. "It was easy."

"What? Why? How dare you—" George sputtered, his voice getting louder.

"Hush! Put these on," Catherine said, handing each of them a canvas life vest.

Freddie tried to fit Annie with an adult vest, but it was a bit too large.

"Mother, that will never work. It's enormous," George said, tightening the straps of his vest and retying Annie's straps until she squeaked like a dog toy.

"You're straggling me!" she cried.

"Strangling." He backed off the knot a bit. "How's that?"

Annie nodded and took her mother's hand.

Freddie pulled the belt off her coat and wrapped it around her little sister, holding the vest in place and leaving a tail to act as a leash. "There. Quite a fashion statement," she said. Annie smiled and slowly twirled like a ballerina watching her new tail.

"It will have to do," Catherine said, tying her vest. "Let's go before the ship comes to life."

Catherine took one final look around and turned off the cabin lights. Opening the door a crack, she checked the passageway. *No one.* "Let's go," she whispered.

"Would you care to disembark, Madam?" George whispered, holding the door open to let them pass and bending over with a flourish.

Catherine led them down to the right—toward the starboard side of the ship. Twenty steps later, they found themselves at a dead end. Backtracking, they chose another corridor, and then another, searching for a ladder to take them to an upper deck. Unlike a luxury ocean liner, there were no familiar directional markings or guiding lights to lead the way to the outside decks or the lifeboats—at least none that they recognized.

"Mother? Look," Freddie whispered as she pointed to the metal bulkhead. "It's a Dan Henry drawn in chalk. I remember from our bike race last summer."

"Are you sure?" Catherine asked just before she saw it. It *was* a Dan Henry, a way to mark running or bicycle courses. To the untrained observer, the symbols appeared to be simple circles with a line but pointing in the desired direction.

"This way," Freddie whispered, waving them toward her. "There's another. And another," she said, encouraging everyone to follow—left, then left again, and finally up a steel staircase.

They soon arrived at a heavy steel door with enormous dogs[14]. It was marked by a circle with an X in the center. Opening it carefully, they finally smelled fresh sea air, but the cold still air spanked their cheeks and encouraged them to button their coats and shield their faces.

"At last," Catherine sighed. She dreaded meeting anyone and had no idea what she would do if someone tried to stop them. That wasn't in the plan.

Once on deck, they found a moonlit sky painted with a glorious field of stars, and below, a thick sheet of fog blanketed the bay and everything on it, including the ship as if it were floating in a layer of meringue. To the south and west, tiny dots of lights outlined a small seaside town. *Perfect.*

Following the Dan Henrys, they continued toward midship looking for a gangway, and found it had been lowered against the starboard side, but the last twenty feet were completely obscured in fog. Catherine pulled Freddie aside and whispered in her ear.

"Really?"

"You know how, don't you?"

"Of course. Father showed me last summer."

"Do it quickly."

Catherine lifted a large white life preserver off its hook and handed it to George. "Down," she whispered.

"Where's Freddie?" George asked, mounting the first step.

"She'll be along. I'll take Annie." Catherine replied, lifting her youngest with one arm and holding the rail with the other.

As quietly as they could, they descended the wooden stairs, cringing at each squeak and clank. At the bottom, buried in the

---

[14] On a ship, the watertight doors are held in place with door 'dogs.' These are latches (usually one near each corner) that secure the door.

fog, Catherine rejoiced to find one of the ship's lifeboats waiting for them. They all got aboard.

"Where's Freddie? You aren't going to leave her, are you?" George whispered.

Catherine looked up, "She'll be along." *I hope.*

A seemingly endless five minutes later, they heard the stairs creaking. "Someone's coming," George whispered. A moment later, they saw Freddie's legs pierce the fog.

"Get it done?" Catherine asked, hugging her eldest.

"Easy," she replied.

"Good girl. Let's shove off," Catherine said.

Once everyone was aboard, they worked nothing like a seasoned crew, but figured out how to get the boat untied and pushed away from the ship. It soon disappeared into the fog. Catherine was thankful no one had fallen in and no one on the ship had raised the alarm—but they weren't free yet.

"Hoist the sail," Freddie said, pulling on the halyard.

"No, better not," Catherine said. "The fog is hiding us for now, the sail might be seen above the mist."

"And there's not a puff of wind," George said. "It won't help. We need to row. Grab an oar, sis."

"George, you and I will row; let Freddie handle the tiller," Catherine said, knowing Freddie was an experienced sailor and crew coxswain, but George was stronger.

Keeping low, they repositioned to their new duty stations, making sure not to awaken Annie who had fallen asleep in the bow, her leash lashed to the life preserver. *Another blessing.*

"Where to?" Freddie asked.

"Head toward … there," she said, pointing to what appeared to be a distant cliff.

Freddie nodded as her crew pulled on the oars. While it took a bit of coordination, they eventually got the rhythm, and the small boat began coasting across the glassy water at a fair clip.

Suddenly, the repetitive sound of a ship's bell clanged an alarm that echoed off the cliffs. *What's going on? This wasn't the plan.* Ahead of them, a searchlight cut through the fog and moved their way and ducked below the gunwales as it passed. In the cold, still air, Catherine could hear what must have been the ship's officers ordering another boat to be launched. Even with their head start, she knew the ship's experienced oarsmen would quickly catch up.

"Row!" she commanded just above a whisper, and George pulled harder to match his mother stroke-for-stroke.

Freddie kept the lifeboat pointed at the cliff but had a funny look on her face and finally let out a short laugh.

"What are you sniggering about?" George asked. "This isn't funny."

"Nothing," Freddie said, still smiling. "Just row."

"What have you *done?*" Catherine asked as if she didn't know.

"Mommy, I was naughty."

"*Fredricka.* What *have* you *done?*"

"I removed the other lifeboat's seacocks.[15] Hopefully, they won't notice in the dark."

"Naughty girl," Catherine said with a grin.

As her arms grew weary, Catherine continued to pull on her oar and listen as the other lifeboat was lowered and got under way. "Keep pulling George. I know you're tired."

"I'm okay… mom," he puffed between strokes.

"I can have Freddie take over if you're too—"

George pulled even harder. "I'm fine."

---

[15] Seacock: A valve used to permit water to flow into or out of the vessel.

A bit later, they giggled to themselves at the mens' startled cries. Laced with profanities, their chaotic responses told them the other ship's crew had discovered they were taking on water.

"What *is* this place?" Freddie asked as the rocky breakwater came into view. "It looks like something from one of Bram Stoker's vampire stories."

"Dry land and safety," George said, as they approached the barnacle-covered pilings of what was once a long pier.

"I'm not so sure," his mother said. "We don't know where we are or anyone who lives here, and they might not be particularly welcoming to foreigners. We need to be on our guard."

"We will," Freddie promised. "Maybe they speak Thai."

"Funny," Catherine said, looking up at the sky. "That's the North Star and … no, I don't know enough about the stars to know more than we're still north of the equator." She kept rowing.

"At least that's something," Freddie said.

"And we can't use our real names. Once we get ashore, let *me* do the talking. Pretend you don't know the language and keep Annie quiet. She tends to—"

"Talk too much," George and Freddie said in unison.

Catherine realized in a heartbeat that guileless Annie would give them away at her first opportunity. She kept rowing into the foggy darkness.

"We're getting close!" Freddie warned. "Can't you hear the breakers?"

Nineteen—The Ascent

*T*hey *were* close. All at once, they arrived—their boat impaled on the rocky jetty, throwing them all forward into a heap. Still about ten feet from shore, Catherine was happy to have made it this far. While expecting to have to swim ashore, Catherine was thrilled that they had managed to get to dry land—well, almost—without suffering any more than the indignity and discomfort of wet stockings. She felt especially proud of herself and her novice crew, but she knew their odyssey to find safe refuge for her family was not complete. "Well done. You make a great crew," she said.

Catherine immediately surveyed where they had unceremoniously made their landfall. In the misty moonlight, they found themselves near the base of a towering cliff. A handful of stone buildings clung to the top of the escarpment ten stories above, but with no signs of life. *It's too early.* To the north, she saw a few streetlights and the moving glow of headlights. *The cliff, the stone building, it all seems to fit. I think we've found it. It's a miracle.* "Is everyone all right?" she asked.

"I'm fine," George said, massaging his overworked shoulders.

"Me too," Freddie said, making her way forward to help with Annie, who seemed too sleepy to be frightened.

"Let's get under cover," Catherine said, scanning the sky. "It looks like a squall is blowing in. It may start pouring any second."

"See those old pilings?" George asked, "This could have been a boat landing or a pier. There *must* have been a way up that wall. Maybe there's a stairway to the top, unless it rotted away like the dock."

"I don't suppose there's a lift or a funicular?" Freddie asked.

"Or a concierge?" George quipped. "Porter, will you be a good fellow and collect these bags?"

Catherine chuckled. "I doubt it, dearest. But I think you're right, there must be stairs somewhere," Catherine said, stepping out on to the rocky shore and steadying the boat. She knew there was. Everything had been just as Richard had described. *Now to find the stairs and Richard.*

"There," George pointed. "See? There was a ramp here at one time. It's long since washed into the bay."

Freddie picked up Annie and, watching each step, carried her over the jagged rocks and on to a level stretch at the top of the breakwater. "Annie, just stand here a moment," she instructed. The child nodded and made a lollipop of her thumb.

Having a flair for the dramatic, George tried to make a great leap off the boat but slipped on the gunwale, ending up in a twisted heap on the rocks. Grabbing his lower leg, his scream echoed off the stone wall.

"George!" Catherine cried as she and Freddie scrambled to his side, tenderly cradling his head and using a life vest as a pillow. Catherine's fingers told her George's leg was injured—very badly, and almost certainly broken. "Can you put any weight on it?" she asked, but she already knew the answer.

He tried. He couldn't. "It's probably not that bad," she lied, trying to convince herself and keep from frightening her son. Their grand plan was already falling apart. They hadn't counted on anyone getting hurt, certainly not their children. Annie knelt at George's head and brushed away her tiny tears. "Georgie owie?" she asked.

"Yes, sweetie, he's hurt his leg," Freddie said. "We'll take care of him."

To make matters worse, a freshening squall began washing away the fog as the wind picked up from the south. The once-calm bay had evolved into a rolling line of white-tipped waves that threatened to carry their lifeboat out to sea. Catherine knew if the fog cleared, it would make it easier for the men on the ship to find them and foil their deception. They had to move out of sight—and quickly.

Catherine closed her eyes for a moment to think. *We have to get off this jetty.* She studied the cliff and looked for 'an arched doorway,' as Stephen had described. *There.* "A door. There's a door at the base of the cliff," she pointed.

"Where does it lead?" Freddie asked.

"Off this rocky jetty, I hope. We'll have to take the chance. Freddie, take off your life vest and I'll help George with his. Get our things out of the boat," Catherine said as she removed their life vests. The boat had already begun shifting off the rocks.

"Next the boat. Let's push it out into the current." Catherine instructed. "We don't want to leave any clues to show where we came ashore."

"Yes, ma'am," Freddie said, stepping out of the boat with their bags. "I sure hope we can get through that door."

"I'm sure we can," Catherine said. "Now push."

Freddie waded out and pushed. "I just opened the fore-word seacock," she said. "I figure if they don't find the boat, they'll think it sank."

"Now you're thinking," Catherine said.

Once Freddie was back on dry ground, she picked up one of the life vests. "And these?"

"Throw them and the life preserver into the current. With any luck, they'll think we all fell overboard and drowned."

"Great idea, mom. I didn't know you were that devious," Freddie said.

You have no idea, my dear.

With considerable effort, Freddie threw the vests into the water where they began their journey out to sea. They all stood together for a moment to watch the boat disappear beneath the murky water.

"Good job. Let's get your brother and sister to shelter. George, you ready to get off these rocks?"

"More than ready. Let's go," he said.

With some assistance, George was on one foot and moving toward the door. He gazed into his mother's eyes. "Are we having fun yet?" he asked with a thin smile. His face was a disturbing shade of gray.

"Aren't we, though. It's quite an adventure. You'll be all right," she assured her son. "I promise." His eyes were closed as he seemed to be pushing back the pain. She fought back an impulse to scream in frustration and fear as his anguish became hers.

"Up there?" Freddie asked, pointing to the top of the wall. "We're going up there? It must be a hundred feet high."

Her mother nodded. "Let's head for that door. It looks like the only way."

"Mommy, I'm hungry. And I need to go potty," Annie announced.

"You'll have to wait a bit, pumpkin," Catherine said as they reached more level ground where the going was a bit easier. Looking north, she finally made out what might be the ship. "Let's keep moving…"

"I hope it's not locked," Freddie said, sounding winded.

"So what? You can pick the lock with…your barrette," George said with a derisive sneer and a wince.

As they helped George hop on one foot the last twenty yards to the door, Catherine tried again to convince Annie she could wait a few more minutes to go potty. After another dozen feet, and an equal number of pleas, Catherine gave up. "Freddie…"

"Sure. Come on Annie." Taking her sister aside, Freddie helped Annie empty her bladder while the others kept moving as best they could.

"Feel better?" she asked.

Annie nodded, straightening her clothes, and reached down to pick up a dead fish she had found rotting on the rocks. "Look mommy!" she said, holding up her prize to her mother. She dropped it when she saw her frown, wiping her hands on her dress.

"Why didn't you go before?" George asked, clearly in pain.

"No one heard me ask," Annie said.

Freddie reached the door first and pulled at the handle. It didn't budge.

"Locked?" Catherine asked as she helped George sit with his back against the cliff.

"Yes Ma'am—it seems so. Do you want me to try to pick it?"

"No, go fetch the bags off the jetty while I take a crack at it; perhaps it's just stiff," Catherine said, walking over to the door and discreetly pulling a large key out of her coat pocket.

Freddie headed back for the bags and Annie tagged along, but paused again to gather another treasure. "Annie, put that down," Freddie said sternly. Annie held up the rotting carcass of a large rat covered with hungry maggots.

"Leave your… new rat friend there." Returning with the bags, she brushed off her sister's hands and dissuaded her from further explorations. "Come on sweetie, let's get up closer to the wall, and out of the rain," she said softly.

While they were distracted, Catherine tried the key in the lock. *It fits. Wait. It's unlocked.* She inspected the door but didn't see hinges. Putting her shoulder to the door, she found it opened easily—well, easy-ish. *This must be the way.*

"We're in luck," she said to her kids "The door was just stiff." She looked inside, but the passage was impossibly dark, the smell indescribable and unrecognizable to a genteel person not raised near the sea. She could tell the floor just inside was covered with seawater and silt. *Not in the plan.*

"Now where?" George asked.

"Let's get you inside and out of the rain," Catherine said, nodding to Freddie to help lift him. "Come on, Annie."

Catherine stepped though the doorway and felt the walls. *Cold, wet, stone and… yes. The wooden base of a torch.* She felt the top. *Cold.*

"I don't suppose any of you have any matches or a flint?"

George shook his head. "Sorry, no. I gave up smoking for Lent."

Freddie smiled and extracted a packet of heavy matches from her bag. "Will these do?"

"Where on earth?"

"They were in the lifeboat. I also found a work knife, a chunk of what appears to be food, a whistle, some flares, and a length of rope."

George grinned and begged a chunk of hardtack off his sister.

She willingly complied and cut off a piece. "Anything for Tiny Tim."

Catherine tried to light the torch and after the third match, it ignited, throwing flickering yellow light up the void. To the left, a dark corridor led up and inclined to another mystery. To the right, another door. *Locked. Left it is.*

"Mother, what's going on?" Freddie asked. In the torch-light, her mother could see worry deepening the furrows in her daughter's brow.

"Are they going to chase us up here?" George asked.

Catherine closed her eyes. She had no idea why the men her husband had trusted were chasing them. They were supposed to let them slip quietly off the ship. Crippling their life-boat had been done on instinct—it was not part of the plan. She would have to tell her children eventually, but even she didn't have all the answers.

"I hope not. I... I just don't know what to tell you. All I know for certain is that we can't let anyone know who we are or where we are from. At least not yet."

"Why?" George asked.

"George, you'll just have to trust me."

"Not even father?" Freddie asked.

"Not even your father."

"What about–?" George began.

"And none of your friends."

"They'll be worried sick," Freddie said.

"I expect so—at least for a time. This is crucially important. If we tell anyone who we are, we risk being snatched up and that will put us and your father in even greater danger." *Us and the country.*

Catherine let her children sit, rest, and contemplate their new predicament for a moment as she collected her thoughts, which seemed as scattered as a broken string of pearls. Finger-ing the pistol in her pocket, she renewed her resolve to follow the plan.

"First, we need to get George's leg splinted. Freddie, did you see anything on the beach we could use?"

"Like a wooden crate? There's one off that way," she said, pointing down the jetty.

"Run and get it; and stay low."

And she did. While out of breath, she arrived back with a small wooden apple box and a board. "Will this do? Maybe he could use the board like a crutch—like this," she said, tucking the board in her armpit to demonstrate her find.

"It's perfect. Break off two long slats. We'll use the rope to lash them to George's leg."

"Where did you learn how to do that?" George asked.

"Oh, mothers know a number of things you might find useful," Catherine said.

"Like where to find a blanket and a warm bed?" George asked.

"We'll get you comfortable as soon as we can, honey," Catherine said, her heart crying for her injured son.

While Freddie held the torch, Catherine fashioned a suitable splint—despite George's protests.

"There. Good as new. Ready?" Catherine finally asked, but she had already made up her mind—they had to find a doctor at once.

"I'm not up for a climb," George moaned, trying to use the board Freddie had found to hold himself erect. It was almost working.

Catherine pushed the door closed behind her and threw the bolt.

None of them said another word as they slowly felt and limped their way in the torch-lit darkness. The passageway's air was as foul as any Catherine had ever smelled. The floor, slimy from years of unrestrained moss, was not easy for any of them to manage—George least of all.

Still hopping on one foot and bracing himself against the makeshift crutch, he slowly made his way into the darkness. Even Annie, now dead weight in Catherine's arms, was silent—her head planted on her mother's shoulder.

Freddie had been tasked with carrying her mother's and Annie's bags.

"Mother, why is your bag so heavy? What do you have in here? Twenty sacks of doubloons?"

"No, only six, and a few other essentials. Try not to drop it. We might need the contents before the day is done."

"Really?" Freddie asked.

"Really. Here, give it to me. I can carry it for a while. Try to get Annie to walk."

Ahead, a steep flight of stone steps appeared out of the shadows. Timeworn with age, they posed another more daunting but dryer challenge. "We should have known we would eventually have to climb," she said.

"Brilliant," George said in his typical sarcastic tone. "So, no lift?"

"Let's rest here a bit," Catherine said softly, sitting on the first stone stair.

"I'll go on ahead," Freddie volunteered, "...to see how much further we have to go," She set down the bag and started climbing. "Is that okay?"

"Farther," Catherine said, correcting her English. "Go ahead."

"Farther. I hope we don't have too much further to go," Freddie said with her own sarcastic tone.

Catherine smiled and nodded. "Just be careful, and grammatical."

"Are you sure you'll be all right here in the dark?" she asked.

"Just hurry. If this one wakes up, things will get a lot harder."

Freddie nodded. "I'll leave the matches and the flares."

Catherine smiled and watched Freddie take the torch and quickly climb out of sight on the near-vertical spiral staircase. Freddie's heel clicks told her she was making steady progress ascending the stone steps for a while, and then there was… silence. Figuring she was resting somewhere above or out of earshot, she did not worry in earnest until …

"Where's Freddie?" Annie asked sleepily. "I'm hungry."

"Looking for breakfast, I expect."

"I hope she hurries," Annie said. "Are there cupcakes?"

"She's probably found another book to read," George mumbled.

Without the torch, there was little Catherine could do but wait. There might be any manner of pitfalls ahead. *We should have stayed together. What can we do now?* Getting on her hands and knees, Catherine carefully felt her way up the next step. "George, you and Annie try to follow. Annie, just hold on to my skirt."

"Are you sure, mother?" George asked.

About this time, Catherine heard Freddie's scream. "Fredricka?" she yelled. "Are you all right?" She heard no reply. "We can't wait here. Freddie might be in trouble up there." When she realized that George was unable to get up, she bent down and put her arm under his to steady him on his good leg and tried to scale the steps to rescue her eldest daughter.

෯෯෯

One hundred and ninety steps above, Freddie found a small window that looked out on the bay. Outside, she spotted the Sutherland with a narrow black stream of smoke coming from her stack. The wind and rain had changed the placid bay into an angry uprising of whitecaps and waves punishing the rocky jetty. Turning to restart her climb, Freddie saw something at her feet. "Curious," she said as she picked up what appeared to be a small hat; pointed and about the right size to fit over her index finger.

"Curious?" a tiny voice asked.

Freddie was not one of those easily frightened girls who would scream at every spider or mouse, but she had considerable difficulty stifling her alarm, so yes, she screamed, albeit briefly. *Oh my God!* She pushed herself back against the wall and waved the torch at the floor, searching for the voice.

"I'm sorry, did I startle you?" the voice said calmly.

"I... who... *what* are you?" she searched back and forth but didn't see anyone in the flickering light. *Ghosts?*

The flash of what must have been a tiny match illuminated the face of a small man, no taller than her ankle-high shoes. He casually lit a long pipe, puffed, and smiled, blowing a stream of fragrant smoke into the shadows. When the match went out, the glow from his pipe softly illuminated his round, bearded face with each breath. The aroma was unlike anything she had experienced. No, it wasn't tobacco like her father had smoked, but fragrant and... nice... and soothing.

"Miss, my hat, if you please." The man reached out a tiny hand.

"Are you a... a leprechaun?" Freddie asked, handing him his hat.

"If it were not for your ignorance, I might take great offense at that remark." He pulled the hat down over his unkempt hair and frowned. "I should leave you to the belluas that frequent this passage."

"Oh, no, sir. I meant no offense. I'm new to this... town and not acquainted with the local inhabitants." She had read and adored *Gulliver's Travels* and figured they might have landed on the shores of Lilliput.

"Then you apologize?"

"Of course. We have not been properly introduced. My name is…" Freddie remembered her mother's admonition about revealing who they were. "… most people just call me 'Freddie'."

"Nice to make your acquaintance, Miss Freddie. I am called Alred, among other honorifics, titles, and denigrations."

"And I am honored to meet you, sir."

"Are there more of your party attempting to ascend into our domain?"

"Yes, my mother, brother, and little sister are below."

"No more?"

"No others. I assure you."

"So not a Hessian invasion?"

"No, not an invasion."

"And not armed?"

"No, not armed." She dared not mention the lifeboat's folding knife she fingered in her pocket.

"We cannot be too careful." He blew another cloud of fragrant smoke toward the low ceiling. It seemed to bring Freddie a new sense of peace with every breath.

"I understand. We come looking for a doctor, accommodation, food, drink, and friendship."

"You can find a suitable hotel or boarding house in the town; unless you have a small child."

"But we do. My sister is only four—nearly five. Is that too small?"

"I was only jesting," the elf said with a smile. "I could hear her cries from down below."

"I see… Is the whole town populated with… with people your size?"

"Seldith? Hardly. There be precious few of us remaining."

While she ached to learn more about Alred and his friends, something made Freddie remember her mother and siblings. She had lost track of time and knew she should go back with the torch to help them climb. "I must help my family. They'll need the torch."

"No need. Just wait a moment."

"Oh?" Before Freddie could blink, the little man had disappeared into the darkness, but a moment later, a line of overhead lights made the spiral stairway easier to see. It was then that she noticed there were two stairways, one with a smaller elf-size stairway next to the human-size steps.

"Is that better?" Alred asked, appearing again at her feet.

"Much."

"When you reach the door above, just knock soundly. It's a bit early, but the mistress of the house will answer presently."

Freddie heard her mother calling from below and turned to answer, but when she looked back, Alred had disappeared. She headed back down toward the others.

"Are you all right? Who were you talking to?" Catherine asked as Freddie appeared.

"You won't believe me," Freddie replied, helping George climb.

"Did you find a switch? The lights really help."

"The little man turned them on."

"There's someone up there?"

"A minute ago—a man about as tall as a teacup. He said his name is Alred, and we should knock on the door at the top of the stairs."

"There're more stairs?" George lamented.

"I'm afraid so." Freddie raised her torch a bit higher. "It spirals up quite a way from here."

"Perhaps you should go ahead again. We'll soon need to rest again."

"Mother, I think this place is enchanted."

Her mother just smiled. "Wait, get closer."

Freddie leaned over. "What's wrong?"

"Have you been smoking?"

"What? What makes you… think. Wait. The little man was smoking a pipe."

"That's not tobacco, and it explains the leprechaun," Catherine said with a smile.

"He hates to be called a leprechaun. They like to be called *Seldith*."

"I'm sure. Let's get off these stairs. We can talk about your drug habits later."

"Mother, *really*. I think…" Freddie realized that she would have a tough time convincing her mother that she had seen an elf, especially since she had spent her lifetime telling stories fabricated from her imaginative mind.

"Of course dear. Go on. We need to get your brother some help and we're all getting H U N G R Y," she spelled.

"And I'm hungry," Annie said, plopping her cheek back on her mother's breast.

Freddie left them the torch and scaled the stairs until she found the door Alred had described. Tapping politely at first, when no one answered, she pounded until her fist was sore. Still, no one came. Exhausted and cold, she sat on the cold stair and tried to come up with another way to get in—and get help for her brother and mother, and a cupcake.

As the dawn began to shed light on the coastline, Officer Plutarch stood on the bridge of the Sutherland. Scanning the coastline with his binoculars, he could see no sign of anyone— not even the lifeboat. *Nothing.* Their charges had slipped away and had taken two of their lifeboats. The captain wasn't about to let them launch another. There was no need.

At this instant he saw it; someone framed in the light of a torch. Not from the town, but from an opening in the wall. *Someone has scaled the stairs.* He promised himself to keep this to himself until he could telegraph Europe.

Twenty—The Castaways

*I*t wasn't quite dawn when Trudi was awakened by an insistent pounding. Pulling on her robe, she made her way to the workshop and listened. The pounding began again. "Who's there?" she asked as she took the key off its hook.

"We need help. Can you *please* let us in?"

Trudi was as confused as she was concerned about letting a stranger into her home. But the voice described a girl about her age, and it sounded like she was in trouble. "Yes. Give me a second," she answered.

"Mother, there's someone here. Just wait there. I'll come down to help with George in a minute," the girl's voice said.

Trudi didn't hear the response, but the girl's voice sounded even more desperate. Unlocking the door and pulling it open, she found a bedraggled, dirty-faced teen. She might have thought she was a street urchin if it was not for her fashionable coat and dress showing the wear and grime of an arduous journey and an equally hard climb.

"Come in, come in. You look exhausted, and frozen," Trudi said.

"Thank you so much. My name is…Freddie… Barnes."

"I'm Trudi. Please, come sit in the kitchen and I'll set a fire and make tea."

"No, no. My mother, little sister, and brother are still down there. He's badly hurt and is having considerable trouble walking. I need to—"

"Rest. I'll go down and help them up." And Trudi set off at once, making her way back down the stairs. She was not surprised that Freddie followed close behind.

"Is this castle haunted?" Freddie asked.

"Haunted? It could be, I guess. Did you see something down here?"

"I… I think I saw a little—"

"Freddie, am I glad to see you!" Catherine said, giving her daughter a hug. "You had us so scared."

"I'm fine, mom. This is… "

"Trudi. Please let's get you all upstairs where it's warm."

"Thanks, so much. I'm Mrs. Smithe, my daughter Annie, and this is my son George. His leg is—"

"Broken. We'll need to get a doctor for him."

"And for your kindness, we would be eternally grateful," Catherine said.

"What happened?" Trudi asked as she helped get the boy to his feet while smiling at the very sleepy child clinging to her clearly exhausted mother.

"Our boat got blown on to the rocks and George got hurt coming ashore. We found the stairway and attempted to climb. It's like scaling Mt. Everest."

"I can imagine. I've climbed these stairs myself. Let's get you all upstairs and in front of the stove."

With a Herculean effort, they got everyone up the stone staircase, and George made as comfortable as possible in the kitchen, warming his feet by a newly laid fire. He seemed to enjoy the pampering and his color had improved, albeit marginally.

"We need to get a better look at his leg," Catherine said.

"I agree. I think we're going to have to get that makeshift splint and his pants off," Trudi said, gazing down at their patient. "Can we slip them down? I would hate to have to cut such fine fabric." She wasn't smiling.

"I agree," Catherine said.

"What's the plan?" Freddie asked as she came in with the bags. She plopped in one of the kitchen chairs; still breathing hard from her climb.

"We have to remove the splint and his pants, so perhaps you should take Annie…" Catherine said, looking at Trudi.

"Upstairs," Trudi said. "Second bedroom on the right. The bed is clean. She can nap there until we get things sorted down here."

"Come on, Annie," Freddie said, reaching out for her sister's hand.

Once she heard the upstairs door close, Trudi nodded to Catherine, who loosened George's belt and unzipped his trousers. As she tugged on his cuffs, he cried out in pain.

This was not the first time she had undressed a man, having had to help her grandfather into the tub or help him on the toilet on occasion. To protect his modesty, she fetched a crocheted quilt, and with eyes averted, she laid it over George's lap.

George's leg was badly swollen and had turned various shades of magenta. About six inches above his ankle, it had taken a swollen detour, but the bone had not broken the skin—yet. *That must really hurt.* For some reason, her own leg began to ache.

"Can we get more light?" Catherine asked.

"Of course," Trudi turned on another light and took a closer look at the boy's lower leg. "No, it does not look good," Catherine and Trudi said almost at once.

"Ow," Freddie said, looking at George's leg as she rejoined them. "Annie fell asleep at once."

"Thanks, honey. You're a treasure," Catherine said.

"I'll call Doc Stewart," Trudi said.

"I think that's best. But before you do, a word please," Catherine said. "We… we don't want anyone, I mean *anyone,* to know we're here. I know it's a lot to ask, but we think there may be people trying to…"

"I don't know how we're going to avoid that," Trudi interrupted. "However, I've known Doc Stewart my whole life—he delivered me and I'm sure he can be trusted to be discreet."

Catherine nodded. "Then please call him."

Trudi went into the shop and picked up the receiver. Ernestine answered at once.

"Good morning, Miss Trudi. It's early for—"

"Good morning, Ernestine. Could you please ring Doc Stewart?"

"Is everything all right?" Ernestine asked.

"Not a thing for you to worry about, thanks," Trudi said. Everyone knew Ernestine was the biggest gossip in town, but she also knew the juiciest details, so it was not wise to tell her any more than was absolutely necessary.

She waited while the line rang, and rang, and rang. "Should I let it keep ringing? It's early for him."

"No, I'll just step over there. It's only a few blocks. Thanks."

"I hope everyone is okay."

"Nothing serious. Lady issues," Trudi said as she hung up the receiver. She rushed upstairs to dress. A few minutes later, she was descending the stairs, buttoning her blouse. Taking a deep breath, she stepped into the kitchen, pulling on her coat.

"He's not answering. I need to go over there. It's not far," she said. "I'll leave the shop door locked. I'll bring some groceries as well. There isn't much food in the house, as I hadn't planned on hosting a family. I won't be long." She didn't say that she had almost emptied her larder to feed the entire Seldith clan.

"You're most kind. Here. This should help," Catherine said, reaching into her bag and handing Trudi a stack of coins.

"Don't dream of it. I'm glad to help."

"I insist. Is there any ice? It might bring down the swelling."

"I think there is some the fridge," Trudi said, dropping the coins in her pocket. Doc Stewart would be far more interested in coming and being discreet if he knew he would be paid cash in advance.

"Can *I* go?" Freddie volunteered. "You fetch the doctor, and I'll shop for breakfast and food for later."

"Yes, that would be great. We could use groceries. Bread, milk, butter, bacon, lunchmeat, vegetables, potatoes, and pastries. The Friday farmer's market will be setting up in the town square. It's only about four blocks away," she said, pointing with her arm. "…up the hill off to the northwest. You can't miss it."

"Do you have money?" Catherine asked, knowing full well it was a silly question. "Here. This should be more than enough." She handed Freddie a stack of coins.

Freddie smiled, dropped them in her pocket, and was gone. Trudi locked the door behind her and gave Freddie last-second directions and advice. "…and watch out for pickpockets."

❧❧❧❧

"Can I have my pants back?" George asked, nibbling on a cold scone.

"I'm afraid not," Catherine replied. "We're lucky we didn't have to slice up your trousers. We'll find you a dressing gown of some sort. At least you have on clean underthings."

"Mother!"

All Catherine could do now was wait. Things weren't exactly going as planned, but her experience in tough situations had prepared her to deal with unexpected contingencies—the stuff in life that just happens. What made her mind race was thinking through the contingencies, the what ifs, and what-will-we-do-if-someone-finds-us concerns. Their plans had put her entire family in jeopardy, and it was all on her to protect them. She realized that the person Richard expected to host them was nowhere to be seen. *I'll need to ask Trudi?*

It didn't take long for her to start wondering if they were *really* being pursued, and what she would do if anyone tried to recapture them. *Would this make a difference?* she asked herself, fingering the pistol. *Why did they raise an alarm and launch a boat?* Along with the same thought, she was sorry they had sunk both of their lifeboats.

Perhaps I should go down to see if the ship is still there.

She considered descending the tower stairs to the landing to get a look at the bay, but that would mean leaving Annie and George alone, and those stairs were arduous. *No.* She settled on locking and bolting the stairway door and pocketing the key. As it clinked in her pocket, she remembered she already had a key. Richard had given it to her months ago as they made their escape plans. Hesitating a moment, she pulled out both keys and laid them side-by-side. *The same.* She decided to return one of the keys to the hook over the door where she had found it. *Interesting. This is most certainly where we were meant to go. I wonder why? Richard has not told me the whole truth about this place. And Trudi. She looks… familiar somehow.*

At that instant, she thought she heard something move. She turned and clicked on the light. *Nothing. Probably vermin. Great, rats. Filthy, flea-infected plague vectors.* She imagined tiny eyes watching her every move from the shadows. They were. And not just rats.

Twenty-one—The Doctor

*T*rudi's head was still spinning when the brisk air hit her face. *Who are these people? Freddie looks so familiar.* Opa had told her the sea door and stone stairway led to the old docks on the bay, but besides her confusing foray down there, no one besides her grandfather had used the passage in her memory. Not even granny. She never imagined it would be an escape route for desperate refugees, if indeed that's what they were. *Where are these people from, and why the mystery?*

Trudi wasted no time walking through the dew-silvered streets with barely a soul to distract her. She had almost finished polishing her speech to explain their desperate circumstances by the time she knocked on the door under a virtually unreadable shingle. *Dr. Donald Stewart–General Practice.* Impatience compelled her to also pull on the chain, ringing the bell inside.

Above, a yellow glow appeared in an upstairs window. *He's up.* Everyone knew the old doctor's reputation for competency and compassion when he was in a good mood, and gruff behavior when he was not. They also knew why his mood sometimes detoured into shaded valleys of depression—it all began after his wife of three decades had passed.

Trudi was about to knock again when she heard footsteps inside. Her patience had worn as thin as her tattered winter coat. When the door opened a crack, an old man wearing a disgruntled scowl peered out, pulling on a housecoat and pushing back a mop of unruly silver hair. When he recognized Trudi, a warm smile crossed his face, and he opened the door wide, beckoning her to enter.

"Trudi, my child, come in out of the cold. What brings you to my door at this hour?"

Before she could speak, he ushered her by the elbow into his surgery and turned on a light. The room was… tidy, but not as she would have expected for a doctor's surgery.

"There's been an accident. A boy, a friend, has hurt his leg; it looks badly broken," she said.

"So, you're the doctor now?" he said with a smile. "And a boy?" His smile broadened into a grin.

"It *looks* broken, just above the ankle. The fibula, the big bone, looks displaced just above the ankle but hasn't broken the skin."

"Is he able to walk on it?" he asked, gathering bandages, a splint, and a few brown bottles into a black leather bag.

"No. Not at all."

"Is your patient someone I know, a long-lost cousin, a new boyfriend?" he asked, looking over his shoulder—one eyebrow raised.

"Doc, I *just* met him. He, his mother, and two sisters just showed up at my doorstep, just before dawn."

"I see. Trudi, you're too trusting for your own good. They could be wanted criminals, vagabonds, or international spies. There might even be a reward posted for them."

"They said to pay you this," she said, holding out a stack of coins in her palm.

Doc Stewart briefly studied the coins and closed Trudi's hand over them. "There will be time enough for that. You need to get back home before they carry off your shop."

He's right. They could be anyone. She had been too trusting again, and she had left them alone in the shop. *They could be robbing me blind.* She bolted for the door. "Come as soon as you can."

"Should I dress first?" he asked, looking down at his nightgown under his housecoat.

"As quickly as you can. Thanks."

Trudi nearly collided with a police officer as she burst into the street. She didn't pause even when he called after her—heading straight back toward the shop.

Out of breath, Trudi found George still sitting by the stove, looking a bit less bedraggled but still deathly pale. "Where's your mother?" she asked.

"She's dealing with Miss Piddly Pants," George said.

Trudi cocked her head, not understanding.

"Annie had to use the loo again. She drank too much apple juice. They're upstairs in the lavatory."

"The doctor is on his way. Is there something *you* need?" she asked, heading for the staircase. She was still uncomfortable with having strangers in the house, especially in her private rooms. Catherine met her coming down the stairs.

"We had to use your facility. I hope you don't mind," she said, helping Annie down the steep staircase.

"That's fine. Is there something else I can help with?"

"Not a thing. Is the doctor—"

"On his way. I got him out of bed," Trudi said, still breathing hard.

"Thanks. You're an angel—most kind and generous," Catherine said, pausing to take a long look at her saving angel. "Honey, where are your parents? Are you here alone?"

"It's just me. My…" she began, but decided to keep her personal life behind the curtain until she was more certain of her new guests' agenda.

"I see. Let me know how I can help make it easier for you."

"Of course. I will." Trudi didn't know how to ask her new guest the questions that still distracted her. She just stared at the older woman, her hands digging holes in her pockets—finding only lint, a candy wrapper, and a stack of coins.

"Here. Doc Stewart said we can settle up later," Trudi said, holding out the coins.

"Keep them for your trouble. It's the least I can do."

"I won't hear of it," Trudi said, stacking the coins on the kitchen table.

"I sincerely appreciate your continued generosity. You *must* be wondering where we're from," Catherine said.

Trudi nodded.

"I—" Catherine hesitated. "We're—"

Trudi could sense the fear in her eyes—the terror in her voice. Something was wrong, horribly wrong. Trudi didn't want to know, and she could see Catherine didn't want to tell her. *Did it matter?* "Don't," she said, a tear forming in her eye. "Don't tell me. It doesn't matter. I didn't mean to pry."

Catherine closed her eyes for a moment and wiped away her own tear. "My dear, it's probably best for everyone that you *not* know," she said. "Just understand that we would never put you in jeopardy. Not if we can help it. I would also not blame you if you sent us packing this instant."

"Trudi?" a voice came from the shop.

Trudi went into the shop to find Doctor Stewart.

"Where's our patient?" he asked. Trudi was relieved that he looked far more kempt and, well, more like a doctor than he had a few minutes ago.

"He's in here," Trudi pointed as Catherine led the way.

George looked quite relieved to see the doctor.

"Let's take a look," the doctor said, taking the boy's wrist. "And what's your name?"

"George," he said, not seeing his mother's troubled look.

"Doctor, is it really broken?" Catherine asked.

"We'll see. We'll see…" he said in that uncommitted tone that doctors perfect in medical school.

While the women hovered nearby, the doctor examined George and his leg, gingerly moving it, but not saying a word—just the usual "uh huh" from time to time, punctuated with an occasional "hmmm."

"*Is* it broken?" Catherine asked again.

"And you are?" Dr. Stewart asked, giving the boy a small bottle of dark liquid. "Drink a bit of this. Not too much," he said to George, who looked up at Catherine.

"I'm his mother, Mrs. Smithe. What are you giving him?"

"I see. Well, Mrs. *Smithe*, his leg *is* broken. Badly. It'll need to be set, and he'll need to be taken to the hospital at once. And that's a laudanum compound. It will temporarily relieve the pain."

"To hospital?" Catherine asked, giving Trudi a frightened look.

"It's serious. I think he'll need a few days there to stabilize the leg and ensure there aren't any complications."

"Complications? What complications, pray tell?" Catherine asked.

"Yes, without going into detail, there are a few things…"

"Can he be treated and recuperate here?" Trudi asked.

The doctor didn't answer. "Trudi, can I talk to you a minute in private?"

Trudi's stomach tightened. "I guess. Sure. Let's go into the workshop." She looked back toward Catherine who looked most concerned.

"Excuse us for a moment. We need to wait a few minutes for the sedative to take effect." Trudi and the doctor pushed through the beaded curtain.

"Who are these people? I've never seen them before. They look English by their dress, those British coins—and wealthy."

"They're friends—strangers cast on my doorstep in the storm. Opa would have taken them in—in a heartbeat."

"Yes, but they could be dangerous or in serious trouble."

"They could be innocents," Trudi said. "They *are* in trouble. They need my help—and yours."

Doctor Stewart just stood there and frowned.

"Are you going to help them or let that boy lie there suffering?" Trudi asked, her voice breaking.

Something seemed to come over the doctor. With no way to be sure, Trudi thought that perhaps it was his Hippocratic oath, his conscience, or his oversized heart, but he began to smile. "Of course. I'll do whatever I can. I'm just sincerely worried about *your* safety. You must promise me to be especially careful."

Trudi smiled and gave him a hug. His coat had the comforting aroma of pipe tobacco, like her grandfather. "Thank you," she whispered.

When they returned, Catherine was putting on her coat and bundling up Annie. She had George's coat and trousers over her arm.

"Where are you going?" Trudi asked.

"We don't want to be a burden. We'll find a hotel."

"Nonsense," Doctor Stewart said, rolling up his sleeves. "I'll need hot water and a place to work. Can we get him into a bed? He won't be moving much for a few weeks."

Catherine's face morphed into a thin, hopeful smile.

"Opa's room is right through there. George is welcome to use his bed," Trudi said, opening the door to the small bedroom which had not been used since her grandfather's passing. She hesitated a moment in the doorway, briefly imagining Opa lying asleep in that bed. Clarence pushed by her as he darted in to inspect and ensure the room was free of four-legged visitors.

Over the next two hours, Trudi and Catherine aided the doctor while he set, splinted, and bandaged George's leg. Thanks to the judicious use of ether, which Trudi was taught to administer, George seemed all but oblivious to the pain. In the end, the air was sweet with its heady aroma.

"He's going to be in considerable discomfort when the ether wears off and he wakes up," Dr. Stewart said as he washed his hands. "I'll leave a bottle of laudanum here, but only give him a few drops in a glass of water or wine every few hours—no more."

"I'm familiar with laudanum," Catherine said.

"So you know it's an opium derivative and can be quite addictive if taken injudiciously."

"Of course." Catherine nodded and took the bottle, slipping it into her pocket.

"How much do we owe you?"

"Whatever you think is fair," the doctor said.

Catherine counted out a dozen coins and offered them to him.

The doctor picked out four and smiled. "That will be more than enough to cover the supplies and my services with my friends and family rate. I'll be back this afternoon to check up on him."

"Thank you so much, doctor," Catherine said, shaking his hand as he left.

Once George was tucked into Opa's bed, Annie tugged at her mother's skirt.

"Where's Freddie?" she asked.

Twenty-two—The Freed Eagle

*F*reddie felt like an eagle escaped from the zoo as her feet all but flew her up the hill to forage for food on her mission of mercy. Finally able get out on her own, she had been liberated from the airless confines of the small cabin and the suffocating supervision of her parents. This latest ordeal, the kidnapping, if that's what it was, and the orchestrated escape all seemed so… so bizarre, so contrived. It didn't make sense. Now that she was out of reach of her mother and siblings, she was ready to kick up her heels, spread her wings, and soar into the heavens, or at least into town.

As the child of a diplomat, everything she did cast a shadow on her father and the country he and his family represented. Everywhere she went, everything she said or wrote, every action or inaction, reflected on her and her family and invariably made it back to her parents' ears. Stories of other diplobrats being severely punished, arrested, or their families deported, and the terrible consequences that resulted, were not lost on her. But today, she saw herself as a winged cherub on a holy mission, skipping across the wet pavement that began with her uphill search for the town square.

All around her, the shop windows all but sang Christmas and celebrated the holiday season. The red and white and green decorations, the gayly wrapped packages stacked under Christmas trees, and the mistletoe hung over so many doorways—they all made her long for her adopted home in England and the friends she had been forced to leave behind without a single goodbye. While she had not settled on a particular boy, she had a few more persistent suitors like who buzzed around her like bees circling a spring flower wishing to taste her pollen. They must think she had been murdered, kidnapped into white slavery—or worse, she was just ignoring them. Pushing these thoughts out of her mind, she lingered at a millinery shop window admiring the hats, pretty ribbons, feathers, and bows, and flitted off to another. Shoes, dresses, purses, and fabric shops all caught her eye and briefly slowed her pace as she haltingly continued up the hill. *Focus, girl. You're on a mission.*

I really must figure out where we have landed. What is this place? She realized that she couldn't just walk up to someone and ask where they were without drawing attention to herself. Instead, she looked around for any signs or anything that would give her a clue. *There—a flag. The Stars and Stripes. We must be in the United States, but which one? There are forty-eight of them.* The street signs in English substantiated her theory, and the advertisement for repairs on the cobbler's shop window gave another hint.

"Resole your shoes: $.05 a pair."

Dollars. Wait. Canada also uses dollars.

She passed a real estate office with pictures of homes for sale.

"Marvelous Seaside Views."

Yes, we must be somewhere on the East Coast of the US or Canada. Mom will be so pleased—she's back home. As Freddie walked by a newsstand, the vendor stacked papers from all over the region. She stopped dead in her tracks. A headline in *The New York Times* screamed the news.

AMERICAN DIPLOMAT'S WIFE AND CHILDREN MISSING

She dared not stop to read the rest of the story for fear there might be pictures of the family. *Everyone is looking for us. Wow. And Billy, Roy, and Alex will all be worried senseless. I have to get a message to them. But how? Telegram?*

At once she realized she had to get back to the clock shop—with food and the unsettling news. Freddie followed an older man laboriously pushing a cart of fresh vegetables up the cobblestone road, thinking he would lead her to the town square, but when the road steepened and his pace slowed, without a word being spoken, she helped him push his cart. Once they reached the peak of the hill, she bid him a good morning. "Where is the town square?" she asked.

He smiled and touched the brim of his hat. "Just ahead miss, another three blocks. Thank you," he said, smiling.

"I'm in need of a few vegetables. Could I buy some of these and these?" she asked pointing to the potatoes, onions, and carrots.

"Of course, miss," he said, bagging a handful of each in a string bag.

"Thanks so much! How much do I owe you?"

"Let's just call it even for the help up that hill," he said.

"Oh, you're too kind. And thanks again," Freddie said.

Not far ahead, Freddie found the square filling with people of every ilk erecting colorful canvas awnings, and stacking tables with canned and fresh farm truck, and hard goods—pots and pans, brooms, tools, and used clothing and *books*. Judging by the number of signs mentioning Klippenburg, she concluded that was the name of the town.

The wonderful aroma of freshly baked bread and sweet rolls mixing with exotic spices, roasting meat, and ladies' perfume, made her light-headed. Her mouth watered, reminding her she hadn't eaten since they were aboard ship last night, and then, not much, having to share their meager rations with her family. *I shouldn't have given all that hardtack to George.* Eyeing a freshly baked roll drizzled with white sugar frosting and dotted with what looked like crushed pecans or black walnuts, she reached out.

"Pay first," the shopgirl, who was about her age, snapped.

"Of course," Freddie said, opening her coin purse. She handed the girl a half shilling coin—more than enough for the roll; she could get a dozen for a shilling back home.

"Real money." The shop girl handed her back the coin with a scowl.

"It's real. That's a sixpence. It's *perfectly* good," Freddie insisted.

"You take me for fool? No good money, no Brot," the girl snapped.

An older woman dressed in a colorful peasant dress and a patterned scarf approached Freddie from behind, pushing in close. "What are you trying to pull?" she demanded, nudging Freddie toward the stall.

"I just wanted to buy the sweet roll. The girl won't take my money."

"Show me." The woman held out her wrinkled hand, which reminded Freddie of the witch in Snow White.

Freddie held up the coin between her fingers but wasn't about to give it up at this point. "See? It's a sixpence. It has an image of the King and everything."

"You not from here. We don't sell to *foreigners*." The woman spat out the word like a moldy chestnut.

Freddie stepped back, deciding not to raise a fuss. The word 'diplomacy' crossed her mind. There were plenty of other stalls. "Fine. I'll take my business elsewhere."

"You must pay. You touch, you pay," the woman said.

Choosing to ignore her, Freddie turned and kept walking before realizing the money her mother had given her may not be accepted anywhere. She reached into her pocket; it was empty. *Someone must have…* Then she remembered; the old woman had brushed up against her.

"Thief!" she shouted. A few curious heads turned—albeit briefly.

The peasant woman's scowl grew deeper and angrier. Her hand was jammed in her own pocket clutching something. "You... you *go!*" she all but shouted.

"Gib es zurück, Mutter," the girl said to her mother. While her grades in German weren't the best, Freddie understood the girl wanted her mother to return the money.

Her antagonist shook her head and told her daughter to be silent. "Sei still!" she said.

Freddie decided to tip her hand. "Gib es zurück, oder ich rufe die Polizei," which she hoped meant "Give it back or I'll call a policeman. "Verstehen Sie mich?" "Do you understand me?"

Her German seemed to be good enough to wash the arrogant smirk off the woman's face and get her attention. She reacted by picking up a long bread knife. "Verschwinden Sie hier zum Teufel, Sie räudige Hündin!" she cursed.

Freddie was fairly certain the old woman had told her to leave, with an unwarranted expletive added for emphasis. Her eyes were as terrifying as Sister Krause from the Convent school—a woman not to be crossed. She backed away, her hands held up, wanting no part of this craziness.

For some reason, her assailant's countenance suddenly softened, and she tucked away her knife.

Freddie was about to flee when someone stopped her, firmly grabbing her arm and turning her around.

"What's this fracas?" said a man—his tone firm and commanding like her own father's.

Freddie turned to be ensnared in the arms of a man about twenty, dressed in black and wearing a badge, shiny black boots, and a tall hat—a policeman. *Oh great.*

Trying not to bleed courage, Freddie broke free and struggled to regain her composure. "Officer, I... I think this woman *robbed* me. My mother gave me a number of coins not twenty minutes ago and I believe this woman removed them from my pocket."

"Frau Becker, are you up to your old tricks again?" the officer said, regaining his grasp on Freddie's wrist.

"Officer McNally, me? I no take nothing," the old woman said.

Frau Becker looked away for a moment, as if she were plotting an escape route. Around her, several townsfolk had been drawn to the commotion. "Elke! You take poor girl's money?" the woman asked her daughter.

"There! Officer, look in her hand," Freddie pleaded.

Frau Becker pulled out her hand—it held nothing.

"She put them in her pocket. I heard them tinkle."

"Come on, Frau Becker, empty your pockets," McNally ordered. "Now."

"These? Mine," she said when her hand opened with the contents of her pocket.

"Let's see," the officer said as Frau Becker backed into the table. He grabbed her wrist and examined the coins. "Give them back," he ordered.

"Mine!" she screeched.

"Somehow, I don't think so. Those coins are from England. Where did *you* get them?"

"That's my mother's money," Elke interrupted. "It's all we have."

"English touch the roll and not pay," Frau Becker said.

"All right, Frau Becker, let's all sort this out at the station."

"You arrest? Und mein Brot?" she protested. Other words passed her lips which Freddie understood but did not translate for the policeman—things were already going her way.

"Frau Becker, you should have thought about that before you stole her money. This is not the first time you've been caught pickpocketing, and I expect the sergeant won't be so easy on you this time."

"Ich kann das Brot aufpassen," Elke said.

"Elke said she can watch the bread stand," Freddie translated.

The policeman smiled. "So, you understand German?"

"Ein bisschen, a bit," Freddie replied. "Genug zu wissen, wenn ich betrogen werde." *Enough to know when I'm being cheated.*

The old woman bristled at the remark.

Elke seemed far from distressed as if she was glad to be tending the bread stall on her own. Freddie recognized another over-protected daughter—a kindred spirit, or perhaps she wanted to reap a bigger share of the sales.

As tensions eased, Freddie had no desire whatsoever to waste the morning in the police station where unanswerable questions would doubtless be asked, and non-existent identity papers may be demanded. She had to think fast. She might try to run, but the growing crowd wouldn't make that easy, and she still didn't have her mother's money or the food she was sent to fetch.

"Officer, if she just returns my money," Freddie pleaded, "I think we can settle this. I won't press charges." She addressed the old woman. "Geben Sie mir einfach mein Geld zurück." *Just give me back my money.*

The old woman's face softened a bit, but it seemed she sensed Freddie's reluctance to be taken into custody.

"Give it back," the policeman said firmly, holding out his hand.

The old woman slowly dropped the coins into his hand as if they were Elke's dowry. As the last one clinked, the policeman stiffened his glare.

"And the rest."

Frau Becker produced five more coins—the larger denominations—which she had skillfully spirited into her other hand.

The policeman turned to Freddie and held out his hand. "Here you go, Miss. Are you sure you don't want to press charges?"

Freddie smiled and accepted the coins, and after a quick count, stowed them away in her coin purse. "Thank you, officer. No. I'm in a hurry anyway."

"Glad to be of service. And you, Frau Becker, I'll be including your name in the report. I'm sure the sergeant will want to have a chat with the city attorney."

The old woman put her hands together and pleaded for mercy.

"No more pickpocketing," he said firmly.

"Ja natürlich."

"One other kindness?" Freddie asked as they walked away.

"Yes, Miss?"

"If I had exchanged my English coins for the local currency, this problem might not have occurred. Can you recommend an honest establishment that could exchange these?"

"Dollars. The local currency. Yes, that bank on the corner opens at ten."

"Thank you so much," she said, glancing up at the town tower clock. *7:50. Great. Over two hours.*

"You don't look happy."

"My mother sent me to buy food and we haven't eaten in a while," she said.

"And she sent a girl into a strange town without an escort?"

"My brother is… incapacitated… unable to walk; and I'm perfectly capable of dealing with strangers. I grew up in a big city."

"And so it appears… in Europe?" he smiled, raising an eyebrow.

"Yes… in… Europe," she said, not wanting to reveal anything more truthful. Freddie's nausea reminded her she needed to get something to eat, and soon—a buttery crescent or a crust of stale bread would tide her over. Her hands had begun that tremble which had often preceded her fainting spells, and the delicious smells cascading from the surrounding stalls were not helping.

"I guess I'll just have to wait," she said, gazing into his eyes. The tactic usually worked with her father, perhaps it might work with this handsome young policeman. "You could, or I could exchange a bit of your money—enough to get breakfast."

Freddie blushed when she realized the officer was going out of his way to be kind. "Would a pound be too much?" she asked, figuring that would be enough.

"I don't know the rate of exchange—let's just make it a loan. You can come by the station to repay me when you get settled. Ask for Officer McNally, Sean McNally. Where are you and your family staying?" He gave her a dollar in coins from his pocket.

No. Her fists tightened. "At… at a hotel near the river," she blurted out. She regretted the lie—knowing that lies are invariably exposed and corrode trust, but her mother's admonishments about giving their real names echoed in her mind— even in this quaint port town.

Officer McNally cocked his head. "Which hotel?"

"I forget the name. It has a view of the bay."

"The only hotel in that part of town closed years ago, and it was a… a place a decent girl like you would not frequent." His expression had changed back to that of a cautious police-man.

Freddie looked at her feet, fearing her eyes would betray her.

"Perhaps I'll need to escort you back to the station after all," McNally said. "…for your own good." His smile had disappeared as his hand wrapped around her arm.

❧❧❧

A half-hour later, Freddie found herself sitting on a hard bench in a small, cold cell—still unfed. In the office across from the cell, a plainclothes officer sipped a cup of coffee as he slowly devoured a large, iced pastry, no-doubt confiscated from Frau Becker. Her eyes followed a morsel as it fell to the floor. That's when Freddie's world went black.

❧❧❧

"Miss? Miss?" someone was saying as her eyes fluttered open. She could barely make out the face of a middle-aged man with a five-day beard—his strong hands pushed through from the adjoining cell held her upright on the bench. "Hey, officer. Can we get some help in here?" the man shouted. "This girl has fainted. What have you done to her?"

A moment later, Freddie found herself slumped on a chair as Officer McNally offered her a cup of lukewarm coffee. "Drink this," he said softly, like a concerned brother. She took a long drink and smiled. It tasted strong, overly sweet, and heavenly. "Thanks. I haven't eaten in some time. I get kinda woozy when… I skip meals."

He offered her the rest of his sergeant's pastry, which she gratefully accepted and ate in three large bites before the incredulous plainclothes officer could object.

"Feeling better?" McNally said. "I'm sure Sergeant Driscoll won't mind."

"I won't?" Sergeant Driscoll asked.

Freddie smiled. "Dwamaticawally, fanks," she said, through her dough-impacted smile.

"I'm Sergeant Driscoll. You've met Officer McNally, and that's *my* breakfast you ate."

"Thanks. You're most kind for sharing," she said, licking her fingers.

"Now what's this nonsense about your papers? How old are you?"

"Eighteen…seventeen, sir."

"All right, as a minor, you don't need to carry identification documents, but we'll need to see you're returned safely to your parents. You *do* have parents?"

Fortunately, Freddie had been thinking about a better, more believable story while being escorted to the station and sitting in the cell, so she thought she was ready. "My family and I are on holiday, visiting a distant relative of my mom's. We're staying for a few nights at the old clock shop above the bay."

"So not a hotel?" the sergeant asked.

"I was confused. It's not a real hotel. You see, English is not my first language—Verstehen Sie vous?" she replied, trying to fake a German accent, but it came out more French than German.

"I see, so you know the old man who runs the shop. Mr. Sanduhr?"

"Sanduhr? Why…" she caught herself before telling another lie. Talking to the police had become a daunting challenge—like walking on a partly frozen river. Each word, each step, had to be taken gingerly. "No, I don't recall anyone by that name, but there was a sweet young woman about twenty who took us in. Trudi?"

"Of course. Miss Trudi is just the type to take in strangers. Her grandfather passed away not long ago."

It was a trick question—meant to get me to step through the ice. "But we're not really strangers. My mother went right to her house when we arrived—she *must* know them." Freddie wanted to get back on firm ground, so she didn't elaborate further. It occurred to her that her mother *had* led them right to that obscure door that led up those stairs to the clock shop. *What's going on? She had planned to come here. Why?*

"I see," said the Sergeant.

"I saw Miss Trudi this morning coming out of Doc Stewart's, just before I went on duty in the square," the officer said. "Anything wrong?"

"As I said, my brother is hurt. I think she went to get the doctor."

"Is it serious?"

"Nothing—ah, nothing catching. He fell and broke something. He'll probably be fine, but I really need to get back there. I was supposed to take them food ages ago. They'll be worried."

"I see," McNally said, but his tone told her he was still unconvinced of her veracity.

"Let's get your money changed so you can buy some food," the sergeant said. He opened a newspaper and scanned the financial section. "Yes. There it is. The exchange rate is .2141 pounds to the dollar. So, a pound sterling is worth about $4.67," he said doing the math on the edge of the newspaper.

"I see. I have…" Freddie began, counting her coins, "…so a shilling would be about twenty-five cents in your money and five pence is worth about a dime so about two cents per penny."

"Yeah, a shilling is about two bits."

"So, eighteen shillings and twenty-four pence so that works out to almost five dollars."

"Quite a sum. So yes, Miss, you need to be more careful with your money."

"Can you change some of it, say, ten shillings?"

"How much is that exactly? You Brits have such strange money," the sergeant asked.

"It's 120 pence."

The sergeant blinked vapidly.

"About two dollars thirty?"

The sergeant's eyes glazed over. "I'm not sure I can spare that much."

"How about these two half crowns here?" Freddie picked out two large coins. "That's about a dollar fifteen. A half crown is two shillings and sixpence."

"Done. I hope we did the math right," he said, exchanging the coins for a dollar bill, a dime and a nickel.

"Thanks. Am I free to go?" she asked, handing him the coins.

"I'll have Officer McNally escort you back to the clock shop."

"I really need to visit the market first, to get some food."

"Of course," he said. They both seemed happy with this outcome—at least Freddie was.

As they passed the cells, the man who had helped her spoke in a hushed tone. "Feeling more like yourself now, Miss?"

She turned to see it was her cellmate who had sought help for her. She paused. "Yes, thanks for your help."

"Anything for a St. James," he whispered with a smirk. He bowed and tipped his non-existent hat. "Where did you say you were staying?" he asked.

A chill ran down Freddie's spine, but before she bolted, she noticed a faded tattoo on his lower arm—an anchor wrapped with a snake. "I didn't," Freddie said, moving quickly out the door. *How did he know me?*

As Freddie and Officer McNally walked back toward the market, she felt relieved she was all but free, but even more questions ricocheted off the corners of her mind. *Who was that reprobate?*

"What's there to do here in… Klippenburg? What's the main attraction?" she asked, trying to get the officer to relax.

"Klippenburg. Well, I expect it's a bit less exciting compared to the big cities in Europe like London. But Maine is a beautiful state—green and lush and the people are warm and generous to a fault."

"London is in the UK—the United Kingdom," she said with a smile. "Small-town life can be fun too. Most folks make their own fun."

"We do have a few night spots and some nice restaurants. but they're expensive when the tourists are in town. They just reopened the Roxy Theater a week ago."

"So what should I buy for breakfast and lunch?" she asked as her nose told her they were approaching the market. And there it was. There were even more shops and stalls set up selling everything imaginable.

"Take your pick," he said.

"It's like Piccadilly. I could spend all day here."

"But you need to get back home, and I need to get back to my beat."

"Of course," she said. When the elaborate clock in the city tower that overlooked the town square chimed eight thirty, it reminded her that she had been gone far too long. She paused only a moment to watch the animated figures dance about the clock tower.

"They look so lifelike. Like nothing I've ever seen—even in Europe—with the obvious exception of the clock in St. Mark's Square in Venice."

"We're quite proud of it. It was made right here by Miss Trudi's grandfather."

"I'll have to ask her about it."

"Have you really been to Venice?"

"Yes, a few times, and several of the capitals in Europe and The British Isles. To Edinburgh, Dublin, and Cardiff."

"Cardiff?"

"The capital of Wales."

"Why so much travel?" he asked as they paused at a fruit stand.

Freddie froze. *He's probing for information.* "My father travels in his business and takes us along when it suits him. Those look like some especially nice beans, and the squash looks delicious."

"If you like squash and beans," he said.

As they shopped, he helped her buy breakfast pastries, a few cannoli, bacon, fresh eggs, apples, bread, and a half-pound of black tea—all loaded into another string bag which he carried as if they were a couple. Frau Becker briefly glared at them from across the square. As they passed a bookshop, an unseen force compelled her to turn and go inside.

Officer McNally began to say something but just shook his head.

The shopkeeper was placing a sign over the Samuel Clemens book *Adventures of Huckleberry Finn.*

BANNED IN NEW YORK.

Freddie could not resist, wondering why it had been banned. As she reached for a copy, the shopkeeper eyed the officer.

"Are you going to let her buy that?"

"If she has the money," he said.

Freddie smiled and handed the man a dime. He just shook his head and muttered. "Kids."

"Is that all you need?"

"Almost," she said.

"Almost?"

"I need some way to repay your kindness."

"For arresting you?"

She smiled. "Well, let's overlook that. For getting my money back and helping me negotiate with the shopkeepers."

"Think nothing of it. You're a nice, polite, well-bred, young lady. Ready to head back to your mother? It's been over an hour. I expect she's beyond frantic by now."

"Yes, of course. I guess we should head back. That way?"

"Sure. Down the hill and follow Cliff Street. It's only about six blocks."

"I'm sure I'll find it," she said, reaching for the bag.

"And I'm sure the sergeant will have me scrubbing toilets if I don't escort you to your doorstep."

"But I'll be fine. I don't want to keep you from your duties."

"Yes, and I want to make sure. I could not forgive myself if you came to harm." He held on to the bag and offered his elbow. She nodded and put her arm through his as they continued down the winding streets toward the clock shop.

"The town really seems to be ready for Christmas," she said, gazing into a brightly lit storefront. The display had a wooden army of toy soldiers arranged as if ready to go into battle, with a miniature electric train circling the scene. Compared to the shop windows in London, these displays seemed a tad pedestrian.

"We enjoy the holidays. Winters can be gray and long. We expect it to snow any day now."

"Really, perhaps we'll have… a… white—"

"Is there something wrong, Miss?"

"Just remembering the friends I left behind back home, and how they loved to play in the snow. And call me Freddie. Everyone does."

As they approached the clock shop, she paused. No, she didn't want him to come in—not wanting to have her mother know she had been detained by the police and not wanting the officer to learn any more she hadn't inadvertently shared. Freddie took the bags and their fingers lingered. "You've been more than kind," she said, looking into his soft, brown eyes.

"Shall I see you inside?" he asked.

"Please, no. I don't want to frighten my mother and have to explain why a policeman had to bring me home."

"I understand. Are you sure you'll be all right?"

"Of course. Thank the sergeant for his pastry and you …"

"McNally. Sean. If there's something you need while you're in town, let me… ah, *us,* know."

She smiled and nodded, reaching for the doorknob.

"Wait," he said, touching her shoulder.

She froze.

"Freddie, what's your last name?"

Suddenly, the door opened. "Where have you been? We've been worried," Catherine asked. She wrapped Freddie in a warm hug and pulled her inside. "Thank you, officer," she said, closing the door behind her, leaving the policeman standing outside.

"I'm fine mom. See? I bought breakfast."

"And lunch and dinner from the looks of it. Is that a brace of lobsters? What took so long? Oh, you must have found a bookstore."

"There was a bit of a problem with the money. The stalls didn't want to take our British coins. I had to exchange a bit for the local currency."

"Oh, I'm so sorry. I'm proud you were able to sort it out."

"It was easy," she lied with a grin.

"And the policeman? You didn't think I would notice?"

"Oh, he was just bringing me home from the station. He had to detain me. Isn't he adorable?"

"What?! You were arrested?"

Freddie kept unloading the string sacks onto the kitchen counter. "I'm afraid so—well, sort of. No charges were filed." She kicked herself for revealing that confidence. She slipped the new book under a newspaper and kept talking as if nothing had happened.

Catherine had what seemed like a dozen questions and each answer led to another dozen, so Freddie told her the abridged version of the story, leaving out how she thought the policeman was quite handsome and had been flirting with her.

"… and some strange guy in the cell knew my last name," she whispered.

"Wait." Catherine turned her around. "What? How did he know? Did he recognize you? You didn't give them your real name, did you?"

"No, mother. Not to anyone. The sergeant said I was a minor and didn't need papers. Sean had *just* asked me for my name when you interrupted him."

"Sean? The officer? And we slammed the door in his face? Don't you think he'll be suspicious?"

"Perhaps. Perhaps only curious or was just being nice."

"Oh, my God. It's a nightmare."

"We'll be fine, mother. I think he's just sweet on me."

"Does he know you're only seventeen?" Catherine looked her in the eye.

"I'm nearly eighteen, and he's only about nineteen or twenty. He's just joined the force."

"Still, he's… it's…" She just shook her head.

"Dangerous. Yes, I know. I didn't tell him anything he didn't already know. He knows we came from the UK because of the money, and he knows I'm with my mother and brother and he's hurt. Wait. How is George? Is he better? Did the doctor come?"

"He was treated by the doctor but he's not doing that well now that his pain medicine is wearing off."

"I'll look in on him. So, the police. They don't know much, so I think we're fine. No one *really* knows who we are," Freddie said. "At least I hope not."

"Once the news spreads that we're missing, that might bring them back here if they can add two and two."

"About that. There is a headline story in the New York Times about us. I didn't dare buy a copy. Is there anything in the local newspaper—besides saying that we're missing?"

"There was a brief story," Catherine said, picking up the paper revealing Freddie's new book.

"If they know, they know. Let's not start packing or panicking yet. We just got here." Freddie slipped the book under her jacket.

Catherine turned to stare at the stove. "Breakfast. It's been years since I cooked anything. I hope I still know how."

"Like riding a bike. So, the doctor came?" Freddie asked, taking a nibble of the sweet cannoli and slicing some bread.

"Yes, he's been seen by the village doctor. As we suspected, he said his leg is badly broken, and Trudi and he wanted him to go to hospital for observation."

"And?"

"We convinced the doctor that we would watch him carefully. Hon, it's a tough call but we can't afford to risk it."

"The unanswerable questions, the forms, the attention. I understand."

"We'll all—"

"Have to take care of him. Yes, I know. I'll do my part and more," Freddie said.

"I know you will. And we *will* take him to hospital if he gets any worse."

"How's Annie?"

"She's oblivious. She's under a table in the workshop and quite content playing with a doll she found—dressing and undressing her. Let's let her play in peace. I expect she'll soon want a nap."

Relieved her brother and sister had been tended to, Freddie turned her attention to helping fix everyone a nice meal. "So, where's the girl, our host? Trudi?"

"Trudi went out looking for you."

"Did you know her grandfather just passed away? Apparently, the whole town knows him—and this clock shop. It's been here forever."

"I could tell. These clocks are really something special—like none I've ever seen."

Just then, Freddie remembered—the little man in the stairway. "There's something else."

"After we eat. I don't need any more surprises—not until I've had some strong tea and another one of those pastries."

"I'll make a plate for George. Is he awake?"

"I'll go check," Catherine said, disappearing behind the bead curtain. A moment later, Freddie heard her mother scream.

Twenty-three—The Healer

*F*reddie rushed toward the screaming to find Catherine standing in the doorway of the bedroom off the workshop. She was pointing at George's leg. "What in the name of all that's holy are you doing to my son?" she shrieked.

Freddie pushed her way into the room where she saw Alred, the tiny elf she had met on the spiral staircase, standing on the bedside table looking as concerned as Catherine, but he said nothing. Another elf, a woman, knelt next to George's lower leg, her tiny hands laid on his bandaged wound glowing beneath her fingertips. George seemed to be unconscious—either dreaming or mesmerized—but still breathing and apparently not in pain.

Freddie tried to move forward but found her feet were too heavy to lift. "What are you *doing?*" she asked.

Alred put his index finger to his lips. The other elf did not look up—she also seemed to be in a trance, and now, her own leg was softly glowing beneath her long peasant dress. "Please. A few moments of silence if you please," Alred begged. "It will be over very soon."

"I… I don't understand. Who, what…?" Catherine tried to ask, nearly weeping but seemingly unable to move any closer.

"Mother, this is what I wanted to tell you," Freddie whispered.

"I'm terribly sorry, Madam," Alred said. "The boy had a fat clot and was in mortal danger. She's almost done dissolving it."

"We should take him to hospital; at once!" she said.

"If you think that's wise, then of course, but Kenezer is a gifted healer—a powerful empath. She can knit the bone and remove the clot. Just give her a few more…"

"But…you're *leprechauns*," Catherine sputtered, still unable to step closer to her son.

"No mother, they're *not*—they're *Seldith*. I think we can trust them. This little elf helped me, helped *us* this morning on the stairway."

"We're nearly done," Alred said as the glowing subsided. He handed Kenezer an earthenware jug.

"Thanks," Kenezer said softly, taking a long swig. She continued to kneel alongside George as if she could no longer stand.

"Will George be all right?" Freddie asked. "Will *she*?"

"He'll be sore for a fortnight, but perhaps walking by morning. He should not be playing football or chasing young ladies for a day or two.

"And the healer—Kenezer?"

"I expect she'll be fine. She usually heals very quickly."

"Really? The doctor said it would be many weeks."

"And it would have—if he had lived through the night," Kenezer said. "If the clot had broken free, he might have been dead in minutes, and they would have been powerless to save him."

"How did you know?" Freddie asked.

"Watching over the clan and our uman friends is what we do."

"Really? Friends? We've just met."

"We Seldith have helped each other and our uman friends for many generations. Are you not relatives of the clockmaker and his granddaughter?"

"We barely know them," Catherine confessed.

Alred's face showed a strange mix of confusion and discretion—as if he knew more than he should say. "None-the-less, we welcome strangers. Strangers in a strange land are treated as we would wish to be treated. It's one of the fundamental precepts in The Book."

"And the Bible," Freddie said softly.

George's eyes blinked. "What's going on?"

"Are you all right?" Catherine asked, now able to rush to embrace him.

"I had the strangest dream," he said, rubbing his eyes.

"It's not over," Freddie quipped.

George looked down and pulled away. "What the—?"

"Relax, they're friends. She just healed your leg—well, almost."

George ran his hands over his leg to inspect the wound. "It's...a little sore, but not like before."

Alred helped Kenezer limp across the bed. "We need to go. She needs to rest."

"Of course. I can't thank you enough." Catherine said. "If there's something we can do, please don't hesitate to—"

"One thing, there is... spare an egg or a bit of bacon, could you?"

"I expect so, how do you want your eggs prepared?"

"Just raw, don't go to any bother. And one other thing."

"What's that? Anything," Catherine asked.

"Rescue Mrs. Framingham from your little girl, could you? Your little darlin' has been undressing and dressing her for over an hour, and I think the poor dear is quite exhausted by now."

"Annie!?" Catherine and Freddie exclaimed in one voice. George just grinned.

Freddie ran into the kitchen and quickly scooped up Annie and gently freed her "dolly." "I'm so sorry, Mrs. Framingham, so, so sorry," she said, handing Annie off to her mother and a tiny dress and underthings back to the elf.

"Thank you, miss," she said before running off in the buff.

"Honey, let's find Katie," Freddie said as she took Annie upstairs to search for her actual doll. By the time she returned to George's side, the elves had disappeared.

"Where did they go?" Freddie asked.

"Oh, I expect they have a dozen secret doors," Trudi said, joining them in Opa's bedroom. "I'm glad you made it back. Any trouble?"

"Not at all… mostly. It was an *adventure*."

"Freddie, you're back. Brilliant," George said. "What kind of trouble did you get into?

"Just so you're safe. I'm so relieved. I see you've met the elves," Trudi said, standing in the doorway. At this instant, Trudi remembered her promise to Opa. She was never to reveal the existence of the Seldith but it seemed they had revealed themselves. Still knowing she had a duty to protect her new elven friends, she resolved to make sure Catherine and her family helped her keep this solum oath.

"That we have. It seems they're magical, but I have a million questions," Catherine said.

"I expect so. I'll tell you what I can, but I just learned of them myself. It seems they've been watching over us for, well, forever."

The next hour was spent bringing Catherine, Freddie, and George up to speed in regard to the Seldith with admonishments to keep their existence a closely guarded secret.

"Given that we've asked you to keep our secrets, I think it's more than fair that we keep yours," Catherine said. "Right Fredricka?"

"Of course, mother. Of course."

Freddie was compelled to tell of her trip into town with the sordid details pulled out like thorns from a mohair sweater.

"Trudi, do you know Sean? Sean McNally?" Freddie asked at last.

"Sure. He's the beat cop."

"Isn't he dreamy?" Freddie said.

"Yes… he's very sweet," Trudi said.

Freddie detected a slight tinge of green in Trudi's response. "Are you together?"

"Sean and I? Not really…"

She's sweet on him. I can tell.

Twenty-four—The Deliveries

*T*rudi spotted two boxed clocks sitting under the counter waiting to be delivered to their owners. One was the mayor's, and the other was for her mysterious knight. *Perhaps Catherine could watch the shop and collect payment if the knight showed up while she delivered and installed the mayor's clock?*

"Catherine? May I have a word?" Trudi asked. "Can you help get me out of a self-created jam?"

Fifteen minutes later, Trudi had arranged with the mayor's office to install the repaired clock and collect final payment while her houseguests minded the shop—admitting only the man who had bought Anastasia. "I promised to have it ready by noon and it's already after eleven."

"We'll keep an eye out for him," Catherine said. "Go. Go get the mayor's clock installed before he gets back to his office."

When she didn't see Chad's cab outside, she called for another which arrived a few minutes later. As the driver helped her load her tool case and the boxed clock, Weeset surreptitiously slipped into the cab and hid.

Once they were on their way, Weeset landed on Trudi's shoulder. "I thought you might need a chaperone or a bodyguard."

"I'll be all right," Trudi said.

"I'll make sure. I've seen *His Honor's* shenanigans when young women get behind closed doors."

When they arrived at City Hall, and Trudi's driver had helped her get her tool case to the top of the stairs, she discovered the city's seat of government had transformed into bustling, noisy chaos. Gritting her teeth, she made her way through to the mayor's outer office.

"Is he in?" she asked the pretty receptionist.

"He's never in when there are people around," she said. "People mean problems."

"Well, I called. I'm supposed to install his clock," Trudi said, holding up the boxed clockworks. "And collect payment."

"Just go on in. I'm sure it will be fine. He did mention that you were expected but I thought it was an older man who worked on it before. He also left this." She held up an envelope.

"That was my grandfather. He passed away not long ago. It's just me now," Trudi said while she opened the envelope; it held a stack of new bills which she carefully counted. *All there*. "Thanks."

"I'm sorry to hear that. Go ahead. No one will bother you."

"I'll see to that," Weeset whispered from her shirt pocket.

It didn't take long to reinstall the clock, reconnect the counterweights and make sure it was running as it should. While she worked, Weeset spent her time reading every document she found on his desk—and apparently in it.

"What *are* you doing? It's not nice to snoop."

"Oh, I've been doing it for years. I've read some pretty juicy stuff in this office; seen, and overheard more."

"Well, stop it. It will ruin my reputation if my clients, even the scandalous ones, find out I've betrayed their trust."

"Yes'm," Weeset said, as she returned to her shoulder.

"I'm almost done," Trudi said.

"Good. I'm bored."

Minutes later, Trudi was enjoying the relative quiet of the cab ride back to her shop.

"Do you want me to tell you what I discovered?" Weeset asked.

"No, you little pixie. And don't tell anyone else. Promise?"

"Don't make me promise. Faeries can't break a promise."

"Promise," Trudi said sternly.

"I promise." Weeset was quiet the rest of the way.

As they came into the shop, Catherine came out to greet her and Freddie took her case back to the workroom.

"Anything to report? Any customer issues?" Trudi asked.

"The man you described came by and was most disappointed that you were not here. He did bring the rest of the cash. This should put a nice dent in some of these," Catherine said, holding up a banded packet of bills.

Trudi was crestfallen. "I so wanted to talk to him again. I didn't even get his name and where he's taking Anastasia."

"He seemed very nice, and I'm sure he'll take good care of your beloved Anastasia."

"Well, we can also add this to the accounts," she said, holding up the mayor's cash payment. "I never thought I'd see the city pay up."

Twenty-five—The First Supper

For the rest of the day, the houseguests found ways to make Trudi's life easier by doing chores, bringing in coal for the stoves, and sweeping and dusting when the shop was idle. While they were afraid to help with the shoppers for fear of being discovered, they did make a mid-day meal that Trudi seemed to especially appreciate. Even George had helped by being less demanding than usual, which worried Freddie and his mother. Annie had indeed been admonished that she was not to mistreat the "dollies" that she might find. The Seldith clan was likewise cautioned that tiny humans do not fear them, and they should be more cautious when infants were allowed to roam about unsupervised. No one above the floorboards saw any sign of Mrs. Framingham.

After four in the afternoon, the clock shop traffic had evaporated, and Trudi found herself looking through the front window as she watched the world glide by. Large, white flakes of snow had finally covered the town in a downy blanket, creating a wondrous, glimmering scene of streetlamps, Christmas lights, and people shopping or just rushing home with their bundles tucked away with collars pulled high.

It was a pretty time, a happy time for most, but for Trudi, a bittersweet time as well. She missed Oma and her unquenchable enthusiasm for the holidays, her overzealous decorations, the special cookies, and homemade pies, and the roast lamb they all enjoyed on Christmas day. She also missed Opa, and she had not forgotten how he needed so little makeup to convince the customers' kids he was Santa, or at least one of his helpers.

Trudi remembered when she was about ten, Opa had set up a chair in the shop where he would don a red coat and hat, and the customers' children would come to talk to 'Santa.'

"Well, Dorothy, have you been good this year?" Opa would ask, glancing up at the wide-eyed child's mom. "My elves tell me that you're doing well in school, and that you help around the house. Is this true?"

And so it would go. The parents loved to bring their children by, but this year, there would be no surrogate Santa. Trudi knew it would not be the same.

When the clocks struck five, she turned over the sign on the door and turned the lock. Her breath frosting the glass, she just stood there mesmerized by the flakes tumbling to the street.

"You all right?" Freddie asked, touching her on the shoulder.

Trudi didn't turn around. Refocusing on her reflection in the glass, she wiped away her tears and took a deep breath. "Sure. Just reminiscing."

"I miss my dad and friends too. I know how hard it is to have someone you care about taken—"

Trudi turned and embraced her. It was as if she had a new sister.

"Dinner is almost ready. Hungry?" Freddie asked through her own tears.

"Famished. From here it smells delicious."

"Annie helped with the cake, so I would reserve judgement."

"I'm sure it's fine…"

Once the excitement of their first day together had finished echoing in their lives, Catherine, her children, and Trudi sat at the table to a warm supper Freddie and Catherine had prepared, while Clarence found George's lap especially comforting. The feeling seemed mutual.

As everyone settled in around the table, Trudi said a short grace.

"Lord, you asked us to embrace strangers and make them feel at home. Thank you for these new friends and may they find comfort and safety here within these walls. Amen."

And they echoed, "Amen."

"That was…lovely," Catherine said. "Thank you for welcoming us into your home."

Gathering up her courage, Trudi posed the unasked question, the question already on everyone's mind. "How long can you stay?" Trudi hoped it would be for quite some time; she knew she could use the help—especially from those who had the money to buy their own food.

Catherine closed her eyes and paused. "Trudi, we honestly don't know. For your protection, I can't explain our circumstances in much detail, but I fear we will have to remain incognito, at least as much as we can, for at least a fortnight. We couldn't possibly impose on your generosity and hospitality for that long."

Trudi smiled, but said nothing, handing the plate of steamed vegetables to George. He still seemed a bit stunned—perhaps he was not quite over his ordeal with the elves or the newly mended broken leg. He managed a thin smile and a "Thanks."

"Tomorrow," Catherine began. "we'll begin our search for a quiet bungalow or a discreet hostel outside of town."

"Aren't you afraid of checking into a hotel?"

"Of course, you're right. There are too many nosy clerks, too many registration forms, strangers coming and going, too many questions we dare not answer truthfully."

"I see," Trudi said, serving herself a portion of steamed lobster. "Then I can assume you are the family mentioned in the newspaper?"

Catherine's eyes dropped as she confessed. "We are. Can we discuss this after dinner? The kids have been living on short rations for a week, and this is all a bit unsettling."

"Of course, of course. Please. Eat. Enjoy. We don't have to decide anything now, or today, or this week. You're welcome to stay as long as you—"

"As we what?" Freddie interrupted.

"Keep cooking like this. This is a *sumptuous* feast. I have neither the skill, nor the time or the money to prepare meals like this. I expect to look like Mrs. Santa Claus in a month."

"Trudi, we're *so* appreciative of your hospitality. Of course, we'll help however we can and pay you for your trouble."

"Pay me? I should be paying *you*," Trudi said with a smile and part of a warm buttermilk biscuit in her mouth.

"I noticed Klippenburg was all decked out for Christmas," Freddie said. "It was oh so pretty and reminded me of London, of home. I certainly hope we can take Annie and George to see all the lights and decorated storefronts—especially now that it's snowed."

"Yes, the lights and decorations are beautiful around town. We usually have our Christmas ornaments up by now, but…" Trudi mused aloud.

"We understand," Catherine said. "Where do you keep them? Perhaps it would be fun to have us help you put them up."

"Oh, I would *really* like that. Can we?" Freddie asked Trudi.

A smile, albeit a thin, sad one, crossed Trudi's face. "Of course, I would love that, too. The boxes are in one of the storerooms upstairs—the fourth door on the right—I think.

The boxes are mostly labeled in German, so you'll need to look for—"

"Weihnachten," Freddie said with a smile.

"Why, yes. Do you speak German?" Trudi asked.

"Just enough to keep me out of trouble," Freddie admitted.

"Almost enough…" Catherine said. "She keeps overhearing things she oughtn't."

Freddie nodded. "Yes, almost…"

"Are you sure the decorations would not be a bother?" Catherine asked.

"No, really, it would be fun, and it would help business— let's get started after supper," Trudi said.

Once supper was done, and the topics of conversation exhausted, Freddie and Catherine quickly cleared the table, and did the dishes, treating Trudi like visiting royalty in her own home. They delegated George to drying, which seemed more of a challenge for him than it should have been.

Trudi could see they were especially anxious to please, oh so polite, and quite well-mannered, and she didn't mind keeping an eye on Annie. She surmised that Catherine was well-off, as whenever any expense was incurred, she was eager and able to pay—albeit in British pounds. Any regret Trudi might have had taking in these mysterious strangers from the bay had disappeared like the last morsel of Annie's cake—which wasn't that bad.

Once the supper dishes were dried, put away, and the fires banked, Annie tugged on Trudi's skirt.

"May we do Christmas now?" she asked.

"Of course, dear. Let's go find the boxes," Trudi said, taking Annie by the hand. She led her and Freddie upstairs to the long hall of numbered doors. Their own guest bedrooms were off this corridor, but they had not explored any of them.

"Was this a hotel?" Freddie asked?

"Well, yes, and… the building had a few other… purposes."

Freddie smiled. "Oh."

"Here's the room we're using as a storeroom," Trudi said, opening the door marked "Sechs."

"Sex?" Freddie asked with a big grin.

"Ja, sechs, einer mehr als sieben[16]" Trudi said, getting the play on words.

Inside the musty room were rows of boxes, most marked with faded German labels. After a short search, they found five boxes containing Christmas decorations. Trudi paused for a moment, gazing into the first box. It contained the last ornament placed on the tree—the Christmas Angel. She fought back more tears as she recalled her final Christmas with Oma and Opa. That was a sparse year, but despite the hardships, she had been given a pair of knitted socks, and a special set of tools. Opa had made them to help her do her own experimenting with her robotic toys. It was an especially happy time.

Gifts. I'll need to make Catherine and her family Christmas presents.

"We'll need a tree," Freddie said, fingering a string of lights.

"I'll call Mr. Tannenbaum. He'll bring one by—he's an old friend."

"Not too tall," Freddie warned. "Last year, father bought an enormous tree that didn't fit in our living room."

Trudi laughed. "Let's get these downstairs. I can't wait to put them up."

"Me too," Freddie said, grabbing a pair of boxes.

---

[16] "Yes, six, one more than seven."

After several trips, they discovered that Catherine had made hot chocolate. As they sipped, they planned how the large shop window would look and how the clocks and music boxes could be decorated.

"We could use more of these mechanical toys," George suggested, fingering a toy caribou he had found in one of the boxes. "Do you have all nine of Santa's reindeer?"

"Nine?"

"Dasher and Dancer, Prancer and Vixen, Comet and…"

"Cupid, Donner, and–"

"Blitzen!" they all said at once.

"And Linterna," Annie said.

"And Linterna," Catherine echoed. "You can't forget Linterna."

"Linterna?" Trudi asked. "She's new to me."

"She has a magic nose. Santa has her light the way, so he doesn't get lost in the dark," Annie said with considerable authority.

"Oh, I see. I might just have to make a few more reindeer this year," Trudi said. "Including one with a bright, shiny nose."

Among the decorations, they also found a few Christmas books, including *A Christmas Carol, Als der Nikolaus kam*[17], and a well-worn Advent calendar—its candy treats long since gone. Each discovery triggered new, fond and emotional memories for Trudi, and it seemed for her houseguests. "Opa would read this one to me in German."

"What's it about?" Annie asked. "Can you read it to me?"

"It's the story of the night before Christmas when a little girl's father heard the sound of tiny reindeer on the roof."

---

[17] The night before Christmas.

"Santa Claus!" Annie said. "Daddy read us that book. How did it get here?" she asked, reaching for it.

Catherine smiled. "This is Miss Trudi's book that her grandfather read to her."

"So can Miss Trudi read it? I can read. Can I try?" Annie said, paging gently through the faded illustrations.

"If you're careful, you can try, but it's written in my Opa's language. His family came from Austria, where they spoke and read German," Trudi explained patiently.

Annie studied the colorful pictures, but the words seemed to confuse her at first—but only for a moment. "It was the night before Christmas," she began.

"Annie, how did you do that? Can you read German?" Trudi asked.

"She has heard that story read to her countless times. She knows it by heart," Freddie whispered.

They all sat sipping their cocoa as they marveled at Annie translating the German *Als der Nikolaus kam*, with only a few imaginative embellishments. When she was all but done, it was clear she was ready for bed so Freddie took her upstairs to tuck her in. The rest put the shop back in order and retired. It had been a long day.

As Trudi turned off her bedside lamp, she whispered: "Thanks, Opa and Oma, I knew you had your hand in this."

Down the hall she heard Catherine. "Good night, Freddie."

"Good night, Mama; good night, George," Freddie said.

"Good night, Freddie; good night, Trudi," George said.

"Good night, all," Annie said.

Trudi was barely awake when she heard a familiar voice whisper, "Good night, Miss Trudi." *Alred.*

"Good night, my elven friends."

Twenty-six—The Betrayal

efore the shop opened that crisp Saturday morning, Trudi sat at the kitchen table reading the morning paper. "Catherine?"

"Yes?" Catherine said, looking up from the shop's books.

"I think you need to hear this." She read the article aloud.

MRS. ST. JAMES AND CHILDREN LOST AT SEA

"According to sources in Southampton, UK, the entire St. James family, including Mrs. Catherine St. James, their daughters Fredricka and Annette, and their son George, was lost in a tragic accident at sea. Given the limited information available, it appears that their lifeboat overturned off the State of Maine in the United States. Life preservers from their ship HMS Sutherland were found adrift, along with a few items of personal clothing. No explanation was available to explain the reason the family was in the lifeboat or even why they were aboard the cargo-laden steamship. Authorities have been unable to contact the ship, as it continued on its planned course after the incident. It is not expected to return to port for another three weeks. The Honorable Richard St. James, Mrs. St. James' husband, American Charge d' Affairs, and father of her children, could not be reached for comment as he too has not contacted the American Embassy in London for several days. While his whereabouts are unknown, he was not reported to be on the Sutherland. The reward of £500 ($2,335) for information regarding the location of the Honorable Richard St. James is still in effect."

"Well, I must say that was…" Catherine began.

"Unexpected?" Trudi asked.

"No, not really."

"So you're really the family of the missing diplomat—Mr. Saint James aren't you?"

"Yes, but I expect you had already figured that out. A family of four, showing up at dawn with a sketchy story and a desire for confidentiality; it would be hard not to link us to the newspaper stories."

"I knew you were in trouble, but I didn't realize you were the missing family until… well, it took a few hours," Trudi said.

"We intentionally tried to make it appear that we were drowned; to deter those looking for us."

"I overheard. We're dead?" Freddie asked, incredulously.

"They think so," Catherine said.

"So, they're not looking for us," George said. "That's good, right?" His voice confirmed his malaise. The fact that he had barely any appetite further concerned Trudi, and, she suspected, his mother.

"Or so it appears," Catherine began, "but without bodies washing up on a beach somewhere, they might keep looking." Catherine didn't take her eyes off her son.

"What will daddy think? He'll be frantic," Freddie said.

"I… I expect so," Catherine said.

"I understand why you still want to remain hidden," Trudi said.

"Exactly. If someone recognizes us, we'll all come back to life."

"But none of the papers have pictures of any of you. Unless you're recognized by someone you know—"

"Someone, like that guy who spoke to me in jail?" Freddie asked.

"Are you sure he recognized you?"

"Quite sure. He called me by name."

"That makes it even more important we stay out of sight," Catherine said.

"And that reward. $2300 and change is a fortune. It might tempt even the staunchest friend to turn us in," Freddie said.

"I…" Trudi began.

"No, no, I didn't mean you. I didn't think that for a second," Freddie said. "Please forgive me."

"There was nothing to forgive. It's the truth. It's a lot of money—a great temptation to anyone. These are desperate times, and anyone might want to collect the reward—anyone."

"I should have never gone into the village," Freddie said.

"Dumb move, sis," George chimed in.

Freddie gave him a dagger glare.

"Perhaps we can *encourage* the man who spotted you to be silent," Trudi suggested. "This town's gears are greased with money," she said, rubbing her thumb and forefinger together.

"It's worth a try, but we can't approach him. Freddie, can you describe him? Perhaps Trudi could recognize him."

"Ah, let's see. A man, forty or fifty maybe, about this tall," she said, holding up one hand. "Five seven? Dressed like a…a street criminal. Dirty shoes, unkempt, soiled suit, greasy hair, hard, calloused hands, and dirty fingernails."

"That describes most of the non-professional men in this county, and the professionals too, after a weekend of gardening or fishing. A common seaman or cannery worker?" Trudi asked.

"A tattoo. He had a tattoo of an anchor wrapped with a snake on his forearm."

"That narrows it down a bit. Perhaps we can get your policeman friend to identify him. Once we have his name and whereabouts, we might be able to approach him."

"If he's not in prison or has skipped town," George said.

"But we can't let anyone recognize me. I'm more widely known and photographed than you children," Catherine said. "We've seen to that."

"Can you wear a disguise?" Trudi asked.

"Yes… yes, I can," she replied with a mysterious smile. "Did your grandfather keep any henna around? Perhaps as paint for his clock figures?"

"I think so; it's in the workshop. Why do you… oh. I understand. I think you all will need it. I don't know if there is enough for everyone."

"What?" Freddie asked. "What are you thinking about?"

"How would you like to be a raven brunette?" Catherine asked. "At least for a while."

Freddie just stared at her mother unable to fully grasp what was about to happen.

"And with shorter hair. What if you had two sons?" Trudi asked.

"Intriguing. They're looking for a woman my age with a teenage daughter and son."

"And an infant."

"And an infant. Let's boil some water."

"I'll go to the chemist. I need a few other things too," Trudi said.

As the clocks struck nine, a customer rapped on the shop door. Trudi got up and her day began. She was thrilled to have so many customers, but this was expected as it was only a week before Christmas. Then again, she wanted to help Catherine and her family in any way she could. By the time the clocks struck ten, the shop had cleared out and Catherine approached her.

"Here," Catherine said, handing Trudi several British banknotes.

"No," Freddie said. "I got in enough trouble trying to spend your British coins. We need to get that exchanged."

"That may be tricky. As soon as someone sees the money, they'll wonder where it came from."

"Right. I should have thought of that," Catherine said, putting the bills back in her purse.

"I think I have a solution to that problem," Trudi said.

"Oh?"

"When you want to do something under the table, hire a criminal or someone who works with them."

"You know someone like that?"

Trudi just smiled. "Besides the mayor? Give me what you want to exchange. I'll take care of it." She thought back and realized that few people beyond her own grandparents had trusted her with something this important.

Catherine handed her the banknotes.

"Officer McNally told me the rate of exchange is $4.67 to the pound," Freddie said.

While Freddie kept one eye on the shop, they verified the banknotes added up to exactly fifty pounds and slid them into an envelope.

"£50, so, $233.50," George said after doing the conversion just before laying his head on the table.

Freddie nodded, after cross-checking the math. "Right. George, are you all right?" Freddie asked.

"Tired. Very tired. And my leg is aching."

Freddie looked at her mom.

Catherine nodded. "George? Let's get you back into bed and get that leg elevated." She reached over and felt his forehead. "A bit warm. Freddie, would you get him a cup of tea and help me get him undressed?"

"I'm fine," George protested, but in a voice that said just the opposite.

"No fuss. You're not well and the doctor is coming in the morning. Let's make sure you're better by then or we'll all want to stick you in hospital."

The next few minutes focused on getting the patient in his pajamas, hydrated, and settled into his bed. He was asleep before the clocks struck ten-fifteen in nearly perfect unison.

"So now what?" Freddie asked.

"We find a discreet fence," Catherine said.

"Let me see what I can arrange," Trudi said.

With the banknotes bulging in her jacket pocket, she stepped out on the street. *We're in luck.* She put her fingers to her lips and let out a shrill whistle. A moment later, Chad pulled his cab up to the curb.

"Chad, do you have some time for an important mission?"

"Anything, Miss."

"We need some money exchanged."

"I can take you to the bank."

"But we don't… can't let anyone know where the currency comes from."

"Stolen, Miss? Really?"

"No. No. *No.* It *isn't* stolen," she said adamantly. "It belongs to a friend. She's fleeing… an abusive husband. He can't find out where she's gone." One of Trudi's acquaintances had told her a tall tale is easier to believe if it's at least thirty-percent true.

"I see. All right, I know a wealthy gentleman who trusts me to exchange his money from time to time. He's a British tourist though. I might imply that I'm doing it for him—but if it's not pounds, that would—"

"Be perfect. Here: fifty pounds. We figure the exchange rate is—." She handed him the bag of coins.

"Close to $240. I exchange money for the British tourists all the time. That's quite a bit, Miss."

"It is," Trudi said, as her impression of this cabbie improved dramatically. "I've trusted you with my clocks and my confidences before and I know I can depend on you and your discretion."

"I… I really appreciate the confidence. I won't let you down, Miss."

I know just how you feel. "I never doubted you would. So, can you take me to the chemist, and then you can go to the bank?"

"Of course, Miss. Are you ready now?"

"Give me a moment. I'll lock up and be right back."

Chad nodded and Trudi went back into the shop.

"I'm off to the chemist," she said across the shop to Catherine. "I have a safe way to get the money exchanged so they won't be able to trace it back to us."

"Safe?" Catherine asked.

"Safe-ish…" Trudi replied with a raised eyebrow.

"I hope you're right. Thanks. Can you also pick up a bottle of aspirin and a pair of good hair-cutting scissors?" Catherine asked.

"I expect so. I'll lock the shop while I'm gone."

"Perhaps that's best. We'll stay out of sight."

"Until you're all brunettes," Trudi said with a wink.

When Trudi returned to the curb, her heart all but stopped. Chad was gone. Her stomach turned over as she looked up and down the street but there was no sign of him. There were a few cabs and several other cars, men pushing carts on the road, and a few shoppers, but no sign of Chad.

Her heart racing, Trudi rushed back into the shop and picked up the phone, jabbing the switch hook until the operator answered. "Ernestine, this is Trudi. Do you have Chad's address handy? It's important." She grabbed a pad and pencil. "240 9th St.? That's over by—yes. Thanks. You're a gem."

"Did you hear about the—?" Ernestine began.

"Sorry, I don't have time," Trudi replied and hung up the phone.

"Is there something wrong?" Catherine asked, standing out of sight.

"I hope not," she said as she locked the shop door and raised her arm to hail a cab. A newer cab pulled up.

"Take me to 240 9th St." she said, as she got in the back.

"That's Chad's house—you know, the cabbie?"

"Yes, how did—"

"It's a small town, Miss Trudi, I know where almost everyone lives. Chad is still with his parents in the old Carson place."

"Can you take me there? I'm in a hurry."

"Of course, Miss," the driver said, flipping down the flag.

"How do you know my name?" she asked.

"As I said, it's a small town; cabbies get to know more than most about what's going on."

"Then you know Chad."

"Sure, we've been buds since we were kids in school."

"Is he reliable? Can I trust him?"

"Is the Pope Catholic? His father is a police sergeant—or was."

"So, you would trust him."

"He owes me money, so yes, I guess I do. He would have joined the force too if he had passed the physical."

For reasons Trudi didn't understand she was still unconvinced. She sat on the edge of the seat while her mind wove a tapestry of treachery, deceit, and betrayal. *This is so unlike him.*

"This is it, Miss. That's his cab. I hope things work out."

"I hope so too. Can you wait?" She glanced over to his hack license. "Thanks, Howie."

"Of course; it's a slow morning."

Trudi sprinted up the stairs to the door. Inside, she could hear people talking quietly. Her knock eventually brought a young woman about her own age to the door. She was wearing a black shawl and gazed back at Trudi through tear-clouded eyes. "May I help you?" she asked softly.

"I'm looking for Chad. I'm Miss Trudi Sanduhr, but I can see this is an inconvenient time. I can come back later."

"Miss Sanduhr? Of course, Chad has spoken about you so often. I'm his sister, Denise. Please come in."

"No, I don't mean to intrude. I just need to talk to him for a moment about an important matter."

"The bag. Yes, please come in. He thought you might be worried about it."

Trudi stepped inside, not knowing what to expect. She was greeted by a dozen distraught faces, tears, and an older man stretched out on the dining room sofa, his arms crossed over his chest. Dressed in a police uniform, the man had the pallor of a corpse. Chad didn't look up from where he knelt beside the body, gripping the man's hand.

Oh my God. Trudi stepped back, but Denise took her hand.

"It's our father. He was shot and killed while trying to stop a robbery at the bank."

"Isn't… wasn't he a police sergeant?" A cold shudder flowed through her body.

Denise nodded.

"How awful," Trudi whispered.

"The doctor said he died ... quickly."

"I'm... I'm so sorry for your loss. Just tell Chad we can talk later."

"No. He insisted that I take this to you without delay," Denise said, discreetly handing her an envelope.

Trudi realized the contained the bank notes. A sense of shame washed over Trudi like a fall storm of guilt, soaking her to the soul. *I was wrong. Chad had only rushed home to console his family.*

"Can I help with the funeral expenses?" Trudi whispered.

"We wouldn't think of it. The chief said they would pay for everything. But thank you for offering—it's most kind."

In a daze, Trudi said her goodbyes and walked back out to the street.

"Something wrong, Miss?" Howie asked.

"Chad's father was... killed by a bank robber."

"My God, that's a... shame. They... were quite close."

Trudi could tell Howie was shaken at the news. "Can you take me back to my shop?" she asked.

"Right away," he said, helping Trudi into the cab.

They had not gone far before Trudi spoke. "Let's stop at the chemist first."

"There's one open on Third; it's on the way."

"Thanks." Trudi tried her best to clean up her face in the side window's reflection and realized it was *she* who had betrayed Chad's trust. She had chosen to believe the worst, based only on the thin evidence that he had rushed off without saying a word. Even then, she felt that was no excuse for what she did. Under slightly different circumstances, she might have reported a theft and asked the police to arrest him. By the time they reached the chemist, she felt no better—still wracked with guilt and grief for his family's loss.

She wasted no time finding the supplies they needed. Near the checkout counter, she saw an ad for a new type of hair dye. She put the bottle on the counter. The radio was broadcasting a news report about the robbery.

"Thinking of going darker?" the girl behind the cash register said with a smile. She was one of those clerks who had an irritating case of perky.

Trudi didn't reply, still listening to the radio whispering a story about a missing family. "Can you turn that up?"

"The hair color? Sure, It's easy. They have lots of other colors and it styles nicely." The girl flipped up her long hair to illustrate her point.

"No. The radio."

"Yes, Miss." The clerk twisted the dial. "…and the diplomat has still not been located. The public is encouraged to keep a lookout for him. He's forty-three, graying hair, and about five ten…"

"That family. It's so tragic," the clerk said, talking over the radio. "I think you would look lovely with red hair."

"I… " Trudi began, still trying to hear the radio.

"But your hair is darling as it is," she said. "I'm surprised you want to change it. I would kill for hair like yours."

Trudi just smiled and as the girl rang her up, Trudi added a few popular movie magazines and the latest editions of the out-of-town newspapers. The magazines might help her houseguests get some styling ideas and makeup tips, and the newspapers might have more details about their disappearance.

Still in a daze, Trudi finally made her way out to the street, happy to be out of earshot of the chatty salesgirl who never seemed to stop talking about nothing. Howie was waiting for her. Once back at the shop, a few customers were congregating at the door.

"Good morning, folks. Mrs. Bradshaw, thanks for being patient." Trudi said, not offering an excuse, and not wanting to betray the privacy of Chad's family. She quickly reopened the shop and caught sight of Freddie hovering behind the bead curtain. She took a moment to give her the sack of supplies as the shoppers ambled in.

"Thanks. This is marvelous," Freddie whispered.

Trudi turned to go back to the shop.

"Is something wrong? Have you been crying?"

Trudi paused. "Let's talk later." She wiped her face with her hanky, put on a brave smile, and returned to the shop and her customers, who seemed unaware of her angst.

Just after one, Trudi closed the shop for lunch. All morning, she had tried to find a way to understand what had made her mistrust Chad. In her mind, she realized how losing Opa had been so different than the vigil she had just interrupted. Chad's entire family and a host of his father's friends had gathered to support, mourn, and celebrate his father's life with him. Looking back, she realized that her own family had either passed away or was missing. She had no one with whom to pray, no one to share her grief, no one to weep with her, no one to help with the final arrangements or assist with the shop—not until Catherine and her family had arrived as if sent from heaven. It had been a challenging, confusing, dark time made brighter with their unexpected arrival.

Clearly, her ordeal was not over. Kneeling behind the shop counter, she put her face in her hands and wept. She didn't know how long she cried, but she looked up when she heard someone approach. She tried to compose herself.

"Trudi, are you well?" Catherine asked softly.

"I'm fine," she said. But she wasn't.

"Really?" Catherine helped her to her feet.

"Not really. I… Chad… my friend. He does my deliveries. His father was… killed… in a bank robbery," she said between sobs.

"Oh my God, my dear. That must be hard on you."

Trudi nodded and looked longingly into Catherine's eyes. A heartbeat later, she was being embraced and found herself weeping against her breast. She missed her own mother, Opa, and Oma. Warm fingers stroked her hair and whispered. "Just cry—let it all go."

And she did.

"Let's just close up for the day," Catherine said.

Trudi felt her head nod as someone led her into the kitchen. Warm hands gave her a cup of tea and encouraged her to sit at the table. Putting her lips to the cup, she looked up where three oddly familiar strangers sat and stood around the table—each with a look of concern. *It's the Saint James.* With darker, shorter hair, and drawn-in beauty spots, it was harder to recognize them. "My… goodness. Someone is good at disguises," Trudi said, regaining her composure.

"Are you feeling better my dear?" Catherine asked.

"Yes. Thanks. I guess I'm not quite through mourning."

"Have you even begun? Have you taken any time to just sit and release your emotions or talked to anyone about your feelings, about your loss?"

Trudi shook her head. "No," she heard herself say. "I just got caught up in the shop, the repairs, the bills, and the daily routine."

"Do you have relatives who could come and help for a few days—until you get back on your feet?"

"No, not really. Granny was an orphan and what's left of Opa's family is living in the old country. I expect they don't even know he has passed."

"And your parents?"

"My mother died in childbirth."

"And—?"

"My father? He disappeared well before I was born—or so I'm told."

"So, you're like me," Catherine said. "An orphan. My parents died of the flu when I was about your age, and my relatives were scattered across the globe like dandelion seeds."

"Perhaps you could adopt an orphan," Trudi heard herself say. Her mind and words were still not making a lot of sense to her. "Did I say that aloud?" she asked.

"Let's get to know each other a bit better before we take any big steps," Catherine said, with a smile. She refilled their teacups.

"Mother was in the theater," Freddie interrupted while admiring her newly dyed and styled hair in a hand mirror. Her long, light brown, straight hair was now much shorter and chocolate brown. "How do you like it?" she asked. "Isn't it cute?" Her new Jean Harlow style was a radical departure from her more conservative chest-length hairdo.

"You and your mother look really different; and Freddie, you look more like a twenty-year-old and less like a naïve schoolgirl. What do you think Officer McNally will say when he sees you?"

"Oh, my Lord," Freddie said. "I hadn't thought about that."

Someone tapped on the shop door. Trudi urged everyone to be quiet as she wiped her face and went to the door. It was Chad's sister, Denise.

Twenty-seven—The Exchange

"Miss Kent? How can I help you?" Trudi asked through the open door.

"It's Denise. Please, all my friends call me Denise."

"Denise, please come in," Trudi said, ushering her inside.

"Thanks. Chad wanted me to help get your British money exchanged. He told me how he does it, so if you still want it changed into dollars, I can do it—or, I think I can."

Trudi felt the envelope pressing against her thigh and her conscience. *The least I can do is trust Chad's sister.* "Of course. Please come through. There is someone I want you to meet."

Denise nodded and followed Trudi into the kitchen where the St. Jameses were folding drop cloths, sweeping up hair, and rinsing bowls. "Folks, this is Denise Kent, Chad's sister. She has offered to get the money exchanged. Would you like to introduce yourselves?"

Catherine smiled and walked over to shake hands with Denise. "I'm Mrs. Mary Bridget," she said in a Scottish brogue. "This is my daughter Frances, and my son Gerald. That's Annie on the floor at your feet. My eldest daughter Fredricka was called away to Boston to stay with her father."

"She's my twin," volunteered Freddie—except she has lighter hair."

Trudi was taken aback by Catherine and Freddie's stories and their new accents. *They're skillful liars. Perhaps the stories they told about their situation was another elaborate lie?* "Miss Kent, we're so grateful that you offered to exchange our money. I would do it myself, but—"

"No need to explain, Mrs. Bridget, it's no trouble at all. I apologize for the confusion."

Trudi smiled when she rationalized that her new house-guests had already conspired to confuse those who would be searching for them. *Now if I can just keep these new aliases straight.*

A few minutes later, they were standing at the shop door. "I really wish I could go with you—in case there's any trouble," Catherine said.

"But you can't. I understand. To keep your husband at bay, this transaction cannot be traced back to you."

Trudi nodded and handed her the envelope. Catherine nodded her approval.

"Please. Count it out," Denise pled.

"I trust you," Trudi said.

"And I trust you, but I would feel more comfortable if we counted it," Denise insisted.

"Opa, my grandfather, taught me to spend my trust sparingly and have faith it won't be betrayed. It's a currency easily spent but far, far harder to earn."

"Your grandfather was a wise man," Denise said, tugging on Trudi's hand, drawing her to the front counter. She took out the banknotes and counted them. Inspecting the bills, she soon shook her head. "I'm glad we did this. I've never seen money like this. "Fifty pounds, right?"

"Yes, £50 should return $233.50 based on the exchange rate in the newspaper."

"Can you show me? I want to be prepared," Denise asked.

"Sure. Of course. Mother showed me." Freddie fetched the financial section and looked up the exchange rate. "Yes, 4.67 dollars per pound," she said, circling the rate.

"But banks don't always exchange at the published rate," Catherine said. "They often reduce the valuation to feed their bottom line. But it should be close."

Denise's face wilted as she steadied herself on the counter. She set the envelope down on the counter as if it were a fine crystal wineglass.

"What's wrong?" asked Trudi, touching her hand.

"It's… it's so *complicated*. I've never seen that much money in one place in my whole life—much less held it in my hand."

"That settles it. I'll go with you," Trudi and Freddie said at once.

"I think that's wise. It *is* a lot of responsibility," Catherine said.

"But you can't," Denise protested, her lip quivering.

"While we probably shouldn't go into the bank, we can stay in the cab and remain nearby. If you have any trouble at all, we'll come to the rescue."

"Are you sure?" Denise said. "That would be so comforting."

"Of course. Let's go."

"What time is it?" Denise asked.

Trudi smiled. "Honey, you're in a clock shop."

Denise looked up at one of the clocks. "One forty—" She was interrupted by the clocks striking the three-quarter-hour.

"Five," Trudi said.

"Wait," Freddie began. "I just thought of something. The bank was just robbed. Will they be open?"

"I'll ask Ernestine. She'll know." Trudi picked up the phone and talked to the operator. "Great, thanks," she said after a brief exchange. "They've decided to open anyway— something about being afraid of a run if they close unexpectedly."

Once they were outside, Trudi, Freddie, and Denise settled into a cab and found Howie driving.

"Howie, we meet again. Can you take us to the bank?"

"Ah… sure, Miss Trudi," he said as he got the cab and meter started. He turned back to Denise. "I'm so sorry for your loss. How are you all holding up?"

"Hour-by-hour Howie. Thanks," Denise said.

Trudi suddenly realized that she should never have accepted Denise's offer. There was too much on her mind. "Denise, I feel awful asking you to do this," she said softly. "And going back to the bank…"

Freddie didn't say a word.

"I… I must try to be brave and keep living my life," Denise said. "Actually, it's a blessing. I needed to get out of the house. The grief was smothering me, and if I can do this to help Chad, so much the better. Don't worry about me."

"Are you sure? We can figure out another way, someone else to do the exchange," Freddie said. "…or I could go in."

"No, I've thought about it quite a bit. I want to help to… let's just do this."

"If you're sure," Trudi said.

Denise nodded.

As they pulled out on Main, Howie looked up in the mirror. "Have they found who robbed the bank?"

"And killed my father?" Denise answered.

"And, yeah. Killed your… father."

"Not yet, but they have some leads. There were several witnesses who gave good descriptions. He was masked, so they didn't see his face, but they're watching the highway, the train station and the port; searching, and interviewing everyone leaving town."

"I expected as much," Howie said.

"We think he's just laying low, going about his day as if nothing had happened. All the shopkeepers know to report anyone with a lot of extra spending money."

Howie kept his eyes on the road.

"They'll catch him. I know they will," Denise said.

After several minutes of silence, the three women quietly went over their plans and the signal to use if Denise sensed trouble. "So, I pull my ear, like this?" she asked quietly, tugging her left earlobe.

"That's it. Simple," Freddie assured her.

"We're here," Trudi said as they pulled up in front of the bank. "Howie, can you park and wait here?"

"I… guess. For a while, Miss, at least until the cop shows up. They're a bit nervous about us hanging around outside the bank even *before* the robbery."

Denise walked up to the bank. The guard held the door open for her and greeted her by name. They had a brief exchange and she moved on to the first cashier.

"There she is—at the third counter," Freddie said.

"Do you think she can do it?" Howie asked.

"I hope so. She was as nervous as a new kid at school; for good reason."

"She's shaking her head. She's in trouble. I'm going," Trudi said.

"Wait. Give her a chance," Freddie held her arm as they watched Denise through the window.

"Good morning, ladies," someone said

Apparently, none of them had seen Officer O'Malley approach.

"Howie? You know it's against the law to park here in front of the bank. Wait. Oh, Miss Trudi, I didn't see you back there, but who is that with you?"

Trudi's stomach turned over, but before panic set in and she could reply, Freddie stuck her head out the window. "I'm a friend of Miss Sanduhr," she began in her Scottish brogue.

"Miss Frances Bridget. Can't we linger here for a few minutes officer? We're waiting for Miss Kent—Chad's sister."

"Miss, would you both please step out of the cab?"

"Why? What for?" she began.

Trudi motioned for her to comply and got out to join Freddie at the curb. She took her hand and gently squeezed.

"I'm a bit puzzled, Miss Sanduhr, your friend here looks most familiar. I know I've seen her before, but with light brown hair and not cut like… that," the officer said, his brow curling.

"Let me handle this," Freddie whispered. "Keep an eye on Denise." Trudi nodded.

❧❧❧

Freddie was surprised Officer O'Malley had seen through her disguise as if it were a paper mask. Taking a chance on their budding relationship, she decided to try to enlist the officer's help. She also didn't want to chance having her troubles spill over on Trudi or Denise.

"Can we speak frankly?" she said sweetly.

"Of course, Miss. That's usually best," O'Malley said, not taking his eyes off the cab.

"I'm not Frances Bridget."

"I know. What you don't know, is that I recognized you at once. You have the same eyes as a young lady I detained not so long ago—a young lady who never gave me her full name."

"My eyes? You recognized my eyes? How remarkable," Freddie said with a shy smile, deflecting the attempt to learn her name.

"Every eye is different—even left to right—unique to each person. My mother says our eyes are windows to the soul."

"Fascinating," she said, oozing charm.

William Vaughn

"And eyes as blue, as pretty as the sky on a clear winter day, would be impossible to forget," he said with a smile.

He's flirting.

"I didn't get your name when I dropped you off at the shop. I better not make that mistake again or my sergeant will have me doing beats in Shantytown."

"My name… they call me Freddie."

"Is that how you sign your name Miss 'Freddie'?"

"Freddie. Fredricka St. James," she said softly. *I've got to trust someone.*

"I thought so."

"I suppose that means you know we're the family they keep blabbering about in the newspapers."

"I do. I've known from the beginning. All of us knew."

"I also suppose that means I have to return with you to the station."

"Have you broken any laws more serious than riding in an illegally parked cab?"

"No, but…"

"I looked into your family—quietly, mind you—and discovered that you're not wanted by the authorities. While half the lawmen and all of the newspapers in the world are looking for you all, they say it's only to ensure your safety and report on your location."

"It's not that simple," Freddie said.

"I didn't think it was. My dad taught me that nothing is as simple as some would make it or like it to be."

"There are people out there who wish to do us harm—we think my family, including my father, are in mortal danger. I suspect these foreign elements want to use us as leverage to influence my father or silence him."

"These are especially dangerous times in Europe, and I expect here too before long."

"You're not only a handsome young man, but you're smart as well," Freddie said, turning her charm knob a notch higher.

"Freddie?" Trudi said, nodding toward the bank window.

Freddie turned to see Denise tugging on her earlobe. She was still standing at the clerk's desk with a panicked look on her face. "Officer, I wonder if you could intervene on my behalf… again."

"In what manner? Wait. Don't tell me. It's that English money again."

"Brilliant. We looked up the correct exchange rate for the money and it appears my friend is having trouble with the clerk."

Officer O'Malley turned to see Denise still madly tugging at her ear. "I see. Perhaps I *can* be of assistance. I suggest you remain here."

Howie, Freddie, and Trudi watched as the officer entered the bank and walked straight past the guard and to the third teller cage. In a single motion he managed to catch Denise who all but fainted as he approached. As if viewing a silent movie without the Wurlitzer accompaniment, Freddie watched as O'Malley calmed Denise and interact with the clerk, whose face drained of color. A moment later, a man in an expensive suit appeared and shooed the clerk aside with an ominous glare. Their body language, nods, and gestures told Freddie they were in luck. After warm handshakes and an exchange of pleasantries and cash, Officer O'Malley returned to the curb with Denise on his arm.

"What happened?" Freddie asked.

"Well, the clerk tried to *cheat* me," Denise began. "He was going to give me only $37 for the banknotes. *$37.* I knew that wasn't right, but he insisted a woman would not know better than a bank clerk."

Freddie could feel her fists tighten into balls. "And *then*?"

"Well, he said I should just take the $37 and go, or he would call the police. That's when I began tugging on my earlobe."

"That stronzo," Freddie murmured.

Trudi looked at her with a puzzled expression.

"Don't ask," Freddie said.

"When the officer showed up, I nearly fainted," Denise continued. "I was terrified. My father would have been mortified if I had been arrested."

"You're Sergeant Kent's daughter?" Officer O'Malley asked.

"Yes. Yes, I am. Did you know him?"

"Of course. He was my training officer. He was a fine man. I'm so sorry for your loss."

"Thank you, officer, you've been especially kind."

"So, what happened then?" Trudi asked.

"I explained what was going on to the officer and he summoned the bank manager—Mr. Lefkowitz. He came over and a moment later, he had uncovered the clerk's scam. Apparently, it had not been the first time that clerk had been caught, but Mr. Lefkowitz made sure I got the right amount. We all counted it out *twice*. $233.50," Denise said, handing Freddie an envelope with the crisp bills and change. At Denise's insistence, they counted it together. It was all there.

Freddie turned to thank Officer O'Malley, but he was gone. Looking inside the bank, she saw him talking to Mr. Lefkowitz and taking notes. Freddie's mind raced forward and realized that the officer might arrest the clerk for fraud. If he did, that would mean more trips to the police station for everyone, more questions, and more exposure. "I think we should return to the shop," she said, opening the cab door. "Howie, you ready to take us back?"

"Yes. Let's go," Howie said, not taking his eyes off the officer.

"So, you're not Frances," Denise said quietly as they got in the cab.

"Not really. Everyone calls me Freddie."

"I know. My brother told me everything. He's known all along."

"It *is* a small town," Freddie said. *That's what I'm afraid of.*

❧❧❧

Once they arrived back at the shop, they had no sooner stepped inside before the sound of police sirens shredded the quiet. A squad car careened around the corner and blocked the street as another came up from the other direction, surrounding Howie's cab. Even from inside, they could hear the police demand that Howie get out with his hands up.

"My God," Denise said. "What's going on?"

Trudi was stunned, while Freddie stood there speechless.

Howie hesitated for a moment, his hand no longer on the wheel, but his cab's motor was still running.

"Don't even think about it, Howie. If you want to live, keep your hands in plain sight," someone shouted.

Trudi held her breath and prayed. *Don't do anything stupid. Anyone.*

Howie slowly reached out the window and opened the door from the outside. A swarm of officers forced him to the ground and handcuffed him.

As Trudi and the others watched, Catherine appeared from the back rooms, but turned around immediately, taking Annie back toward the kitchen.

"I wanna see too!" Annie cried.

"I'll tell you all about it later, hon," Freddie said over her shoulder.

It wasn't long before the police found a flour sack containing a few bundles of bank notes and a gun.

"They found a *gun*. We were just in that cab. Oh my God," Trudi said.

"Four rounds fired. Two left," Officer McNally said, inspecting the gun with his fingertips.

"Where's the rest of the loot, Howie?" another policeman demanded.

"Who'd you split it with?" said another.

"It will go easier on you if you tell the truth—while you still can."

Howie just stood in the street, his face cast in stone, his hands behind him handcuffed. He looked over at Trudi and Freddie as if *they* had betrayed him.

"Get him and his hack back to the station," Sergeant Driscoll said.

"I know that sergeant from the station," Freddie said.

"The one with the sweet roll?" Trudi asked.

Freddie nodded as Officer McNally joined them in the shop, hat in hand. "I'm sorry you had to see that," he said. "I thought I spotted the butt of his gun on the floor when I first approached the car, but I didn't want you ladies to be put in jeopardy, so I had the bank manager call the station to set up the capture after he dropped you off."

"He was quite brazen to keep driving his cab," Trudi said. "Especially with the evidence stuffed under the seat."

"I expect he figured that if he suddenly left town, everyone would put two and two together and realize it was him."

"Was that all of the stolen money?" Denise asked.

"No. Only about a hundred bucks—one packet of new ones. The thieves took over a thousand according to the bank manager. Someone is still holding the rest."

"Or running like the wind," Freddie said.

"That would be hard, as the town was cordoned off within minutes of the robbery," McNally said.

"Unless he lives here in town," Trudi said.

"We'll catch him," the officer said, returning to duty.

The now-shaken young ladies retreated into the kitchen where Catherine stood waiting. It didn't take long for the trio to tell the entire story, including the kerfuffle at the bank.

"And you're all right?" she asked.

"Yes, my heart is still beating like a greyhound's," Denise said. "…but Chad and my mom will be glad they found the robber."

"And here is your money," Freddie said, handing Catherine the bank envelope.

"Shall we count it?" Denise asked.

"I trust you," Catherine said, putting the envelope in her enormous purse. "Let's have a cup of tea and relax for a few minutes to unwind. It's been quite a morning."

No one objected, except Annie who wanted to hear the story again… and again.

Twenty-eight—The Message

"*I* simply *must* have more clothes to wear," Freddie moaned while she and Trudi washed their delicates in the dishpan the next morning. "I've had to wash my only under-things so many times, they're nearly falling apart," Freddie continued, wringing out her bra. "…and this skirt and top are still stained and tattered from the lifeboat *excursion*. It's not fair to keep borrowing your things."

"I don't mind really, and since you're helping with the laundry—" Trudi began.

"Yes. You're right," Catherine interrupted. "We all need new things, from the skin up. But it's dangerous for us to be seen all over town shopping. What if someone or the local police figures out who we are?"

"Mom, you weren't *listening*. When I came home the first day, Sean had already figured it out. He's exceptionally bright."

"Sean?"

"Officer McNally. They all know—at least the police know. And Sean says they aren't telling anyone, and the newspapers have stopped carrying our story on the front page. As far as they're concerned, we're dead."

"Even so, we shouldn't press our luck."

"Then only *I* will go. I know your and Annie's sizes, and I can guess at George's. Just make a list. I know where the shops are; I found them on the first day. I'll have American money this time and—"

"I'll go with you," Trudi volunteered. "To iron out any wrinkles. I need a few things too. I'm *so* tired of this outfit Oma chose for me before I had a shape."

"Then it's settled. Trudi and I will go this morning," Freddie said with an excited aura about her. *Free again.*

"Wait. Are the shops open on Sunday?" Catherine asked.

"Of course, they open just after church," Trudi said. "We open at one. This gives me a chance to catch up on my chores."

"I want to go," Annie said, appearing from underneath the table with Katie dangling under her arm.

"Not this time," Freddie said, checking under the table for elven clothing. "We have a lot to do, and you'll get tired."

"No," Catherine said. "It would be best if you took Annie along so I can watch the shop without her getting underfoot."

"What about someone recognizing you?"

"While that ship might have sailed, I can maintain that I'm Mary Charlotte Bridget, Trudi's distant cousin from Scotland. That explains the British money and makes sense."

Trudi thought for a moment but could not find any gears that did not mesh in her story. "Sure. Cousin Bridget."

Freddie plopped in the chair across from her mother. "Moooom." Her vision of a carefree girls' day with a new friend had been shattered.

"It will be fun," Trudi said. "Let's take her. I've never had a little sister to mind."

"You don't know Annie."

"I do know she's very well-behaved for someone her age. She'll be fine."

"All right, all right. What should we get?" Freddie asked.

"Toys, dollies, and cupcakes," Annie squealed.

"If you're a good girl. I saw some cute dresses in the magazines you bought and in the newspaper ads."

Freddie and Trudi retreated into their own world where they planned what stores to try and where to go to lunch.

Annie did her best to be included as she hovered around the two teens planning their outing. Freddie finally came up for air with a question: "How much can we spend?"

"Well, I think four or five dollars should be more than enough," Catherine said. "And don't forget about George. He's going to need a new pair of dress slacks, a pair of denim trousers, a few shirts, and of course, new socks and underwear."

"You want me to buy boy's *underwear*?" Freddie asked. "Really? Oh, I *couldn't*. I would be mortified."

"Oh, I bought Opa's underwear for years and all his suits and clothes after Oma died. I know just the place."

A few minutes later, the list was made and amended a half-dozen times. "Wait," said Trudi. "We should invite Denise. She might like the diversion."

"What a great idea," Freddie said. "We could get her a thank-you gift."

"I'll call her." Trudi picked up the phone. "Ernestine? Can you ring Chad for me? Yes, his home." A moment later, someone picked up. "Denise? This is Trudi. Yes, fine. How are you? Up for a shopping jaunt and lunch? Freddie is paying," she said jokingly. Freddie nodded and gave a thumbs-up. "Oh. I hope she gets to feeling better. Perhaps another time."

A moment later, Trudi hung up with a frown. "She has to take care of her mom. She can't go."

"That's a shame. Mother, we're off," Freddie said over her shoulder, and the girls were off with a warmly bundled Annie in tow.

❧❧❧

Thinking about the last few minutes, Catherine recalled it wasn't the first time her teenage daughter wanted to go shopping with a friend. It was one of Freddie's favorite pastimes.

She had studied Trudi and Freddie as they cleaned up after breakfast and realized how similar they were in some ways, and different in others. One raised as an orphan in a small town, naïve, yet worldly. Her daughter raised in privileged society, sure of herself, but frail in other ways. *Sisters from another mother.*

"Thank you, Mrs. Vigoureux. I know you'll love that music box. Come again," Catherine said as she closed and locked the shop door. Trudi had spoken of Mrs. Vigoureux's generosity. She was a delightful person and would have loved to chat, but the time was getting short.

Now that the clock shop was finally empty, Catherine quickly fetched her traveling bag and retreated to the kitchen. Unsnapping a false compartment, she extracted what looked like a large family Bible. Opening it revealed dials, switches, and a Morse key. She plugged in a glass tube, strung a length of wire across the room, and plugged the 'book' into an electrical outlet. Putting a headset over one ear, she threw a switch and watched the tube glow as she listened. She heard nothing but the rush of static.

Good. It's working.

Checking her watch, she waited, and at the appointed time, she threw the transmit switch. The book began to hum as she tapped out a quick sequence on the key before switching to receive. Again, the headset hissed random static that sounded like a leaking steam pipe.

Nothing.

She waited another ten seconds, threw the switch again, repeated the code sequence, and switched to receive.

Nothing. It's the right time. It has to work.

After the fourth attempt, her heart leapt when a faint series of tones answered her.

There he is.

Carefully twisting a knob, she tuned the receiver to better hear the carrier signal. Tapping on her key, she sent another brief series of tones. To anyone listening, these noises would not mean a thing—even an experienced radiotelegrapher might recognize dots and dashes, but the code was not Morse—it was one of her own—their own. Only two people in the world knew it: Catherine and one other person: her husband. Another long series of tones were followed in quick succession. While others might hear individual dots and dashes, she recognized each word, each pause, each nuance. A thin smile crossed her face and a tear rolled down her cheek. She could tell it was him—if only by the way his fingers operated his code key—his 'hand.' She imagined reaching out to touch his finger tapping the key.

He's not coming. Not yet. But alive.

Deciphering the last bit of code in her head, it said "Stay where you are. Help is nearby. I love you. Your Saint."

Hearing someone rap on the shop door, she brushed away her tears and scrambled to conceal the transmitter. She quickly checked on George before returning to the shop.

༺༺༺

"Do you think she's a spy?" Martine asked, ducking back inside the tunnel that came out in the kitchen.

"She might be. But on which side?" Glenda asked.

"Does it matter?"

"It does, if she's helping Hitler. That uman has already done so many evil things."

"All umans do evil," Martine said.

"Do they? Miss Trudi is not evil. The new family seems nice and generous to a fault."

"Except for that Annie. Just ask Mrs. Framingham."

"Annie is a yenesem. She had no idea Mrs. Framingham was a living creature. She didn't hurt anything but her pride."

Martine stared at her for a long moment. "You're right. They could have squished us or destroyed the whole village."

"Not all umans are bad," Glenda said.

"No. Not all. But some."

"What was that box? The one with the glowing glass?"

"I don't know, but it made her cry."

"I'll go back and check on the boy. Alred seems worried about him."

Twenty-nine—The Market

$\mathscr{I}$t was a lovely crisp day, so Trudi, Freddie, and Annie decided to walk up the hill toward the market square instead of taking a cab. In hindsight, Freddie realized that was their first mistake. On the way up, she was reminded of how nice it was to have a friend almost her age to share her secrets and discuss boys they met along the way. Trudi made it abundantly clear she felt the same.

"Don't walk so fast," Annie pleaded.

"It's not *all* uphill, sweetie," Trudi said, pausing long enough to take Annie's hand.

Freddie took Annie's other hand as they continued at a bit slower pace. "Too tall," Freddie said softly as a boy their age approached on the other side of the narrow street.

"All boys are tall, and yucky," Annie said.

"Oh, I like them tall," Trudi whispered, giving the boy a smile. "Hi, Dan," she said in passing.

"Hi, Trudi, who's your friend?" the young man said, as he slowed.

"My cousin. Call me," Trudi said over her shoulder.

"You know what they say about tall boys?" Freddie asked.

"Yeah. Big…"

"Feet," Freddie laughed.

"Nice day, ladies," said someone walking up from behind.

Freddie recognized Officer O'Malley's voice. *Sean.* She stopped and smiled. "Top of the mornin' to you officer," she said with a terrible Irish accent.

"Off to take advantage of the Sunday Christmas sales?"

"That we are," Trudi said.

"I hope you brought real money this time."

"Indeed, we did. We also have these gold doubloons and pieces of eight rattling around in my purse," Freddie said, shaking her handbag.

"Stay out of trouble, ladies," the officer cautioned with a smile.

"Officer, might I ask you another small favor?" Freddie asked.

"And what would that be?"

"When I visited your fine accommodation, I encountered a man with an unusual tattoo, an anchor and—"

"A snake. Yes, I recall the man. What do you need to know?"

"Oh, I would… just like to… thank him. Yes, thank him for his kindness to me. There's no telling how long I would have laid on the floor unconscious if it were not for him alerting you of my distress."

"I see. I'll inquire at the station. Perhaps they can supply his current lodgings, but I expect he's been encouraged to leave town."

"Was he a vagrant or ne'er-do-well?"

"That was unclear, but by the time the word came down to release him, I don't know that any charges had been filed."

"So, they let him go?"

"I expect so. I have not seen him since."

Freddie's face must have shown her disappointment as the officer continued to probe her interest in the man. "I just wanted to thank him. Nothing more, other than to see that he had a healthy meal."

"I'll inquire as to his current situation."

"Thank you again, Officer O'Malley. Have a good day."

"Sean. My friends call me Sean."

"Thank you, *Sean*. We need to get our shopping done." Annie was already tugging on her sister's hand, urging them to keep walking toward a gayly lit toy store up ahead.

"You all have a good day as well. I'll come by the shop if I hear any news."

"You may call *any* time, Sean," Freddie said as they walked on toward the market square.

"He really likes you," Trudi confided.

"I think he likes *you* better," Freddie said. "He's so cute."

"What makes you say that?"

"His eyes. He never missed a chance to steal a glance your way."

The rest of the morning further cemented the friendship Freddie and Trudi had created while Annie was… Annie. By early afternoon, as their arms were loaded with packages and shopping bags dangled from every arm, Chad drove by in his cab.

"Do you ladies need help?" he asked through the window.

"Oh, yes. You're a Godsend, Chad. I'm *so* glad to see you working again," Trudi said.

"Yes, Miss Trudi. I'm at your service—now that I know you're flush."

"Flush?" Trudi asked.

"I heard about that trip to the bank from my sister. She mentioned you might need help shopping—*she's your angel.*"

"That's sweet. Trudi, we have an aspiring businessman here," Freddie said. "Could you follow along and carry the packages as we shop? We have several more stops to make. Of course, I'll pay for your time."

"Sure," he said, hopping out and loading the trunk with the boxes and bags they had already bought.

"How are you and the family doing?" Trudi asked quietly, touching Chad's arm.

"I was shocked to hear about Howie. I've known him all my life and I can't believe he would…"

"Shoot someone? Me neither. He seemed like a… honest, trustworthy, helpful, person, but not a bank robber."

"He's no saint, but he's not a killer," Chad said.

"No. Not a killer. There must be more to this than it appears."

"I went down to the jail," Chad began. "They let me chat for a few minutes. Howie said he doesn't know where the gun and money came from. I believe him."

"Did someone identify him? One of the bank customers or clerks?"

"No, the robber was masked and pretty average. Their description could match Howie or any of a hundred men in town and some of the women."

"Does he have an alibi? Where was he at the time of the robbery?"

"Howie said he was across town."

"Any way to prove that?" Freddie asked.

"Apparently, not. But they said the man ran out of the bank and fled on foot. My father was there to make a deposit and tried to stop the robber. The coward shot him without warning. Everyone was too scared to follow. The inspector thinks Howie could have picked him up somewhere nearby."

"Maybe the robber left the gun and some of the money behind just to make Howie look guilty," Trudi said, still being tugged along by Annie.

"So, the real killer might still be out there," Freddie said.

"Or Howie is lying," Chad said softly.

At this point, Annie was able to drag Trudi away toward another store that had caught her eye.

"How are your mom and Denise holding up?" Freddie asked.

"We're still a bit numb, but being a policeman's family, it's something we thought we were prepared to deal with. We were wrong. And to find out it may be a friend… we're pretty shattered."

"I'm so sorry for your loss—we all are. Let's hope it wasn't Howie."

"Thanks. Can I just tag along as you shop? I could use the company."

"Sure. Of course, but could you do me a favor?" Freddie asked.

"Of course, Miss. Anything."

"Can you buy my brother some underwear, t-shirts, and socks? He's a bit smaller than you but…"

"Underwear? You want me to buy boy's underwear."

"If you don't mind. If you don't think it's too… forward."

Chad smiled and blushed. "I know just the place. Keep shopping and I'll be right back. How many pairs?"

"As many as a couple of dollars will buy. And whatever else you think a teenage boy would like to wear—shirts, slacks, or maybe a nice sweater." She handed him two one-dollar bills.

"Fine, I'll be back as soon as I can."

Freddie's stomach turned over when she saw the cab disappear around the corner with all their packages and her mom's money. *I know better than to trust strangers.*

"Where's Chad?" Trudi asked, coming out of the shop, another bundle tucked under her arm and Annie in tow.

"I sent him off to buy George's socks, underwear, and a few shirts."

"My, you *are* trusting for a big-city girl," Trudi said.

"He'll be back in a few minutes," Freddie said. *I hope.*

"You have nothing to worry about. *Nothing,*" Trudi said.

"Can… may I have a cupcake?" Annie asked. "…Please."

"Since you asked so nicely, I think we can follow our noses toward that bake shop," her big sister said.

"I think that's a great idea. I get kinda lightheaded when I put off eating," Trudi said, trying to keep Annie from sprinting away. They followed Annie into one of Trudi's favorite bakeries.

"Me too. I told you about fainting in the police station," Freddie said, taking a bite out of a doughnut. A rim of sugar gave her a confectioner's mustache.

"You did. I expect there's more to that story than you shared within earshot of your mom."

Freddie smiled. "There is." At this point, Freddie told the whole story, including the scene with the German pastry vendor.

"Freddie, what's it like to have a mom and dad?" Trudi asked softly. "I know I had Oma, and Opa, but I never knew my mom and dad. I've always wondered what it would be like to be guided along with folks who look after you, and gently cushion your path through life."

Freddie closed her eyes and tried not to cry. She reached over and laid her hand on Trudi's. "It's… wonderful, and… challenging. While it's wonderful to be unconditionally loved and pampered, it's challenging to get them to let me go, make mistakes, and learn on my own."

"Can I have another… may I have another?" Annie interrupted.

"Later. We need to save some for George and Chad," Freddie said, using her mom voice.

"And that's something else I've missed. When I have kids one day, I'll want to know how best to raise them. You have such a good role model. Your mom is great. I wish she were mine."

"Be careful of what you wish for," Freddie said. "She can be very controlling and strict at times. But your grandparents seem to have done a great job."

Trudi smiled. "There he is," she said, pointing out the window.

Freddie rushed out to flag Chad's cab and asked him to come inside to share the sweet pastries.

"Your change, Miss," Chad said, handing her twelve cents. "I hope I got the right sizes. The receipt is in the package if you want to exchange anything. I would be happy to do it for you."

Looking over his selections, Freddie thanked him profusely and gave him a brief hug. "Thanks again, you saved me from mortal embarrassment. Keep the change."

"Thanks, and think nothing of it."

With Freddie sitting beside Trudi, they all chatted about their purchases and Frau Becker, the pastry huckster. At one point when Chad was distracted, Trudi leaned in and whispered. "You have another conquest. I'm having trouble keeping up!"

"He's all yours. I can tell," Freddie whispered. "I may be new, but his heart is in your hands."

"It's getting late. Shouldn't we be getting Miss Trudi, you, and this rambunctious monkey home before her sugar high wears off?" Chad said.

"You're right. Lead the way to our chariot," Freddie said.

Exhausted, the shopping expedition finally arrived back at the shop in Chad's cab loaded to the gunnels with packages and boxes. Freddie spent the last of the money paying Chad for the use of his cab, including a generous tip.

"Thanks, ladies. That was appreciated. I needed a distraction in my life just now," Chad said in parting.

"How did it go?" Catherine asked as she helped sort through the packages on the kitchen table. "It looks like you got everything and a bit more…"

"It was… fun. It was so good to get outside and… fun. Just fun."

"I see you got George's underwear. These will do fine," she said, looking through the bundle. "Wait. What's this? I think this is for you, Freddie." She handed her a note written on the butcher paper used to wrap the shirts.

Freddie opened the note and read it to herself.

Miss Freddie, thanks for trusting me. Call if you would like to go to a movie and dinner some evening. Chad

Freddie blushed and tucked the note in her top. It occurred to her that Trudi liked Chad. He was taken, as far as she was concerned.

"What was that?" Catherine asked. "No. You don't have to tell me. Can you put Annie down when you take your things upstairs?"

"Can I check on George first?" she asked.

"I just looked in on him. He's resting comfortably for once, but his temperature is up a bit."

"Okay, come on Miss Annie, let's go upstairs for a nap."

Strangely enough, Annie did not protest but had to be carried the last few steps. Freddie helped her go potty, laid her in bed, took off her shoes, and covered her with a blanket. Trudi stood in the doorway gazing longingly at the tender scene.

"Trudi, can you come to my room? I want to show you something," Freddie asked.

When they were alone, Freddie showed her the note.

"I told you he was sweet on you," Trudi said. Her face betrayed her disappointment.

"He's just in love with my money."

"I'm sure that's it," Trudi laughed.

"Do you ever wear makeup?" Freddie asked, freshening her lipstick.

"Oma never did and Opa didn't approve, so no. I'm afraid not."

"Do you want me to show you? I've been wearing it for just ages."

Trudi nodded. "Just don't go crazy. I don't want to look like one of the former… residents."

"The seamstresses?" she replied. "You won't. It doesn't take much at all if you do it right. I just bought the right brushes and the cosmetics my mom uses. We share all of it. She's great at makeup and disguises."

"What about perfume?" Trudi asked, taking a whiff of an unopened bottle of scent Freddie had chosen.

"It takes just a puff. Too much and you risk smelling like you're trying too hard."

"Freddie…" Trudi said, looking her in the eye. "This has been the happiest day I've had in a long, long time."

"Me too," Freddie said, taking her hand.

"It's nice to finally have a friend, a sister."

Freddie reached out and embraced her new friend. "Let's try on that new dress. I can't wait to see it on you."

"Do you think Chad will like it?"

"Or Sean?"

Thirty—The Count

*A*n elderly man, calling himself Count Rudolph von Schlager, sat alone at his desk studying the obituaries by the light of a desk lamp. His thin-lipped grin exposed crooked, tea-stained teeth. *Yes. It's time. She won't know what hit her.*

"Parkins!" he bellowed, rousting the pigeons dozing on the windowsill. He listened for footsteps but heard nothing. "Parkins!" *Where is that fool?* A moment later, he laid down the paper, crossed the room, and opened the office door. Peering out, he saw no sign of anyone or any light burning in the corridor or adjoining rooms. Listening intently, he was startled by the old clock striking ten. *That slacker must have gone to bed. The nerve of that ingrate. He knew I was working late.*

The Count climbed the narrow staircase and surprised Parkins in the corridor outside his one-room bedchamber. The middle-aged man, dressed in a gray ankle-length night-shirt and knit cap, came to a stop like an army private when meeting his captain.

"Sir? Is there something I can do for you?" he said, fighting off a yawn.

"I need you to foreclose on a tenant."

"Tonight? Sir, it's after ten."

"Not tonight, you idiot. At first light."

"Of course, sir."

"I'll leave the details on your desk. See to it and report back to me when you return."

"Of course, sir. Will that be all?"

"Why is it as cold as a spinster's tomb up here?"

"You're too cheap to heat these rooms… sir," the man whispered to himself knowing that his employer was hard of hearing.

"How's that?" The count cupped his ear.

"We're economizing on coal, sir."

"Ah. Rightly so. I'll speak to you in the morning."

"Of course, sir. If that will be all…"

ৰৰৰ

As the animated clock in the town square struck seven, kickstarting the town on another nearly winter day, Henry P. Parkins, a man about forty who looked a decade older, tied his neatly polished shoes and inspected himself in the mirror. He straightened his tie for the third time, his collar for the fifth time, and finished by dusting invisible specks from his lapels. The person he saw in the mirror wasn't happy. *A job is a job.* His heavy sigh fogged the mirror. It was mornings like this when he had to serve papers on some poor wretch, that he realized that he had sold his soul to the Devil. He ate a day-old boiled egg he had kept cool on the windowsill and followed it with the crusty end cut from a baguette.

Collecting up a stack of legal papers, he looked over the address and details of the contract. It seemed his employer had paid the past-due taxes on another property in the old section of town just above the bay. Thanks to a law that The Count and his political friends had pushed through the Council, he could take possession of the building and its contents with virtually no notice. He slid the papers into a worn leather case—flipping the cover closed and tucking it under his arm in a single motion.

As the city shuffled to its feet like a hobo who had decided to endure another day, he hailed a cab. He knew he would arrive at the property before it opened, but experience had told him it might be the only time he could be able to talk with the owner in private.

"Who's the victim this morning, Mr. Parkins?" the cab driver asked through the window.

Parkins handed him a slip of paper with the address.

"Not this cabbie, fella. Get someone else to take you to torture that sweet kid." The cab roared off, the slip of paper blowing skyward in the draft.

Parkins had known better than to tell a driver the actual address of his next foreclosure, and his momentary lapse had cost him a ride. Not saying a word, he walked toward the nearby cab stand, but the driver had arrived ahead of him and both drivers refused to take him across town. He would have to walk the three miles. *At least it's not raining.*

As he passed the first block, the skies parted and a deluge of sleet began pelting him in earnest, as if sent by the Furies to deter him. He fussed with his old umbrella, but by the time he got it partially open, he was soaked to the skin. He tossed it in the gutter where it floated away with the rest of the litter.

A long, cold walk later, Parkins arrived at a small shop with lace curtains and several antique clocks in the window decorated with Christmas lights and tinsel. The aging building looked like it dated back to the first settlers in this forgotten backwater. Looking more like a stone fortress than a suitable place for a quaint shop, he wondered why The Count would be remotely interested in the property. The sign on the door said "Closed" so he had no choice but to wait when he saw the smaller sign that showed the hours. "9 AM to 5 PM weekdays and Saturdays until noon." Checking his pocket watch, he realized he had another thirty minutes to wait. He looked for a nearby café or sheltered lobby to wait. Finding none, he decided to simply stand under the narrow eave to catalogue his fate. He accepted with some degree of certainty that if he lost his job working for the Count, he would be joining the nameless, homeless wanderers who huddled in the sheltered stairways and doorways all over town. He had encountered several on his long hike across town. *There go I but by the grace of…The Count.*

Mr. Parkins' lips were the color of blueberries when he spotted a light in the back of the shop. He tapped on the doorframe. "I nnnneed to speak to Missss Sanduhr," he stuttered, loud enough to be heard through the glass and draw the attention of a woman hiding behind a window shade across the street. A long minute later, a young woman pushing back bedraggled hair came to the door.

"Can you come back at nine?" the woman pleaded through the glass, holding up nine fingers. "We're closed."

Parkins held the papers against the wet glass. "Notice to Vacate" was written in large script across the top. "It's important."

Trudi's countenance changed from mild irritation to a witch's whisker short of anger. Her eyes narrowed as she stared back at the gangly skeleton of a man like a woman scowls at a street masher. She showed no sign of opening the door.

"Miss, I… I don't have alllll dayyyy," Parkins said, shivering out the words. He again motioned for her to unlock the door. She did not comply. Realizing he would have to conduct his business from this side of the door and using as much compassion as a butcher dispatching a steer at a packing plant, Parkins introduced himself and his employer from where he stood. "Miss Trudi Sanduhr, you have seven days to vacate these premises."

Decades of experience had purged Parkins of any attachment to the parties with whom he dealt—if he once had any empathy, it had deadened long ago by thick callouses on his soul. At times like this, he wondered if he ever had any. These were simply clients, names, and property descriptions, like old, tired horses to slaughter, their carcasses dissected, their meat ground into dog food, and their hooves rendered into glue. Like it or not, it was his job.

"According to the terms of the contract, a week from to-day we take possession of these premises," he said with the compassion of a hangman. He shoved a copy of the eviction notice through the mail slot, where it fell at the young woman's feet. Trudi picked it up but did not try to read it—her eyes locked on the predator on the other side of the glass.

"A week? Are you serious? My grandfather has just passed. He—" she all but screamed.

"Quite serious, Miss Sanduhr," Parkins interrupted. "My employer has instructed me to either obtain the back taxes he so generously paid or expedite your departure in one week's time—even that is generous."

"If the taxes are repaid, may I keep the shop?"

"Well, yes, assuming the principal and the *interest* are repaid in full," Parkins said, consulting a small black book he kept in his coat pocket. "…in the amount of…" he showed her the book.

Trudi's face crumbled just short of tears.

Parkins' expression did not change, as if cast in gray pewter.

"This time next week, I'll be back with the police and a crew to begin demolition."

"Demolition?"

"Of course, Miss. My employer desires to erect a more modern building on this site. I think he's considering a river-side tavern and entertainment." Parkins realized he had said too much.

Trudi couldn't respond.

"I'll be back in a week." Parkins turned his back and recorded the details of the meeting in his notebook, his numb fingers barely able to hold the pen. He resisted the temptation to turn around to see what effect he had on the Count's latest victim. He rationalized that, while he had delivered the blow, it was the Count's sword he was wielding. He raised his arm to flag an approaching cab. It passed by without stopping but at the last second, veered to the curb to drench him in cold slushy water.

৵৵৵

"Did you hear that? She's in trouble," Martine said from his lookout spot overlooking the shop.

"What can *we* do?" Glenda asked.

"Know any leprechauns with a spare pot of gold?"

"Let's go report back to Alred. Perhaps he'll have a suggestion."

Martine just watched Trudi's tears fall on the document.

"Are you falling in love with her?" Glenda asked, touching his back.

"Of course not. I just hate to see someone we all care about go through so much torture and grief—and now this."

"Me too. Let's find Alred."

Thirty-one—The Plan

*T*rudi stood at the door staring at the document, her eyes glazed over from the pages and pages of fine print and legalese. At first, it didn't make any sense, and then it did. Opa must not have paid his taxes and the "Count" had. Thinking back, she remembered watching her grandfather use unopened letters to light the stove—and so did she, not realizing the consequences. *Some of those could have been dunning notices.* She felt violated, as if a thief had robbed her in the night. She accepted that this was her fault—*she* had been handling the bookkeeping since Oma died. *I'm going to lose the shop and my home. Everything. And it's not even mine…*

"What is it? I heard someone knock," Catherine asked, tying the belt on her robe.

Trudi handed her the eviction notice.

"My dear Lord," Catherine muttered as she kept reading.

"I could lose everything," Trudi said quietly.

"Not if you repay the taxes—"

"And interest."

"And…interest. Wow. Eighteen percent is criminal usury. You've had a fairly good week; how much have you saved?"

"Some. About a third of what they want, but to come up with the rest in a week will be all but impossible. I'll bet he knew that."

"You might consider a Christmas sale to raise the balance."

"That's risky too. And besides the current stock, I don't have other things to sell. Building clocks takes time."

"Granted, but it's something to think about. How about borrowing the money?"

"Wouldn't that just delay the inevitable?" Trudi asked, taking back the document and heading for the kitchen.

"Perhaps long enough for you to come up with a more profitable business plan."

"And who would lend money to a woman my age who can't even show she owns the roof over her head?"

"I'm afraid you're right. Banks don't generally lend money to women even when they have collateral and sizeable assets. I would lend you the money, but I don't have near enough."

"I know precious little about business, as you can tell. I love and adore bringing clocks, music boxes, and toys to life but managing the ledgers and dealing with creditors and tax collectors is a tooth-pulling chore."

"But I *do*. I come from a long line of businessmen, and I've picked up a thing or two," Catherine said. "Trudi, one does not need to be a man to run a business. Women have been doing that since the dawn of time. Based on what you shared with us, this very building once hosted one such enterprise."

Trudi quickly grasped what she had implied. "I guess you're right." She looked down at the omelet and sliced apple Freddie had just placed on the table. "Thanks. You're too kind, but I don't have much of an appetite."

"Anything for my new sis," she said.

While Trudi ate, she spotted another article on page six of the newspaper. Mr. St. James had not been found and a sizable reward was still being offered. *Perhaps there is another way to come up with back taxes. $2300 would more than cover the bill. No. I could never.*

ﻌﻌﻌ

At the stroke of nine, Trudi had dressed and managed to open the shop. The rest of the day went smoothly, but each tinkle of the bell tightened her stomach as if bracing for another blow. Each tall man who passed by on the street made her think the Count's henchman was returning to demand his pound of flesh. *I've got to do something.* She pulled out a pad and wrote a list of ways to raise the money. She purposefully did not write down her thoughts about the reward for fear the wrong eyes might see it.

Take in boarders. *No, the St. James are living in the spare rooms and the others are in squalid condition.* While the building was once a modest hotel and even a thriving brothel (or so it was said), and there were plenty of rooms upstairs and a large attic, she couldn't afford to renovate them to accommodate regular borders or guests. *Well, you have to spend money to make money but I don't have the time.*

Auction off the antique clocks. *I might have to, but I hate to see these old friends leave the shop—they give the shop character and charm. On the other hand, Opa was right. This isn't a museum where you pay for admission. Perhaps it could be.*

Charge more for repairs? *Times are hard. My customers are already complaining about the prices and how electric clocks don't need cleaning and regular repair—and if they break down, they toss them in the trash. No.* She crossed out the entry.

Sell something else. *After all, this is a good retail space on a busy street—even The Count thinks so. What if we sold… pastries, clothing, appliances? No. I would have to hire a cook and buy ingredients. Hard goods?* Her mind tumbled with the possibilities. *But what would be my added value?* She didn't really know how to cook anything fancy, or anything about clothing, vacuum cleaners, toasters, or other appliances. *All I know is clocks,* she said to herself, absent-mindedly winding her dancing duck.

When the doorbell tinkled, she looked up to see Mrs. Barnes. Her delightful ring-curled girl skipped up to the counter. "May I please play with Donnie Duckie?" she asked politely.

"Of course, Nancy, since you asked so nicely."

Nancy reached up to the counter and took the duck to the corner. She sat there cross-legged and set the duck walking and dancing to its own tune.

"She so enjoys coming here. It's a shame you don't sell them," Mrs. Barnes said.

"Then you wouldn't need to come by and visit," Trudi quipped.

"Oh, I enjoy the shop so much, I would be back."

"So, how much would they be worth?" Trudi asked.

"The mechanical toys? Oh, there is a store in Camden that has wind-up toys, but they aren't as cute as yours, don't hold up, and aren't as well animated. The kids are so hard on them."

"I've heard of the shop. Anderson's?"

"Yes, that's right. They sell theirs for about fifty cents, but I would give you…say, seventy-five or eighty cents for the duck. He's quite special."

"If he was for sale," Trudi said, watching the duck spread its wings and try to fly.

"If it was for sale," Mrs. Barnes said with a sly grin.

Trudi turned a page in her notebook and jotted down what it cost her to make Donnie. But then she realized that it would be cheaper and take less time if she made the parts in batches and had Privi assemble them. *Perhaps the elves could help? I might be able to make them for less than thirty-five cents.*

"Miss Trudi?" Mrs. Barnes said, trying to get her attention.

Trudi looked up and snapped back to the real world.

"How much is this beautiful mantle clock? I think my grandmother would enjoy it."

"Clarise is a lovely piece. My grandfather made her about fifteen years ago. The case is hand-finished walnut and one of my favorites. Is three dollars fair?"

"That seems a bit much for a mechanical clock, even a nice one."

"She's been carefully maintained and cleaned on a rigorous schedule, I assure you. With four jewels, she keeps excellent time, and her chimes are delightful." Trudi moved the hands to eight o'clock to trigger her song. Clarise did not disappoint. Even Nancy looked up and seemed to enjoy the melodious chimes.

"It is lovely. Will you take three fifty?"

"That's more than generous, but I said three."

"For the clock *and* the duck," Mrs. Barnes said, holding out the cash.

"Will you give us a moment?" asked a voice behind her.

Trudi turned to see Catherine walking toward them. "Trudi, can we chat?" she whispered, gently pulling Trudi aside.

"That's fifty cents for the toy and a fair price for the clock."

"But that duck is one of a kind. All the kids love to play with her. I can't sell her."

"Can you make another?"

"Well, yes. I suppose I could."

"Do you recall who was at the door this morning?"

Trudi remembered vividly how Parkins grinned at her as he handed her the eviction notice. "Yes, but I love that duck."

"You'll love the next one you make too—and so will the children who get them as Christmas gifts. And so will the little girl's friends who will want their own."

Trudi looked into Catherine's eyes and then back at Nancy and Mrs. Barnes. "That will be fine," she said, accepting the money and ringing up the sale.

"Is it mine?" Nancy asked.

"It is," Trudi said. Her mother nodded.

At this, Nancy wrapped her arms around Trudi's legs in a hug. "Thank you, thank you, thank you," she said.

After she carefully boxed and wrapped the clock and saw that Donnie Duck had found a new home in Nancy's coat pocket, Trudi said a final goodbye to both Donnie and Clarise, who had been ticking, chiming, and dancing in her shop for the last five years. It was like parting with a child she had raised, loved, and cared for most of her life. Now she knew why Opa was hesitant to sell many of the older clocks. They were his children; children who would never betray him, who might have problems, but with a gentle touch, he could always fix. *I'll miss him.*

Thirty-two—The Sergeant

*I*t was about one in the afternoon when Trudi looked up to see Sergeant Driscoll come into the shop. *Oh, dear Lord he's come to evict me!* "Sergeant, don't I have a week to pay?" she said before he had crossed to the counter.

"Good morning, Miss Sanduhr. The grapevine tells me that Parkins, the Count's stooge has made a call."

"Word travels fast. But I thought you'd be made aware. Who told you?"

"Let's just say you have a lot of cabby friends in this town. So, it's true?"

"It is. He said I have a week to pay up or face eviction."

"I'm afraid that it's true. Do you have a copy of the eviction notice?"

"Of course. Why?" Trudi said, fingering through the papers she kept under the counter. "Here…"

"I want the City Attorney, Gene Lennon, to look over this contract. I can't promise anything, but we don't want to have to evict you."

"Well, that's a relief," Trudi said.

"I know Judge Carstairs. He presides over these cases, and he might be encouraged to rule that the document is unenforceable."

"Thank you so—"

"However, before you start popping champagne corks, you still need to settle with the county for your outstanding taxes."

"Does that mean we still have less than a week to come up with the balance?" Trudi asked.

"I'm afraid so," the sergeant said. "until we can get a stay. For that, I expect you'll need to hire an attorney."

"Well, to do that, I'll need to get a few more customers to pay their outstanding debts. Thankfully, I was able to get the mayor to pay his bill."

"You mean the crook who's still pinching young girls and padding his pockets with shady deals?"

"The same," Trudi said. "If you know he's dirty, why can't you get him into one of your cells?"

"We would have a better case against him if we could get a look at his other set of books—they say he keeps a journal of his deals and skeletons in a safe in his office—sort of an insurance policy, but no one has ever seen it."

About this time, Trudi felt something move in her breast pocket. She turned away and realized that Weeset had taken up a listening post. "Why are you snooping?" she whispered.

"Sergeant, would you excuse me for a moment?" Trudi said, stepping into the workshop so as not to be overheard. "It's not polite to snoop. Haven't I told you about this?"

"You made me promise not to repeat what I've seen at City Hall. And Faeries can't break a promise. But I do need to tell you something important." Weeset's eyes sparkled with a gleeful mischief.

"Well, then, I release you from your promise," Trudi said, with reluctant curiosity.

"I've seen it," Weeset whispered. "I've seen it lots of times."

"What? Do you know what he writes in that black book?"

"That's what I'm trying to tell you. Every time one of his friends comes in to make a payment, or arranges one of their deals, he writes it all down in the book. It's like a personal diary with names, dates, and numbers."

"Are you sure?"

"As sure as I'm a nosey pixie."

"Could you repeat that to—"

"Oh, no. I can't be seen by just anyone. You know that. They would squash me in a second, or I'd end up in a cage."

She's right. I'll have to do this alone. I've seen his ledger too… when he opened the safe. Still, should I tell anyone about a customer's private home and their personal business, or keep it to myself? But he's such a creepy, crooked man, and… Trudi stepped back into the shop.

"Sergeant, may I ask you a question?"

"Of course, I might not be able to help, but…"

"Suppose a person, a workman, visited, say, a certain office and saw, for example, a black binder as you describe in a safe in that office."

"Was that person the only witness?"

"No, but the other… witness was afraid, unable to come forward."

"I'm not afraid!" Weeset whispered. "I'm not afraid of anything."

"Hush," Trudi admonished, and buttoned the flap on her breast pocket. "But the other… person could not say anything for other reasons."

"All right, but that would make it harder to prove in court, if it came to that. But what's the question?"

"Would she, or he, have to keep the combination to the safe that contained the book, private?"

"I'm not a lawyer, so I don't really know, but…"

"But?"

"However, your… this fictional person's other customers might be hesitant to let them enter their homes for fear they might reveal some confidence they would rather not be made public."

Trudi thought back to her conversation with Chad about the mayor and his cronies and remembered reading the newspaper stories of the recent bank robbery—and what Weeset just told her. But no, she dared not risk her reputation. But then… "Sergeant, I can't provide you with anything more in your inquiry and maintain my standing in the community—other than the date the civil war ended."

"May ninth, eighteen sixty-five?" the sergeant asked.

"Correct. And I can say no more."

"I see, and this is relevant, how… oh. Yes. I understand." The sergeant smiled and jotted down the date. "I appreciate your dedication to keeping our government on the straight and narrow. I'm going to show this contract to the city attorney and get it back to you with his decision as soon as I can. You still need to be rounding up the back taxes in any case."

"Thanks, Sergeant," Trudi said as she walked with him to the door. At this point, Trudi's breast pocket looked as if something inside was trying to kick its way out. Resisting the urge to cry out, she quickly unbuttoned her pocket. "Stop that, you little vixen."

An instant later, Weeset jumped out and flew away, where she chastised Trudi in a language she had never heard but the tone was clearly obscene.

"Weeset, I'm sorry, but we were having a serious conversation. I thought you didn't want to have them find out about you?"

"I was sufrecating in there. I hate being trapped!" Weeset said, flying angry figure eights around Trudi's face.

"I'm sorry, but you weren't suffocating."

"Perhaps I can arrange for *you* to be stuffed in a tiny sack."

"Trudi, who are you talking... Is that… a Faerie?" Catherine asked.

Weeset zipped off into the shadows before Trudi could turn around. "Faerie? Perhaps the light was playing tricks on you."

"Trudi, I know what I saw. And I know about the little people living here with you and how they tried to heal George's broken leg." Her expression told Trudi she was upset about something serious—more serious than tax debt.

Catherine touched her arm. "Trudi, I'm really worried about George."

"Now that's something I can help with. I can check him into the hospital under an assumed name as my…cousin."

"That… that would make me far more at ease. Thank you."

"Consider it done. Let's go fetch him. I'll introduce you as my aunt."

"You're a—"

"Friend. A friend doing what any good friend would do."

The next three hours were a whirlwind of activity as George was whisked off to the local hospital.

Hours later, Catherine paced in George's private room as Dr. Stewart and his colleagues diagnosed his condition.

"Trudi? I think you should turn us in for the reward," Catherine said.

Her earnest tone told Trudi that she was quite determined. "What? No. I could not live with myself."

"It would be best for everyone. If the town already knows about us, it only make sense for *you* to get the reward."

"I won't hear of it. I'll get the money some other way. It's settled."

Catherine and Trudi debated the strategy for some time and after what seemed like an eternity, Dr. Stewart came in.

"Well, is he going to be all right?" Catherine asked, getting to her feet.

"The X-rays showed that his leg fracture has miraculously healed," he said. "I've never seen anything like it."

"So, he's okay?"

"I'm afraid not. There's an ugly shadow on the fibula. It might just be a non-malignant cyst, or it could be osteogenic sarcoma—bone cancer. I think a similar cyst weakened the tibia and made it far easier to break. It's rare, so we'll need more tests. The fact that he's still running a low-grade fever is troubling, so I'm concerned about septicemia. We're testing his white-count and ..."

Catherine stopped listening when she heard the "C" word. She reached back for the chair and felt Trudi guide her down. A moment later, she handed her a cup of water.

"Catherine, I know it's a shock, but we don't really know how to proceed until we do more tests. We'll do a biopsy and other blood work before we will know how to proceed."

"Did *I* do this? If we checked him into the hospital at once, would he have caught cancer?"

"Not at all. One does not 'catch' cancer—it's not like a summer cold. These growths can take months to years to develop. A few days one way or the other would not have made any difference to his outcome or treatment."

"We just wanted to keep our presence here secret..."

"I know. Many of us knew who you were almost at once. Rest assured, we're all on your side. We'll keep your secret safe."

"Should I stay?" Trudi asked.

"No. You really need to get back to the shop and please, please reconsider your decision."

And as she rode back to the shop, Trudi thought about the reward and how coming forward might put Catherine and her children in mortal danger. *Thirty pieces of silver is not worth it.*

ৰৰৰ

Later that afternoon, Gene Lennon, the city attorney, was shaking hands with Judge Morgan Carstairs and reminiscing about their days in law school and discussing an upcoming pheasant hunt. "Gene, you must have something on your mind besides trying out that new Purdey," the judge said.

"I do. I assume you're familiar with 'The Count'?"

The judge expression darkened. "Yes, that scallywag has been a thorn in the county's side for decades. Which widow has he foreclosed on now?"

Gene pulled out the papers detailing Trudi's obligation to the Count and laid them out for the Judge to examine.

"Oh, I've seen his nonsense before. It's generally unenforceable, but The Count keeps intimidating people with it. Anyone who hires an honest attorney can get it nullified. It's against state law for a handful of reasons."

"I thought so. I was ready to do a hard sell on the legal issues."

"No need. He's in cahoots with the mayor, and several of the Council members—they all get a cut from the profits—or so I hear."

"Is Chief Brown in on it too?"

"No, I seriously doubt it. Brown's one of a rare breed—an honest cop. Chauncy and I have known each other for decades—we went to school together. I know your office is constantly doing battle with those reprobates—at your own peril, I might add."

"We've never been able to get any hard evidence to convict them on anything substantive. The Chief is lucky he's elected and not appointed," Lennon said.

"Let's get Chief Brown over here. I might have a way to give his effort a bit of help," Gene said.

"Oh?"

"Yes. The day the Civil War ended."

Thirty-three—The Warrant

*A*n hour later, Trudi was glad to see Catherine pull up to the shop in a cab. "How is he?" she asked as Catherine walked up to the counter. She seemed drained. "Let's go into the kitchen. I'll make you a nice cup of tea."

"That would be...heavenly," Catherine replied. "They're keeping George for the time being to run more tests."

Once the tea had been brewed and Freddie and Annie joined them, Trudi spotted Weeset perched cross-legged on a rafter with her own tiny cup. "Well, what's going on?"

"So, the doctors don't really know what's wrong with him. And we won't know for at least a day. It could be serious... cancer."

"I'm so sorry," Trudi said. "It might not be cancer at all."

"Let's pray it's not."

Freddie appeared catatonic—just staring into her teacup.

"When is George coming home?" Annie asked, standing by the table. "I need him to fix Katie. Her arm came off again."

Freddie picked her up and cuddled her close. "George is not feeling well. He's going to stay in hospital for a few days," she whispered.

Annie laid her head on Freddie's breast. "I hope he gets better soon. I miss him, and so does Katie."

"We all do honey," Catherine said. "We all do."

When the phone rang, Trudi went to answer it.

"Trudi's Clock Shop," she answered. "Chief Brown? Your wife already picked up Esmerelda—" She listened for a moment. "I see. Yes, of course. We can come down if it's that important." She hung up and just stared at the phone for a moment, trying to process what she had just been told.

Catherine came in to fetch her bag. "What is it, dear?"

"Chief Brown wants me and Freddie to come down to the police station. He said it was important."

"Did he say what it was about?" Catherine asked.

"Just that it was important and that we should come straight away."

"I'm coming with you," Catherine said flatly.

"That would be most comforting. I'll want people who are on my side."

"I can stay here with Annie," Freddie said.

"He wants you too. He said to bring Freddie. I think we'll also need to take Annie with us."

"Do you think he's going to foreclose?" Catherine asked.

"Oh, I hope not. Sergeant Driscoll said he was going to try to get that quashed, or at least delayed."

"What's getting squashed?" Annie asked as Freddie helped her sister button her coat.

"Quashed, honey. It means nearly the same thing, but not as messy," Catherine said.

Trudi quickly called Chad's home in hopes that he could take them. She needed all the support she could muster, and Chad had been a faithful ally. She hung up after a brief conversation and looked up. "Chad's also been summoned. He's going to take us."

Five minutes later, they were in Chad's cab. "What's going on?" he asked. "Chief Brown didn't say why he wants me at the station. Is it about the robbery?"

"Oh, I hadn't thought about that. It could be," Trudi said, now feeling guilty about not realizing other people also had life-altering problems. "We thought it was about the eviction notice."

"Eviction? Who is getting evicted?" Chad turned to ask. When he looked back, he had nearly hit a horse cart. He swung back into the middle of the street, keeping his eyes on the road.

"Opa didn't pay his taxes and The Count somehow paid them off so… it's complicated."

"That's tough. We have a bit of money; can we lend you some?"

"A couple grand? That's what we're short," Trudi said.

"I was thinking a couple hundred," Chad said.

"Thanks, you're sweet. But we need a philanthropist with deeper pockets, I'm afraid." Trudi made a mental note to add one of her wealthy customers to the list of people to ask for a loan.

"This is it," Chad said, pulling up in front of the police station.

As they queued at the sergeant's desk, Catherine spoke up for them. "Chief Brown asked us to come in."

"Yes, ma'am. Officer McNally will take you back."

With Annie in tow, the troupe paraded in silence into the inner offices of the station and into the chief's conference room. "Please, make yourselves comfortable. The chief will be joining you momentarily."

Trudi and the others took places around the long conference table—Chad took a seat to the right of Trudi and Catherine sat at her left. Officer McNally stood guard at a nearby door. He kept his eyes on Trudi… or was it Freddie?

"Trudi, I noticed you answered the phone as 'Trudi's Clock Shop'," Catherine said softly.

"I guess I did. I've been thinking about it for some time. It's a lot easier to say than 'Sanduhr's'."

"And it says that it's your craftsmanship they're coming to admire and buy."

"You have a point," Trudi said feeling a familiar movement in her breast pocket. As she was about to investigate, a door opened, and Chief Brown walked in. She knew better than to button her pocket. "Behave," she whispered.

"Thank you for coming so promptly," the chief said. "I'll bet you're wondering why I invited you here."

"To foreclose on my shop, I suspect... sir," Trudi said.

"It had better *not* be," Catherine began.

The chief held up his hands as if to deflect the verbal assault about to be unleashed. "No, ladies. It's not about your tax arrears. It's far, far, more serious."

"Oh?" Trudi said.

"About twenty minutes ago, we served a search warrant on the offices of the mayor. Marshall Babcock resisted and was subsequently arrested for obstruction and assaulting a police officer, but after we searched the contents of his safe, we will be adding to those charges—including felony conspiracy, bank robbery, witness tampering, bribery, assault, solicitation, and the list keeps growing."

No one said a word, but the silence was broken by a tiny voice screaming "It's about <unintelligible> time!" emanating from Trudi's pocket.

"Yes, I agree," Chief Brown said. "Without the help of a certain person in this room, who will remain anonymous, we were able to open the mayor's safe before he could hide the evidence."

Trudi leaned over and whispered into her pocket. "Well done, you."

"We have also discovered that Babcock had hired a man we have yet to apprehend to carry out the bank robbery and subsequently attempted to frame a local cab driver."

"Howie?" Freddie asked.

"Yes, Howard Barnapple. He's been released and the newspaper will exonerate him this afternoon."

"None of us thought he was guilty," Trudi said.

"They're going to kill him?" Weeset said. "Really?"

"Exonerate. It means to tell people he's innocent, you silly pixie," Trudy whispered.

"Oh, never mind," Weeset said.

"Neither did we," said the chief. "The evidence didn't add up. When we found more of the bank loot in the mayor's safe, we were made certain of Howie's innocence. It seems it was too hot to fence."

"We're all quite happy this was all wrapped up, chief. But what about that 'contract' the Count has been using to intimidate Trudi?"

"It's bogus. We've interviewed his henchman, a Mr. Henry P. Parkins, and he was able to provide us with a detailed list of people The Count has defrauded—in exchange for a more lenient sentence."

"So I don't owe the county a pile of money?" Trudi asked.

"Oh, you still have to pay your taxes, Miss. We all do."

Trudi's spirits crashed like a porcelain vase dropped on a stone floor.

"But," the chief continued, "because of a key bit of information that dates back to the Civil War, it turns out the city owes *you* about ninty dollars. That's the amount left over after your overdue taxes were deducted from the bank robbery reward money."

"Yipeeeee," said a tiny voice somewhere in the room. It was echoed by a host of others congratulating Trudi.

Trudi was on top of the world. The shop now out from under the shadow of a crippling tax burden. *Too bad it doesn't belong to me.*

Officer McNally appeared at Freddie's side. "Can we talk?"

"Sure," Freddie said, and followed him into the chief's office.

"You asked me to find out about that man in the next cell."

"Yes, what did you find?"

"He said his name was Jasper Hoffman. We picked him up for vagrancy as he was seen hanging around station with no means of support, but without any other charges, he was released the day I met you."

"So just a guardian angel."

"It seems so, but with a checkered past—a fallen angel."

"Thanks," Freddie said.

After the celebration wound down, Catherine suggested they all go out to eat at the nicest restaurant in town. "My treat."

"Can you join us?" Freddie asked Sean.

"I'll try. Perhaps the Sergeant will let me have the afternoon off."

"Let's hope so," Freddie said, noticing he was blushing.

Chad and his cab appeared out in front of the station and ferried them over to The Maine Inn—renowned for its steamed clams, lobster, and authentic seafood.

Their dessert had just arrived when the waitress came to the table. "Mrs. Walton has a call. Is she in your party?"

Catherine got up without a word.

Trudi realized this was Catherine's current alias.

"You can take it in the manager's office. Right this way," she said.

A few minutes later, Catherine returned to the table. "I have to go. I've already paid the check."

And she did.

"Something about George?" Freddie speculated.

The revelry was more subdued, and for some reason, their desserts did not taste as sweet. Chad didn't get them back to the shop until around five. Catherine was there waiting for them to return.

Twenty minutes later, Sean brought Freddie home—her lipstick a bit smudged. When she got inside, Catherine gave her a knowing smile and encouraged her to "freshen up," as she had a surprise.

"What's going on?" Freddie asked, coming downstairs, sans lipstick.

"Hey, hot date?" George asked.

"George, how? Are you okay? What did the doctors—?"

"They still have to do more tests, but they gave me a transfusion and jammed a bunch of antibiotics in me. I'm feeling a lot better. The trouble was, I have a rare blood type."

"So is it…?"

"Cancer? They won't know for several days," Catherine said.

"They have to send stuff back to Bangkok," George said.

"Bangor, sweetie, not the capital of Siam. We're going to pamper him from here," Catherine said, giving him a hug.

Freddie, standing behind him, was making faces. She looked like she wanted to explode.

Trudi pulled her aside. "Well, did you two *do* it?" she asked.

"What? God no. He kissed me… okay, I kissed him. He was a perfect gentleman. Well, almost," she said, blushing.

"Come tell me all about it," Trudi demanded, dragging her up the stairs.

Exhausted by the time she finally went to bed, Trudi spent the evening sharing boy stories and reliving the exciting day with Freddie, George, Sean, and Catherine—a day that had solved so many problems, but still left so many unresolved. This pleasant distraction from their shared concern for George was a welcome relief. However, every phone call, every tinkle of the shop bell, brought back the specter of his unknown diagnosis and the worries Trudi kept bottled up inside about her future. Her father, Dick Heiliger, the mysterious man who held title to the building and everything in it, was still missing. The reward money had paid her taxes and given the shop a temporary lease on life, but she still needed to find a way to keep the business, her home, and her livelihood in the black—and pay next year's taxes and overhead.

As the clocks struck eleven, Trudi was tugged out of her slumber by an unfamiliar sound from outside. She sat up in bed and gazed out on the bay. On the parapet that topped the cliff, a man in dark clothing looked up at her window. She tried to make out the face of this voyeur. When he stepped under the streetlight, she recognized him. *Sean. He must have traded his afternoon of revelry with a graveyard shift on patrol.* Then it hit her. That 'anonymous' revelation had indicted two of the most powerful men in the county. *Wait. Sean said he would keep an eye on the shop for a few days. What a sweetie. Freddie is lucky to have him at her side.*

❧❧❧

"Good news?" Alred said, looking up from his dinner.

"Yes. According to Weeset, Miss Trudi has settled the tax debt," Glenda said. "And that crook in the mayor's office is behind bars."

"So, we won't need that pot of leprechaun gold after all."

"Was he really going to go?"

"I would ask him…" Alred said.

Thirty-four—The Seldith Helpers

*T*hat evening, as Trudi took a clock to be repaired into the workshop, she found Privi hard at work. Even more surprising, she found a team of elves working hand in hand fixing clocks. "What's going on?"

`FIX CLOCK`

`ELF HELP`

"I can see that. Who wound you up?"

`BOY`

Trudi turned to see George bringing a small plate of food cut in tiny pieces. "Dinner," he announced. Squeals of appreciation began their dinner break.

"George, no one asked you to do this," Trudi said.

"No one had to. It's the least I can do. The elves came to me and asked if they could help. I owed them a favor, so I let them get started. They seem far more capable of fixing the clocks than I am."

Trudi just shook her head and took her usual place at the workbench where she began disassembling the clock while overseeing the work of her helpers. George was right. If this shop was to stay ticking, she would have to enlist help from wherever she could get it. Having helpers who knew the clocks as well as she did made sense—even if they were elves. She knew she would be hard-pressed to find skilled helpers who would work for food, a place to live, and protection from the outside world.

It wasn't long before the tiny helpers were chatting and joking with one another as they returned to work after their dinner. It occurred to her; they worked like a happy army of Santa's elves. *Toys. They could make toys.*

"Toys," she said aloud "Could we make… toys?" she asked.

"What kind of toys? Elven toys?" one of the older sems in a long coat asked, not looking up from his clockworks.

"Perhaps, but what about toys for little human boys and girls? Like Donnie Duck, The Captain, the dancing reindeer, zoo animals, teddy bears, little cars and trucks, and toy soldiers?"

"And electric trains?" George asked with a wide grin.

"Perhaps, a little far afield. We would need to do some research I expect."

George continued beaming at her. "All your helpers need now are pointed hats, a sled, and eight tiny reindeer," he said, but he seemed to have something else on his mind.

"Exactly."

"George? Are you in the way?" Freddie asked as she came in from the kitchen.

George looked up at Trudi.

"Not at all," Trudi said. "It's nice to have someone out here helping."

PRIVI HELP

Trudi turned to Privi and embraced his head. "Yes, I love how you help. George and the elves can help too." She rewound him, being careful to not over-tighten his mainspring.

BOY HELP

"What do *you* think about us making toys?" George asked Freddie.

"Here in the shop? Oh, that sounds like fun, but Christmas Eve is only two days away."

"Aren't there toy stores in the village?" George asked.

"I didn't see one," Freddie said. "But I only walked up a few streets into the center square."

"I think I've seen a few cute wooden toys," Trudi replied, "but they're pretty simple and not as well made as they could be. Some folks go over to Bangor or Waterville, but it's quite a trip."

"Are there many children here in town?" Freddie asked, stepping closer. She seemed fascinated by the little helpers making quick work of repairing the clocks and music boxes. She smiled as one of the teams started to play a repaired music box—dancing to the tinny song.

"Children? Yes, we see far more on the streets in the summer, and on the big sledding hill when it snows," Trudi said.

"Back to work fellas. We'll be here all night," the older elf said, his voice kind and encouraging.

"Are you the foreman?" Trudi asked.

"I am, Miss," he said. "They call me Galario."

"How long have you worked with clocks?"

He gave Trudi a knowing smile. "Miss? It's what we do. It's what we *all* do. And we've done it for generations."

"I'm so pleased that you've all come up to help. Please let me know if there is anything else I can do for you all."

"I came in to get you two for supper," Freddie said. "Mom says it's ready."

"Then we had better go," Trudi said. "Come on George, we'll come back after we've eaten."

"Don't worry about a thing, Miss," Galario said. "I'll see that the work gets done."

"I really appreciate the help. I think we need to renegotiate our arrangement if you plan to help this much."

"That's not up to me, Miss. We enjoy being up top and out in the open. And one other thing," Galario said.

"What's that?"

"Bring them out," Galario said, waving his arm.

A moment later, Donnie Duck waddled toward her on the table. Following along in close succession, a herd of reindeer, a tiny (albeit ferocious-sounding) lion, a polar bear, a penguin, and a formation of toy soldiers marched in close unison. Following these was a perfect replica of The Captain, Trudi's favorite.

"My goodness. You made all of these?"

"We've been working on them for some time, but this batch was made in the last two days. We took the liberty of copying your designs."

"But how? Your workshop seems so small."

"You only saw the first level. There are four levels below and another two above," Galario said, nodding toward the ceiling.

"This is marvelous, miraculous, and so special. Thank you so much."

"Excuse me, Miss, we need to get back to work," Galario said.

"Of course, of course," Trudi said, anxious to share the news with the others as she scooped up Clarence, who was sitting a bit too close, and pushed through the beaded curtain. "I think you need to stay out of there for a bit," she scolded. The tom protested and squirmed a bit, but finally relaxed as they entered the kitchen with the prospect of his own dinner.

Catherine and Freddie had prepared another sumptuous feast with a tablecloth, napkins, a centerpiece, and flatware arranged in the right places—just as described in one of Freddie's Jane Austen novels. The platters of meat, stewed potatoes, vegetables, and baskets of fresh-baked bread smelled heavenly. Trudi felt she really had something to be thankful for.

"Catherine, this… this is overwhelming," Trudi said, her eyes watering with joy and nostalgia.

"It's what moms do, Trudi. Please sit there."

"No, Catherine, I can't. That's Opa's chair," she said, hesitating to sit.

"This is *your* place now, Trudi. You're the lady of the house."

That revelation washed over Trudi like a rogue wave. She settled into the wooden armchair she had never dared use and fought back tears. *He's really gone. He's left me alone with the shop and … still, it's not really mine.* The waves turned to ripples—of joy, of sorrow, and of happiness.

It took a moment to absorb Catherine's words. She again realized how she missed her mother, a soul, a female presence, a mentor, a friend she had never known. It was as if a piece was missing in her own clockworks—a cog she had not known she had needed until now.

"Here, drink this," Catherine said, handing her a glass of red wine. "Just a sip. It will help."

In blind obedience, Trudi took the wine glass and let the aroma fill her head as the liquid flowed into her mouth. The warmth soon pushed through her body and softened the world around her.

"Trudi, I don't know why fate brought us to you, but I can see now we need each other, in so many ways."

Trudi didn't say anything at first. She took another sip. "Yes. I think so too. I… I would like…"

"No. Don't say any more now. Let's not make any commitments past the dishes tonight. We're all tired, and …"

"Hungry," George said.

"Hungry," Catherine said.

"Yes, may I say a blessing?" Trudi asked.

"Of course," Catherine said, taking her seat and bowing her head.

"Lord, you have taken Opa to rest at your bosom, and brought these kind people to my door. Thank you for this wonderful meal and these new friends, and especially the smaller souls who look after us all. Amen."

"Amen," they said in unison.

"Amen," said a few tiny voices from somewhere above them.

"Mother?" Freddie asked, helping Annie cut her food. "What do you know about toys?"

"And marketing?" George asked.

"About toys, not much, but a bit more than your average mother about marketing. My father and brothers manage enormous businesses and quite a bit has rubbed off on me. Beyond that, not much. Why?"

"Because Trudi wants to expand into toys."

"I do?" Trudi asked.

"You do," Catherine said. "Yes, you do."

"Yes, I do. I came to that conclusion about five minutes ago. I can't wait to tell you what the elves have made."

"Mommy, someone's tapping on the door," Annie said.

Thirty-five—The Stranger at the Door

*T*he dinner table conversation paused long enough to confirm that someone was knocking on the shop door. "I'll go," Trudi said. "Please keep eating."

Outside the shop door, a stranger stood waiting. He was a gentleman, tall and graying, wearing a long, albeit dirty, tweed coat and a fedora dusted with snow. He looked cold and tired.

"What do you want? We're closed," she said through the glass door.

"Is Mrs. St. James staying here?" the man asked.

"There's no one by that name here," Trudi replied, retreating from the door as a chill ran down her back.

"I'm Richard St. James."

Oh, my God. It's Catherine's husband. "Do you have any identification?" she asked, studying his face through the frosted glass. *He does look somewhat familiar.*

"Is she here? Tell me," the man demanded. His face had morphed from the visage of an amicable traveler to the countenance of someone capable of doing her and everyone else harm.

"I'm calling the police," Trudi said, backing away to the counter and reaching for the phone.

"Please…" he said, his eyes dropping. "Please. I've been traveling for days. I just want to find my wife and children. Are they here?" he pleaded. "Just get her. She'll recognize me."

"Just wait there," Trudi said firmly. "Just wait." She stepped into the kitchen, and everyone looked up—even Clarence.

"Who is it?" Catherine asked. Trudi's look of concern quickly spread to her face.

"A man. He says he's Mr. Richard St. James. I have no way of knowing whether he is or not. I thought it best to ask you before I call the police."

Catherine got to her feet. Every eye in the room was fixed on her.

"Is it Father?" Freddie asked, standing next to her chair.

"Sit. Don't move—all of you. Don't say a word. It might be someone pretending to be your father."

"Really?" George said.

"You heard me. Trudi, what does he look like?"

"He's tall, wearing an expensive coat, hat, and shoes. He seems prosperous, with a two-week-old beard and a full mustache."

"It *could* be him. Wait," Catherine said, opening her purse. A moment later, she retrieved a small black case and revealed the photograph of a middle-aged man. "Is this him?"

"If you add the beard, yes, it could be."

"It's still too dangerous. The agents pursuing us would be very clever and adept at disguise," Catherine said, closing her eyes.

"Isn't there another way to get him to identify himself? Something that couldn't be forged? Is there a question you could ask that no one else would be able to answer."

"Trudi, you're a genius," Catherine said. She pulled out a piece of paper and wrote down a few words.

"Daddy!" Annie said from the shop.

Trudi looked up to realize the child was walking toward the glass door.

"Annie! Stop. Right. There," she said with considerable authority.

Annie paused and turned, pointing at the man behind the glass. In a heartbeat, Trudi scooped her up and took her to her mother.

"Daddy is outside," Annie insisted, looking over Trudi's shoulder.

"He might be, honey, but we have to make sure," Catherine said. "Show him this, and tell me what he says, but before you go, we're going to lock ourselves behind the sea door, just to be sure."

Trudi looked at the paper.

Ser bork bazit mart candu

She didn't recognize any of the words. "This is nonsense," she said.

"My husband won't think so," Catherine said, leading the children with Annie in her arms through the sea door.

Trudi pushed the door closed with her shoulder and heard the lock turn from the other side.

Returning to the shop door, Trudi noticed that the man calling himself Mr. St. James was still waiting. "Well?" he asked. "That was my daughter, Annie. *Please* let me in."

"She asked me to have you read this," Trudi said, holding the paper against the glass.

The man studied the paper. He smiled. "Tell her yes. Tell her I have since that day on the Boston Commons when we first held hands."

"Okay. I'll have to ask you to wait."

"But… it's me," he pleaded.

"Just… wait." Trudi returned to the sea door and tapped. "Catherine?"

"What did he say?" Catherine asked through the door.

"He said 'yes.' He said 'he has since that day on the Boston Commons—'"

"It's him," Catherine said, her voice breaking. She emerged from behind the sea door with Annie still in her arms but had trouble keeping up with Freddie and George who rushed past her into the shop to unlock the door and welcome their father.

"Father!" Freddie cried, embracing her father who welcomed the whole family with open arms as he was drawn inside out of the cold and into their loving embrace.

Trudi stood nearby and witnessed the touching reunion, their affection overflowing into the room like a warm fire. All along the rafters and shadows, little eyes and smiling faces reveled in their joy.

A cold wind and a threatening voice pushed its way in from the doorway. "Herr Saint James, I'll have those documents."

Trudy looked up to see a rough-hewn stranger threatening them at the open doorway with a pistol in his hand. She took a step back into the shadows.

Richard immediately put himself between the gunman and his children. "Get them out of here," he said to Catherine, his hand sliding under his coat.

"Nobody goes anywhere, and this Luger has a hair trigger mein Herr. Keep your hands where I can see them," Jasper said, gesturing with the pistol.

Too stunned to act, everyone froze, everyone but Annie. "Go away, leave us *alone*," she cried.

"Just hand over those documents you stole from the Reich, and no one will be hurt. Not even your darling child."

Trudi tried to get to the telephone and she had almost made it to the counter.

"Stay where you are mein fräulein," Jasper commanded, pointing his pistol at her.

Trudi slowly raised her hands and looked up at the rafters, her eyes begging for help from above.

"I think you had best leave," said a small but firm voice coming from somewhere in the shadows.

Martine. My Seldith knight.

Jasper looked around. "Who said that?"

"Someone who protects this home."

"Show yourself or I shoot."

"As you wish," the voice said.

An echoing bang and a blinding spark enveloped Jasper in a shimmering blue light. In desperation, he fired his pistol, spinning Richard around. Jasper collapsed to the floor; his pistol sliding across the shop coming to rest at Trudi's feet. Catherine pounced, pinning Jasper to the floor with her knees while Richard and the others joined in to restrain him.

"We need some rope," Richard shouted, working hard to keep their assailant disabled.

Racing in from the workshop, Privi arrived with a thin strip of spring steel trailing behind him. Trudi picked up Jasper's gun as she watched the robotic boy help bind the hands and feet of their assailant. As Jasper regained consciousness, he began thrashing like a trapped leopard, straining against the bindings and cursing in German. A moment later, Alred and a cadre of armed elves appeared out of the woodwork to join Martine who stood guard over Jasper with his sword still glowing.

"Richard, are you all right?" Catherine asked as they got to their feet.

"My coat will need some mending, but I'm unhurt," he said, showing them the bullet hole. "That's Privi. One of Trudi's inventions," Freddie explained. "Where have you been, father? We were all worried."

"Yes, why didn't you—" George began.

"All in good time, all in good time. I think we need to deal with this Nazi before we do anything else," he said.

"But not before this," Catherine said as she embraced and kissed her husband making it clear she was glad beyond words to see him safe.

Mid-kiss, Richard caught sight of the growing cadre of elves assembling in the workshop—many of whom were armed with spears, bows and arrows, and even pots and pans.

"What… who are… leprechauns?" he sputtered.

"Not leprechauns, father, *Seldith*. This is their home," Freddie said.

"We'll explain it all in good time," Catherine said. "Let's get this brigand into the hands of the police."

"Martine, are you all right?" Trudi asked as Martine joined Alred on the floor, noting that he was rubbing his wrist; his hand still gripping the sword. "That was amazingly brave."

"It's the price for casting a spell, Miss Trudi," Alred said. "He'll be all right. Perhaps Martine won't use so much force next time. He'll learn. Do you know this intruder?"

"I have no idea. I'm calling the police," Trudi said as she headed for the phone.

"That's the man in the next cell," Freddie said. "He knew my name."

"Nice friends, Freddie," George sniped.

"I never said he was a friend," Freddie replied with a glare.

"We're missing someone," Richard said, gazing down at his family's smiles.

"Annie. Oh, my God, she was here a second ago. Wait, she wanted to finish her dinner."

And that's where they found her—quietly having tea under the table with Mrs. Framingham (fully dressed), her doll Katie, and Captain.

"Daddy!" she exclaimed as she ran into his arms. "Is that really you? Mommy said you were just putending."

"It's really me. Give me hug punkin."

"You have an assailant, Miss Trudi?" Officer McNally said from the doorway.

"Oh, I'm so glad you came, Sean," Trudi said, as dozens of little feet quietly scampered into hiding.

"Mrs. Porter from across the street and several others called it in. They heard a couple of gunshots. Miss Parker from next door said it sounded like a Jimmy Cagney movie."

"Michelle tends to exaggerate. There's your criminal," Trudi said, pointing to Jasper still writhing on the floor as he tried to escape.

"The jailbird from the other day," Sean said. "I might have guessed."

"He tried to shoot Mr. Saint James," Freddie began. "He wanted father to—"

"He's a German intelligence operative," Richard interrupted. "Jasper Hoffman here and his Nazi agents have been trying to intercept me for over a week. I caught sight of him at the station yesterday and thought I had lost him, but he must have followed me here."

Catherine held out the Luger but not before she deftly removed the clip and emptied the chamber.

"Let me take that," McNally said, raising an eyebrow. "Was anyone hurt?"

"No, just threatened, and scared. We'll be okay," Catherine said.

"I'm glad no one was hurt. So, Miss Trudi, do you want to add this Jasper to your growing list of houseguests? Perhaps he could stay for the night and you could feed him breakfast, or should I take him back to the precinct?"

"Oh, we have a pretty full house," Trudi said. "Why don't you provide him an accommodation at your place for the next decade?"

Sean turned to the trussed-up man on the floor. "Mr. Hoffman. We meet again. Armed assault this time? I guess we'll have to see how well you like our cells in the county lockup. I'm sure the Feds want to have a word with you as well—espionage, I understand. Shall we?" he asked as he applied a vice-like grip on Jasper's arm and lifted him to his feet.

"Wir sehen uns zuerst in der Hölle," he said and continued to ramble about something he called "fae" and "Winzige Elfen."

"I suppose you know what he said," Sean said to Freddie.

"You don't want to know. His English was perfect five minutes ago. I expect he's hallucinating," Freddie replied.

Trudy smiled at her and mouthed "Thanks." Weeset buzzed by Freddie's ear "I owe you one," she whispered, figuring that the faerie had prevented him from speaking in English.

"How did you get the best of him? He looks like a pretty tough character," McNally asked, as he helped Jasper stay on his feet.

"Oh, magic. I cast a spell on him. It's one of my lesser-known talents," Trudi said with a smile.

"By the looks of these scorch marks, I would say he had an electrifying experience."

"Shocking," Trudi said. "Just shocking."

McNally got Jasper to the front door where two more officers waited. They loaded him inside a waiting paddy wagon. As Sean closed the door, he turned to Trudi.

"Trudi, I'm glad you're all right. I would hate to have harm come to any of you. I'm sorry I wasn't here to stop him, but the station recalled me about twenty minutes ago thinking the threat was over."

"Thanks," she said, "Stay safe."

"You too."

☙☙☙

"That ended well," Alred said. "I'm quite proud of you Martine. It's clear what your herditas is."

"I'm not so sure," Martine said as Glenda wiped salve on his wrist. "I think I would rather be a master machinist. There are fewer lightning swords involved."

"I think it's time we started addressing you as 'sem,'" Alred said, putting his arm around his grandson. "Or apprentice wizard."

Thirty-six—The Reunion

*R*ichard walked alongside Trudi as his family made its way into the kitchen. "I don't think we've been introduced. I'm—"

"Richard Saint James. I know. Your family has told me a lot about you. They were worried sick," Trudi replied as she paused in the kitchen doorway.

"And you are?"

"Oh. I'm Trudi Sanduhr, my grandfather and I ran this shop for... since I was about fifteen. I started working as his apprentice at age nine."

"William Sanduhr? May I speak to him?"

Trudi paused a moment to collect her thoughts and craft a polite reply. "He's... he died not long ago."

Richard appeared shaken. He stepped behind the counter and sat on the stool. "I'm so... so sorry. I really admired him and his clocks, his masterpieces of mechanical wizardry. And... I was deeply in love with his daughter Maria."

Trudi's knees felt rubbery, and as if Richard sensed this, he offered her the stool. "You loved my mother? When did you know her?"

"We dated one summer about twenty years ago when my family was living nearby. Every moment we spent together made it clear that we were meant for each other. We were both very much in love."

Trudi's mind raced trying to connect the dots, adding these details to what she already had discovered about her mother and father. "Do you know a Mr. Dick Heiliger?"

The color drained from Richard's face just as Catherine appeared at Trudi's shoulder.

"Richard. You're very tired. You need to get some hot food. We're all waiting. Can you—"

Richard looked up into Trudi's eyes. "Honey, I'll be there in a minute."

"I'll keep a plate warm," Catherine said softly as she backed away.

"I used that name when I dated Maria. How did *you* know about it?"

"I need to show you something. It's important, so just wait here a couple of minutes. Please," Trudi begged.

Richard nodded and Trudi ran upstairs just as the clocks began to strike seven. Before the last chime rang, she was back with a stack of letters. "I found these hidden upstairs. I've read them all, so I know how much my mother loved a man she called 'Dick.' Is that you? Are you the man who left her pregnant and disappeared without a trace?"

"Oh…my…God," Richard said softly.

"So, you *are* this *Dick* she wrote about? Are you my father?"

"That's… that's a name I used to keep Maria from knowing about my family—at least when we first met. I wanted her to love me for me, and not for my name, my fortune, or my reputation."

"Your reputation? As a playboy? As a scoundrel?" Trudi said, her tears welling up.

"Trudi, I… I swear, I didn't know Maria was pregnant. I really *didn't*. I was about to ask her to marry me, to tell her my real name, to take her to meet my parents, to share the rest of my life with her."

"What stopped you? Did you get scared or have second thoughts about marrying into a working-class family?"

"No. No, not at all. I was working for the State Department. I was a diplomat with unique skills. They needed me to go on an important mission; a mission that could not wait a day or even another hour. I was rushed off to work undercover in… well, I can't say. Not even now, years after the mission. But I was cut off; kept incommunicado to protect me and my family. I didn't hear about your mother until the mission was over. And then, all I could find out is that she had died."

"You had no idea that she died in childbirth. None?"

Richard took Trudi's hands. "None. If I had known she was pregnant, I would have done right by her, mission or no mission. I was devastated. Sometime later, I met Catherine at an official function in Boston and we grew close. In the next few months, she helped guide me through my grief. When I was reassigned to an important post in London, I didn't want to make the same mistake, so I proposed. We were married, and the rest you know."

"So, you're my father," Trudi said, squeezing his hands.

"Can't you tell? We have the same eyes, the same cheekbones, the same... and from what I've seen, the same courageous, generous heart."

"Who told you about me?" Trudi asked.

"Trudi, you took in my family as if they were your own. You sheltered them, fed them, and welcomed them into your life without knowing anything about them. That took courage and generosity. Not everyone would be so kind."

Trudi blushed at the praise. "And I have two sisters and a brother?" Trudi asked with a little smile.

"That you do. And a new stepmother."

"And a new mother. I already love her; I already love them all," Trudi said as she embraced her father for the first time. She breathed in his aroma and felt the warmth of his arms.

"Richard, what have you done to this child?" Catherine asked.

"Catherine, meet Trudi—my long-lost daughter."

"Really?" Catherine asked.

Both Richard and Trudi nodded. "It's true. I know it is," Trudi said.

Catherine smiled. "I suspected as much."

"What? How could you know?" Trudi and Richard said almost at once.

"Let's just say I know my husband's eyes when I see them. Come on. Your dinner's ready, there are lots of stories to tell, and everyone is waiting."

Thirty-seven—The Dinner

"What a feast," Richard exclaimed as they settled around the kitchen table. Trudi's mind was still trying to make sense of having real parents for the first time in her life.

"It is, or it was. I expect it's cold by now," Catherine said.

"Who cares? I'm starving. I haven't eaten anything substantial in two days," Richard said. "May I?" He asked as he reached for the meat platter.

"Please, help yourself. I'll reheat the gravy and get you a hot cup of tea," Trudi said.

"That's my job," said Freddie.

"Before we get started, I think I need to say grace," Richard said.

Everyone paused and fell silent.

"God, thank you for your mercy, and your protection as our families have safely reunited in more ways than one. And most of all, thank you for my new daughter, without whom we would not be as joyful as we are tonight. Amen."

"What?" Freddie said.

"Is mother pregnant?" George asked.

"No," Richard said with a smile. "We just learned that Trudi is my daughter. Say hello to your new sister."

Freddie and George just stared at Trudi as if seeing her for the first time. In a way, she realized she was seeing *them* for the first time as well.

"I knew it," Freddie said, embracing Trudi. "I could feel the bond at once."

"My sister?" George began. "Ewww. I had a crush on her."

"Really, that's sweet," Trudi said. "Still?"

"Not so much," George said, blushing.

When the laughter had died down, the rest of the evening was spent telling and retelling the stories of their epic journeys with embellishments that rivaled the tales of Odysseus. Trudi was especially enraptured by Richard's account of the events that triggered their need to escape back to the US and end up here.

"Why here? Why come to this town, this clock shop?" Trudi asked.

"Because I... as I said, I dated the owner's daughter one glorious summer. She had shown me those back stairs that led to the rocky beach and that's where we—"

"We get the idea Father," Freddie said with a smirk.

"When Catherine and I made our evacuation plans, we needed an unknown place, a safe harbor where the family could hide until I could get the documents to Washington."

"So, Catherine knew about Maria?" Trudi asked.

"I did," Catherine said. "Richard became all but catatonic when he learned that she had passed. He had such high hopes for their future."

Richard's account of his secretive trip to Washington lacked details, but he recalled how he managed to get there and back to Maine before Jasper finally spotted him. "I expect they thought I would come here before going to the District so they kept watch on the trains."

"That sounds exciting," George said.

"It sounds frightening," Catherine said.

"What was in those documents?" Freddie asked.

"You know better than to ask a question like that," Richard admonished. "Did you have a pleasant crossing?"

"It was better than our White Star cabin when we went on our honeymoon," Catherine said with a wry smile.

"It was awful!" Annie began, "Je veux un cupcake au chocolat pour le dessert."

"She speaks French now?" Richard exclaimed.

"And how to ask for cupcakes and bathrooms in several other languages. Father, it was horrible," Freddie replied.

"I never want to see another raw carrot in my life," George added.

"It must have been quite an ordeal," Richard said. "I'm sorry you had to go through that."

"As a family, we came out stronger in the end. We learned we could work as a team, a family, and get though some tough times."

"Tell me, what happened once the ship dropped you off?" Richard asked.

At this point, Catherine told the story of their debarkation and all of the events leading up to Richard's arrival. Freddie, George, and even Annie had to add color to some of the details, but by the time the story was over, the food had all but disappeared, the dishes washed and put away, and Annie had curled up under a crocheted afghan laid out on the window seat, having refused to be separated from her mommy and daddy.

"Freddie," Richard began, "we still need to have a heart-to-heart about why you were arrested."

"Detained, father. Protective custody. No charges were filed," Freddie said in her defense.

"A technicality, my dear," he said, giving her a hug.

"But how did Jasper spot you?" Trudi asked.

"Well, I expect he had been hiding in town looking for strangers that matched our descriptions. The German agents circulated those newspaper stories and posted the reward to get people to reveal your whereabouts. When I got off the train, my three-week beard did not disguise my appearance very well."

"You *said* you were going to shave off your mustache and dye your hair," Catherine chided. "You never were very good at disguises."

"I couldn't bear to shave it," Richard said, twirling the end of his mustache. "Anyway, Jasper spotted me in the train station, but I saw him before he saw me, so I hid out in town until nightfall. It seems he was still able to trail me back here."

"I'm so glad you weren't captured… or worse," Trudi said.

"Trudi, it was your selfless hospitality that rescued us all. Thank you so much. I am forever in your debt."

About that… Trudi thought. "They've all been a delight and a Godsend, Mr. St. James," Trudi began. "I'm so glad our paths through time crossed, as I was like a clock with the wrong pendulum after my grandfather died. When I needed them most, Catherine and your children appeared like magic to help me in so many ways. I can't thank them enough."

"So, it seems we have rescued one another," Richard said.

"Richard, Trudi is going to have to reinvent herself and the shop to survive," Catherine said.

"That sums it up nicely," Trudi said, pouring Richard another cup of tea. "But there is more good news in that regard."

"Oh?" he asked.

"There are some new friends you should meet," Trudi said. "But that can wait until…tomorrow," she said with a yawn.

❧❧❧

By the time the moon had tucked itself under a thick quilt of downy clouds, Trudi was gazing sleepily out the kitchen window. The snow tumbled out of the sky as if to doubly ensure there would be a white Christmas. She had so looked forward to this time of year and she vowed to make it as happy as possible despite all that had happened.

George had long since gone to bed. Catherine and Richard sat next to each other at the kitchen table; their soft words unheard, their cheeks all but touching.

"Should we tell them now?" Trudi asked Freddie, quietly adding more wood to the stove.

"Let's let them enjoy each other for a bit longer. The idea can wait until morning," Freddie replied, looking back at her parents gazing longingly into each other's eyes like a pair of newlyweds, their hands intertwined on the table.

"You're right. It can wait until morning. Let's go to bed and let them catch up." Trudi took Freddie's hand and tugged her toward the stairs.

"I'll see you two in the morning," Freddie said to her parents.

Richard didn't take his eyes off Catherine's face. "Good night, ladies. Get some rest. We'll go up in a while."

"Goodnight all," Trudi said as she turned up the stairs.

"Goodnight Trudi, sweet dreams." Catherine said.

"Glad to have your dad back?" Trudi asked Freddie as they stood in the upstairs hall.

"Over the moon. I've missed him so much and I'm so glad he's… safe."

Trudi could not look away as her tears pushed their way down her cheeks.

"What is it?" Freddie asked, taking her hand.

"I'm looking forward to having a father to be there when things go wrong."

"And when things go well," Freddie said. "...someone to be proud of you and show that pride, someone you know is always there, ready to catch you when you stumble."

"Yes, I missed that."

"Wasn't your grandfather a dad like that?"

"In a way, but it was not the same. Opa was kind and he taught me a lot, but he wanted me to be independent and fig-ure things out and stand up for myself, so he usually let me fail and…"

"Trudi, you're describing our father. Remember, he's also *your* father. I hope you learn to love and respect him as much as I do. Let's get some rest," Freddie said, giving Trudi a long hug. "Sleep well, sister."

Thirty-eight—The Plan

*T*he shop clocks had just struck five when Trudi realized her toes were all but frozen. She kicked the duvet and tried to find a warm place for them to no avail. Unfortunately, her mental gears had been grinding through her problems for most of the night. While her eyes had been shut, she had hardly rested. *Christmas is next Sunday. I really don't want to disappoint my father or his family, but how am I going to manage Christmas on my own? What would Opa or Oma do? Nothing is getting accomplished from here. Mist.*

She stuck her leg out, but her foot recoiled when her toe touched the cold floor. It took a concerted effort to try again, but she did. Realizing that everyone in the house would be just as cold, she decided she needed to get her day and the heating stove started. Once washed, dressed, and downstairs, she gingerly placed the kettle on the stove, as she tried to get something warm inside her without waking everyone.

"Couldn't sleep?" Catherine asked quietly.

"Oh, my lord; you scared me," Trudi whispered, spinning around and nearly dropping the teapot. She took a deep breath. "No. No, it was a hard night. So much to do, so little time before Christmas."

"I couldn't either," Catherine said, peeling strips of bacon into a frying pan.

Neither spoke for a few minutes as the aroma reached up through the ceiling to lure the rest of the family. When their bacon, eggs, and toast were ready, the apples sliced, and the tea poured, they sat down next to one another.

"Do you have a plan, a goal?" Catherine asked.

"To survive Christmas," Trudi said.

Catherine smiled. "More specifically. How do you intend to accomplish that goal? What are the key results along the way?"

"Well, we usually decorate the shop, and we've already done quite a bit of that, but... I think we need to shift the store's focus. Clocks, music boxes, and the like have limited appeal and we're low on stock. The clocks and music boxes are mostly for adults, especially those with money."

"I think you're right. So, what would draw in more customers and replenish stock?"

"Build more things that *children* enjoy," Trudi said.

"Such as?"

"Toys, I think. The kids love my animated toys, but we have so few of them. We would need many, many more—dozens maybe hundreds. George and the elves have already started on some, but I can't see how we can make enough."

"He told me. I'm glad he's finding a way to help, and I think he wants to build a massive train layout."

"You might be right. He does love his trains."

"So what's holding back this plan?"

"We're short on metal for one thing, but mostly we're short on time."

"That's ironical for a clock shop."

"I need to figure out how much sheet metal and wood we'll need, not to mention the other supplies like paint, varnish, screws, brushes, and the like. And then, I worry that the suppliers won't be able to fill the orders."

"That's quite a bit. Besides raw materials, what else do you need? Labor?"

"Labor and *time*. Privi and I can only work so fast. If he breaks down, or something happens to me..."

"So we'll have to keep you two healthy and rested. All right, let's do some figuring," Catherine said, laying out a long sheet of wrapping paper on the table. "We need to be smart about this project."

Over the next hour, Catherine and Trudi put together the basic framework of a schedule that showed what each item would require as far as raw materials, parts, and labor, and most importantly, time were concerned. They then computed what they would need as a return for each to make a profit. "We're not a charity," Trudi said, erasing the price for her high-end captain animated toy and writing in a higher number.

"You're not. You're a business woman. Make it higher. Captain's a winner."

They then calculated how many of each they needed and how many they could make in about five days. As they worked, Trudi began to doubt she could do it, but she poured another cup of strong tea and continued.

"I wish George was here," Catherine said. "He's a genius with figures."

"He needs his rest," Trudi began. "I've used the intricate clock parts Opa designed for the animations, and some of my own designs for the rest. I hope we have enough."

There were footsteps on the staircase.

"Good morning my darlings," Catherine said, not looking up from the sheet

"Is it morning already?" Freddie mumbled, apparently drawn downstairs by the smell of bacon.

George was close behind and took a glancing look at their figures. "There's a multiplication mistake. There," he said pointing. "Is there any tea?"

Thankfully, both teens understood what was going on and after they had fed themselves and fired the stove in the workshop, George returned with a few prototypes for the newly minted toys and Freddie went back upstairs to check on Annie.

"Thanks George," Trudi said, inspecting a darling brass and copper penguin.

"It's a great plan," he began. "But you've left off a critical factor."

"Oh?" said Catherine. "Another math mistake?"

"The workers. The Seldith. They should be involved in the planning. Only *they* know how many toys and components they can make in the few days we have left."

Trudi and Catherine looked at each other. "You're right," they nodded.

"It's going to be a challenge," a tiny voice said from a waist-high shelf nearby.

Trudi turned to see Alred and Galario peering down at their plan.

"How long have you been there?" Catherine asked.

"Several hundred years, I think," Galario said with a grin.

Alred nodded. "Not that long for me, but for quite a while."

"A challenge? Does that mean you can build that many toys before Christmas?" Trudi asked pointing to the sheet.

"With a bit of magic..." Alred said, and Galario nodded.

"What's going on?" Richard asked as he trudged into the kitchen. Do you know what time it is?"

"This is a clock shop father. We know," Trudi said, rising to give him a hug as all the clocks struck six; all but one. *Janice.* She made a mental note to check her out. *After Christmas.* "I'll make you some breakfast."

"Sit down, hon," Richard said. "I can fend for myself. What can I do to help? I didn't mean to interrupt."

"Well, you can look over Trudi's plan to get ready for Christmas."

"Sure. Another set of eyes rarely hurts," he said, leaning over to study the charts and diagrams spread out on the table. "Humm. How do you plan to get enough people into the store to clear this volume of inventory?"

"Good question," Catherine said.

"I've always wanted to advertise—especially in the summer during the tourist season but Opa didn't think we could afford it," Trudi said.

"Let me take care of that," he said with a pensive expression.

"I hate it when he gets that look," Catherine said.

And so, Trudi's day began. She had discovered to her delight that she didn't have to do this all alone. With her extended family's help and a little magic, they just might pull it off. In less than six days. *With a little magic.*

Thirty-nine—The Surprise

*A*gain, unable to sleep a minute past six, Trudi awakened to the realization that Christmas Eve had finally arrived. Five frantic days ago, they had put up an enormous chart to track the daily tasks. Someone had to go to Bangor for sheet copper and brass, a foundry at the port for steel, exchange more British money, and Richard had disappeared for a day to who knows where on another mission he couldn't (or wouldn't) talk about. Last night, with everyone exhausted, they had checked off the next to last task.

☑ Christmas Eve-Eve: Everyone get a goodnight's sleep.

I hope we're ready.

Trudi bathed, brushed her hair into submission and dressed, trying not to disturb anyone still sleeping. Worrying dreams for much of the night didn't help her feel as perky as she needed to be on this, their last and most important day of sales before Christmas.

With his "good morning" meow, Clarence pushed open her bedroom door and made it clear that he had waited long enough for his breakfast. "I'm up," she whispered. "Let's get us both something to eat but keep it quiet. We don't want to wake the others." In the dim early morning light, she stroked his tail as he walked beside her down the stairs. Near the bottom, she thought she saw one of the Seldith children about the height of a radish peering around the corner.

"She's coming!" the yenesem said, nearly shouting— which for an elven child was more squeaky than loud.

Trudi picked up Clarence and stepped more cautiously down the stairs, not wanting to step on the little creature, and wondered what was going on. As she turned the corner, she took in a startled breath. What she saw laid out across the entire shop was, "Unbelievable," she said aloud. "Oh, my God. What… how… who…?"

The shop had been redecorated with a resplendent display of shiny new toys. At her feet, a score of Seldith elves stood waiting for her.

"Good morning, Miss Trudi," Alred said. "What do you think?"

"Did you do this?"

"No, I can't say that I did; well, I can't take much of the credit. I simply recruited a few of Santa's helpers, but everyone helped. They've been working all night to finish."

"Surprise!" said Freddie, George, Catherine, and Richard as they popped up from their hiding places. A moment later, Annie was hugging her leg. "Surprises!" she said.

"Have you been up all night too? I thought you all had gone to bed," Trudi said. "This is… is wonderful; beyond my dreams. The displays, the clocks, the toys. The toys! Where did you get all the *toys*? Have you really made that many?"

"We've been working on them for some time after Galario suggested we make more of your favorites," Martine said. "But that was weeks ago."

"The clan was more than happy, thrilled even, to work on something besides clocks," Alred added.

"And they had so many great ideas to add to your favorites, I hope you like them," George said.

"Oh, I'm sure I will," Trudi said, picking up a mechanical penguin that flapped its stubby wings as if it was trying to fly. "This is so sweet. Whose design is this?"

"Mine," said Sondrah. "I'm glad you're pleased."

"I am, I am, and thank you all. It's… it's overwhelming."

"And I made sure they were quiet," said Weeset as she hovered at arm's length from Trudi's face before flitting off to land on the Christmas tree, now sparking with new lights and silver tinsel.

"But there is more," Alred said.

"More?" Trudi asked as the St. Jameses gathered around and Freddie picked up Annie.

"Watch," Alred said. "Okay, everyone, take your places."

As Trudi watched, a host of costumed elves, the older sems, as well as the young nesems and yenesems, climbed into the displays.

"Weeset, we're ready," Alred said.

At his command, the shop lights softened, and tiny spotlights highlighted one display after another, and in each vignette, the elves pretended to be mechanically animated creatures like the ones which had decorated the clocks for so many decades. They danced, wound the toys, and marched in unison.

Trudi was speechless. Her eyes were drawn to each vignette which seemed even more special than the last. In the end, the lights went off for a moment and when they came back up, most of the elves, save Alred, Glenda, and a few others had disappeared as if by magic.

"I'm so, so impressed. You all have done such a wonderful job of... wait. The scenes. The twelve days of Christmas! How wonderful. But what about the music?"

"I told you we needed the music," Glenda chided.

"We thought we would leave that up to you, Miss Trudi," Alred said. "You're the master craftswoman of music boxes."

Trudi was touched and especially pleased that she could contribute to the glorious show of artistry. "Of course, I think I can reprogram Natasha."

"We thought so; she's laid out on the workbench," Galario said.

"Thanks, I'll get right on that…"

"But there is more," Alred said, nodding at George.

"At our home in London, I loved to play with my electric trains. I had worked on the engines and layouts quite a bit."

"Endlessly," Richard said as Catherine nodded.

"Ceaselessly," Freddie said.

"So, with Galario's help, and leveraging a bit from Marklin, the German electric train masters, I was able to create my own engine, and thus I give you… trains."

At this, an electric train tooted its tiny horn and entered the shop from a mouse-hole-sized opening near the ceiling and choo-chooed its way around the shop. It appeared like the engineer was waving his arm as it passed, and the fireman was stoking coal.

"Are those sems?" Trudi asked, looking closely. They appeared to be.

"Yes, we had so many who wanted to be the engineer and fireman that we had to draw straws," George said. "See? We even have a conductor in the caboose."

All of this was more than Trudi could take in as she found a place to sit and just watch the St. Jameses and the elves have fun playing with and re-arranging the displays and vignettes. *Marvelous, simply marvelous.*

Trudi had been a part of getting ready for this day as she worked on creating new toys and reconstructing her favorites. She had seen the bits and pieces, the prototypes, and the failed experiments for the last four days but had only dreamed that it could all be done in time. *It's magic. It must be.*

"Well, Alred, you and your Seldith clan have outdone yourselves," Trudi said. "I assume that's all. I'm simply overwhelmed at the artistry, imagination, and execution of it all."

"Well, actually, there is one more surprise," Alred said.

"Trudi," Richard said. "Would you join me in the kitchen?"

"Of course, but you sound so serious. Is it more bad news? Do you not like what we've done with your shop?"

"Just sit down with me. Please. We need to have a private chat."

Trudi felt her heart skip a beat as she followed Richard into the kitchen. She looked back into the shop and caught Catherine's eye. She nodded and mouthed "It will be all right."

Richard gestured for her to sit in Opa's chair and he sat next to her taking her hands in his. His were warm and comforting.

"Trudi, I have to confess a great sin," he began.

"What could you—"

"Please, let me finish. Trudi, you have a new family who clearly cares about you and your welfare. You now have two stepsisters, a stepbrother, and a loving stepmom, and a dad who is keen to catch up on all the years that he's missed."

Trudi gazed deep into his eyes.

"I've asked someone to join us," Richard said softly.

"Richard, Mr. Brook and his assistant are here," Catherine said.

"Can you ask him to come through?" Richard asked. "…and can you join us?"

Trudi sat up and wiped away her tears. Mr. Brook came in carrying his leather briefcase. "Sir, can you identify yourself?" he asked Richard.

"I can," Richard said as he produced his passport.

Mr. Brook examined it carefully, comparing the picture Trudi had given him with the passport. "This looks like a match," he said. "Miss Trudi Sanduhr, do you accept this man Richard Saint James as your father?"

Trudi looked Richard in the eye and nodded. "I do."

"Very well, then let us begin," Mr. Brooks said.

And at that, the documents that officially handed over the rights to the building, the land, as well as the designs and inventions created by her grandfather and his ancestors, were signed over to her and witnessed. Promises of secrecy were made, non-disclosures were signed, hands were shaken, good-byes were said, and Mr. Brook departed but not before congratulating Trudi and wishing her a bright future and offering his services if the need ever arose.

"Well, the shop and everything is all yours, Trudi," Richard said, as he handed her the documents. "Congratulations. You're a shop owner."

Trudi was numb. It had all happened so quickly and without the court fight she had been fearing. "So, all of this is my responsibility, and it's all my fault if it fails."

"And you get the praise, profits, and prizes," Richard said.

Trudi hugged Richard, and Catherine, and her father again. "Thank you," she said. "But there is one other... issue."

"Oh?" Richard asked.

"The Seldith. I promised Opa that I would keep their existence secret. He was rightly worried that if people knew about them, they would be victimized, taken off to study or worse."

"I completely understand. The Seldith are truly remarkable, and their magic could really be used for evil purposes," he said solemnly. "So what do you propose? The Seldith are fully committed to the Christmas display. It's your decision. Should we tell them it's too risky to—"

"No, I think it's up to them. If we plan it well and keep the lights down, we can always say they're just realistic mechanical figures," Trudi said.

"Very realistic," Freddie said.

"Going forward, we should continue to discourage them from being seen by the public."

"That makes sense. Let's see what we can do to better protect their anonymity," Catherine said. Richard nodded.

"Well, Alred, what do you think?" Trudi asked as if he was listening.

He was. "I can speak for our clan as we have discussed it at length. While we agree that there is a risk, and while there are ways to protect our existence with... well, fairly drastic means, we think for this one magical day, we can go forward with the plan."

"I'm so glad," Trudi began, but wondered what these 'drastic means' might be. "We have a lot to do before we open. Let's make this a Christmas the town will never forget."

"Breakfast. That's first, then we need to get the shop door open. We might not get to eat all day," Catherine said.

"Have you seen the newspaper?" George asked, as he came into the kitchen, now bustling with too many cooks.

"No, I've been... busy. Did they say the family is safe and sound?" Trudi asked, realizing that it was her family too.

"Something more exciting," George said, handing her the newspaper folded to show the half-page ad on page four.

TRUDI'S CLOCKS AND TOYS GRAND CHRISTMAS SALE

> *Come to the reborn Sanduhr Clock shop on Cliff Street to discover a delightful assortment of hand-made toys and trains, clocks, and music boxes. On Christmas Eve we're offering a 15% discount on our unique line of mechanical toys*

> *while supplies last.*
> *Doors open at 9A.M.*

"Wow. Another first. I could never convince Opa to advertise or offer any discounts. Whose idea was *this?*" Trudi asked.

"Guilty. I hope you don't mind. As they say, you have to spend money to make money," Richard said. "I had to take the train into Bangor to talk to the paper to get this done in time."

"Make sure you invoice me," Trudi said.

"It's a Christmas present, hon. Don't worry about it."

"Thanks... dad. That's generous, but what are we going to do if half the town shows up?"

"Let's burn that bridge when we get to it," Catherine said. "Sit. Eat. Enjoy. We still have a lot to do before we open at nine."

Forty—The Christmas-Eve Sale

"Everyone ready?" Trudi said as she stood poised to unlock the door. Her hand trembled as she reached for the latch. Outside, the sidewalk was crowded with more people than she had ever seen waiting. *I hope they're not disappointed.*

"We're ready," Catherine said.

Trudi took a deep breath and opened the door. She wisely stepped back as her friends, new and old customers, pushed in. The expressions on their faces were contagious. An instant later, their wide-eyed gazes and smiles had spread to everyone. It was as if they had never seen anything like what Trudi's new family and the elves had created.

Making her way through the happy throng of adults and children of all ages, Trudi greeted everyone she recognized and welcomed those who were new to the store. She noticed many were carrying newspapers—but some papers were from other nearby towns—even Portland and Bangor. *Richard must have gone overboard.*

Taking up her post behind the counter, Trudi was soon busy packaging selections and making out sales slips. Catherine stood at her side handling the money and ringing up the sales while Freddie and George answered questions and demonstrated the toys. Even Richard, put in charge of Annie, seemed all but overwhelmed by the questions and attention from the women. Before long, the cha-ching of the cash register became music to Trudi's ears.

As the last clock struck ten, the lights dimmed. An audible gasp flowed over the shoppers. A moment later, the show began, accompanied by *The 12 Days of Christmas* being played on Trudi's custom music box. Each vignette was appreciated with gasps of amazement, laughter, excited cries, and applause.

What Trudi had not expected was the customers joining in by singing the lyrics.

"Are there any more of those darling penguins?" Mrs. Brown asked once the lights came back up.

"I'll have someone check the back stock," Trudi answered. Motioning to Freddie, she asked, "Do we have more penguins?"

"There are about a dozen still in the back; I'll bring some up."

"Thanks, could you get a *special* one for Mrs. Brown?"

"Why certainly," Freddie said with a smile, knowing the toys were all but identical.

Trudi noticed Chad, was captivated by the electric train. Making her way over toward George, who was proudly showing him the engine he had designed, she got Chad's attention. "Chad, your clock is fixed. You didn't come by to pick it up."

"Thanks. I've been so busy. I enlisted, you know."

The news was as startling as a cold snowball in the face—running a shiver down her back. She remembered the broken veterans in shantytowns all over the country—those who had fought the last War to End All Wars. They had been no older than Chad when they went off to fight. So many, far too many never returned.

"Enlisted? When do you report?"

"Not for another week. I'm going to try to fly for the RAF."

"I thought you had a condition that kept you off the police force?"

"That condition was my mom's insistence that I not follow my dad into the force. I'm old enough to make my own choices."

"I'm so… proud of you. I always knew you had more courage than most. Well done, you."

"Thanks. If it's inconvenient, I can come back later for the clock."

"It's no problem. Let's get it," she said, reaching under a counter and handing him the clock. "Merry Christmas. The repairs are on me. It's the least I can do for the kindness your family has shown."

"This is so… generous; my mother will be thrilled," he said.

"Is anyone else going with you? Someone I might know?" she asked.

"Sean, Officer McNally is going too. We've struck up a real friendship."

Standing a few feet away, Trudi noticed that Freddie had overheard their conversation. She could tell that the news hit her hard; she could understand why. Not everyone was oblivious of the dangers of young men, of loved ones going to war, perhaps never to return.

"Thanks for everything, Miss Trudi. I've asked Howie to fill in for me for your deliveries."

"That's great Chad. Take care of yourself and Sean."

Freddie pushed through the beads into the workshop and Trudi followed. She found her standing near the workbench where the elves and Privi were still finishing and packaging toys.

"Freddie? Are you okay?"

"Sean's throwing his life away," she said. "He's a fool."

"It's his life. If the country goes to war, many, many of our young men will have to go. Those who go in now before the fighting starts will be the leaders and officers who will have some of the most important jobs to do."

"But… I wanted him to stay here."

"Freddie, isn't your family going to go back to the UK or at least be transferred to DC or some other embassy?"

Freddie nodded. "Maybe… probably."

"He's not leaving for a week or so. Make that time with him precious and memorable."

"Should we get married?"

"Good Lord no. You're not eighteen and too young to marry, and you've only known Sean for how many days?"

"You sound more like my mother than my sister," Freddie said.

"Marriage is a life-long commitment and should not be entered into lightly—not without a lot of impassionate thought and planning—and certainly not until you get to know one another a lot better, and I don't mean in bed."

"How did you get so wise?" Freddie asked.

"I don't know that I am, but that's how I was raised. I've seen too many children get married, or have to, and those marriages often end badly, with more than enough pain for all concerned. How many of your books have stories about unhappy marriages or girls that get in trouble?"

"Too many."

"So have fun with Sean, but don't go too far or let your passions get the better of you. Tell him you'll write—keep in touch, and when he comes back from the war, you'll both be wiser and know what to do."

"Ladies, we have a store full of customers. Should I tell them to come back some other day?" Catherine said, poking her head through the beads.

"Dry your tears, and let's get back to work," Trudi said.

Freddie squeezed her hand, "Let me get another armload of toys…"

And they went back to the shop. By three, the mobs thinned out, but a new wave of last-minute Christmas shoppers, mostly dads, arrived closer to five. It was then that Trudi looked up to see Sanders, the mysterious stranger come into the shop making a beeline to Richard. They shook hands and talked quietly before he left without saying a word to anyone.

"Can you hold the fort for a minute?" Trudi asked Catherine.

"Of course, dear," she said.

Trudi slipped through the customers to stand at Richard's side. "You know that man? Mr. Sanders?" she whispered.

"Yes, why do you ask?" His eyes never left the shoppers, as if he were looking for someone.

"You two acted like you knew one another."

Richard grinned. "Guilty. He's just a friend. He's been keeping an eye on Catherine and you kids. He's with the Secret Service."

"So why didn't he—?"

"Meet me at the train? He was ambushed by our visitor and ended up in hospital."

It became clear that there was a lot more to the St. James family than met the eye. "You'll have to fill me in on the details later."

Richard's eyes returned to scanning the customers. "Someday," he said. "In my memoir."

Ernestine, the telephone operator, came up to Trudi with a sad look on her face. "You're all but out of toy soldiers," she moaned.

"Well, Ernestine, if you had been here an hour earlier, we would still have a wide selection. Those four are all we have left, and I expect that's our last Captain. Sorry," Trudi said.

"I had heard so many people talking about the cute penguins and ducks, I had my heart set on those, but when I saw the soldiers... Okay, I'll take them—all."

"We'll have more by mid-week—at least by New Year's."

"Can you hold some for me?" she said. "You really need a catalog, so I could order over the phone like Sears."

Trudi smiled and nodded. *We're going to need more elves.* "A catalog is a great idea, but don't tell Catherine. She'll have one in national distribution before the weekend."

It was about seven when Mr. Snodgrass had finally finished shopping, and he was having trouble carrying everything. Trudi locked the door behind him. "Finally," she said, plopping into a chair at the kitchen table.

"What a day. Did anyone eat any lunch?" Freddie asked.

"I had a piece of bread about two this afternoon and seven cups of tea. You all must be beat. Should I call out for Chinese?" Catherine said.

"Too late," Richard said as he came into the kitchen carrying a bag loaded with paper containers steaming exotic aromas. "It was just delivered. I got some of everything except raw squid."

"No squid?" George said as he started opening the containers and dolling out the chopsticks and fortune cookies. Clarence saw his opportunity to jump up on the table but was lifted off by three gentle sets of hands.

"You hate sushi and raw fish, and you know it," Freddie said, laying out plates and glasses.

"I closed out the register and put the cash in the drop safe," Catherine said, bringing in the ledger.

"Thanks. I simply don't know what I would have done without everyone's help. I can't thank you enough."

"And the elves. They were marvelous," Freddie said.

"Did I see a fairy flitting by, or am I just that tired?" Richard asked.

"Weeset's real enough, but she's a bit shier than the rest. Just keep her out from under your hat—and your pockets; she hates that," Trudi said.

"You're doing quite well," Catherine said, glancing up from the ledger and eyeing an eggroll.

"Enough to pay y'all a salary?" Trudi asked.

"Enough to give you a nice nest egg, do a bit more advertising, and hire more staff once we're gone."

"So, you're thinking about leaving?" Trudi asked, but not really wanting to hear that her suspicions were true.

"Trudi, the world is about to go back to war," Richard began. "I'll be needed in DC, as my knowledge of Europe and the UK will be invaluable to the State Department and the President. I just heard that I'm ordered to head out on the early train."

"Don't worry," Catherine said. "…we'll stay and help out here until after New Year's unless some unexpected or untimely event comes up. I would rather stay and help than live in a drafty hotel in DC."

They were interrupted by a tap on the shop door. "I'll go," Freddie said. Trudi followed her into the shop where she saw Sean outside, brushing snow off his shoulders. "Sean?" Freddie said, opening the door. "Come in out of the cold."

They took two steps into the shop before Sean took Freddie in his arms and kissed her. "Merry Christmas," he said.

"Is this good-bye?" she whispered.

"It doesn't have to be," he said, holding her hands.

The End

Reviews

Every author depends on feedback from their critics, editors, and their family but especially from their readers. In my case, I don't mind if you write a review that's less than flattering. It's like a chef who has worked tirelessly to prepare a sumptuous meal. He stands at his patrons' table and asks... "Well, folks, how was it?"

The lady looks up. "It's… it's fine," she says, looking to her husband.

The gentleman hasn't eaten much. "Did you mix up the sugar and salt?" he begins. "And what are these blue lumps? They look like eyeballs."

The chef smiles. "I appreciate the feedback sir. And yes, those are lamb's eyeballs. They're quite a delicacy."

Which of these reviews are most useful to the chef? They both are.

Yes, authors love five-star reviews, but we especially like to hear what worked in the book and what didn't, what made you smile, laugh, brought you to tears of anger or pathos. No, even the best authors can't please everyone. In my case, I tend to make a certain segment of society a bit miffed, to say the least.

Reviews are a critical factor in making a book successful in the marketplace. After an Amazon book gets fifty reviews, Amazon will begin to advertise it themselves to encourage other buyers. So, as with any Amazon author, I would love to hear your feedback, even if you think I mixed up the sugar and the salt or you don't recognize the blue lumps and yes, even if you really love it.

Thanks,

William Vaughn

The Seldith Lexicon

Herditas	An inherited skill, often magical, like healing, wizardry, or fire-master, or simple, like carpenter, weaver, cook, or swordsmith.
Protector	A soldier or police officer.
Seldith	Nomadic forest elves about as tall as a mushroom.
Sem	A form of address for an adult male Seldith. Equivalent to 'man'.
Nesem	A form of address for an adult female Seldith. Equivalent to 'woman'.
Yesem	A form of address for a young Seldith male before reaching adulthood. Equivalent to 'boy'.
Yenesem	A form of address for a young Seldith female before reaching adulthood. Equivalent to 'girl.'
Yene	An abbreviation for 'yenesem'.
Uman	The Seldith term for humans.

Made in the USA
Monee, IL
15 October 2023